The Starlight Medallions

The Starlight Medallions

F. H. Wallace

iUniverse, Inc.
New York Bloomington

iUniverse books may be ordered through booksellers or by contacting:

iUniverse
1663 Liberty Drive
Bloomington, IN 47403
www.iuniverse.com
1-800-Authors (1-800-288-4677)

ISBN: 978-1-4502-0052-3 (sc)
ISBN: 978-1-4502-0053-0 (dj)
ISBN: 978-1-4502-0136-0 (ebook)

Printed in the United States of America

iUniverse rev. date: 02/03/2010

For Sean, Matthew, Laura, Ray, Hannah, Ryan,
Bryan, Beth, Michael, Sophia, Will, Trevor, Andrea,
Libby, Connor, Colleen, Zach, Rowan and Keenan
for whom and with whom this story was written.

Contents

Acknowledgements		xi
Chapter 1	The First Medallion	1
Chapter 2	The Man With The Crooked Face	9
Chapter 3	An Ancient Forest	14
Chapter 4	Secondhand	20
Chapter 5	Lorces	24
Chapter 6	A Distiguished Visitor	30
Chapter 7	Saturday	35
Chapter 8	Thunderhead Cliff	40
Chapter 9	The Cave	46
Chapter 10	The Witch of Thunderhead Cliff	51
Chapter 11	Ginger Ale and Cookies	56
Chapter 12	A Robbery	61
Chapter 13	Cows in The Pomeroy Room	69
Chapter 14	Dr. Asneth Pleever	75
Chapter 15	The Girl on the Oracle Stone	80
Chapter 16	Making Plans	87
Chapter 17	Nightwalking	93
Chapter 18	A Letter from the Smithsonian	100
Chapter 19	Treasure in the Attic	105

Chapter 20	Amanda's Smile	112
Chapter 21	Researches	119
Chapter 22	Greta Breaks The Code	126
Chapter 23	Lost, Oh Lost	133
Chapter 24	Operation Ringneck	138
Chapter 25	Toadstools and Cream Soda	146
Chapter 26	Nathaniel	151
Chapter 27	Guna-Guna	156
Chapter 28	The Reception	160
Chapter 29	Sagittarius	164
Chapter 30	Telling Secrets	170
Chapter 31	More Secrets	175
Chapter 32	A Successful Operation	181
Chapter 33	Dinner At The Pomeroys	186
Chapter 34	A Viking	192
Chapter 35	A Case of Mistaken Identity	197
Chapter 36	A Note From Travelstar	204
Chapter 37	Pegasus	209
Chapter 38	Bulldozers and Cranes	216
Chapter 39	Four Medallions and a Seagull	222
Chapter 40	The Graveyard	230
Chapter 41	Gold-Tipped Smith	238
Chapter 42	Kolbrúnarskáld	245
Chapter 43	A Tomahawk	252

Chapter 44	Behind The Northern Lights	260
Chapter 45	Starspinner	265
Chapter 46	The Runaway	271
Chapter 47	Dreamwalking	277
Chapter 48	Protecting Hazel	283
Chapter 49	Netting The Rhododendron	287
Chapter 50	A Wormhole	291
Chapter 51	The Eight Medallion	299
Chapter 52	Sailing On Starlight	305
Chapter 53	The Northern Lights	309
Chapter 54	Traped In Time	313
Chapter 55	The Coast	318
Chapter 56	Six Hours Till Twelve	326
Chapter 57	The Starlight Medallions	330
Chapter 58	A Skippeer of Stars	335
Epilogue		339

Acknowledgements

First to Scott Carson who, after I had spent several Thursdays working with his fourth grade on creative writing, asked if I didn't have something of my own to read. I returned the next week with the first chapter of *The Starlight Medallions*. "Let me see your beautiful eyes," Scott would say when he wanted the class's attention. Those beautiful eyes are what this story is about. To my agent, Carrie Hannnigan, who devoted many thoughtful and caring hours helping me get the story right. To my copy editors, Chuck Bennett and Kathy Brandes. To Rick Pacelli for help in understanding the celestial canopy and especially star clusters, and to my father who once adopted a basset hound and named him Walter.

... existence is of little interest save on days when the dust of realities is mingled with magic sand, when some trivial incident becomes a springboard for romance. Then a whole promontory of the inaccessible world emerges from the twilight of dream and enters our life, our life in which, like the sleeper awakened, we actually see the people of whom we had dreamed such ardent longing that we had come to believe that we should never see them save in our dreams.

Marcel Proust
"Remembrance of Things Past"

Chapter 1

The First Medallion

Sim Spotswood was supposed to be on his way to get measured for braces the day he found the first of the medallions. But when he turned right at Market Street to get to Dr. McCreedy's office, he saw Denny Dumont coming out of Bob's Sweet Shop. Denny was a bully with a small following of goons who laughed at everything he said. When Sim was younger he had made up stories about the father he had never known: that he was a shipwrecked prince, for example, who had returned to his own kingdom. Some day he would return, Sim said. Denny never failed to tease him, telling Jack and Carl that Sim's father was just another drunken sailor in port for a weekend.

Sim quickly retraced his steps and walked down Threadneedle Street, then across the bridge that spanned Lost River as it opened into the cove.

It wasn't only Denny and his goons. Sim didn't want to have his teeth straightened and was glad for an excuse to walk the other way. And it wasn't only his teeth. He had argued with his mother about other things as well – small things that didn't really matter. And he had this sense something was about to happen. He couldn't so much as open a door without preparing himself for what might be on the other side.

Sim stopped in the middle of the bridge and looked upriver. It was a sunny September day that held more the memory of summer than the promise of fall. He shifted his eyes to the corrugated steel sheeting just above the town pier. It contained a Viking ship whose ribs had been exposed after a storm years earlier. The steel box had been constructed so that the river water could be pumped out and archaeologists could expose the ship and its contents. There were rumors of treasure and the ghosts of disturbed spirits, but all anyone could view were a few blackened timbers resembling the charred skeleton of a dragon.

At the end of the bridge Sim walked down to the clam flats that bordered Lost River. It didn't take much looking to find a couple flat stones. He skipped one out over the calm river. One, two, three, four, five, six, seven. Seven skips. He was out of practice. He adjusted his posture and skipped the second stone. Twelve.

A few feet away, a seagull poked in the sand with his bill. Probably after a clam, Sim thought. The bird looked at him, its head cocked to one side. Something wasn't the way it should be. There were hundreds of gulls in Lost River Cove. You couldn't be anywhere near the water without seeing ten or twenty of them. That was it. That's what was different. If you saw one you'd see another and then another. But there was only this one. Looking at him. Sim walked closer.

The gull stepped back from the place where it had been digging.

"Where are your friends?" Sim asked. The bird turned his head and looked back at the bridge. Sim followed his gaze.

A man walked quietly toward town, a small boy sat upon his shoulders, his legs crooked under the man's arms. Sim felt a familiar sadness, a catch at the back of his throat. He wasn't in the mood for silent fathers or weird birds. He turned back to the gull. "Get lost," he said. picking up a stone. He tossed in the direction of the bird. The gull ignored him and scratched one more time in the sand.

Sim approached and knelt not two feet away from the strange bird. He dug with his fingers where the gull had scratched. Something was there. He removed what looked like a coin. It was a little bigger and heavier than a silver dollar. He started to scrape away the sand and then dropped it, stepping back. The thing had moved in his hand. No, not moved; hummed, purred. Like the sensation of touching a refrigerator when it was running. The gull cocked his head. Sim picked up the coin again, carefully. Maybe it had been his imagination. No. There it was again. Like it was alive. Or magnetic. Or some special kind of metal. He looked over at the ribs of the Viking ship. Maybe it had come with the Vikings. That must be it. Maybe there were others. He dug again in the sand. Nothing.

He heard a flutter of wings and looked up. The gull had taken flight. He watched as it flew higher and higher until it disappeared into the afternoon sky.

He walked to the river to wash the coin. As he looked down he caught his breath. Where the bank should have shelved away, there were now bottomless depths of clear water. It was like standing at the edge of a quarry. Gingerly, he stepped back from the impossible edge.

He picked up a stone and tossed it into the water. It landed as it should have, just beneath the surface. He tossed another. It was as if there were two depths of water: the one that should be and another that seemed to come and go the way trick images did, depending on how you focused your eyes. He took off his shoes and, more fascinated than frightened, stepped carefully into the shallows. It was almost October and the water, which never got very warm even in August, was now bone-chilling cold, the kind of cold that makes your feet ache and your skin go numb. And yet it was an oddly pleasant sensation, like something he had felt now and then in a dream. He walked out farther, up to his waist, to see what it would be like. "It's not a bad way to go," his mother had said once of a winter drowning reported in the *Lost River Clarion*. Like lying down in the snow, he thought, but his dreamy thought was suddenly interrupted.

"What are you doing? Are you crazy, Sim?" It was Amanda Pomeroy. She was standing on the shore behind him.

He turned. "How long have you been there?" he said, a little annoyed at having been seen doing something foolish.

"I just got here. I saw you from the road. You're crazy."

"It's great. Come on in."

"You are going to get P-neumonia." That was the way the Pomeroys said it, as if it had to do with taking a leak. It was one of Mr. Pomeroys' expressions. He had lots of them. He was a fun father to have except when he pretended to know more than he did, which was fairly often.

Sim walked out of the water. "I can hardly feel my legs," he said.

The Pomeroy twins, Alex and Amanda, were two of Sim's best friends. Their father had never worked a day in his life, but was busier than any man in Lost River Cove. The Archaeological Society was one of Mr. Pomeroy's causes. The Fisherman's Museum was another. The library still another.

"You are honest-to-god crazy," Amanda said.

Sim pulled on bis shoes. "I've got something to show you,"

"What?"

"Let's go to Bartlett's." He walked back toward the bridge, Amanda following.

Bartlett's Restaurant was just on the other side of the bridge. There was a booth at the back with high-backed benches and it was there that Sim and his friends liked to gather because it was so private. And free for Amanda, Alex and their friends. Mr. Pomeroy had bought Bartlett's two years ago because he had never owned a restaurant. Homer Dunn ran it for him. Homer had run it for the previous owners as well. Homer didn't like change. He didn't like the Viking ship being dug up in the harbor and he didn't like all the out-of-towners it attracted. Sim suspected that he probably didn't like Mr. Pomeroy either, but that was just a guess. Homer wiped down their table with a not-very-clean cloth and took their order. Two mugs of hot chocolate. When Homer left, Sim took the coin out of his pocket and laid it on the table. "Feel it," he said"

Amanda picked it up but showed no surprise as she rubbed her finger over the shiny black surface. "What are the bumps?"

"I don't know." Sim hadn't really noticed them before, his mind taken up with the feel of the thing. But now he could see them. Like grains of sand under a shiny black coating. "Can you feel it?"Amanda wrinkled her nose. "The bumps?".

"No, the way it tingles. Like it's electric or something."

"No." She handed it back to Sim. It purred in his hand. What was happening didn't make any sense. He couldn't decide what to say.

"What is it, Sim?"

"It sort of purrs," he said. "Like Sophonsiba." Sophonsiba was the Pomeroys' Siamese cat.

Amanda reached out and touched it again.

"It's magic," she said matter-of-factly.

"You can feel it?" he asked, feeling a surge of relief.

"I'm not supposed to. It's only magic for the person who finds it. Like Aladdin and his lamp."

Sim usually smiled to himself when Amanda spoke about magic. He was too old for stuff like that, but it was as much a part of Amanda's world as homework or macaroni and cheese. Amanda was the only person Sim knew who had actually seen a gnome, or so she claimed. He told her about the seagull and how the water was deep and then not deep.

Before she could respond Homer arrived with their hot chocolate. Sim quickly covered the coin with his hand. "Thanks, Homer," he said. Homer nodded and returned to the soda counter.

"I looked for you after school," Amanda said. "Where'd you go?"

Sim told her about Dr. McCreedy and Denny."

"Are you getting braces?" she asked. The tone in her voice revealed more than mere curiosity. If Sim was getting braces and had not told her, it would have been a serious breach of their friendship and Sim knew that.

"No, I'm not. Which is why I didn't go."

"Well, why did you have an appointment?"

"My mother thought I was going to."

"Your mom's going to be boiled. This is not going to be a good afternoon for you, Sim, unless...."

Sim looked at her hopefully.

"Unless this is a lucky coin. It depends on what kind of magic it's got." She picked up the black disk and looked at it again. "Maybe you're supposed to make a wish. You could wish that everything will be OK with your mom." She hesitated, turning the coin over in her hands. "Of course if you get only one wish, that wouldn't be a very big one."

Sim knew what his wish would be. The same one he had made on every shooting star he had ever seen, lying at night on the widow's walk at 413 Fisher Lane. He thought of the man and the boy on the bridge. There one moment and gone the next. "Yeah, I'd better save it." He put the coin into his wet pocket and realized how cold he was. "I think I better head home," he said, finishing his hot chocolate. He suddenly felt guilty about having shown the coin to Amanda. She was one of his three best friends but it had been secret for maybe hundreds of years and now here he was disturbing its rest, showing it around, letting people have theories about it. Sim had a habit of giving thoughts and feelings to things that really couldn't have them. He was the kind of person who felt sorry for trees after an ice storm and worried about the moon when it couldn't see through the clouds.

"Yeah, me too," Amanda said. They finished their hot chocolate, said thanks to Homer, and walked out to the street.

Walter, Sim's basset hound, was waiting outside the restaurant. Usually he met Sim at the corner of Maple and Fisher Lane as Sim walked home from school and Walter finished his afternoon rounds. Walter wasn't a sit-at-home dog. He had friends to see and business to conduct from one end of town to the other. He'd share a donut with the barber; a piece of beef jerky with the postman; several dog biscuits of various flavors and sizes at selected sites and the vegetarian scraps from Colleen Gardner's lunch table. Walter was a low-riding kind of dog with very sad eyes and long, soft ears. Sim knelt down and gave his ears a rub. "Sorry, Walter. I forgot to tell you about my appointment."

"OK, well I'm goin' down the hill," Amanda said. "I'll see ya tomorrow."

"OK. Oh, about the coin."

"What?"

"Don't mention it to anyone."

"OK."

"I'm really serious, Amanda. It's important."

Amanda gave the secret sign that sealed a promise, a sign that only she and her brother and Sim knew. Then she turned and walked down the hill toward Pomeroy Hall.

Chapter 2

The Man With The Crooked Face

Sim turned and started toward home. Walter waddled along beside him.

"I'm in a little hot water, Walter," Sim explained as they walked. "I hope Mom is in a really good mood."

He turned into the Parish Church cemetery, which filled an entire block in the middle of the town and had gravestones going back to 1620, the time of the Indian massacre. Some of the inscriptions warned against sin and damnation and were decorated with angels or tormented souls. You couldn't walk through the cemetery in one breath, but you could breathe very carefully, which seemed to work well enough.

Sim didn't want to do things that would upset his mother. She had enough on her mind as it was. She had lost her job three months before, and her savings were getting smaller and smaller. He had been trying to come up with ways to help. Last night before going to sleep he had dreamed up a hot-dog stand and a pet-washing business.

They had not always lived at 413 Fisher Lane. Once they had been in a trailer in the Sea View Trailer Park, which was nowhere near the ocean. Then Mrs. Goodwin, a very nice old lady who Sim's mother had helped out with shopping and house cleaning, moved into a place for old people and rented her house to them. They had been there now for four years but Mrs. Goodwin was very ill and not expected to live very long. Then the house would go to her son who lived in Boston. He would sell it. He had heard his mother talking on the phone to her friend Tricia. She was worried. It was hard not having a father.

Sim opened the door and walked in. He could hear his mother in the kitchen. He quickly ran up to his room and changed his pants. He took the coin from his pocket and laid it on his pillow. Ridley Raccoon, his one-eyed and somewhat threadbare sleeping companion, watched. Ridley had shared Sim's pillow for as far back as he could remember. Missing his appointment was going to be hard enough to explain. Walking into the river he couldn't even explain to himself. He slipped the coin back into his pocket.

When he walked into the kitchen his mother was unpacking groceries. "Hi, Mom, I'm home," didn't feel like the right thing to say, so he just took off his jacket, walked to the kitchen counter and sat on one of the stools. His mother had taken him to Dr. McCreedy for his annual cleaning two weeks earlier. That was when the subject of braces had come up. They made an appointment and she was to meet him there after school, but he had said he wanted to do it alone. After all, it was just measuring; and Sim had recently felt a need to do things on his own.

"Dr. McCreedy's office called," she said. He could tell, even though she said it in a sort of throwaway voice, that she was upset: she put the milk in the cupboard and the canned tomato sauce in the refrigerator.

"I missed my appointment. I forgot about it. Amanda and I went to Bartlett's and we got talking and then I remembered but..,"

"But?"

"It was too late."

She looked into the grocery bag as if something that was supposed to be there wasn't. It was a feeling he often had. His father would have understood about braces. Sailors didn't get braces. Sailors had gold teeth.

She crumpled the bag. Sim could almost feel it. "I don't want braces, Mom."

"So you didn't forget."

"Well, not exactly."

"Not exactly."

Miss Blenden, his teacher, did that too. Repeat what you said. It meant "tell me more." Sometimes. Now it meant something else. There was a rule about lying. "I like my teeth the way they are," he said, sitting on one of the stools, putting his elbows on the counter. "They're part of my personality."

"I am only thinking of your own good," she said. "Lord knows we have better things to spend the money on."

The fact was that being gap-toothed had its advantages. Sim could whistle louder than any boy at school and, with a following wind, he could squirt a stream of water four feet three inches. Braces threatened to change all of that.

"Do you know how much braces cost?" she asked. "And I'll have to pay for today's appointment. Did you consider that?"

Sim didn't consider it because he was pretty sure it wasn't true. He could tell when his mother was adding flourishes. They always ended with, "I'll bet you never thought of that!" which Sim took as a good clue that she hadn't either.

Sim was going to launch a protest, but doing that might lead to stage two, whose warning words were, "And another thing...." In stage two, depending on the level of his mother's annoyance, how things had gone with job-hunting and other variables, which remained a mystery to Sim, anything could happen. Matters totally unrelated to his most recent bad thing would reappear like old underwear at the back of a closet, to oppress him: chores not done, things left out to be tripped over. He decided to try a different strategy.

"I think it's too expensive. Think of all the things we need."

"Like what?" His mother put the empty bags with the other recyclables and turned, with her hands on her hips and a very firm mouth.

"Like getting the dent in the car fixed.".

A hit-and-run shopper at Ben's Grocery Mart had put a crease along the passenger-side door one day while his mother was shopping. His mother took care of the little red Toyota as if it were her other child, and she had been devastated by the calamity. Claiming the insurance, she said, was out of the question; her rates would just go up.

"I think you are a little more important than a car," she said, the edges of her mouth softening slightly.

"OK. But I can wait. The twins aren't getting them till next year." It was always good to use the twins as an example. His mother was glad that they were his friends and did everything she could to encourage the friendship.

Sim put his head in his hands and looked his mother right in the eyes. "They're too expensive, Mom. I'll make a deal. Fix the car and next year I'll get braces. I promise."

"You're really serious about this, aren't you?" she asked.

Sim nodded. Speaking now would have been risky. The little bit of serious concern he saw in his mother's eyes made the issue of braces even more important than he had realized at 2:30, when he had seen Denny and walked the other way.

"OK. But next year. Same time. Same station. September 27th. That's the day of your first appointment with Dr. McCreedy."

"OK."

She reached across the counter. "Shake on it," They shook on it. Sim slipped his left hand into his pocket and crossed his fingers. He felt bad about that, but who knew what the future might hold? You had to keep your options open. He felt the coin in his pocket. It seemed fuzzy. He wondered what the black stuff really was. And the bumps. It's just because I'm still cold, he thought. He was cold. His feet were cold. His legs were tingly. He started to take the coin out of his pocket to show her, but something made him stop.

Then the doorbell rang. It was the kind of doorbell that only happens in the black-and-white movies his mother liked to watch. It was jarring. Walter immediately began to howl. But not just howl. He growled and he was not, temperamentally, a growling kind of dog.

"I'll get it," Sim said, glad for a chance to be useful.

Under most circumstances, Sim was a very polite boy. He knew, for example, that it was rude, to stare and that appearances were deceptive. Often people who had the brightest smile and most winning ways turned out to be selfish and cruel. And people who were unpleasant to look at might well have a generous and lovable nature. But all of this knowledge flew right out of his head when he opened the door and for the first time saw the man with the crooked face.

Chapter 3

An Ancient Forest

First it was the eyebrows. They exploded above deep set eyes that seemed to peer as if from within a cave. And they didn't match. Not the eyes or the eyebrows. One nostril was more flared than the other. There was a scar in the center of the stranger's upper lip and his mouth seemed shaped into a perpetual frown. It was as if one half of the man's face was lower than the other, as if it had been taken apart and carelessly put back together.

Walter was standing beside Sim, still growling though more softly. The man looked at him with what, on an ordinary face, might have been a smile, Sim thought. It didn't work.

"Nice puppy," the man said, reaching out a hand. There was a ring with a large red stone on one bony finger. Walter was silent. Sim stepped between them. The man looked at him and Sim realized that he was staring, which he knew was rude.

"I'm sorry," he said, "I was expecting someone else."

"People usually are," the man said, rubbing his hands together slowly. Sim tried not to look at the ring. He looked up. The man was studying him. It was a penetrating look, which made Sim uncomfortable. "I deal in antiquarian objects," he continued, as if he were reciting something learned for class. "Treasures in your attic. Ancestral trunks, old jewelry, knick knacks, snuffboxes, and coins. He emphasized the word coins, and, narrowed his eyes.

"We don't have any ancestors."

"Everyone has ancestors," the man said. Of course Sim knew that. What he had meant to say was that they hadn't left any trunks behind.

"I mean we don't have any ancestors with trunks." Sim sneaked a glance out to the street. There was no vehicle there; the man had walked from somewhere.

"Even the change in your pocket can contain treasure," the man said.

Sim clutched the coin in his pocket. There was no question about it. It felt strange. Stranger than it had when he first dug it up. There was a tickling sensation on his chest and he felt light-headed. The man looked at Sim and smiled. It was a smile of satisfaction. Sim started to speak, but as he did the entire scene before him started to dissolve. In its place he saw a forest of trees larger than any he had ever seen before. The lawn, the street, the town faded to ghostlike shadows in a dense silent forest. The man reached out a bony hand and touched Sim's shoulder. "It's you," he said.

Sim awoke on the sofa. It must have been no more than a few minutes. His mother was talking to someone on the phone. She hung up and rushed back into the room. The front door was closed.

"What happened?" Sim asked.

"You fainted," she said.

"The man with the crooked face," he said.

"Sim, that's not the way we talk about people. Think what it must be like for him. And then to have you faint."

"Did he say anything to you?" Sim asked.

"He just apologized. You probably frightened him more than He frightened you."

They went up to his room

As he changed into his pajamas his mother found his wet jeans lying on the floor. She picked them up. "What's this all about?" she asked.

"I was looking for something in the river," he said.

"In September?"

"He was about to make up a story but just then the doorbell rang. Dr. Harvey checked him over. Hearing the story of Sim's dip in the icy waters of Lost River Cove, the doctor diagnosed a case of delayed shock brought on by mild hypothermia.

It wasn't that, Sim wanted to say. It was something else. It was seeing things that weren't there. After Dr. Harvey left his mother scolded him. But it was a what-would-I-do-if-ever-anything-happened-to-you scold rather than an angry one.

"You know those old wharves up past the second bridge?" he asked.

"The ones across from Miss Gardner's house?"

"Yeah. They're really old, aren't they?"

"They'd have to be. Before the bridge. When the river was still deep enough for ships."

"How old?"

"Maybe a hundred years old. Maybe older."

"And the Viking ship was here even before then."

"Long before then."

"How long?"

"I don't know, Sim. Maybe a thousand years. A long time ago."

"Then the river would have been really deep," he said.

"Really deep," his mother responded. She pulled the covers up around Sim's neck and tucked them in tight.

"And there wouldn't have been any town here. No roads, not even any docks. Nothing but...." He hesitated.

"Trees. Giant trees of a kind we will never see. Chestnuts. Great groves of chestnuts and beech and king pine. All gone now."

"Except in stories."

"Stories and dreams," his mother said. Then she kissed him good night and turned out the light, leaving the door open a crack the way he liked it.

Sim looked for the pattern in the wallpaper opposite his bed. He knew it by heart – clipper ships and flags –but the night was dark and the images were hidden from sight. When there was a moon and a night breeze moving the branches outside his window, the ships would set sail through a sea of shadows. Tonight Sim would have liked to see a moon. He had never been afraid of the dark, even as a child, but tonight he was. Was there a darkness in the darkness he wondered, as earlier there had been in the cove, depths beneath the depths?

When Sim was frightened, he thought of his father, a man he had never seen but who stood superhuman in his imagination. He was a sailor. His mother had been called in to look after him. There had been a shipwreck. He had come from another land and spoke a language that no one could understand. Magnus Siglandi was his name. His mother imitated his voice, hitting her breastbone with her fingers. "Magnus Siglandi," she said. "Magnus Siglandi," she repeated with a far-away look in her eyes.

"What did he look like?" Sim would ask her.

"Like a god," his mother would reply. "Blond with deep blue eyes."

"Was he big?" Sim asked.

"He seemed big, but no. He wasn't much taller than I," she said.

"How old was he?"

"Maybe twenty. Maybe younger."

Then she would look at Sim strangely, lost for a moment in her own thoughts and say, "He looked just like you, Sim. He had your eyes. You will be just like him some day."

How could you love a father you had never seen, who didn't even stay long enough for you to be born, who had never come back to see how you had turned out, Sim wondered, as he had often before. How could his mother love a man who had left her alone with a baby? She did. That was the thing.

The stories his mother told him, he learned quickly, were not stories that he could repeat to friends as he became old enough to have friends and to have his own story. Only to Amanda, whose tireless search for wonder helped Sim enlarge upon his mother's description of his father being "like a god." He probably is one, Amanda explained. People in history are always being fathered by gods who don't stick around. "But do they come back?" Sim wanted to know. Amanda couldn't say.

All he had of his father's was a stone hung on a leather cord, which his mother had found on the bedside table where his father had stayed. It was a little larger than the coin he had found in the sand that afternoon, but thinner. Usually it was a soft grey, but sometimes it changed colors, especially when he slept on the widow's walk beneath the stars. Then it was like rain sliding down a window in colored sheets. His father had left it on top of a drawing: two stick figures, one inside the other. "I didn't understand until I realized I was carrying you," she told him. '

"And I knew he had left it for you." "Lucky," his father had called it. "I thought he didn't speak like we do," Sim said when his mother told him the story. 'He didn't have many words, but he had that one," she said.

The stone was his most prized possession, his only link to his father, and it had kept alive the hope that someday his father would return.

The feeling of expectation that he had felt earlier remained with him in the dark. Once again he saw the man and the boy so strangely silent on the bridge, the gull as it watched him, and then as it disappeared into the sun. They shared a secret: he and the gull. He couldn't have said that, but he could think it.

"It's you," the man with the crooked face had said. What had he meant? How could you be somebody you didn't know you were? Why hadn't he told his mother any of it? Not even about the coin. It felt strange suddenly to have so many secrets - strange and, in a way that he wasn't sure he liked, exciting. He reached under his pillow to touch the coin. There was that feeling again, as if it were alive. As if it were purring. He held it and soon, comforted, he was asleep.

Chapter 4

Secondhand

The next morning Sim brushed the same teeth he had brushed the day before, ran the same comb through his hair, and saw in his mirror the same slightly freckled eleven-year-old boy he hadcome to know and mostly approve. It seemed that things were back to normal.

Sim's first thought as he awoke had been that he would tell his mother the whole story: of the coin, the deep dark of the river, and the great forest behind the man with the crooked face. But then he remembered all the things she had on her mind already: mostly her worries about money, but also himself. It's a hard world, she told him. There's no such thing as luck, unless you make your own. You're getting too old for that, she had said one morning when he told her about a shooting star the night before and how he had made a wish. How could he tell her that he had found a magic coin?

He reached under the pillow where he had put the coin the night before and examined it. It didn't look valuable, blackened as it was and pimpled with little dots. Probably just sand, he thought.

He got up and walked over to his desk, opened the drawer, and took out his jack knife. Mr. Pomeroy had given it to him on his tenth birthday. It was just like Alex's. Mr. Pomeroy was the most generous person Sim knew, and he was glad for the knife. But now and then it made him sad to see it. He would like to have had a knife from his own father.

He opened the knife and chipped at the black stuff covering the coin. A piece broke away over one of the bumps and revealed a tiny gem. He took the coin to the window and tilted it so that the gem caught the rays of the sun. It sparkled and filled with a blue light.

Then he dressed as he did every morning in a plain-colored shirt and bib overalls. He and his mother shopped at a second hand clothing store in Bailey, twenty miles to the north. You couldn't buy second-hand clothing locally, she explained. People might stop and stare at you, recognizing something they had just cleaned out of their closet and dropped off at the thrift shop.

Sim favored overalls because if they weren't exactly the right size it didn't matter. And he liked the pockets in the bib. He kept a notebook and a pencil there. Shirts were easy. There were always piles of them. He concentrated on socks and neckties. You could get very interesting neckties for not much at all, and neckties were his trademark. If you had a really good necktie, no one would notice the rest. He put the coin and the jackknife in his pocket and pulled on his high-topped sneakers. One of the laces was knotted in two places and you could see the big toe on his right foot. He wiggled it. It worked the way it was supposed to. That was reassuring. He looked over at Walter. "You're second-hand too, you know," he said. "Even your name."

If Walter was awakened by Sim's preparations for school, he didn't show it. Walter had two speeds, *on* and *off*, and for much of the time *on* wasn't all that different from *off*. Walter didn't waste energy. Walter was independent, but he was also a good friend who kept the secrets Sim told him.

When he was eight, Sim had pleaded with his mother to let him have a puppy. He was old enough, he insisted and, since there was no father, it would be a good thing to have a dog that could look out for trouble. There was a litter of beagles at the pet store in Bailey. But they were expensive, his mother explained, and there would also be the cost of food. As always, there wasn't much money, even for the things they needed. "Maybe next year," she said.

Then one evening Walter appeared at the kitchen door. Sim gave him the scraps from the table and a bowl of water and sat on the back steps watching as he ate. Of course he wasn't Walter then; he was just a bedraggled hound with a tear in one of his ears, a limp, and eyes that were sadder than any Sim had ever seen. Walter wasn't a puppy. He was gangly, like an adolescent, but whether from lack of nourishment or age was unclear.

"If you feed him, he'll stay around," his mother said. Sim wasn't sure he wanted this sad-looking stray to stay around. He still had his heart set on a playful puppy. So, having fed and watered the visitor, he went to bed and lay there troubled in ways that were new to him.

When he awoke the next morning, he opened the kitchen door and the dog was still there, only now he had a different look in his eyes and wagged his tail.

It was the next day, when they drove to the animal rescue league in Bailey to find out about shots and learn why Walter limped, that he got his name. They were sitting in the waiting room when the vet's assistant called out,

"Walters?" "Jenny Walters?"

A large woman with what Sim thought might have been a schnauzer or a small terrier stood up. But not before Walter, who limped to the counter trailing his rope lead behind him and wagging his tail.

"Is your name Walters too?" the assistant asked.

Walter barked. It was the first sound Sim and his mother had heard him make.

"It's just plain Walter," Sim said, surprising himself. "Here, Walter," he said. "It's not our turn yet."

When it was their turn they learned that Walter had been shot. There was a pellet near his left eye that the vet thought it better not to remove and several pellets in the muscle above his left leg that the vet did remove.

"Why would anyone do that?" Sim asked. The vet just shook his head. Then he looked at Walter's teeth and thought he was about three years old.

This was the first time that Sim learned how sometimes the events that choose you are better than the ones you choose for yourself.

"OK, Walter," Sim said, standing up and turning off the light in his bathroom, "Breakfast time."

For many dogs of Sim's acquaintance, chow call brought on an explosion of enthusiasm, of running in circles, jumping up and down, and barking. Walter merely lifted his head and looked around as if to say, "What? Breakfast already? Where does the time go?" Then he got slowly to his feet and followed Sim out the door and downstairs to the kitchen.

His mother greeted him with an awkwardly long hug and appeared to be on the verge of an "if anything ever happened to you" commentary; but she recovered herself and announced that she wouldn't be home when he got back from school. She had an interview for a job with a catering firm. She knocked on wood and so did Sim.

Sim fed Walter, then himself, put the lunch his mother had packed into his backpack, kissed her goodbye and, with Walter at his heels, walked into Friday morning the 29th of September.

Chapter 5

Lorces

Walter followed Sim as far as the junction of Chase Lane and Oak Streets where Sim bent down, gave his ears a good rub, told him to behave himself, not to over-eat and sent him on his daily rounds. Then Sim continued up Chase Lane to Lost River Cove Elementary School, known to everyone as LORCES.

Sim went to his classroom where Miss Blenden, his teacher, was writing the daily greeting on the easel pad that stood outside the door. It asked for everyone to write his or her middle name. They were going to discuss how people got names.

"Good morning, Miss Blenden," he said.

"Good morning, Sim," she said, adding a smiley face to the upper corner of the greeting where it said Good Morning, Starfish. (Every classroom at LORCES was named for some sea creature.) This Is Friday the 29th of September. When she finished she handed Sim the marker. He took it without thinking and realized he had nothing to write. Miss Blenden smiled at him in the patient way she had with the more challenged members of her class. Here he was faced with a moral dilemma even before school began. He felt it was going to be a long day.

If he told Miss Blenden the truth – that he had no middle name – she would feel terrible, the way you would feel if you said to someone, "Hey, watch where you're going," only to discover that they were blind. Once she had asked a new boy what his father did for work and the boy had said his father was in jail. Sim felt sorry for the boy but he felt more sorry for Miss Blenden who was so very careful never to hurt a person's feelings. Telling her that he didn't have a middle name would be like that. She would feel awful, say that she was so sorry and probably erase the whole morning greeting for fear of putting yet another of her pupils in the same position. Then there was the other side: lying, making up a name so that she wouldn't feel bad. In his imagination he had taken his father's name, Magnus; but it wasn't official. It wasn't written down anywhere except on his desk at home.

He was relieved of his dilemma by the arrival of Morty Glick, who, reading over the announcement said, "I don't have a middle name. My parents ran out of names after Tyler." Then Morty smiled, turned and went into the classroom. There were six Glick children, Morty was the youngest. It made sense. Miss Blenden seemed unfazed.

"Me neither," Sim said, "Except the ones that I make up."

"Those are the best kind. I remember that for a long time when I was your age I was Leticia."

Sim smiled, thought for a moment, and wrote Magnus in the space provided. Then he handed her the marker, left his pack in his cubby, and went out to the playground. There were still fifteen minutes until school started.

He found Alex Pomeroy at the corner of the basketball court waiting for someone to pass him the ball. You could wait a long time if you weren't among the select few who considered themselves pro athletes. You waited until someone missed a shot and the ball came your way. Alex was bored with waiting.

"So what's this about a magic coin?" he said.

Sim looked quickly to see if anyone had overheard and furrowed his eyebrows. "Not here.".

They walked across the grass to the fence.

"What's the big mystery?" Alex asked.

"First of all, it's not magic. Where's Amanda?"

"Capa-wierdo."

"Capoeira," Sim corrected.

"Whatever." The PE teacher at LORCES, Mrs. Knight, was a martial artist and she offered a class in Capoeira before school on Mondays and Fridays. Mostly girls took it. Greta, his other best friend, was in it too.

"Well, I never said it was magic."

"You told Amanda it was."

"Amanda said it was. Anyway, you know Amanda. She likes things like that."

"So it's not magic?"

"Not exactly." Sim had to stop and think what he could say that would make sense to Alex whose mind was opposite to that of his twin. When Amanda looked at the stars, she saw constellations. When Alex looked at the heavens, he saw big rocks. Amanda wanted to meet aliens; Alex wanted to name an asteroid. He tried to find the kinds of words that Alex used.

"It has certain properties," he began, but then he didn't know where to go.

"Like making you jump in the river."

"I didn't jump in the river. I was investigating. This strange thing happened."

Sim told the story from the beginning: about the water and the man with the crooked face but Alex was most impressed with the story's ending.

"You fainted?" he said. "Cool."

"It wasn't cool, Alex. It was definitely not cool."

"This is a lot of stuff. So this guy, what did he look like?"

"It was his face. It didn't fit together. One side was higher than the other. Like it had been split open and stuck back together but not quite right."

"Mr. Splitface," Alex said, pleased with his invention.

"Yeah, Splitface." Sim nodded. "That's him. This is top secret, Alex."

"Except Amanda."

"Right. And Greta. I haven't told her yet."

"So did you bring it?"

Sim showed Alex the coin. "How come this chip is off?"

"I chipped it off. I wanted to see what the bumps were."

"That is a definite no-no. Never mess with something that is old. There was this guy on television. He had this little fox made out of metal on a stand. It was old. I mean it was really ancient, probably even before my father was born. Guess how much it would have been worth if he hadn't cleaned it?"

"A million dollars."

Alex ignored Sim's less than serious response. "Two thousand dollars," he said. "But he cleaned it with something. I don't know, something you clean sinks with and then you know how much it was worth?"

"A thousand dollars."

"No, not even that. I don't remember. Not very much."

"How are you supposed to clean it?"

"Chemicals. They have special things that don't damage the surface. My dad would know what to do," he said, half-heartedly. Sim looked at the coin. Mr. Pomeroy meant well enough. He was all eagerness and willing to take on just about anything, whether he knew something about it or not. His specialties were lepidoptera, mycology and early English kings before Alfred. Butterflies, mushrooms and kings other than Arthur Pendragon were not among Sim's interests.

"Your father's a really brilliant man, but I think we ought to deal with this ourselves. If an adult had found the coin that would be different, but I did. I think it should be a kid thing. I think the coin would want it that way."

Alex peered at him out of the tops of his eyes. Sim recognized the look. It was a habit his friend had for showing that he thought someone wasn't playing with a full set of checkers.

"I didn't mean that like it sounded," Sim quickly added, realizing as he spoke that it was exactly what he had meant. "I just mean that the world the coin came into is our world. OK?"

"OK."

Sim looked again at the coin and put it back into his pocket. "Greta would know what to do." Greta was the smartest person in their class. After the first month, Miss Blenden, their teacher, had nicknamed her Einstein. She always said it in a humorous way, but Sim suspected that Miss Blenden had not done it entirely out of respect. Greta had seen much more of the world than Miss Blenden had and knew a great many things that even Miss Blenden didn't know. Greta was not above correcting people when they were wrong, even teachers. You could be jealous of Greta's brilliance but you had to like her. She made being at school more fun. Even on a gloomy day she sparkled.

Alex looked away. Sim followed his gaze but saw nothing there. Alex was having his thoughts. That was Amanda's expression. Sometimes Alex went quiet.

It seemed to Sim, though Alex denied it furiously, that his friend was a little bit jealous of Greta's brilliance. Certainly he was competitive with her. But there was more than that. Something dreamy now and then in Alex's eyes when he watched her. It was something Sim thought about a lot. About how complicated and wonderful friendships were. Amanda and Greta were as different from one another as fractions from football and yet they were best friends. Alex and Amanda were opposites and yet they were twins. And Sim? Where did he fit? Perhaps in the middle. Not a bad place.

"So what do you think?" Sim asked.

Alex nodded. "I guess so. Her father's got that lab in their basement where they clean up stuff from the Viking ship. Yeah, that's a good idea."

The bell rang and everyone headed to line up at the door.

Chapter 6

A Distinguished Visitor

The bell rang and they followed the crowd to the building. Over to the side, out of sight of the teachers, Denny Dumont was talking to a boy named Conan. Conan and his family were new to Lost River Cove. They were from Ireland. Conan's father had been hired by a bank to run their on line banking operation. Sim could see that Conan was trying to make the best of a bad thing. He was a small boy with the energy of a wind-up toy. He couldn't sit still. He sat in front of Sim and squirmed all day long. Conan thought that friends were people who laughed when you misbehaved. Denny, who nicknamed him Conan the Barbarian the first week of school, played with him like a remote-control car. Sim had seen at once what was happening, but Conan had not. He thought that having Denny Dumont as his champion would score points for him. But, as Sim well knew, Denny was nobody's champion except his own and took his pleasure only from the misery of smaller people. Now, a month into the year, it seemed that Conan wanted out from under Denny's thumb, but there was no getting away.

As Sim and Alex watched, waiting to enter the building, Denny was trying to give Conan something that he didn't want to take. Jack Thorpe and Carl Rudd thought it was side-splittingly funny. Then Denny whispered something in Conan's ear and Conan took whatever it was and put it in his pocket. As the crowd at the door thinned, Denny and his friends left Conan standing there and followed the others into the building.

"Good morning, Mr. Carraday," Denny said in his most polite voice, as he passed the vice principal. Sim took one last look over his shoulder as he passed into the building and saw Conan wipe at his face.

"Get a move on there, Conan," Mr. Carraday said.

"He's got something on him," Sim said to Alex as they entered the building.

"What? On Conan?"

"Yes. That's the way he is. Like the stuff he got on me."

Denny's mother had broken her hip two years earlier and his father had hired Sim's mother. That was when practical nurses could still get work, before the visiting-nurse program came to town and hired only registered nurses. Sim's mother had told Denny's mother about the stories he made up as a child in order to explain his father's absence. She had also mentioned buying clothes up in Bailey. Denny had overheard and made great use of that information at Sim's expense.

Sim figured out that the best defense was offense. That was when he started wearing neckties. You didn't get neckties unless you went to a thrift shop or a second hand store. It was a way of turning something that might have been embarrassing into an advantage. After awhile Denny's teasing didn't have the same sting. Sim had outsmarted Denny, however, and that wasn't something you got away with for very long.

"What do you think he's got on Conan?" Alex asked.

"Who knows? Something mean."

When the students had settled at their desks and everyone was holding up two fingers for silence, Miss Blenden announced that on Sunday morning there was going to be a lecture at the library. A man from the Smithsonian Institution was coming to Lost River Cove to talk about the Viking ship.

"Does anyone know what the Smithsonian Institution is?" she asked the class.

Four hands went up, including Greta's and Alex's. Miss Blenden called on neither of them. She called on Conan, who said it was where the space museum was. Miss Blenden was standing near his desk, as she often did when it appeared that Conan might be about to add some special effects to a statement – like turning himself or his pencil into a spaceship, Sim thought, smiling. Miss Blenden put a hand on his shoulder and he merely made a funny face.

"That's right, Conan," she said. "And several other museums as well. In fact, it is quite possible that the artifacts from the Viking ship in the harbor may end up there."

"No," Alex said. "My dad's going to build a museum right here."

"I didn't see a hand raised," Miss Blenden said, smiling at no one in particular. "Class, did anyone see a hand raised?" There was general agreement that no hands had been raised. Alex raised his hand. "Yes, Alex, did you want to say something?"

"There might be a museum right here," he said.

"Well, that would be even nicer, wouldn't it?" Miss Blenden said. "As I was saying.... As I might continue to say if people weren't talking and looking for things in their desks. Morty, is there something you need right now?"

Morty shook his head.

"Good, then if I might have your attention. My goodness, if you are this restless at eight in the morning, what is it going to be like here at two in the afternoon?" Opinions were offered and several demonstrations as well. Riot, for one moment, ruled. Miss Blenden clapped her hands three times.

The class came back to order. "This will be a wonderful opportunity for all of you to learn more about the history that is unfolding right here in our village. I'm sure that Greta will be there. As you all know, her father is the chief archaeologist of the dig. How about others of you?"

Amanda and Alex stared at the ceiling. Sim could feel Miss Blenden's gaze shift and land on him like a laser beam. "Sim, I think you are doing your report on the Vikings, aren't you?" It wasn't really a question. Miss Blenden was good at making things sound like questions. He looked up, as if drawn suddenly out of deep concentration.

"Huh?" The class laughed. He saw a smirk cross the two nearly identical faces of the twins.

"I'm sorry, Sim. Was that the sound of a goat or a boy?"

"Sorry. I wasn't paying attention."

But Miss Blenden had moved on. "Now who else would like to go to the lecture? I understand it will be illustrated with slides."

Morty Glick wanted to know if there would be any Vikings there. "No, just pictures of what they might have looked like," said Miss Blenden. "Billy? Good. Sarah, Felice. Very good. Any others?" Several students said that their families had other plans. Amanda explained that she had a French lesson.

Alex raised his hand and looked over at Sim with a sympathetic if slightly annoyed smile. A friend is a friend, his smile seemed to say. If you have to do Vikings I'll do Vikings with you.

It was when the class came back from art class at 1:30 that they found Miss Blenden in a fury. Bob Tate, the janitor was cleaning something up from the floor near Conan's desk. All the windows were open, a fan running at high speed in one of them. The smell in the room couldn't have been given a name. Flannery Daley covered her mouth and ran into the bathroom. Miss Blenden herded the class out into the hall and closed the door. Some minutes later, she found Conan hiding in the art room closet. Sim looked at Alex. Alex looked at Sim. Skunk perfume. Denny had made him do it. That's what he had handed to Conan on the playground. Whatever it was that Denny had on Conan would remain, for a little while longer, a secret between them.

Chapter 7

Saturday

Sim woke up the next morning with the happy realization that it was Saturday. It felt to him like an unexpected gift.

The first clue was silence. There was no noise from downstairs. No clatter of last night's dishes being put away. Nothing except the scurrying of a mouse in the wall behind his bed, a predictable event whatever day of the week it might be.

"Hey, Walter," he said, "it's Saturday. What do you think of that?"

If Walter thought much of it, he kept his enthusiasm hidden. He opened one eye, yawned, and closed it again.

Sim remembered that he had had a dream. At first it was one of his familiar and comforting dreams: he and his father were fishing off the wharf at the McCrory building. Then it morphed into something that wasn't really like a dream at all. Instead of being on the pier with his father he stood in front of the old McCrory building, which had been closed up since Putney Publishers had gone out of business a year earlier. It was night. Three or four cars drove past him as he stood there and several people ambled by without apparently noticing him.

Sim had never really looked closely at the building before. It looked out on the street with the eyes of a blind man, its two large street-front windows having been whitened to hide the now empty rooms within. The second and third stories of the building each contained four stone-silled windows, revealing nothing. There was a light on the third floor. It wasn't very obvious and Sim assumed it must have come from the back of the building. There must be somebody there, he thought. He could remember no more than that. He decided that it was the most boring dream he had ever had. He was also upset that it had interrupted his other dream, the happy one about being with his father.

The phone rang and he heard his mother's voice, then footsteps.

"Sim, are you up?"

"Yup."

"It's Alex."

Sim ran down the stairs and took the receiver from his mother. "Hey, Alex," he said.

"Hey, Sim, what's up?"

"You are, for one thing. What are you doing up so early? It's Saturday, you know."

"Right. Saturday. We're going to the beach. Or have you forgotten?"

"I thought we were going after breakfast?"

"It *is* after breakfast, Sim, it's nine o'clock."

"It can't be."

"It is. You must have slept late."

"I guess so."

"We'll be over in a few minutes."

"OK." Sim put the handset back on the receiver and yawned. It didn't feel like 9 a.m, that was for sure. He went back upstairs and dressed, putting the coin into the pocket of his overalls.

"So?" his mother said when he arrived in the kitchen.

"We're going to the beach. I guess I overslept," he said, opening Walter's food bin and filling his dish. Walter looked at it as he did each morning with an expression that said, "There must be some mistake here. This isn't what I ordered." Then, receiving no response, he walked to the bowl and munched a few of the kibbles, turning again to let Sim know that there was still time to correct this mistake. It was no use. Sim was filling a bowl with Nutritious Nutcake Cereal. He poured on the milk, sat on one of the stools at the counter, and watched his mother. She was frying up sausages for spaghetti sauce.

"Do you want to make your own lunch or shall I?" she asked.

"It's OK," he said. "Ponidi always makes it for all four of us. He even puts in a treat for Walter." Ponidi was the Pomeroys" caretaker, cook and baby sitter all rolled into one. He was also descended from a long line of *dukuns*, which were, Amanda insisted, Indonesian wizards. Alex said they were just medicine men of some kind. Sim had often thought that if the Pomeroy parents were to go away for three months, nothing would change in the lives of the children. It was to Ponidi that they looked for most everything that affected their lives. Ponidi was a person to whom Sim could say anything and know that he was being taken seriously. He felt the coin in his pocket. Maybe even that.

Walter had abandoned the kibbles and sat hopefully beside Sim's stool. "This is people food," Sim said. "You wouldn't like it." He knew that wasn't true even as he spoke. The only thing Walter didn't like was celery.

"No going in the ocean," his mother said, "not after the other night."

"No way," Sim said. "We're just going to mess around in the river." Messing around in the river meant exploring, building dikes and diversions in the sandbars, racing seashell boats, and scampering among the rocks at the end of the beach where the land began to climb into what would become Thunderhead Cliff, a mile south. When the tides were right, the sandbars, which made a small maze at the Sandy River's mouth, would warm the water. It was much more interesting than an ordinary beach.

"You and the twins?" she asked.

"And Greta," Sim said.

Sim heard the front gate open. He quickly finished his cereal and kissed his mother, something that it was getting less easy to do in the presence of his friends.

"Take a jacket in case it gets cloudy," she said.

"It's in my pack," he said. "C'mon, Walter."

Walter returned to his bowl and emptied it with great efficiency while Sim stood waiting. Then he followed Sim out the door.

With help from Ponidi, Sim had made a cart for Walter, whose legs weren't designed for keeping up with a bicycle. The cart was attached to the post under Sim's bicycle seat by a long curved piece of aluminum pipe. The axle was made from another piece of pipe, the wheels from a bike long abandoned by one of the older Pomeroys. The cart was finished off with a small oriental prayer rug donated by Mr. Pomeroy,

The twins knew not to ring the doorbell. Alex knocked just as Sim was about to open it.

"Hey," Sim said.

"Hey," Alex said. "You ready?"

"All ready."

"Let's mosey then." Alex turned and walked back toward the gate. Sim looked at Amanda and shaped without speaking it, the word Alex had just introduced. "Mosey?" his mouth said. Amanda rolled her eyes. Alex was a great asset to vocabulary building. If he picked up a new word in conversation, on television or in a book, he would use it at the earliest chance.

Walter climbed up onto his cart, rotated three times and lay down. He was sharing the space somewhat reluctantly with a collection of tools for the construction of sand castles and bridges.

"Where's Greta?" Sim asked.

"She's meeting us at the bridge," Amanda said, hopping on her bike and leading the procession down Fisher Lane, past the cemetery and along Water Street to Lost River Cove.

Chapter 8

Thunderhead Cliff

Greta joined them at the bridge and they began the five-mile ride from the Lost River Cove to Sandy River. Several years earlier the road had been resurfaced and, at that time, a bike path had been added on the east side of the road. It was another one of Mr. Pomeroys' projects. He had circulated a petition, the twins explained, and gotten the plan on the town ballot. Sim didn't know what a petition looked like. He imagined it was something that blew around until someone managed to get hold of it with a ballot. What any of that had to do with a bike path was beyond him. He was grateful to Mr. Pomeroy, however, because Shore Road would otherwise have been off-limits to children on bicycles. It was a road where drivers often paid more attention to occasional glimpses of the ocean than to where they were going.

Sim and his friends had made the trip to Sandy River many times, always taking the precaution, after they climbed the hill to Thunderhead Cliff, to stop and rest. They did so now. Sim was breathing the hardest because he had been hauling Walter behind him.

"Ready?" Alex asked after a couple of minutes. Sim nodded. Just ahead was the Wentworth Estate, home of Winifred Chit, the Witch of Thunderhead Cliff. Sim took a deep breath. The others did likewise. You couldn't let your breath out until you were well past the witch's lair. The Wentworth Estate was haunted. It wasn't just that Winifred Chit was 111 years old and a witch. The mists that gathered there when the wind blew and the waves thundered against the granite fortress of the headland bore the spirits of drowned sailors. People said that if you listened carefully you could hear them moan and if you watched with a patient eye you could see the mists take human shape. To breathe the air was to invite trouble.

Walter had no superstitions about the Wentworth Estate or witches and now, to Sim's great surprise and just as they took their breaths, he stood up in his cart and started barking. Instead of pedaling faster until they were safely past the witch's lair, Sim stopped.

Greta, Amanda, and Alex, several yards ahead, heard the racket and stopped. Greta, who didn't hold her breath and said the whole thing was nonsense, turned. "What's he doing?" she asked.

Sim shook his head.

"He's barking at something," Greta said. "What do you think it is?"

Sim let out his breath with a near explosive force. "I don't know," he said. "Walter! No!"

Walter not only ignored Sim's command but now put his front paws up on the cart's drop-back and struggled to get out. Sim got off his bike and tried to calm Walter, but it was no use.

"Maybe he has to pee," Greta said.

Sim shook his head. "I don't think so."

"Maybe it's a bear!" Amanda said. She had stopped holding her breath even before Sim.

Alex was the last to give in. "Or you-know-who."

In fact, this wasn't a very precise statement because there were now two you-know-whos, so no one could say who this particular you-know-who was. There was Splitface and there was Witch Chit.

Sim didn't believe all that was said of Winifred Chit – the part about luring sailors to their deaths, for example. But there was a history book in the library that spoke of shipwrecks and how, in at least one instance, nothing had ever been found of crew or cargo. Only the crushed timbers of the hull and two of the masts, one of which could be seen today in front of the post office serving as a flagpole.

Afraid that Walter might injure himself trying to jump out of the cart, Sim let down the back. Walter made a dash for the woods, broke through the bracken at roadside, and disappeared. Sim looked at his companions with a helpless shrug of his shoulders and stood there waiting. Just ahead was the driveway to the Wentworth Estate, darkened like a tunnel by a canopy of bittersweet vine.

There was no question of calling Walter, except in the smallest whisper, which would have been pointless. Anything louder might reveal their presence.

"Didn't there used to be more cars on this road?" Alex asked.

"Lots more," Amanda said.

"Maybe the road's closed up ahead," Alex said.

"Why would the road be closed?" Greta asked.

"I don't know. Maybe there's something in it."

"Something like what?"

"I don't know. Something big. Maybe the thing that Walter smelled."

"Maybe if this is where it started, it will circle back," Amanda suggested.

These unpleasant thoughts were put aside when Walter's head appeared from the roadside bracken.

"Thank goodness," Sim said. "Come on, Walter, let's go. Good dog! Come on, boy."

But Walter, instead of advancing to the road, turned, his wagging tail momentarily in evidence, and headed back into the forest.

"No, Walter," Sim pleaded. "Come, Walter. Come!"

Again Walter's head emerged, then again his tail, and again he disappeared.

"He wants us to follow him," Greta said. Sim was surprised at her tone of voice. It was almost approving. Of course Greta had not grown up in Lost River Cove as Sim and the twins had. Things that were pretty well set in Sim's mind were, in Greta's, open for investigation. Greta had lived in places Sim and his friends had never even heard of. For one year in a place called Mongolia. Another time in a place with a jungle. Once, exploring a cave with her father on an island she had found a tooth. She had shown it to Sim. It was from a saber-toothed tiger. Now Greta got off her bicycle and walked up to where Walter had once again disappeared.

"Maybe he's found something important," Sim said.

"Yeah, and I don't want to know what," Alex said.

Sim got off his bicycle and joined Greta. He parted the bracken and looked into the forest. It was surprisingly clear of deadfall, unlike most of the woods he had explored around Lost River Cove. And the trees were taller, fatter, and farther apart from one another. It was a forest one could walk through without being swished, cobwebbed, tripped, and sprinkled. He turned to find Greta standing beside him.

"This is ancient," she said in a voice filled with wonder. Sim suddenly felt a strange sense of pride. It puzzled him. Then he realized that it was the first time he had shown or said anything to Greta that she had not already known or seen.

"It's pretty cool," he said.

"I'll bet it's cool," Alex said. "Is there a gingerbread house?"

"No, seriously guys. You ought to see it."

The twins joined him and then all four of them walked through the bracken into the forest. Greta stood, her hands on her hips, surveying the great trees as if about to take her first steps in a new land.

"I'll bet this is a virgin forest," Alex said.

"What's a virgin forest?" Sim asked.

"It's one where nobody has ever cut down a tree."

"Unlikely," Greta said. Greta didn't put people down the way Alex sometimes did. She simply put things right. It seemed to Sim that she saw it more as a responsibility than an opportunity to show off.

Sim looked around and, seeing no obvious mischief among the trees, relaxed.

"It's beautiful," Amanda said.

"But how much can we trust Walter?" Alex asked.

"Pretty much," Sim said, experimentally. "I mean I don't think he'd let anything bad happen to us."

"Unless he's been enchanted," Alex said.

"There's that," Sim said. "But he doesn't look enchanted."

On the contrary, Walter looked very much himself. He marked a couple of trees as if to take ownership of the ancient forest and then set a course directly toward the ocean and Thunderhead Cliff.

"I think he wants us to follow him," Sim said.

Greta turned. "Let's go," she said.

"What about our bicycles?" Alex asked

"Maybe you'd like to stay behind and guard them," Amanda said.

"That's not what I meant," Alex said.

"The bikes will be fine," Sim said.

"And people will know where we went if anything happens," Amanda added.

"I don't think anything's going to happen," Sim said, surprising himself at the certainty of his feeling.

Alex looked at him quizzically. "Yeah, whatever," he said.

Sim, hearing the confusion in Alex's response, wanted to say more but couldn't find words to describe his sudden feeling of rightness, the keen sense of anticipation. It was like that day he had found the coin on the beach.

They had to quickstep to keep up with Walter. Not even a chattering squirrel distracted him from the route he had chosen. They walked for awhile without speaking, and then Sim, who had taken the lead, stopped. There was a sound.

"What's that?" Amanda asked.

"Guns," Alex said. "Big ones. Cannons!"

"Sure sounds like it," Sim said. "But it couldn't be."

There was something. Even Walter had stopped and was sniffing the air for clues. Then they felt it. Beneath their feet, the ground shook. Sim remembered a thunderstorm earlier in the summer. Then too the ground had shaken beneath his feet, but now the sky was cloudless. Walter took a few steps, paused, looked over his shoulder, and continued, cautiously, toward Thunderhead Cliff. The companions followed. No one spoke. As they walked, the light seemed to dim as if there were a forest within the forest. Then they could smell the sea and feel a softness on their faces. The explosions grew louder - some sudden and sharp, others deep and rumbling as if beneath them giants mined the earth with gunpowder.

Chapter 9

The Cave

The forest began to thin and they could glimpse the sea between the trees, but it was a sea Sim had never seen. Thunderhead Cliff was well named. They stood well back from the edge, for a moment speechless at the spectacle. The sea looked like a liquid mountain range, rolling toward the wall of the cliff. Wave after giant wave crashed into the rock wall, its spray rising like a great geyser. It was this that had wetted their faces and dimmed the sky. The artillery, firing round after round and shaking the earth with its recoil, was no more or less than the sea echoing in the grotto below Thunderhead Cliff.

"It's the hurricane," Alex said.

"Hurricane?" Sim asked.

"Not here," Alex said. "Out at sea. My Dad told me about it. Oh, I forgot. I was going to tell you. It's named Simeon."

"Cool," Sim said. "But it's a nice day."

"It's way out to sea. Real far out. But the waves go a long way," said Alex.

"What happened to Walter?" Amanda asked. They had been so preoccupied with the spectacle before them that they had forgotten for a moment about their leader. Sim whistled, but there was no response. Below where they stood and separating them from the cliff edge was a clearing in the shape of a half circle almost too perfect to have been an accident of nature. It looked like a small outdoor theater complete with moss-covered rocks for seats. On one of the rocks stood a seagull, his head cocked to one side, watching them. Sim looked to see if there were other gulls. There weren't. Not even in the sky above.

Rough-hewn steps led down to the clearing.

"He must have gone down there," Sim said, leading the way.

Then they heard his bark, or rather they heard an echo of his bark. Reaching the clearing, they still saw no sign of him. They heard his bark again and he emerged.

"It's a cave," Greta said, approaching an opening in the cliff side just below where they had stood moments earlier. The others followed. Once inside they could see nothing. Sim whistled. The sound bounced and came back to him. "It's big," he said.

"There could be bears in here," Alex cautioned, staying near the entrance.

"If there was a bear, Walter would have discovered him," Sim said. "Anyway it's summer and bears hibernate in winter."

"Yeah, but they have to live somewhere in the summertime too, don't they?" Alex persisted.

"You can guard outside if you want to," Amanda said. It was the second time in fifteen minutes she had made that kind of suggestion, Sim noticed. He caught her eye. "Anyway it's good that one of us is cautious," she said.

"Forget it, Amanda," Alex said. "I'm not ashamed to be cautious."

"I think it's safe," Sim said. "Anyway, there's nothing we can do without a flashlight."

"I've got a flashlight," Alex said. "I'm not sure it still works. I haven't changed the battery for a long time. It probably doesn't. It's not very bright even if it does work." Sim had to smile. Alex couldn't resist being the guy with the right word or the right tool at the right time, but he really wasn't eager to go into the cave. Alex removed the small flashlight, one of several multi purpose implements he carried attached to his belt.

Walter, apparently having found nothing of interest in the cave, wandered over to a log at the edge of the clearing, jumped it, and disappeared along the cliff top.

"Where's he going?" Amanda asked.

"Exploring," Sim said. "It's OK. He won't get lost."

Alex had now detached his flashlight. He tried it. It worked.

"I don't mind going in first," Sim said, holding out his hand.

"Well," Alex said. "It is your cave after all. I mean it's Walter's cave and, well, Walter's your dog." He handed the flashlight to Sim.

Greta had already entered the chamber. Sim followed her with the light. "Hello?" Greta called. "Lo...." came back the answer from the stone walls. Sim whistled. The sound bounced. He whistled again and then again and the cave was filled with bright, sharp sound. Amanda clapped her hands. Alex hooted. It was a big cave, that much was certain. Sim explored the walls with the small beam of the flashlight. At one place there was a passage going deeper into the cliff. Sim focused the light there, but it wasn't strong enough to penetrate the long darkness.

"We need to come back with more flashlights," he said. Then they continued around the wall of the main room.

"Wow!" Sim said.

The other three caught their breath. There on the wall before them were a number of childlike drawings.

"I guess we aren't the first kids to have found this place," Amanda said.

"I can draw better than that," Alex said.

"Look at this," Sim said, directing the beam of the flashlight to one of the drawings.

"It's a boat," Greta said.

He moved the flashlight beam to the right, where there were three drawings of people that looked like this:

"I don't think these were made by kids," Sim said. He scanned the beam around the cave.

"They look like petroglyphs," Greta said.

Amanda turned to her friend, "What are those?"

"They're very ancient drawings," Greta said. "Thousands of years old. They're all over the world. Papa has a book on them."

"What do they mean?" Sim asked.

"Different things. Lots are about hunting and animals. Some are pictures of ancient gods. Sometimes they tell stories."

"I hate to say this, guys," Sim said, "because it's going to sound really weird. But I have the feeling I've been here before."

"How could you have been here before if you've never been here before?" Alex asked. "If you don't mind not being weird just now I'd appreciate it."

"He could have been here in another life," Amanda suggested matter-of-factly. "Anyway, I don't think it's any accident that we found this cave."

"OK, I'm out of here," Alex said turning back toward the entrance. But before he reached it they heard a voice.

"Good dog," the voice said.

Chapter 10

The Witch of Thunderhead Cliff

"Uh-oh," Alex said, looking at Sim. Sim put his finger to his lips and crept quietly to the cave entrance. Then he peered in the direction from which the voice had come. About 30 feet away from the cave out toward the cliff edge, Walter was gazing up at an elderly lady with whom he appeared to be having a conversation. She reached into her pocket and produced a treat that Walter accepted without a second thought. Then she gave him a good firm rub on his ears in a way known only to dog owners.

Dogs don't just show up in the middle of nowhere, and, for all practical purposes, the Wentworth Estate fit that description. It was only a matter of time before the old lady would look around for Walter's owner or, if she knew dogs as well as Sim thought, she might send him to find that owner. Sold out by his best friend! Sim shook his head in disbelief. What was it to be? Hide in the shadows of the cave, waiting to be sniffed out or take the tiger by the tail? He took a deep breath and stepped out into the sunlight, where he stood waiting, hands at his side, the way he assumed you should when trespassing.

Sim again saw the log that Walter had jumped earlier, beginning his explorations. He could see now that there was a path leading back from it along the cliff's edge. The old lady looked up as Walter jumped the log. "Here, give me an arm," she said, looking at Sim, as if it were the most natural thing in the world for a boy to be standing there awaiting instructions. Sim crossed the clearing and held out his arm. She took it firmly, steadied herself, and stepped over the log. Her hand on his arm was as light as a breeze, and it seemed as she alighted that she hardly touched the ground.

She wore brown shoes, brown wool stockings, a brown skirt and jacket, white gloves and a hat decorated with flowers and a cardinal that rocked back and forth. It was a male cardinal, Sim noticed. Bright red. The flowers weren't real and they looked a little dusty. She didn't look at all like a witch, Sim thought. But she didn't look much like a person either. More like a soft cloud in a dress. Then he saw her eyes. They twinkled. She smiled. Walter stood between them, looking at one and then the other, wagging his tail.

It was Sim's first experience with a witch. He decided to let her start the conversation.

"Well, I see you've found my cave," she said.

It wasn't an accusation and it wasn't a simple statement of fact. Sim looked at Walter sitting obediently at her side.

"Actually it was Walter who found it," Sim said.

"And who is Walter?" she asked.

"He is," Sim said, pointing to the self-satisfied canine at her side.

"He is a very resourceful dog. He found me as well, in my garden." She reached into the pocket of her jacket and produced another dog biscuit, which Walter accepted with a surprising delicacy.

"I'm sorry," Sim said. Then, realizing that she might take this the wrong way he quickly added, " I mean I'm sorry he bothered you."

She examined Sim more intently. "Do I know you?" she asked.

I don't think so," Sim said.

"At my age it's always a good thing to ask," she said. "Still, I thought maybe I had. I usually remember eyes. Well, no matter."

"I'm Sim," he said. "Simeon actually," he added.

"Sim," she said, examining him carefully. "Of course you are. And it's time isn't it?"

It was rude to stand with your mouth open but, Sim couldn't think of anything to do with it right at that moment, and by the time he had framed his question, the old lady with the flowered hat had redirected her attention to the cave entrance.

"My goodness," she said. "A troop of cave explorers."

The companions joined Sim, Greta in the lead.

"Are there more still inside?" the old lady asked.

"No, just us," Greta said. "We didn't touch anything."

"You've come to look at the drawings," the old lady said. "Aren't they wonderful?"

"You don't mind?" Alex asked.

"I don't think so," she said, as if moved by Alex's suggestion to reconsider. "Not if you keep them to yourselves. The local historical society can be very tiresome. They're always after me for one thing or another. That Mr. Pomeroy. He's so enthusiastic."

"It's just for ourselves," Amanda reassured her.

"The old lady looked at Alex, then at Amanda, then back at Alex. "Twins," she said "I don't think I know any twins. Have we met before?"

"No," Amanda said. "We're Pomeroys, with the enthusiastic father. I'm Amanda and he's Alex," she said pointing to her brother.

"I once had a twin," the old lady said. She became thoughtful for a moment. "That was a long time ago. My goodness. I haven't had so many visitors for a long time and where are my manners? I am Winifred Chit. Or Hazel if you prefer."

"I'm Greta Hoffner," Greta said, extending her hand. Winifred Hazel Chit took it in her own, examining it as she might a shell from the beach. Then she looked at Greta, all the time nodding to herself.

"Have you made the discovery yet?" she whispered.

"Discovery?" Greta asked.

"I guess you haven't," Miss Chit said. "That's going to happen later." She patted Greta's hand and turned to Alex.

Alex glanced quickly at Sim who understood the glance to say, "She really is a witch."

"I think we probably ought to be getting home," Alex said. "It's ummm." He looked at his watch. "It's eleven o'clock. Almost eleven o'clock. Not quite, actually. Just a little before."

"Nonsense," Miss Chit said. "I haven't had such youthful company in years. You're not going to go running off now, just as we're getting acquainted. We'll have some tea and cookies. Oh, children don't like tea, do they?"

"I like it, Miss Chit," Greta said.

"I like iced tea now and then with sugar," Amanda said. Alex looked at the two of them with disbelief.

Sim was torn. If Miss Chit was a witch, she didn't appear to be a very dangerous one. A little batty, but not obviously evil. Walter seemed determined that they should have met her. And Sim wanted to know what it was time for.

"I can't keep milk," she said, "It goes bad. There may be a bottle of ginger ale. I think Ponidi brought one the last time he brought my groceries.

"Ponidi?" Alex asked.

But Miss Chit was on her way. "Here, give me your arm," she said to Sim, approaching the log. "And call me Winifred, or Hazel, anything but Miss Chit." He helped her over and they started down the path, Walter in the lead, then Winifred Hazel Chit, Sim, the girls, and Alex bringing up the rear, shaking his head.

Chapter 11

Ginger Ale and Cookies

There was nothing in Sim's experience to which Wentworth Hall compared. Nothing in his real-life experience, that is. The Wentworth Estate looked like certain places he had read about and even some places in his dreams. Small, round towers, which once must have been impressive, now tilted at odd angles. Chimneys leaned away from the sea as if ready to take a step. An enormous front porch faced the sea, but what remained of its floor, Sim thought, wouldn't have supported the weight of a fat raccoon. Its roof was a high garden of lichen and moss. The lawns were gone to field and the field well on its way to forest.

But it was not the house to which their hostess led Sim and his friends. It was to a small cottage as different from the great house as day from night. First off, it was made of stone to which time had made much less difference. Its roof, Sim observed, no less a garden of mosses, was firm and straight at its beam. There were window boxes and, most striking of all, a garden in the middle of the wilderness. It looked, Sim thought, like a painting hanging on a tree.

Winifred Hazel Chit opened the door. Sim and the others followed her into a neat kitchen. It was not as neat as Ponidi's kitchen at Pomeroy Hall, or even Sim's kitchen, but it was bright and clean. There was a table with two chairs. Under a long window that let in a surprising amount of light there was a bench piled with books, some needlework, a pair of gardening shoes and a trowel, several hats and sweaters, a burned-out teakettle, a glass jar with a label that said *hollyhock seeds* and a small globe of a winter scene.

"I don't have many guests," she said. "We'll have to move that." Four pair of hands, eager for something to do, pitched in and quickly cleared the bench, carrying its contents as instructed to the adjoining parlor. Sim carried the globe, which suddenly filled with snow as he tilted it. He examined it. It was a simple trick, he saw. White particles in water, heavier than the water, settling slowly.

Their hostess could not find the tin of cookies, but she did produce the remains of a box of somewhat spotted chocolates and the promised bottle of ginger ale that divided itself nicely into five glasses.

"How come you have dog biscuits?" Sim asked.

"I have had dogs," Hazel said. "I have had many dogs, but they keep dying. And they're too rambunctious. The last one I had kept knocking me over." She looked at Walter who, disloyal to the end, had not left her side since the first dog biscuit. "If I had a dog again, I should like to have one like this. Sedate and reasonable, What's his name again?"

"Walter."

"A very sensible name," she said, producing another dog biscuit. Sim wondered which were older, the chocolates or the dog biscuits. Walter didn't seem to care.

"Are you really a witch?" Alex asked.

"I'm not sure," Miss Chit said. " At 111 anything is possible."

"I didn't know people could be 111," Amanda said quietly.

"Neither did I," Miss Chit responded. "And I take no responsibility for it. If I could have my way I'd have been long gone. But promises are promises." She looked significantly at Sim.

Amanda looked at Sim, then at Miss Chit. "How do people get to be witches?"

"I wanted to be famous someday." Miss Chit said, wistfully. "I realized that all famous women had middle names or middle initials at least. If you had only a first and last name, you'd never amount to a row of beans. So I became Hazel W. Chit. When I turned in my school papers that's what I wrote. One day we came back to the school room and someone had written my name on the board, rearranging the letters. It said Witch Hazel. I don't suppose you've ever heard of Witch Hazel in this day and age."

The companions shook their heads.

"Well, I suffered for a few weeks as a witch before I gave up Hazel altogether and decided just to be Winifred."

"You can be Hazel with us if you want to," Greta volunteered.

"I think I will be," she said

"You said it's time," Sim began, but before he had Hazel's attention Alex interrupted.

""How do you know Ponidi?" he asked.

"Well, now, that's an interesting story," she said, taking another chocolate from the box. "Being a witch can be very useful. People keep their distance. Of course, if people don't believe in witches that's another matter. Or if they're out selling encyclopedias or religion. I get a few of them now and then. And then there was Ponidi."

"What did Ponidi think?" Amanda asked.

Hazel chuckled. "He thought we might have something in common," she said. "His grandfather had lived to 105. And dear Ponidi...well."

"He's a *dukun*," Amanda said.

"What's a *dukun*?" Greta asked.

Alex beamed. There was something he knew that Greta didn't. "A medicine man," he said. "In Indonesia. That's where he was born."

"Not a medicine man, a wizard," Amanda corrected. "Isn't that right, Miss Chit?"

"Hazel, please," she said. " Yes, he told me about his ancestry. *Dukun*. Yes, that was the word. I think he was disappointed to find out that I wasn't anything but a very old lady. We had a good talk despite that. And then another one and so on, and then we did have things in common."

"He never said anything about knowing you," Alex said. "He's practically raised us. How could he never say anything about you?" He paused. Sim could almost see his next thought take shape. 'And he never told you anything about Amanda and me?' Alex's disillusionment was painfully clear.

"You're not the center of the world, you know Alex," Amanda said.

"Oh, I'm sure he has mentioned you," Hazel said in an offhand way. "We had an agreement. We both like our privacy now and then. Which reminds me. Delightful as your visit has been it's time for my nap. People my age take a good many naps."

She stood up, looking, for a moment, confused. Sim wondered how anyone could ever have mistaken Miss Chit – no, Hazel – for a witch. "I'll find those cookies," she said, "next time you come." She turned to Walter. "And you too. You are a very good dog. I'll have to ask Ponidi to bring two bottles of ginger ale and some fresh dog biscuits. Unless you'd rather have something else. I could have him bring lemons and we could make some lemonade. Does everyone like lemonade?"

Sim, unfamiliar with conversation that drifted so suddenly, nodded. Hazel ushered them to the door.

"You can walk out the driveway," she said. "It's much more convenient.' She led them out of the cottage.

"You said it was time," Sim said.

"Did I?" Hazel responded, apparently trying to remember. "When was that, dear?"

"When I told you my name. You said, "It's almost time, isn't it"' And then later you said something about promises and you looked at me."

Hazel reached down and rubbed Walter's ears. "You are the clever fellow, aren't you? You knew it was almost time, didn't you?"

Sim could hardly contain himself. "Well!?" he blurted out. It was totally out of place. He knew it the minute he had spoken, but he stood his ground. It was too important to let go.

Hazel looked up slowly. She studied his face. Sim felt the red in his cheeks. "Time will tell." she said. "It always does. We must be patient." And with that she turned, stooped with surprising agility, and pulled out a dandelion from a bed of roses. Then taking it with her, she walked back into her cottage, closing the door behind her.

Chapter 12

A Robbery

Lying on the widow's walk Saturday night with Walter snoring lightly beside him, Sim had another strange dream. The setting was unfamiliar, but not entirely. It was definitely Lost River Cove and it may have been a street on which he had ridden his bicycle one time or another. It wasn't a very nice street. The lawns weren't well kept and there were a number of cars that hadn't been driven for awhile, sitting on back lawns. There was a full moon, just as there had been as he fell asleep, and he could see quite well.

He was standing outside a small clapboard house badly in need of painting. A bicycle lacking its front wheel lay in the driveway. For some reason it was the garage that wanted his attention, and he started to walk toward it when he heard people arguing in the house. A man and a woman and now and then a younger voice, which he felt he knew but could not place. Then the man's voice was louder and the child was crying. Before he could learn more, he awoke and looked at his clock. It was ten. He had been asleep for only an hour.

Sim was up early Sunday morning for the lecture at the library. There was no getting out of it, Miss Blenden would be there, checking on who showed up. Dogs weren't invited and, in any case, Walter had his own visits to make. They parted at their usual corner.

When Sim arrived at the library, he saw Chief Turnbull's police car sitting outside. He didn't pay much attention until he noticed that a crowd of people had gathered by the library's front doors, Alex among them. Sim joined them and watched as the chief stood talking with Fred. Dumont, the library janitor. He was the kind of man who couldn't talk without nodding his head, as if ready to agree with anyone about anything even before an opinion had been expressed. Mrs. Rose, the librarian and Mr. Pomeroy were there too, and a man Sim had never seen before. "What happened?" Sim asked as he joined Alex.

"A robbery," Alex said.

"When?" Sim asked.

"It's not sure." Alex said. "It was from that glass case on the second floor. You know, the one with stuff from when they built the library. Stuff they dug up. Nobody pays much attention to it, but Dr. Pleever wanted to see something that was there, and when Mrs. Rose went to show him, the case was empty."

"Who's Dr. Pleever?"

"The guy from Washington. He's giving the lecture. He stays with us when he comes to town."

"What'd they steal?"

"Some coins and stuff."

"What kind of coins?" Sim asked.

"I only looked at the case once. I remember there were some clay pipes and arrowheads and some kind of jewelry. I don't remember there being coins, but I guess there were."

As they watched, the man from Washington took something out of his pocket and showed it to the others. Mr. Pomeroy looked at it and scratched his head. Sim recognized the gesture that was always accompanied by the words, "could be, could be, very possibly, very possibly." Mr. Dumont saw the thing too and stepped back, bumping into Chief Turnbull. He apologized in an exaggerated and comic sort of way and left the office.

"Dumont's in a pretty big hurry," Sim said.

"You would be too if you'd spent as much time in the town jail as he has and almost knocked over the police chief," Alex said.

"How come?" Sim asked.

"He's a drunk. Dad says you can be a sweet drunk or a mean one and he's a mean one. He hits people and breaks things."

The group dispersed and the chief walked to the front door. Passing the boys, he paused and smiled. "You tell Walter when you see him that I'm sorry I wasn't at the station house for his visit yesterday, Sim. I know he counts on a little treat."

"I'll tell him, Sir." Sim said. He had a sudden temptation to remove the coin from his pocket and ask if it was like any of the ones that had been stolen, but the chief had already passed and was on his way down the steps.

"I wonder if they'll still have the talk?" Alex asked.

A young man whom Sim had never seen before turned, appeared to study them carefully, and then informed them that the lecture would be postponed for half an hour. The young man didn't look much older than Alex's older brother, Jerome, though he was clearly making an attempt. He wore pinstriped pants, an embroidered vest, and a black jacket with a flower in its button hole. A carefully folded white handkerchief peeked from his jacket pocket. There was the suggestion of a moustache on his upper lip. Most remarkable of all, however, was his shiny black gold-tipped walking stick. He looked to Sim like a character out of a movie.

Like his father, sometimes a little stuffy, Alex occasionally played the role of official greeter. "Thanks," he said, extending his hand. "I'm Alex Pomeroy."

"I'm very pleased to meet you," the man said, with a slight bow that made him all the more preposterous. "I know your father. He is a man of most remarkable talents. I think it's fair to say that none of this would be happening" – he gestured with his cane in the direction of the harbor where the Viking ship sat – "without your father's inquiring mind and remarkable generosity."

Then he looked at Sim. "And your friend?" he asked.

"This is Sim," Alex said.

"Sim," the man said. "What an original name. My name is Smith," he said. "Adrian Ahrenberg Smith." He extended his hand.

Sim took it reluctantly. Because of knowing the Pomeroys, he had experience in shaking hands, but it wasn't something he enjoyed very much. You never shook hands with someone your own age and adult hands made you feel small. Not so with Mr. Smith whose hand wasn't much larger than Sim's.

"How do you do," Sim said.

"Very well indeed," the man said. "Until the lecture, then," he said, bowing again and turning away. Alex rolled his eyes.

There were still twenty minutes before the talk and the boys walked out to sit on the Oracle Stone, which dominated the center of the library's front lawn as it sloped down to Water Street. Sim had never been able to understand why a giant rock the size of an automobile was called a stone. There was a story that people told. It had once been a giant's book, when giants still lived. One day a young giant who was always leaving his books out in the rain woke up at night hearing a crack of thunder. Remembering that he had left the book in the field, he ran there. But he was too late. A bolt of lightning hit the book and turned it to stone. It was a shame, because the book had been filled with important knowledge that could never be found again. That was the oracle part, Sim's mother had explained. Oracles were people in ancient times who unraveled secrets.

They climbed up and Alex started talking about the new car his father had just gotten– a 1944 Packard. Mr. Pomeroy collected old cars. Alex told Sim all about it as they sat there, but Sim's mind was elsewhere. He was remembering an earlier time when he had sat where he now sat. There were lots of stories of people asking questions of the Oracle Stone and having the answers suddenly appear in their minds. You had to sit there for a long time, someone had told him, very patiently, concentrating just on the question to which you wanted an answer. Sim had tried.

"Where is my father?" he had asked the stone. "Is he going to come back someday?" He wondered where the answer would come from. Would it just appear in his mind, or would there be a voice, he had wondered. A gull had landed beside him. No vision had come to him, no voice whispered in his ear, no hand ruffled his hair. He had been disappointed and angry: angry at himself for believing in magic, for hoping. He had taken it out on the gull, reaching to knock it off the Oracle Stone. But it had flown away.

"Omigosh!" he said aloud.

Alex, who was still going on about the car, stopped. "What's up?" he asked.

"The seagull," Sim said. He wasn't really speaking to Alex. He was working it out. It was like a film in reverse. Something, a cup maybe, breaks and then comes back together again. It felt like that now. That day when he had found the first medallion. The seagull. The lone seagull, digging in the sand. And the man on the bridge, the boy on his back. Sim had looked longingly at them, sad not to be the boy, not to have a father. Then, too, he had been about to take it out on the gull. He had actually picked up a stone to throw. But the gull was scratching at the sand and looking at him, trying to get his attention.

When he had turned again to look at the bridge, the man and the boy were gone. Vanished. As if they had never been there. Of course that was crazy. It was just that he had lost track of time. For a minute, two minutes maybe. He had felt, just for a moment, the sense of being that boy, of feeling the strong back beneath him. Now it all began to fit together. Asking his question that time years ago. The gull landing beside him. The same gull who had shown him the medallion. The gull and his father were connected. Somehow. And he was the boy on the bridge. And the medallion. His head was spinning. "It's crazy," he said. "Totally impossibly crazy."

"What's crazy?"

"The Oracle Stone," he said. "It's putting stuff in my head."

"Right. And Santa Claus really comes down the chimney and the Easter Bunny hides eggs. It's just a story made up for the tourists. We better head back if we want to get seats." Alex jumped down from the rock and turned. Sim hesitated for a moment. It was true about the Oracle Stone, but no one would ever believe him. He jumped down and followed Alex back up the library lawn.

People started to go into the library for the lecture. Sim saw Greta and Miss Blenden. He waved and Greta waved back. Then she ascended the library steps with perfect posture and approached the door as she did most things in life, with purpose and assurance. Sim smiled to himself. Miss Blenden, clutching a notebook, was right behind her.

"We'd better go in," Alex suggested, "or we'll have to sit in the front row."

They ran the distance to the steps. The lecture was to be held in the Pomeroy Room, named for the library's chief benefactor. A table was set up at one end of the room, with a lectern in the middle. At one end of the table sat Greta's father, Dr. Hoffner. The man from Washington sat at the other. He had white hair that was parted in the middle and came down to the unusually high collar of a shiny red shirt. Over the shirt he wore a black vest and below the vest black trousers and shoes. Everything about him was interesting: a nose that was almost too long and almost too straight but not quite, and eyes that were as restful and secret as tidal pools. Sim realized that he was staring. The man looked back and smiled. Sim looked away.

Chairs had been arranged to provide an aisle in the center. Midway down the aisle was a projector. A screen had been set up behind the lectern. "Greta's over there," Alex said, pointing to the front row. Most seats were filled, as Alex had predicted. All except the front rows. "It's either stand or sit up there," Alex continued, having one more look over the room.

"I don't want to be up front," Sim said. "Let's stand."

They moved to the back of the room. The excavation in the harbor had created a good deal of interest in Lost River Cove. He and Alex weren't the only ones without seats. The room was nearly full.

Dr. Hoffner thanked everybody for coming and made a little speech about how none of this would be happening if not for the generosity of Percy Pomeroy. Mr. Pomeroy stood up and people clapped. Then Dr. Hoffner told about awards that Dr. Pleever had received and held up copies of two of his books – one on the Stone Age and early metal age civilizations and one on ancient languages of Scandinavia. Then he told a joke, which nobody but Greta and Dr. Pleever laughed at, about digging things up on people, and introduced the speaker.

"I'll bet Greta made up the joke," Alex whispered.

"Probably," Sim said, hoping that Alex wasn't going to talk all the way through this the way he did at movies.

Dr. Pleever's voice, it turned out, was even more interesting than his high-collared shirt or his almost-too-long nose. It was the kind of voice that made dead things come to life, the kind that fathers in movies had when they tucked children in and told them stories. He told about the Vikings' ships with their square sails and dragon-headed prows and how they struck terror into the hearts of shore dwellers. They could cross the open oceans under sail and then switch to oars for lightning-fast hit-and-run attacks on undefended towns and monasteries. The secret of the Viking ship, he explained, lay in its construction. Dr. Hofner turned on the projector and Dr. Pleever showed pictures someone had drawn of what it would have looked like to build such a vessel.

He showed other pictures as well. Some of the most interesting were of rock carvings on the north coast of Norway, more than 4,000 years old. They were very simple drawings of reindeer and fish and hunters, and one of a ship. Sim nudged Alex. It was just like one of the drawings on the cave wall.

This was all much more interesting than Sim had expected it to be, so interesting that it wasn't until near the end that he remembered he was supposed to be taking notes for his paper. He took his notebook out of his overalls bib and reached into his pocket for the stub of a pencil he had picked up at the card file on the way in. The coin was there. He touched it. It wasn't just purring, it was tingling, just as it had when Splitface had touched him and he had fainted. Amanda hadn't felt anything when they had been at Bartlett's Restaurant, but now, Sim thought, no one could fail to. He had to test that thought. He took the coin from his pocket and nudged Alex with his elbow. When Alex turned, he handed him the coin. "Feel it," he said.

He realized his mistake the moment he saw the expression on his friend's face. But by then it was too late. The coin fell to the floor with a loud clang and then spun in that annoying way round objects have until it came to rest with a small, apologetic plop.

Chapter 13

Cows in The Pomeroy Room

By the time the coin came to rest, Sim realized that the audience's attention was directed almost entirely to where he stood, smiling weakly. The coin had rolled under one of the chairs in the back row. The man sitting there was the same one who had earlier praised Mr. Pomeroy, the young man with the gold-tipped cane. Now the man reached down, picked up the coin, turned and handed it to Sim, the slightest smile shaping his mouth.

Sim quickly put it in his pocket. Ignoring the interruption, Dr. Pleever went on with his lecture. Once the audience had turned back to the front, Alex looked at Sim and made a comically guilty face.

Then it was time for questions and answers. Someone asked if the ship in the rock carving from the north coast of Norway was the same as the one in the harbor. Dr. Pleever replied that the drawing was really too primitive to allow detailed comparison, but given the number of occupants represented in the carving, it would appear to have been of about the same size as the ship in Lost River Cove. Then he took a small leather case from his pocket.

"One of the joys of working at a place like the Smithsonian," he began, "is the possibility for collaboration. We have so many researches going on at the same time that one often intersects with another and that can be quite exciting. For example...."

He opened the case.

"This interesting little object was brought into the museum by a coin collector who had purchased it in a pawnshop. He knew a good deal about ancient currencies." Dr. Pleever removed a coin from the case. "But..., he began, and then he stopped. His brows furrowed. He started again to speak and stopped a second time. He apologized for being momentarily distracted, took a sip from his water glass and continued.

"But the coin collector was unable to identify it. Our experts weren't able to do any better. The owner agreed to leave it with us so that we could do some metallurgical analysis and carbon dating. The results were as puzzling as the object itself." Dr. Pleever paused the way people do when a room falls silent with attention, then continued. "The first surprise was that this little medallion – as we decided to call it for reasons I will explain in a moment – contains crystals of blue topaz. If there is a gemologist among you, he or she will know that blue topaz does not occur in nature. It is made by irradiating and then heating clear crystals. It is not something one imagines being done during the Pleistocene period, two million years ago. And yet the metals date to at least two million years, perhaps much older."

The audience, which had remained silent, now began to stir. People whispered to their neighbors. Was this a joke? Was this man as strange as he appeared? What was he trying to tell them? What did all of this have to do with the Viking ship?

"I know," Dr. Pleever continued. "It's impossible. More likely is the possibility that it is part of a meteorite that was found and shaped millions of years later, perhaps as a piece of jewelry." The audience appeared to be reassured by these explanations, and Sim could see heads nodding. Dr. Pleever continued. "You're wondering, of course, what this little medallion has to do with your Viking ship. Well, the coin dealer from whom our friend purchased the medallion is just down the coast five miles from here. As it turns out, the dealer contacted me five years later. He had found a second medallion misplaced within his inventory of early Roman coins. It was at this point that we began to think in terms of your Viking ship. Together the medallions begin to suggest a story: Probably they came from Europe, but long before we think of the existence of trade routes of even a rudimentary nature. Some very early exploratory voyage, in all likelihood." Dr. Pleever paused until he saw a few nods of understanding among the audience and then continued: "Very likely on a ship like the one now sitting in your harbor."

Now he looked at Dr. Hoffner, indicating him with his arm. "I called Dr. Hoffner to inquire whether he had discovered anything similar in his excavation of the ship and he said that they had not, but that he recalled seeing once, in a collection of mostly colonial objects here at the library, something that might fit the description I gave him."

Now Sim could detect a mild eruption among the listeners as they put things together for themselves. "The theft," Gerald Smith, who owned the laundromat, said before anyone else had a chance.

"So it appears," Dr. Pleever said, nodding his head.

The man who managed the local bank raised his hand and was recognized. "That theory you told about, the one that they could have been made from a meteorite. Why couldn't they have been used as currency? Like gold or silver?"

"A very good question," Dr. Pleever said. "We should hire you at the Smithsonian,"

There was laughter. Some people, who owed the bank money, probably thought that would be a very good idea, Sim thought.

"You're right. They might have been used as a primitive currency. Currency has value either because of the material from which it is minted or from a stamped image. These objects would satisfy the first condition if there were sufficient, but not a surplus of, the material. Supply and demand. The fact that no such meteorite has ever been found suggests that this one was unique or virtually so. Put simply, there wouldn't have been enough of it for its establishment as coin of the realm, even a very small realm."

Mrs. Rose, the librarian, raised her hand. Dr. Pleever nodded to acknowledge her.

"Perhaps they were religious objects?" she suggested.

"That," Dr. Pleever said, "is our current supposition. This picture is of particular interest." He projected a slide from the rock carvings that he had mentioned earlier. It looked like this:

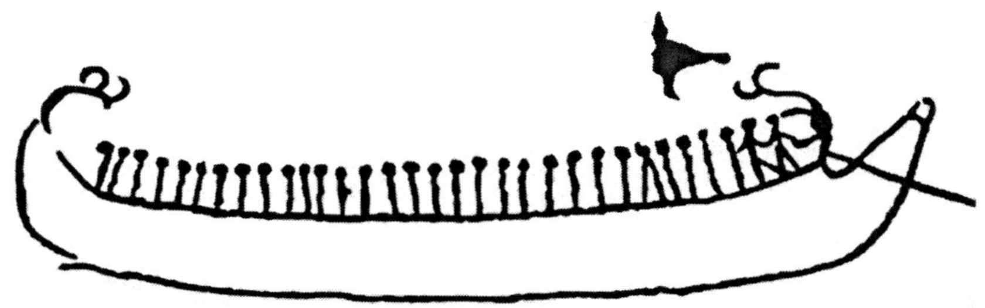

"The figures at the front of the ship you will notice have their arms extended almost as if they were forming a circle. Is the foremost figure a man? Probably. But he appears larger than the others, which may suggest his greater status. Probably he is a shaman."

"What's the black thing that looks like a bird?" the banker asked.

"In all likelihood, just that," Dr. Pleever answered. "Perhaps a god in the form of a bird. Such representations are quite common in primitive Norse art.

"Like the dove in the Bible," Miss Blenden said without raising her hand.

Dr. Pleever wrinkled his brows and then smiled. "Ah, yes," he said. "The dove that returned to Noah with the olive branch. An interesting suggestion. The bird – if indeed it is a bird – might be guiding the ship to a safe harbor." He flashed another slide onto the screen:

"Here the figure floating above the ship is most certainly a shaman. And the line above him? It could be anything. The bird in flight? Are the shaman and the bird together guiding the ship? Protecting it? Is it a real ship or is this a representation of some spiritual voyage?"

"What are the stones?" Miss Blenden asked. "What did you call them?"

"Blue topaz," Dr. Pleever said.

"Yes," Miss Blenden said, as if she had known all along. "Are they valuable?"

"No," Dr. Pleever said. "Actually, it's quite common. Not in the same league as diamonds, even though topaz is nearly as hard. An 8 on the density scale that is used. Diamonds are a 10. No, our thief is unlikely to be rewarded for his trouble."

"Do the stones make any sort of design?" Mrs. Rose asked.

"If we accept the notion that they were smelted from a meteorite, it would seem that the placement of the gems is coincidental. If some other theory emerges ... well, then that could be a possibility."

Sim stepped back against the wall and carefully removed the medallion from his pocket. Cupping it in his hand he studied the tiny bumps. It felt as if an ant was crawling up his chest. And then he looked up to discover a cow grazing about five feet away from Dr. Pleever in a rich green field of clover and grass. There were other animals as well, at a distance. Some sheep, other cows, two or three horses. It was like standing in front of a store window and seeing not only its display, but also the street behind you, superimposed, one on the other. In the middle, just where it should have been, was the Oracle Stone. No library, and only a few buildings along Water Street. It was all much too pleasant to be frightening as the great trees behind Splitface had been, filled as they were with darkness. In fact, it was amusing. Dr. Pleever was so serious, completely unaware of the cow grazing at his ankles. Sim took a step forward, bumped into a chair, and the scene vanished.

"Oh, sorry," Sim said, taking a step back.

The man with the gold-tipped cane smiled at him. There was no way you could explain walking into the back of someone's chair in broad daylight, so Sim didn't try. Instead he returned the medallion to his pocket, turned and walked out of the Pomeroy Room.

Chapter 14

Dr. Asneath Pleever

Sim went into the bathroom and splashed water on his face the way people do in movies when they see ghosts. Then they look into the mirror, shake the water from their hair and reach for a towel.

Things never work out in real life the way they do in movies. For one thing there were no towels, only an air dryer; and when he looked into the mirror, instead of a handsome actor with a day's growth of beard, Sim saw a small boy with a big gap between his two front teeth and a drop of water hanging from the end of his nose.

He left and started back toward the Pomeroy Room.

It seemed that the lecture had concluded. People were coming out into the lobby, taking their hats from the rack and talking about the weather. Greta was with her father and mother. The Hoffners had Sunday rules. Not about going to church, but being together as a family. Greta couldn't even have friends over. It seemed to Sim very old-fashioned, but his feelings were mixed. It made him think about not having a real family, not having a father. He would like to have told her about the cows, but that would have to wait.

Alex came out of the room, spotted Sim, and walked over. "You left in a real hurry," he said

"If I told you why, you'd turn me into the psycho squad," Sim said.

"It can't be loonier than the other stuff. And that coin. I mean that medallion was spooky. So what did you see this time?"

"A cow."

"A cow?"

"A cow."

"You're right. I'm calling the squad now." Alex made as if to walk away and nearly bumped into Dr. Pleever, who had approached, unnoticed, while they were talking.

"Oh, Sorry," Alex said.

"My fault," Dr. Pleever said. "I should have made a noise. It's a very thick carpet."

"My father bought it in Turkey," Alex said. "There was no room for it in the house. Well, there was room, but my mother had things redone and she didn't like it there."

"It goes very nicely here," Dr. Pleever said. Then he turned to Sim. "You left very suddenly. Is everything all right?"

"I had to go to the bathroom," Sim said, wondering why Dr. Pleever should even have noticed. Perhaps because of the disturbance he had caused earlier. "I'm sorry about... you know," he said.

"It focused the audience's attention," Dr. Pleever said. "A little interruption always helps to focus an audience's attention."

The archaeologist extended his hand. "Asneath Pleever," he said.

"This is my friend, Sim," Alex said. "My best friend." Dr. Pleever held Sim's hand a little longer than a person would expect, all the while studying Sim's face. This was getting to be a habit with people, Sim thought. He blushed.

"Sim," Dr. Pleever said. "That must be short for Simon."

"It's short for Simeon," Sim said.

"He who heard." Dr. Pleever said with a pleasant smile.

"I'm sorry?" Sim said.

"Simeon," Dr. Pleever explained. "The name means 'he who heard.'"

"Oh," Sim said. He had never thought of his name as meaning anything.

Dr. Pleever looked like someone you could trust. "Could it also mean saw?" Sim asked.

"Hmmm," Dr. Pleever mused, stroking his chin. "He who saw."

"Sometimes people say 'I see' when they mean, 'I get what you're saying,'" Alex volunteered.

"Good point," Dr. Pleever said. "I guess it could. Are you a person who sees, Simeon?"

"No, I just wondered." Then it came to him why Dr. Pleever was standing here talking with him. He decided to take the plunge: "You knew that I had a medallion, didn't you?" he asked.

"I thought that perhaps you did."

"Because you had one too."

Alex made the sounds of an extraterrestrial ship hovering above a cornfield. It wasn't his best, but it made his point. Dr. Pleever smiled.

"I try to think scientifically," he said. "There is no other way to think. No sensible other way. But then you run into something like these little medallions...." He didn't finish the sentence. "May I ask how you came by it?"

"I found it on the beach by the bridge," Sim said. "I was looking for skipping stones." And then he added for no reason he could have named, "I was supposed to be getting braces."

Dr. Pleever looked at him, a puzzled expression on his face.

"For my teeth," Sim said. "I have this gap." He opened his mouth to demonstrate.

"But instead you went to look for skipping stones."

"Sim has the record for the most skips," Alex said. "Eighteen."

"My goodness," Dr. Pleever said, "that is impressive. I'm quite sure I never got more than eight or nine when I was a boy."

"You stopped talking when you touched your medallion," Sim said.

"The synchronicity effect," Dr. Pleever said. "My medallion was resonant." He stopped, looked at Sim and Alex, and laughed.

"Scientific gobbledygook," he said. "When people can't understand something they give it a big word. The medallions respond to one another. When I took my medallion from its case I realized there was another one in the room. At first I thought it might be the one that had been stolen, but then..."

"I dropped it," Alex said. "It was too weird. What's it called again?"

"Whatever you want to call it, Alex."

"It was like it was electric. Sort of like that."

"That's as good as 'resonant,'" Dr. Pleever said.

Sim was relieved as Dr. Pleever spoke. He wasn't crazy. Or, at least if he was he had distinguished company.

"What makes them do that?" Alex asked.

"We have no idea," Dr. Pleever said.

"Is it a little like magnets?" Alex ventured.

"Yes." Dr. Pleever said, "very much like magnets."

"You said it might be because they all came from the same meteorite?" Sim said.

"That's one theory," Dr. Pleever replied, looking at Sim. It was a friendly look, but it was also an inquiring one.

"There's nothing dangerous about these medallions, is there?" Alex asked, avoiding Sim's eyes.

"Nothing I am aware of," Dr. Pleever said. "The fact that someone wants to steal something doesn't make it dangerous, but it does suggest that the owner take precautions."

"But why would someone want one of these bad enough to steal it?" Alex asked.

"Well, we can't be absolutely sure that was the motive," Dr. Pleever said, apparently wanting to reassure. "There were other objects in the case."

"But you think it was the medallion, don't you?" Sim said. He was surprised to hear himself speak with such certainty.

Chapter 15

The Girl on the Oracle Stone

"How many of them are there?" Sim asked.

"Well, now we know that there are at least three," Dr. Pleever said. "And if indeed there was one in the glass case, that would make four. How many do you think there might be altogether, Sim?"

"Me?"

"Why not you? You're one of the discoverers, aren't you?"

"I guess so," Sim said, tentatively, "but I'm not a scientist."

"All children are scientists," Dr. Pleever said. "The whole work of childhood is in figuring out how things work. The older you get and the more degrees you collect, the more willing people will be to call you a scientist. But a funny thing happens along that road. The more you know, the more you dismiss. You look at a problem and you say, 'Well, we can throw out this and this too. And we know that won't work, and such and such was disproven ages ago and two and two can't possibly add up to five.' And pretty soon you have painted yourself into a corner because you knew too much."

Sim looked at Alex. Alex looked at Sim.

"There's another thing that people do when they get older and think they know a lot," Dr. Pleever continued, with an apologetic smile. "They start lecturing. The fact is we have no idea why the medallions behave this way."

"It's almost as though they want to find one another," Sim said.

"Sim doesn't even need two of them," Alex said.

Dr. Pleever had been about to say something. His hand was already raised as if to make a point. It sat there in mid air for a moment, as if uncertain how to behave, then made its way to the scientist's glasses. He removed and studied them, took a clean handkerchief from his pocket and slowly wiped them. Now he held them to the light as if to check his work.

Sim could sense Alex's impatience and caught his eye. "No more," his expression said. "Let it drop."

When Dr. Pleever replaced his glasses, he looked at Sim as if for the first time. It made Sim uncomfortable. He looked at the carpet.

"I'm sorry," Dr. Pleever said." That was very rude of me, Sim. You see, just for a moment, you reminded me of someone I once knew." He touched Sim's shoulder gently. Sim looked up.

"Will you tell me about it?" Dr. Pleever asked.

"It sort of purrs," Sim said.

"All by itself?" Dr. Pleever questioned.

Sim nodded.

"But it doesn't for Amanda and me," Alex said. "We can't feel anything. Only Sim can. Amanda says it's because he's the one that found it."

"Yes," Dr. Pleever said. It was the kind of "yes" that people said when their minds were someplace else, when they were trying to put things together. "Yes," he said, this time with a nod of his head, a satisfied nod. "What if...." He paused. "What if the medallions were looking for...." He paused again. He was changing course. Sim could see it in his face. "What if the medallions were looking for a young person with an imagination, with time to spend. Someone who wouldn't just stick it away in a drawer or take it to a museum, but make an adventure out of it. Like Jack and his beans or Aladdin and his lamp."

"Or Frodo with the ring," Sim added, a little nervously.

"Or Frodo with his ring," Dr. Pleever repeated. "Yes. Would you be willing to show me your medallion, Sim?" he asked.

Sim felt the slightest hesitation about taking the medallion from his pocket. He couldn't have said why. He liked Dr. Pleever and, despite his earlier reservations about adults, he was glad to have an older friend in this matter. He handed the coin to the scientist, who examined it using a small eyepiece that was on a cord around his neck. "You must be careful how you clean it," Dr. Pleever said.

Sim glanced at Alex. He knew what was coming.

"That's what I told him," he said. "There was this guy on television...."

Alex didn't get to finish his story. Sim interrupted: "If they didn't come from a meteorite, if someone made them, then the way the stones are arranged might mean something."

Dr. Pleever looked at him and nodded: "It might indeed."

"Some kind of code or something," Sim continued.

"That could well be," Dr. Pleever said.

"If you had three or four or five and you put them side by side, then you might get an idea," Sim speculated, half to himself.

"That is precisely what needs to be done," Dr. Pleever said. "That is the way of investigation:" He smiled broadly at the boys and then continued. "I'll tell you what I'll do." He took a notebook out of his jacket pocket and tore out a page. He laid his medallion on the tabletop and, putting the paper on top of it, rubbed very carefully with a pencil.

"We made those in art class," Alex said. "They're rubbings."

"Precisely," Dr. Pleever said, finishing up and comparing the rubbing with its original. "I think that's a fair copy." He handed it to Sim. "Now you have two samples for your investigation. And when I return to Washington, I will copy the other and send it to you." He handed his notepad and pencil to Sim. "You'd better give me your address," he said.

Sim wrote *413 Fisher Lane, Lost River Cove, Maine*. "I don't know the zip code," he said.

"That part I already know," said Dr. Pleever.

"Would you like to copy mine?" Sim asked.

"You wouldn't mind?" Dr. Pleever responded.

"No. That way we can both work on figuring them out." He handed his medallion to his new friend.

Dr. Pleever made a second rubbing. This time he didn't detach the page from his little book. "There," he said, handing the medallion back to Sim. "It's quite excellent, having a field team at work here in Lost River Cove," he added. He put the notebook back in his pocket. "Strictly hush-hush." The boys smiled at the sinister way he spoke, looking over his shoulder to see if anyone was listening. It was theatrical, but Sim could tell it was not entirely unmeant. Then Sim had an idea. "Could I have your medallion for a moment?" he asked.

"Certainly," Dr. Pleever said.

Sim took the medallion. It wasn't encrusted like his own. but it was just as black. The tiny blue topaz stones caught the light.

"I want to see it in the light," he said, indicating the window that looked out onto the lawn and the Oracle Stone.

"Fine," Dr. Pleever said.

Sim walked to the window and held the two medallions in front of him as if he were making an offering. He closed his eyes. "Please don't let me see anything bad," he whispered. Then he opened his eyes. The ant came out of hiding and he felt it walking up his chest. The cows were gone, and the sheep, but the field was there, and the wildflowers. And there weren't as many buildings on Water Street. The Oracle Stone sat there like eternity itself in the middle of the field. Then a girl appeared and walked to the Oracle Stone. She had a kind of pack, which was made of leather and had a strap that went over her shoulder. She opened it and removed a notebook. It had a red cover. Next she did something that Sim couldn't make out. It appeared that she was erasing something written there. Then she closed the book, returned it to her satchel, and jumped down from the stone, disappearing around its side, where Sim could no longer see her. She emerged a few moments later, looked at her hands, wiped them on her dress, and started to walk away. She turned in his direction as if she had spied him out, watching, and as she did, the sun caught her face. Something glistened on her cheek. Sim wondered if it were a tear.

A sound disturbed Sim's concentration. The scene dissolved, and with it the girl.

"Sim!"

The town he had grown up in stood before him once again.

"Sim!" It was Alex's voice. Sim dropped his arms and slowly put his own medallion back in his bib pocket. This was the fourth time. There had been the deep water, then the forest behind Splitface, then the cows, and now the girl. This time he could almost smell the grass and the sea air. The strangest thing, however, was the girl. She was from another, earlier time. There was no way he could have known her, and yet.... He turned. The room was as it had been: Alex, Dr. Pleever and someone sitting in a chair across the room, reading a book. Sim walked back to where they stood and handed the Smithsonian medallion back to Dr. Pleever.

"Thanks," he said. "I just wanted to see what it would be like to have them both at the same time."

"And?" Dr. Pleever asked.

"I think they resonated more," Sim said.

"And that's all?" Dr. Pleever seemed disappointed.

Sim looked at Alex, accurately anticipating that he might blurt something out, and he was right. Alex was just about to say something, but he didn't. He closed his mouth and rolled his eyes.

"I started daydreaming a little," Sim said, turning back to Dr. Pleever. "I was just thinking about things. Vikings and stuff. You know." Sim liked Dr. Pleever and he didn't like lying. That's why he said he was daydreaming. It was a little like daydreaming.

"Well," Dr. Pleever said, replacing his medallion in its leather case. "If you make any important discoveries, do let me know." He reached again into his jacket pocket and produced a business card. "You can always reach me here."

Sim took the card, examined it and put it in his bib pocket. "Thanks," he said. "Are you going to come back to Lost River Cove?"

"If occasion calls me," Dr. Pleever said.

"You mean if they find more stuff?" Sim asked.

"Or if you do. I meant what I said, Sim."

Sim nodded, surprised and more than a little pleased at having a secret sharer. It made the prospect of the adventure less scary. He took the card out of his pocket and looked at it.

"Good," Dr. Pleever said. He smiled again at the boys, He was very pleased with something. It wasn't just the medallions. Sim was sure of that. There was something else.

"OK," Alex said when he had left, "what really happened at the window? You were in outer space."

Hearing Alex's question, Sim suddenly knew the meaning of what he had just seen. He smiled and looked at his friend. "There's another medallion," he said.

Chapter 16

Making Plans

The boys had agreed to meet Amanda at Bartlett's Restaurant after her French lesson. It being a Sunday morning, Greta was homebound. There was a bigger crowd of morning walkers and churchgoers. The booth at the back was empty, however, and, waving to Homer, they slid into it - Sim on the far side so he could keep an eye peeled for Amanda.

Sim told Alex about the girl on the rock, her book, and his theory that she was hiding a medallion under the Oracle Stone. If Alex was skeptical, he kept that doubt unspoken.

"So, are we going to check it out or not?" he asked.

"Not with all these people around," Sim responded. "Especially not with Gold-Tipped Smith around. He gives me the creeps."

"Gold-Tipped Smith!" Alex said. "Cool." Then he became serious. "We should have told Dr. Pleever about Splitface," he continued. "I'll bet he's the one who stole the medallion from the library."

"I thought of that. But then I decided I needed to think about it more. If adults get mixed up in this, it won't be ours any more. I'm the one who found the medallion. I have a responsibility to it. Don't do your spaceman stuff! I'm serious."

"I guess so."

Sim sensed Alex's frustration. It had been apparent when they were talking to Dr. Pleever. It was all happening to him. He was the special one. Alex was feeling left out. He would have given it all to have a father and a brother and sister like the twins, but it would have meant nothing to Alex for him to say that. Instead Sim took the medallion out of his pocket and, covering it with his hand, passed it across the table.

"Here," he said, "you keep it for awhile ."

Alex looked puzzled and a little suspicious. "How come?"

"Because we're in this together, and you're my best friend."

"What about Amanda?"

"She's my best girl friend. And don't you say it. You know what I mean."

Alex slid the medallion back across the table. "It's OK," he said. "When we find the other medallion, maybe I can carry that one part of the time. You found this one, or, like Dr. Pleever said, it found you."

"He didn't say that."

"He was going to," Alex said.

Sim returned it to his pocket.

"So what did you do with the rubbing?"

"It's under the paper liner in my top dresser drawer."

"Cool," Alex said.

Neither of them noticed Amanda until she dropped her French book on the table.

"*Bonjour mes amis*," she said.

"Hi," Sim said, sliding over to make room for her.

"That's the only thing you ever say," Alex said to his sister.

"*Ce n'est pas vrai,*" Amanda returned. "*Je parle français tres bien.*"

"Right," Alex said.

"We did past tense today," she said. "And Madame Valvo talked about her grandfather who was a French nobleman."

"We did the past too," Sim said, trying to introduce some lightness into the twins' predictable rivalry.

"The Vikings," Amanda said. "You went to the lecture."

"There was a robbery," Alex said, playing his high card.

"Where?" Amanda asked, now clearly engaged.

"At the library," Alex said. "One of the medallions was stolen."

"What medallions?" she asked.

"Like the one Sim has. It's not a coin. It's a medallion of some kind."

The two of them related in turns the events of the morning, including the cows grazing around Dr. Pleever, the girl on the Oracle Stone, and Gold-Tipped Smith.

"Gold-Tipped Smith?" Amanda repeated. "What kind of name is that?"

"Sim made it up," Alex said. "It's wicked cool."

"Wait a minute," Amanda said, collecting her thoughts. "What did this guy look like?" Sim described him.

"I've seen him." Amanda said. "He came to the house the other day and spent some time with Dad. I let him in. I don't know what they talked about, but after he left I heard Dad talking to Jerome."

"What did he say?" Sim asked.

"The guy wrote a book when he was young. I mean really young. He's some kind of genius. And he's rich. Dad's trying to get him interested in the museum."

"That explains why he was at the lecture," Alex said.

Homer, who had been busy with other customers, brought their hot chocolate. "Hear your father's got a new old car," Homer said, addressing Alex.

"A 1944 Packard," Alex said. "It's sweet."

"Well, it's nice he has the time for that kind of thing," Homer said. Sim was surprised. He knew what Homer meant. The twins probably did, too. Homer wasn't usually that rude, Sim thought. He took a swipe at the table with his rag and walked back to the counter.

"What's bugging Homer?" Alex asked.

"He doesn't like things to change," said Amanda. "He doesn't like strangers and he doesn't like digging things up, at least that's what Dad says."

"You know what the weirdest thing is?" Sim asked.

The twins waited.

"Gold-Tipped Smith didn't let on that there was anything unusual about the medallion when he handed it back to me, and you know what that means."

"That he's held one before," Amanda said.

"Two," Alex said.

"Right," Sim agreed, trying to think it through. "Anyway, it's for sure that he knows what they do." He thought for a moment. "At least that part of what they do. He might not know the rest."

"Or he might know more," Alex added.

"Right," Sim said.

"I still don't get why you can feel that vibrating stuff when there's only one medallion," Alex said. "Did you see Dr. Pleever's face when I told him?"

"I wish you hadn't," Sim said.

"I thought you liked the guy," Alex said.

"I do," Sim said thoughtfully, "I really do. But... forget it. It's not important."

"It's you," Amanda said. "Like I told you before."

"That's what Dr. Pleever thinks," Alex added.

"Dr. Pleever didn't say that," Sim snapped.

"He was going to," Alex countered.

"Going to what?" Amanda asked.

"He was going to say that the medallions were looking for Sim, but he never finished."

"You think he was going to say that," Sim corrected.

"So do you. And how about Gold-Tipped Smith? He was studying you like you were some kind of rare bird."

"I don't know," Sim said. "Maybe. It's just too weird."

"Anyway," Amanda said, "Dad invited him to the reception."

"What reception?" Sim asked.

"Scientists. To talk about the Viking ship, and to raise money for the museum. Lots of people are coming. It's in two weeks."

"Is Dr. Pleever going to be there?" Sim asked hopefully.

"He's the most important one," Alex said. "So what are we going to do about the medallion under the Oracle Stone?"

"We've got to check it out when no one's around," Amanda suggested.

"Good luck," Alex said

What was it, Sim wondered now, that had made him so certain the girl was burying a medallion. It was a new kind of feeling, like the one he had had when they found the cave. And why was he upset with Alex for telling Dr. Pleever? It was his mother, that was it. How could he be telling a stranger things that he hadn't even told his mother? With Greta and the twins, it was different. But he couldn't tell his mother. She'd explain it all away.

"Earth to Sim. Earth to Sim," Alex was saying.

"Huh?"

"The Oracle Stone."

"Right." Sim put his thoughts aside. "Invite Greta and me for a sleepover," he said.

Alex looked puzzled for a moment and then laughed. "Brilliant," he said, "the medallion revealed at midnight under a full moon."

The middle of the night was not a time with which Sim had much familiarity, except with an upset stomach or a nightmare. But these were extraordinary times calling for extraordinary measures. Circumstances were on their side. Because of the teacher institute, Monday would be a school holiday. Amanda said she would set things up so that Sim and Greta could spend the night at Pomeroy Hall.

Chapter 17

Nightwalking

Sim hadn't thought to ask exactly what arrangements Amanda was going to make about his staying the night, but when he got home he found out. Amanda's mother had called and invited Sim for a sleepover. This was not a good idea. Sim's mother had a thing about being ambushed – the word she used – with plans that Sim had not previously mentioned.

Sim was already a little angry at his mother because he couldn't tell her about the medallions. It didn't make sense, but there it was. He could have told Dr. Pleever, a complete stranger, or Ponidi; but he couldn't tell his mother. Life wasn't a fairy tale, she'd say. You had to be realistic and hardheaded to survive. Sim understood that she was worried about money and wanted to be sure he got on in the world, but it felt like a burden. It felt unfair. So he kept things to himself, things that were fragile and needed protection against being explained away. She should meet Dr. Pleever, he thought. She'd have to believe him. All this was sitting in his mind when she gave him the lecture on not getting other people to do his asking. He got up from the counter, threw up his hands and said,

"Forget it! I don't care. It was Amanda's idea. I don't want to go anyway."

"You don't want to go?" his mother repeated.

He went to the tin and removed a fresh peanut butter cookie.

"It's just the twins," he said. "And Greta and I see them all week anyway."

"Greta Hoffner's invited as well?"

"Yeah. The Pomeroys and Hoffners are very tight. The Viking ship and all that," he said casually, knowing precisely the effect it would have on his mother. He was right.

"The Pomeroys are good friends to have," she said.

"And Cameron's a pain. And Lily and Tad are annoying."

"It doesn't hurt to have friends with position," she said. "You never know when you'll need a helping hand."

Sim knew better than to pursue the argument, for it led into places he'd rather not go – "if anything should ever happen to me" kinds of places.

Then he felt like a rat. He was being dishonest with the only person who loved him. He couldn't finish the cookie.

"There's a dance at the Legion Hall," she said. "I might just have a night out myself." She paused and smiled. "If you make a habit of turning down invitations, they'll stop coming. You'd better call up Amanda and tell her you're coming. It will be good for you."

"I'm sorry," he said.

"About ambushing me?"

"That and yelling."

"Come here," she said.

It was a very long and comforting hug, and he felt much better afterward. So what might have been a problem turned out not to be after all. Maybe his mother would meet some guy, Sim thought. She hardly ever went out. "Why would I want to when I've got one of the two best guys in the world right here?" she'd say. The other best guy was his father. Even after eleven years she was still in love with him. You would have to come back if somebody loved you that much, Sim thought. At least that was what he hoped.

Alex had set his alarm clock for two a.m., when there could be no doubt that the rest of the Pomeroy clan would be fast asleep. Sim got out of bed fully dressed and followed Alex to Amanda's room. She and Greta were already up. They made their way down the back hall and out the kitchen door. Walter was asleep in Mrs. Pomeroys' mint garden. He had always shown a partiality for peppermint. He seemed glad to see them and roused himself with surprising energy at the thought of a late-night adventure.

For both better and worse, there was the full moon that Alex had pictured. No lights showed in any of the houses they passed, nor was there any traffic on the streets, and they made their way to the library lawn without incident. Amanda had brought a garden trowel and Alex a spade. Greta had a plastic sheet to spread on the grass so they wouldn't leave any trace of their trespass. Alex cut the sod with his spade and placed it on the plastic sheet. Just then the headlights of a truck swept the lawn as it drove up Frost Lane. They dove for the grass and lay there until it turned onto Oak Street and headed up the shore. Then Alex resumed his digging.

"No, Walter," Sim said, walking to the other side of the stone.

"What's he doing?" Greta asked.

"He's digging. No, Walter."

"He just wants to help," Amanda said. "Good old Walter. Only you've got the wrong side, boy." She smoothed out the grass where Walter had been digging. "Maybe he knows about the medallion."

"I don't think Walter knows about anything but food. Probably somebody stuck the rest of his lunch there," Sim said.

They removed a good deal of earth without finding anything except a few nightcrawlers and a ball point pen. Sim's companions began asking questions that Sim had answered before. How was the girl dressed? Was he sure she was putting something under the stone? Could she have put it in her pack? They were beginning to lose faith.

"It's here," Sim said, more forcefully than he had intended. "I know it is."

"Maybe somebody else found it," Amanda said.

Sim shook his head, looked back at the library and tried to see again exactly what he had seen when he held the two medallions.

Alex had brought a pocketful of root-beer balls for quick energy. He opened one, popped it into his mouth, and offered one to each of the others. Amanda and Greta took one, but Sim didn't. He was beginning to feel that he had let people down. "No, thanks," he said in a voice designed to convey his frustration. Amanda put her hand on his shoulder,

"It's OK, Sim," she said. "Sometimes people find things and sometimes they don't. Mostly they don't. That's what archaeology is all about. Right, Greta?"

But Greta was lost in her own thoughts and, ignoring Amanda's question, turned to Sim. "Do you remember the way you described seeing the animals in the library?"

"What animals?" asked Sim impatiently.

"The cow," Greta said. "The cows. The pasture. Whatever it was. You looked at Dr. Pleever and you saw a cow from the past."

"I did see it," Sim said. The moment he heard his own voice, he realized he was being defensive. It was as if the entire adventure was being thrown into question now.

"You said it was like looking into a window and seeing a reflection. Two things, you said. What was in the window and what was reflected in the glass."

Suddenly, Sim understood what she was saying. His mouth dropped open. He turned and ran back toward the library. He stood beneath the window from which he had observed the girl with the backpack and the red book. He closed his eyes and summoned up the earlier image. Once again, he saw the girl. It was as if a movie had been stopped. She held the book in her lap and looked toward the ocean. Sim opened his eyes and realized what Greta was saying. "Yes, of course!" he thought. He pumped his arm in the air. "Yes," he said, running back to his friends. "Greta, you're a genius."

"What is it?" Amanda asked.

"It's backwards," Sim said. "It's all been backwards the whole time, but I didn't realize it because it was just trees and cows and fields. But this time there were the buildings."

"I still don't get it," Alex said.

"Gardner's Hardware was on the other side of the bank," Sim said. "We've been digging on the wrong side of the Oracle Stone."

The companions looked at one another, tapped into Sim's new charge of energy, and went to work replacing the soil they had removed carefully packing it back into place. Then they took their tools to the other side and set to work once again.

This time, Greta cut and removed the sod and did the digging. When she turned the third shovelful of sod out onto the plastic sheet, Sim reached to break the clod and felt it. "YES," he said. "YES, YES, YES!" He held it up, brushed away the dirt, and handed it to Greta.

Sim expected her to be startled. After all, it was the first time she had held a medallion when another was present. But she just nodded as if confirming something she had always expected. Then she broke into a smile. "It's cool!" she said. It was the first time Sim had ever heard her use the word. It made him unaccountably pleased.

"Me, too," Amanda said, holding out her hand. Greta dropped the second medallion into her palm. She said nothing, but her eyes went wide. "It's magic," she said. "No question about it."

"Resonance," Alex said authoritatively. "Like magnets."

"No," Amanda said. "Magic."

She wiped it on her T-shirt and held it up to the moonlight. The stones, like those on Dr. Pleever's medallion, had shed any tarnish they might once have had and sparkled in the moonlight as if from some source of their own. Sim looked at Amanda's face. He had never seen her look quite like that before. It must have been the medallion. Probably it was magic. Some kind of magic.

Together they replaced the sod, gathered their implements, and started up the library lawn toward Oak Street.

"Wait! Stop!" Alex whispered, "Did you hear that?"

"What?" Amanda said, and knelt down in the grass. The others followed her lead.

Then there was a loud crash, unmistakably the sound of a trash can lid falling to the ground.

"Cat," said Greta.

"Or a raccoon," Alex said, standing up.

Then there was another sound, this time of a door being closed, somewhere on Water Street.

"That wasn't a cat," Greta said. "Someone was watching us."

"Or maybe just getting home late," Amanda whispered.

"At three in the morning?" Alex asked.

Sim shook his head: "There's no way in the world anyone could know we were going to be here."

"How did Splitface know to come to your house?" Alex asked. And then, as if on a roll, he continued. "And Gold-

Tipped Smith. He zeroed in on you like a hawk that day at the library."

Sim noticed that as Alex spoke, his eyes were fastened on Greta. She looked at him.

"There are a lot of things we don't know yet," she said. "But we will."

Sim took the first medallion from the bib of his overalls, looked at it for a moment, and handed it to Greta, who had assured him in an earlier conversation that indeed she could clean it. He handed the second one to Amanda. "Here, you guys look after this one for awhile ."

"You don't need to do that, Sim," Amanda said.

"It's a good idea," Alex said. "We need to be scientific about these things. See if they only work for Sim. Right, Sim?"

"Right," he said. "That hadn't been his reason for offering the medallion but if it worked for Alex, that was fine. They turned and started up the lawn, Walter trailing behind. Sim waited for him. "Good boy," he said, "you knew where it was all along, didn't you?"

Chapter 18

A Letter from the Smithsonian

The week following was uneventful, a week during which everything was waiting to happen, but nothing much did. Or so it seemed to Sim. Everyone passed the quiz on state capitals, Sim's mother got to do a small catering job with Classy Cuisine Catering Service, and Sim's medallion sat at the bottom of a glass filled with a pale blue liquid, on a shelf in Greta's basement.

As long as the weather held, Sim continued to sleep on the widow's walk. When they had first moved to 413 Fisher Lane, Sim's mother taught him the wishing verse: "Star light star bright first star I've seen tonight/I wish I may I wish I might have the wish I wish tonight." For Sim it had always been the same wish, but as the years passed and he had grown older, he had begun to lose hope that the sailor whose lucky stone lay beneath his pillow would ever return. His mother, who had once been so sure, now spoke rarely of him. She had become, or so it seemed to Sim, more serious, impatient with things like wishes, more worried about everything.

Sim's love of the stars was something that came from deep within him and about which he spoke little. He felt both awe and an intimacy with them. They teased his imagination and offered a landscape upon which he could travel in his dreams. He still said the wishing verse, but now only when he saw a shooting star. Its sudden streak of glory was gone in the blink of an eye, perhaps only his eye. Perhaps he was the only person in Lost River Cove who had seen it and he felt a momentary bond with all the vastness of the sky.

That night, sleeping beneath the stars, Sim had another dreamwalk. This time, the setting was familiar. It was Hazel's cottage. A light in her parlor cast a friendly glow on the shrubbery. Something wanted his attention, just as in his other dreamwalks, but he could not have said what. Then the light was turned off and the dream ended.

As caretakers of the second medallion, the twins had taken turns carrying it during the week, but neither had seen forests, grazing cows, or anything else that they didn't see every day.

When Sim returned from school on Friday, there was a letter for him on the kitchen table – return address The Smithsonian Institution. Inside was the promised rubbing of the museum's second medallion, with a penned note that said, "Good luck with your researches. With fond good wishes, Asneath Pleever." Apart from birthday cards, it was the first letter Sim had ever received. Instead of tossing the envelope in the trash, he smoothed its flap back into place and took it up to his bedroom. He had taken the precaution earlier that week of making a rubbing of the medallion the twins were now carrying, the one from under the Oracle Stone. Earlier he had made a rubbing of the first medallion. With the one Dr. Pleever had made after the lecture, he had had three. Now he had four. He laid the three rubbings on his desk and put the new one alongside them. They looked like this:

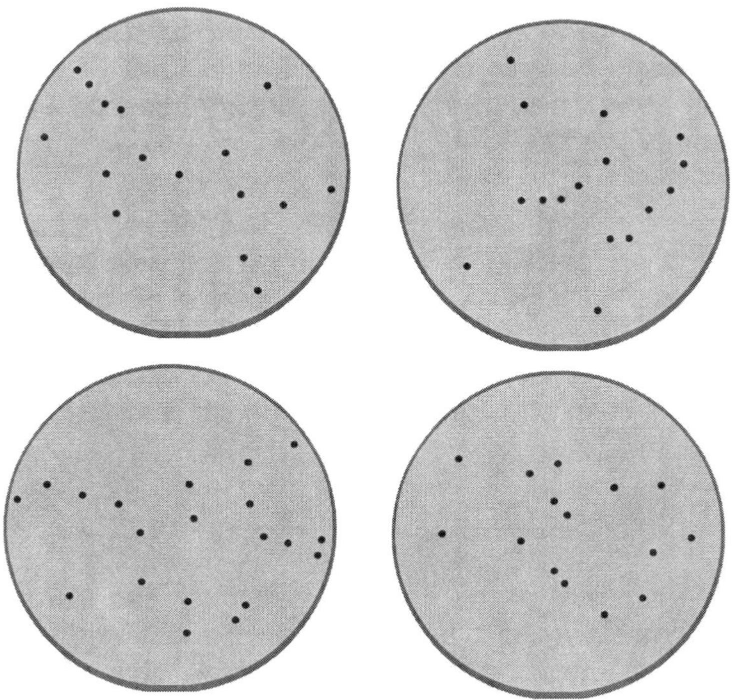

He stared at them for a while without inspiration, feeling a little let down. He had hoped that a fourth medallion would somehow offer a clue to the other three, being more like one of them than the other or repeating a pattern from one of the others. But no matter how he turned them, he could find nothing they might have in common.

Then he reread the note and thought about the word "fond." You could be fond of something, like ice cream or chocolate. And you could be fond of a person. But what did it mean in a letter? He signed Miss Blenden's birthday card, "Love, Sim," but that didn't mean he loved Miss Blenden. He wondered if Dr. Pleever was fond of him. It pleased him to think that he might be. He wondered if the great scientist was somebody's father.

"Sim?" His mother called from downstairs.

"Hi, Mom. I'm up here." Putting the letter and the rubbings back under the dresser-drawer liner, he went downstairs.

"How was school?" she asked.

"Good," he said. "We had hot dogs for lunch."

"And some salad, I hope."

"Salad bar."

"And you had some."

"They had honey mustard dressing."

"And you had some salad under it."

"Mom!"

"OK. Sorry. I see you found your letter."

"Yup."

"From the Smithsonian. You thinking of becoming a member?"

"It was something this guy sent me for my report on the Vikings. The guy who gave the lecture at the library last Sunday."

"I never asked you about that. How was it?" She was leafing through a magazine absent-mindedly.

"It was cool," Sim said, reaching into the cupboard for a cookie. "I really liked the guy. We talked afterward and he sent me this stuff. We're going to keep in touch. He wants to know what I discover about the Vikings."

"He thinks you may break some new ground?" she asked. It was a little sarcastic, not typical of his mother. She has a lot on her mind, Sim thought. He pretended not to have caught the tone of her remark.

"He thinks I have some good ideas," Sim said.

"I'm sorry, Sweetie," His mother said, getting up from the table. "Not one of my better days. I know you have good ideas. Lots of them."

"You didn't get the job?"

"Not this week. But there's a big event at the Pomeroys' coming up. They want me for that and it will pay well."

It being Friday night, with no immediate pressure of homework, his mother suggested that they go down to the video store and rent a movie. They walked. It was a beautiful starry night, and the moon had not yet made an appearance. After the movie, Sim took Walter's bed and his own sleeping bag and pillow up to the widow's walk. He had a small star atlas that he kept in a sealed plastic bag with a penlight, but now he rarely referred to it. He had pretty well learned the night sky. There was Andromeda just overhead. The night air was delicious, with a fragrance from the sea. He closed his eyes and slept.

Chapter 19

Treasures in the Attic

It was Saturday again. Sim awoke to a sunny morning and listened to a bird that he had not heard before. He intended to learn birdcalls the way Mr. Pomeroy had. It was said that Mr. Pomeroy could name any bird in the temperate zone within a minute of hearing its song. Sim could recognize a mourning dove, a starling and a cardinal. Walter lay on his red-plaid balsam-fragranced bed, one eye peeled. Ridley Raccoon lay between them.

"Do you know what day it is, Walter?" Sim asked.

Walter's tail made a very slight movement. Walter knew very well what day it was. Amanda was right. Walter knew a great many things he didn't let on about.

Sim stood up, gathered his sleeping gear, and tossed it down the spiral staircase. Then he tossed Walter's bed, picked up Ridley, and descended, Walter at his heels.

The plan was that Alex would come over after breakfast and that they would explore Sim's attic. What Sim had told Splitface was not entirely true. There were things up there though, as far as he knew, no trunks filled with treasure. He hadn't been up there in several years and probably wouldn't have thought of it except for the strange visitor.

Amanda had an art lesson and would meet them after lunch at Greta's. Then they'd check the first medallion in its cleaning solution.

The wonderful Saturday-morning smell of bacon rose from the kitchen. Sim dressed and went downstairs. His mother was doing a crossword puzzle, last Sunday's. She worked at it on and off during the week as time allowed, but on Saturday mornings it became a major item because the next day there would be a new one. Sim walked to the table where his mother sat and looked over her shoulder. She put an arm around his waist. "Blank raccoon," she said.

"Ridley," he said.

"I don't think the *New York Times* knows about Ridley," she said. "Anyway, it's only five letters."

"Maybe they spell it without the E," he suggested. "What's ten down?"

"Head lizard. Three letters."

"Rex," he said. "*Tyrannosaurus rex*. Can I make the pancakes?"

"They're mixed. You can cook them."

Sim liked to cook. He was good at hamburgers, canned soups, scrambled eggs (without making them too dry) and pancakes. He turned on the stove under the griddle.

"*Rex* is good," she said. "That makes the first letter in 'blank raccoon' an R."

"It's got to be Ridley," he said. "Alex is coming over and we're going to trade cards."

"I'm going out to shop," she said. "I've made sandwiches for you and I'll make a couple more for Alex. What about Amanda and Greta?"

"Art lesson for Amanda. Greta's helping her mother with something. We're going to meet there later on."

The pan was hot now, and he ladled the batter into very small pancakes about the size of a juice glass. That way, they were easier to turn and soaked up more syrup.

"The last letter is *Y*," she said. "From *Starry Night*."

"What's *Starry Night*?"

"It's a beautiful painting by an artist named Van Gogh. You'd like it. Look in the library at school. I'm going to write it down."

It wasn't his mother saying *Starry Night* or seeing the flecks of pecan in the pancake. It was both things at the same time. And having slept beneath the stars. And who knows what all else. Anyway, there was Orion's Belt, three bright stars in the middle of a pancake. He moved the pancakes to a plate, turned off the burner and started upstairs.

"Where are you going?" his mother asked. "Your pancakes will get cold."

"I just thought of something," he said. "I'll be right back," and he ran up the stairs two at a time.

He took out the rubbings from his desk drawer and felt a chill run down from the top of his head all the way to his Achilles tendons. The dots on the paper were the constellation Orion. There was no question about it. He looked at the others. They weren't as obvious. He'd have to work on them. He looked again at Orion and shook his head. Then, as calmly as he could, he went back to the kitchen.

"What was that all about?" his mother asked.

"I just had this idea about my research," he said. "I had to write it down before I forgot."

"The Vikings?" she asked.

"Definitely," he said. "How many pancakes do you want?"

"Four."

"Four? That's hardly any at all. They're small."

"All that sugar. I have to pay attention. Overweight people don't get hired. It's Rocky. Rocky Raccoon."

"Who's that?"

"Before your time. The Beatles."

"I know about the Beatles."

"Well that was one of their songs."

He carried the two plates to the table, along with the bacon that she had put in the oven to keep it warm. She poured another cup of coffee and a glass of milk for Sim. Setting it down, she kissed him on the head. "I haven't seen you so happy in a long time," she said.

"What do you mean?" he asked. "I'm always happy."

Before she could respond, there was a knock on the door.

Alex had had breakfast but agreed to have a few pancakes, a couple slices of bacon and a glass of milk. The boys finished their breakfast and went up to Sim's room. Sim removed the rubbing from beneath the liner of his dresser drawer and handed it to Alex. "I've broken the code," he said, as casually as he could, flopping down on his bed, his hands behind his head. "It's Orion."

"What's Orion?" Alex sounded a little annoyed.

"It's a constellation."

"I know that, but what does that have to do with this?"

"The dots," Sim said. "They're Orion. The medallions are constellations." He jumped up from the bed, got his small star atlas from the top of his desk and opened it.

"Awesome," Alex said. "What about the other one?"

"Haven't figured it out yet, but it's got to be one. It's so cool, Alex!"

"Give me five," Alex said.

Sim gave him five. Then he put the rubbing safely back in its hiding place and they went up to the attic. It wasn't as interesting as Sim had remembered: some dusty boxes filled with old clothes, several broken chairs, a table with only three legs and a pile of old books that wouldn't even get much attention in the free bin at a garage sale. There was one window, now a mass graveyard for dead flies.

"We've got a better attic than this," Alex said, looking around and picking up an old rubber boot. When he straightened it the leg part it broke off. "This is gross," he said, tossing it aside.

Sim felt he had to defend the attic even though it wasn't really in the same league as the Pomeroys'.

"Yeah, but look at all these cool old books," he said, kneeling down by what looked like a big pile of dust. He pushed the dust off the top, sneezed, and picked up the top volume. *"A History of the Willey Normal School,"* he read. "What's a normal school?"

"You know. A regular school. Like LORCES. It means not a school for freaks," Alex said, picking through the pile and coming up with what looked like a diary. It was a small red notebook with cardboard covers, the pages lightly lined as in a composition book. On the cover, in a careful script, was the date 1900. "This is ancient!" Alex said. How long has this attic been here anyway?"

"A long time, I guess. What is it?"

"It's full of handwriting." Alex studied the skillfully sweeping script and shook his head. "It's in another language," he said.

"Let me see," Sim said. Alex handed him the book. He moved his lips trying to sound out the words. "I don't think it's another language," he said. "No one could pronounce these words." He spelled one out: *v.h.f.u.h.w.* "How could you say that? You couldn't. No one could say that." The page Sim was examining looked like this:

Wkh errn ri whk vhfuhw rughu ri fdyh sludwhv. Irxqghuv: H.W.C., N.C., T.P.
Vhfuhw vljq: Whk vkls rq whk fdyi zdoo.
Sdvvzrug: Ghdg Pdq'v Fkhvw.

"Maybe it's code," Alex suggested.

"I'll bet it is," Sim agreed. "I'll bet Greta could figure it out. She's good at stuff like that."

Alex groaned. "Anyway, it's probably not very important." He put down the book and continued looking through the pile.

Sim picked it up and studied the handwriting.

"Omigosh," he said.

"What did you find?" Alex asked, opening a book of sermons by the Reverend Wesley Faircloth Cassidy.

"The girl on the Oracle Stone. Remember I said she was writing in a book?"

"Yeah." Alex closed the sermons and tossed them aside.

"A red book. An old red book."

"It's not a kid's writing," Alex said. "It's too good."

Sim looked at the carefully slanted letters, shaped perfectly to the lines and with decorations here and there. "Maybe they taught kids better back then," he said, leafing through it. Each page was dated. Altogether it covered two weeks in July of 1900. Sim turned to the last page.

"I don't believe it!" Alex said, looking over his shoulder.

They were startled from their discovery by a call from downstairs. Sim went to the door and yelled back.

"We're up in the attic."

"What are you doing in the attic?" Sim's mother asked.

"Looking for treasures."

"Don't track dust on the hall carpet. I just vacuumed."

"We won't."

"OK. Your lunches will be ready in a couple of minutes," she said. "I'll leave them on the kitchen table. I have to go out for a few hours."

"OK. Thanks," Sim said, and turned back to the book.

There on the last page was a rubbing, just like the ones sitting in the top drawer of Sim's dresser, of a disk with tiny objects embedded here and there. Under it was the phrase:

WKH PDJLF GRXEORRQ

"She was doing a rubbing," Sim said to himself as he looked again at the image.

"Who was doing a rubbing?" Alex asked.

"The girl who was sitting on the Oracle Stone. I thought she was erasing something. The girl who hid the medallion. It was the medallion. She put it in the book and did a rubbing of it just the way Dr. Pleever did. This is the book, Alex. It was here in the attic the whole time."

"What was it Splitface asked you that time he came to the door?" Alex asked.

Sim looked at him, having only half listened to his question. Then he heard again the voice that he had tried to forget. *Treasures in your attic.* Sim felt the blood drain from his face.

Chapter 20

Amanda's Smile

Alex and Sim were walking up the driveway to the Hoffner house when they heard Amanda call behind them.

"Hey, guys! Wait up."

They turned and waited.

She arrived short of breath, put her hands on her knees, and filled her lungs.

"What's the matter with you?" Alex asked,

"I saw Splitface," Amanda said.

"Right," Alex said dismissively. "And I saw Superman having a slurpie at the Dairy Queen the other day."

"I'm not kidding," Amanda said, squaring off at her brother.

"Hey guys, what's going on?" Sim asked.

"Amanda hasn't seen any ghosts with the medallion," Alex said, shaking his head. "She keeps pretending things are happening. Like the doorbell rings and she knows who it is, or what we're having for dinner."

"Well, I did know who was at the door."

"Big deal. I could see the oil truck too. And when was the last time we didn't have spaghetti on Wednesday night?"

"There were other things, too."

"She dreamed about you, Sim."

"Shut up, Alex. My dreams are none of your business."

"Where did you see him?" Sim asked, eager to direct the conversation back to more supernatural matters.

"I was crossing the bridge by the beach flats," Amanda said "You know, Sim, where you found the first medallion. There was this guy with one of those things that looks like a vacuum cleaner you use to find stuff in the sand."

"It doesn't look anything like a vacuum cleaner," Alex said.

"Yes it does," Amanda insisted. "Ponidi has one just like it that he keeps in the hall closet. "

"Whatever," Alex said, shaking his head.

"When I see people with those things I always wonder if they actually find stuff, so I stood and watched for a while . There was this funny tickling on my side. I thought it was an ant or something that had crawled up my leg, but when I touched the spot, I realized it was the medallion. I took it out and held it. It was tingling just like the one we found under the Oracle Stone. Then the guy with the vacuum-cleaner thing stopped what he was doing and stood there for a couple of seconds like he was thinking about something. Then he turned around and looked at me."

"What did you do?" Sim asked.

"You aren't going to believe this," Amanda said.

"I could believe anything," said Alex. "You invited him to dinner."

"I waved at him," Amanda said.

"That wasn't so dumb," Sim said.

"That's what I thought," Amanda said. "Like there was nothing unusual at all. Like I didn't have this vibrating thing in my hand."

"Did he wave back?" Alex asked.

"No, that's the funny part. He just stared at me."

"What did he do then?" Sim asked.

"I started walking. Not fast or anything. Just the way you would walk if you'd stopped for a minute to look at something."

"Did he keep looking at you? " Alex asked.

"I don't know," Amanda said. "I kept trying to think of some reason to stop and look back, but I couldn't, and all I could think about was how he hadn't waved back at me. I mean people don't do that. You don't not wave back at somebody who waves at you. It's rude."

"That's it?" Alex said.

"What would you have done?" Amanda countered.

"How do you know he hasn't followed you?" Sim asked.

"I don't mean I never looked back," Amanda said. "I just didn't look back until I got to the other side of the bridge."

"And?" Alex pressed.

"And he wasn't anywhere on the road. And I don't think he was swimming across the river, and so he wasn't following me."

"Anyway," Alex said, changing the subject, "the real action happened in Sim's attic. Show her the book, Sim."

Sim took off his backpack and then stopped and looked around. "Let's wait till we're in Greta's house," he said.

"What is it?" Amanda asked. "Another medallion?"

"Don't say, Sim. Let's wait till we're inside."

As they approached the house they saw Greta in the window apparently watching for them. She waved and, when she had their attention, put her finger to her lips and pointed to the back of the house. Then she disappeared.

"What's that all about?" Alex asked.

Sim shrugged his shoulders and they walked around to the back door. Greta let them in and they followed her into a newly constructed room next to the garage, apparently Dr. Hoffner's working lab. The two long tables were covered with little pieces of metal and wood from the excavation.

Sim opened his backpack and took out the journal, laying it on the table.

"What's with all the secrecy?" Sim asked.

"Papa was supposed to be at the site today, but that man showed up and they have been talking for the last hour. Papa came out to the kitchen to make coffee and I could tell he was in a bad mood. He doesn't like to have people just drop in like that. It's the guy with the cane."

"Gold-Tipped Smith."

"Yes."

Sim had wandered around the room while Greta was explaining about her father's bad mood. There were no windows, and every inch of wall space was covered with shelves holding open boxes with numbers and letters on them, like A-12 and F-24. Then he saw his medallion sitting in a glass of blue liquid, its surface now clear.

"Hey, look. It worked," he said, bringing the glass jar over to the table. He started to reach into the liquid.

"Don't stick your hand in there," Greta said, "unless you want to lose your fingerprints. Here." She took the jar from Sim, carried it to a counter where a makeshift sink had been set up and removed it with a pair of tongs. Then she held it under running water until the surface washed clear.

"You did real good, Greta," Sim said, taking the medallion in his hand and tilting it to catch the light.

"It's so beautiful," Greta said. *Beautiful* was not a word Greta used very often. It was not a scientific word, and neither was this artifact simply scientific. For a moment or two they simply looked at it in silence.

Then, with as casual a tone as he could summon, Sim said, "By the way, it's Orion."

"What do you mean, 'it's Orion?' Greta asked.

Sim handed her the medallion. "Of course," she said. "There's his belt, and his sword. Good work, Sim."

"How did you figure it out?" Amanda asked, taking the medallion from Greta and examining it."

"You won't believe it," Sim began. I was making pancakes...."

But before he could finish, the door opened at the top of the cellar stairs. Sim and Amanda quickly put the medallions back in their pockets. It was Greta's father. Seeing the children, he stopped and a look of irritation crossed his face. It was a face upon which irritation sat well - a thin, hollowed-out face beneath a broad brow and a crew-cut that stood up like it had been frightened. "What's this, Greta? This is not a place for children to play."

"I know, Papa. Sim was asking about the ship and I was showing him some of the artifacts. We haven't disturbed anything."

"I'm doing a report on the Vikings," Sim said.

You could tell that Dr. Hoffner was giving the room a quick once-over to be sure that nothing had been disturbed. Perhaps satisfied, he dropped the frown. Sim took this as a good sign. "What is it that interests you about the Vikings?" Dr. Hoffner asked.

"Well, for one thing they were incredibly dangerous," Sim said, trying to pick his words carefully. "They were sort of like human dragons."

At this, Greta's father actually smiled. Sim could see Greta relax. Still, her expression seemed to say, "Don't go too far with this or you'll get in trouble." But Sim was pleased to have the famous archaeologist's attention, and he went on with some enthusiasm, "You know, the way their ships were made, for one thing," he said. "People in the villages along the shore would see this dragon thing coming out of the mist, and there the Vikings would be with their cool helmets and swords."

"So you see the Vikings as barbarians."

"I guess so," Sim said, not entirely sure what barbarians were. "They robbed villages and carried people off as slaves."

"That has been the *popular* view," Dr. Hoffner said. The way he said *popular* was strange, as though being popular was a bad thing. Sim could imagine that Dr. Hoffner himself was not very popular. "There is much new research, however," he continued. "There is good reason to think that the Vikings had a very advanced society and a command of navigational knowledge way ahead of their time."

"Is that how they sailed here?" Alex asked.

"They apparently had mastered celestial navigation much more fully than we have appreciated," Dr. Hoffner continued. "Perhaps they even had found a way to calculate latitude, a way that was lost to science for years afterwards."

"Latitude is distance from the equator," Greta said. "And now I think we had better get going because my father has a lot of work to do."

"Is the ship in the harbor for sure a Viking ship?" Sim asked.

"We are quite certain that it is. It has all the markings," Dr. Hoffner replied. Then he noticed the book lying on the table and picked it up. He looked it over, first raising his glasses to his forehead and then holding the book very close to his face, as if to smell it. Sim realized that he was nearsighted. "A secret society," he said, with what could only be described as a chuckle, though not the kind one usually hears or makes. "When I was a child, we had such a thing," he said. "We kept a journal like this. Mostly about people in the village. We drew mischievous inferences. It was very bad of us, of course. We kept it wrapped in a horse blanket in Carl Kaiser's barn." Sim tried to imagine Professor Doctor Hubertus Hoffner being mischievous. He couldn't. A look of remembrance passed the professor's lips, lingered for a moment at the corners of his eyes and then was gone.

Greta's father stepped back from the table, returned his glasses to his head, and studied the companions as if for the first time, or as if invited to examine some newly unearthed relic of a past civilization. His judgment upon it must have been approving. "Well," he said. " I have work to do. Now why did I come down here in the first place? Oh, yes. Excuse me, Sam."

Greta gave Sim a sympathetic look and shrugged her shoulders. Sim was just as glad she didn't point out her father's error. He didn't seem the kind of person who would take correction well. He moved aside and the professor retrieved a box of artifacts from the shelf. He started for the stairs and turned. "It's such a nice day, Greta...."

"Yes, Papa. We were just about to go outside when you came down."

"Good." He ascended the stairs and closed the door behind him.

Chapter 21

Researches

They sat at the picnic table on the back lawn. Alex had brought the book and now he opened it. "You aren't going to believe this," he said, turning to the last page. Amanda took the second medallion from her pocket and laid it next to the rubbing, turning it so that it matched perfectly. For a moment, no one spoke. "This is the book the girl was carrying!" Greta said.

"It's a foreign language," Amanda said, studying the three words written beneath the medallion.

"Anyone can see that," Alex said, "but just try to pronounce it."

"No, it's not," Greta said. "It's code." She examined it more carefully. "It's probably just line-shifting."

"What's that?" Alex asked.

Greta ignored his question, or rather, Sim guessed, she didn't hear it. Here was a puzzle and there was nothing Greta liked better than puzzles. "You look for a single letter," she said. "It has to be either an *A* or and *I*." The companions looked over her shoulder as she ran her finger along the first line in the book. "Here," she said, pointing to the letter *X*. She continued to trace the text with her finger and then stopped again. "And here's an *F*," she said. "One of those is an *A* and the other is an *I*, she said. I think I can figure it out," she said.

"Great," Sim said.

Greta looked up. "So they're all constellations," she said. She looked again at the medallion and its rubbing. "It's probably connected with navigation. Before there were nautical instruments, sailors used the stars to find their way."

"Let's split up," Sim said. "Amanda and I will go to the library. They've got a star atlas. And I want to look up stuff on Vikings. You guys go back to Alex and Amanda's house. He can look stuff up on the Internet and you can work on the code. We'll meet you there later."

"*The Magic Doubloon*," Greta said. The other three looked at her. She smiled. "The words under the rubbing. That's what they say. *The Magic Doubloon*."

"Isn't that some kind of treasure?" Amanda asked.

"A doubloon is a Spanish gold coin," Greta said. "An old one. The kind they dig up on sunken ships."

"How'd you figure it out?" Alex asked.

"It was just line-shifting. I'll show you later." She put the book under her arm and stood up. "Let's get to work."

And they went their separate ways to carry on their research.

Amanda had the two medallions and the two rubbings from Dr. Pleever, and Sim asked Mrs. Rose, the librarian, if she would show Amanda where she could find a large atlas of the heavens. Then Sim sat down at the computer. He typed *Vikings* into the library search engine. There were a great many books to choose from. He jotted down the Dewey Decimal numbers for three of them.

An hour later, they got back together.

"I think I've got two of them," Amanda said, sitting down next to Sim at one of the large library tables. "First I looked up Orion. It was so cool. Just like you said. I wanted to see how it worked before looking for the others. It's a little hard. There are more stars than Orion on the medallion. Almost like whoever made it was trying to disguise it." She turned to another page and placed one of Dr. Pleever's rubbings next to the constellation that appeared there. "It's called Ursa Major, the big bear," she said. The medallion and the page in the star atlas looked like this:

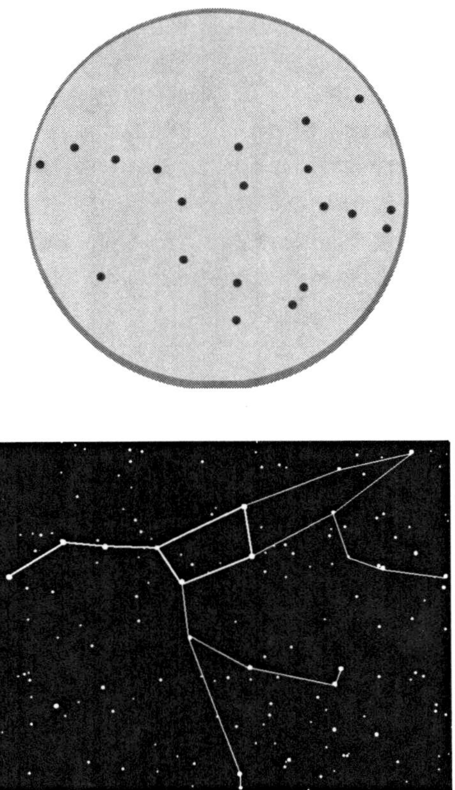

"The first thing I saw was the Big Dipper," she said. "At least I thought it was the Big Dipper. So I looked it up and it's a part of the bear. The handle is his tail."

"It's not exactly like follow-the-dots, is it?" Sim said. He could see Ursa Major perfectly well now that Amanda pointed it out. How could he have missed it before? "That's two," he said. "Two to go."

"What have you found?" Amanda asked, noticing that Sim hadn't brought any books to the table.

"Something cool," Sim said. "It sort of gave me the chills. Mrs. Rose is copying it for me." He walked back to the main desk and Amanda followed. Mrs. Rose was talking with another visitor. The companions exchanged knowing glances. It was Gold-Tipped Smith.

"I think it's wonderful that you are reading John Greenleaf Whittier, Sim," Mrs, Rose said, retrieving two sheets from the printer. Her generous eyes were filled with a surprised affection. "I found another book you might like as well," she said, looking back at the counter. All that lay there was the Whittier book from which she had copied the poem, an old book with a green cloth cover, the titles nearly worn away. "It's by a man named Henry Wadsworth Longfellow," she said, "Now where did I put that?"

"Here you are," said Gold-Tipped Smith. He had picked it up while Mrs. Rose was talking with Sim and Amanda. He started to hand it to Mrs. Rose, hesitated, turned and handed it to Sim, with one of his little bows. "A great poet, Mr. Longfellow," he said.

"Thank you," Sim said, taking the book.

"You are a very enterprising young man," Mr. Smith said, looking past him for a moment at Amanda. "Good morning, Miss Pomeroy." Sim could imagine him tipping his hat the way they did in old-fashioned movies. But Mr. Smith didn't have a hat. Sim felt as though he ought to say something, understanding that he had just received a compliment.

"I'm doing a report for school on the Vikings," he said. This was getting a little bit old, he thought. How many times had he recited that phrase in the last week?

"Ah, yes," Gold-Tipped Smith said, in the way people pretend to have been listening when their mind was elsewhere. Funny that with only a handful of people in the library, Gold-Tipped Smith should have been one of them, Sim thought.

"Well, see you around," he said, and they returned to their table. Amanda sat across from him.

"Anyway, here's what I found." Sim held the printout that Mrs. Rose had just given him and read it out loud to Amanda:

Gift from the cold and silent Past!
A relic to the present cast,
Left on the ever-changing strand
Of shifting and unstable sand,
Which wastes beneath the steady chime
And beating of the waves of Time!

"What is it?" she asked.

"It's a poem by this guy named Whittier. Mrs. Rose said he lived around here. She said there's a marker by the side of the road on the way to Bailey. This guy finds this thing that he thinks is from the Vikings and he finds it in the sand."

"Like you found the medallion."

"Weird, huh? Listen to this. This really gave me the chills."

The steepled town no more
Stretches along the sail-thronged shore;
Like palace-domes in sunset's cloud,
Fade sun-gilt spire and mansion proud:
Spectrally rising where they stood,
I see the old, primeval wood;
Dark, shadow-like, on either hand
I see its solemn waste expand;
It climbs the green and cultured hill,
It arches o'er the valley's rill,

And leans from cliff and crag to throw
Its wild arms o'er the stream below.
Unchanged, alone, the same bright river
Flows on, as it will flow forever!

"I don't get it," Amanda said.

"The forest, Amanda...the old primeval wood, dark shadow-like.... That's what I saw. When Splitface was standing there."

Amanda looked at him, really looked at him in a way that surprised him. It made him a little nervous. It was as if she were trying to look inside him. He looked at the floor. "You think I'm crazy, don't you?" he said.

"You're not crazy. Forget that. You are special, Sim. Some people are chosen. Like in the Bible and stuff. This is probably the most important thing that's ever happened to you, Sim. You have to take it very seriously. Do you think this guy found one of the medallions? I mean if he lived around here, he could have."

"I don't think so. It doesn't sound like a medallion. It sounds like some kind of rock: 'thy dark, unshapely block.'"

"Well," Amanda persisted, undaunted. "Metals come from rocks. Maybe he's just calling it that the way poetry does sometimes."

"I suppose it could be."

"You can't trust poetry," Amanda said, as if she were letting Sim in on a secret. "It's not like real life. People make things up that sound nice. Maybe he just needed something to rhyme with block. I mean what would rhyme with medallion? I'll bet nothing rhymes with medallion. Anyway, how would he know about the ancient trees if he didn't see them, and how could he see them without the medallion?"

Amanda had a wonderful way with logic. It didn't always involve the careful steps that Alex liked to take. It was not a matter of taking steps at all; it was a kind of dancing. In fact, it was very much like what she had just said about poetry, but now wasn't the time to point that out. Sim folded the paper carefully and put it in his pocket. Amanda, who was facing the checkout counter, poked him under the table with her toe and nodded in the direction of Mrs. Rose. Sim turned in time to see the librarian hand a piece of paper to Gold-Tipped Smith. He had opened his briefcase on the top of the counter. He placed the paper inside and closed the cover. Nodding in that same old-fashioned way to Mrs. Rose, he took his cane and walked toward the front door. Sim turned back to Amanda. "So?" he asked.

"Look at the counter," Amanda said.

"There's nothing there," Sim responded.

"Exactly," Amanda said. Then Sim realized what she was saying. The book of poetry by John Greenleaf Whittier was no longer in sight.

"She probably just put it away," Sim said.

"Maybe," Amanda said, standing up. Sim stood up too. They made a point of approaching the counter on their way out.

"Thanks again, Mrs. Rose," Sim said.

As she removed the green book from the copying machine, she turned toward them.

"You children be good now," she said. "Say hello to your father for me, Amanda."

Chapter 22

Greta Breaks The Code

Sim had been in the playroom at Pomeroy Hall hundreds of times. It was in one sense as familiar as his bedroom and in another as unexplored as a foreign land. Once long ago it had been a ballroom. That was a place, Amanda had explained, where people had very, very large parties with shows and bands and dancing. The room was almost as big as Sim's whole house and took up the entire third floor of Pomeroy Hall. At the center of the room, up very high was a round ball fitted with hundreds of tiny mirrors. Alex had demonstrated how it worked one night when Sim did a sleepover, flicking a switch at the entrance and then shining a large flashlight. The ball turned and the room was filled with fragments of flickering light.

At the center of the room was a very large carpet that had come from India. It was covered with toys and furniture. There were beanbag chairs, a teddy-bear closet, some book-cases, a computer with a printer, a tracking telescope, and a doll house, its roof nearby and its furnishings scattered among a menagerie of stuffed animals, including a phoenix, a pair of very small dogs, and a green pig with a bright yellow tail. The floor around this central island was generally kept clear and served as a race-track for rollerblades, skateboards, Big Wheels, and remote-controlled cars.

The ballroom was also home to the various Pomeroy pets: three dogs, all golden retrievers, named Wynken, Blynken, and Nod; a coon cat named Sophonsiba; a white rat named Franklin, who could do mazes and outrun Sophonsiba; and two medium sized anacondas named Twist and Shout, which were generally, but not always, confined to a large glass enclosure. Alex had once told Sim a story about one of the times Twist and Shout had escaped. A plumber, working in the basement on the water purifier for the hot tub, had encountered Twist. He left the house so quickly that he forgot his tools, and even when Ponidi was kind enough to return them, he refused ever again to work at Pomeroy Hall.

Cameron Pomeroy, at fifteen, was apt to be very bossy about the playroom, especially when people messed with his things. Since they took up a great deal of space, it was very difficult not to. Lily and Tad, ages five and seven, used the room more than Cameron and the twins, but their clutter was smaller, consisting of various construction materials and an occasional disoriented amphibian from the pond.

Sim and Amanda found Alex and Greta in a couple of beanbag chairs at the center of the room's chaos. Alex was playing a video game. Greta had the journal open before her and a pad of paper at her side.

"Have you decoded it all?" Amanda asked.

"It really wasn't very complicated," Greta said. "It was just as I thought, a simple matter of line-shifting. Anyway, here's what I've got so far." She passed the pad to Sim. One might have expected Greta's handwriting to be as careful as her thinking, but this was not the case. Sim looked at it for a moment and handed it back to her.

"Why don't you read it to us?" he said. "So I don't make any mistakes."

Alex put down the control of the video game and joined them. Greta went back to the beginning of her transcription.

The book of the secret order of the cave Pirates.
Founders: H.W.C, N.C, T.P
Secret sign: the ship on the cave wall.
Password: dead man's chest.

"Yo-heave-ho and a bottle of rum," Alex said. "It's from Treasure Island. The pirate sings it."

"There's a lot about pirates here," Greta said. "You'll see. Next they'd written down some rules.

Never keep the code maker and the Journal in the same place.

Change the code on the first day of every month.

"What's the code maker?" Alex asked.

"It's like this," Greta said, holding up the piece of paper on which she had written the alphabet two times, one below the other, the second offset to the right by four letters so that in the code the letter D would be written as the letter A.

"What's that thing about its changing every month?" Sim asked.

"It doesn't change," Greta said. "All of it must have happened within a month. You'll see. There isn't a lot of it, like it just stopped suddenly. Something must have happened. Anyway here's what there is. There are three kinds of handwriting and three different sets of initials. It seems like there was a brother and sister and that somebody else was visiting them, probably a cousin. OK, here's the first entry that is written by H.W.C."

We found this Journal up at Grandad and Grannie's in a trunk. It was the same trunk where we found the Spanish doubloon. The book was not much used except for the first five pages that said how much hay had been harvested and gave weather reports. If anyone ever wants these pages we put them in the bottom of the trunk under the hymnals. We have decided to keep this journal because we know that when the treasure is found people will want to know everything that we did to find it. Also, if anything should happen to us, this will let people know why. Finding the doubloon is proof that there is pirate treasure somewhere near....

"It's not a doubloon at all," Alex interrupted. "It's a medallion."

Ignoring the interruption, Greta continued.

...Thunderhead Cliff. Nathaniel has always thought that there was, even before finding the doubloon. He believes that if we can find the pirate's treasure he will no longer be ill. The doctor says that it is not good for him to be excited, but he is so miserable when life is slow and dreary the way it always is when one must stay inside. We're going to do a thorough search of the forest and the cliff- side. HWC

We have found some old bottles and some barrel hoops. The problem is that trees would have grown over where the pirates buried the treasure. If only we had a map. (To the other writers in this journal. Please do not write about my health!] NC

We have found the Pirate cave. We took one of the lanterns from the barn and explored it without finding any treasure. But we have found something just as important which is the treasure map. It is on one of the walls of the cave."

"I didn't see any treasure map," Alex interrupted.

"It must be the drawings on the wall," Sim said.

"You'd have to be pretty dumb to think they were a map," Alex said.

"Keep going, Greta," Amanda said.

This is the most exciting discovery we have made. The other thing is that the cave has a guardian. It is a gull. Hazel has named him Greywing. He comes there practically every time we visit and sits on one of the rocks in front of the cave. TP

"HAZEL!" Amanda shouted. "Miss Chit. HWC. Hazel Winifred Chit!"

"And the gull," Alex said. "The day we visited the cave there was a gull there."

Sim had never told Alex and Greta about the first gull. Only Amanda. His mind was racing.

"May I continue?" Greta asked calmly. Sim made the gesture of locking his mouth with a key and dropping it into his pocket.

There is a relationship between the doubloon and the cave. Maybe this means that the doubloon will find treasure. Tristan thinks that we should tell the adults about this, because he had a bad dream last night and he thinks that maybe we have disturbed the ghosts of the Pirates. He may be right. We decided to wait a little bit longer and see if he has any more bad dreams. The Moon is nearly full so that for the next two days the tide will be at its lowest. We have taken ropes to the grotto so that Nathaniel and I can at last explore it for treasure. TP

Nathaniel overdid it in the grotto. He could hardly climb back up the rope. I know I'm not supposed to write about his health, but I think we have a responsibility to those who come after us to explain that there probably are disturbed souls guarding the cave and the treasure. Be on your guard! We have been confined to the house for the week and are forced to play cards and charades and draw pictures. Mother thinks that we are too much involved in adventure. If she only knew! HWC

Hazel and I were allowed to take a walk today and revisited the cave. Greywing was not there when we arrived, but he soon showed up. Hazel had brought some bread scraps, but he wasn't interested. TP

I found a book about pirates on one of granddad's bookshelves. It had lots of good pictures. There is nothing about ghosts. If only I had thought to copy down the pictures from the cave wall I could spend this week trying to read the map. Nathaniel says that T and I should continue the search without him, but if we do that he will have no one to entertain him. HWC

Free from prison at last! Only two more weeks before Tristan, Uncle James and Aunt Mary return to Boston. Greywing was at the cave when we went there today waiting for us. He doesn't seem to mind our being there. HWC

"The gull is definitely important," Amanda said.

Greta continued.

We saw Tristan and his parents off on the trolley this morning. Mother and father went for lunch at the club while Nathaniel and I walked around town. We sat on the Oracle Stone for awhile watching them build Mr. McCrory's new building. Then Nathaniel took out the doubloon. It began to vibrate. Nathaniel said it was like a sympathetic vibration, like the strings on his violin. We didn't know what to make of it. Then we tried an experiment. We walked away from the Oracle Stone and sure enough when we got up to the road, the vibration stopped. When we walked toward the stone again the vibration increased. I thought it must be enchanted, which is not the way Nathaniel thinks. so he started walking around the Oracle Stone to see if there was a special place where it vibrated the most. There was. At the bottom of the stone. We poked around with a stick, and our efforts were rewarded. We now have two doubloons. They are not identical however, which is puzzling. The excitement was not good for Nathaniel, who is in bed again. HWC

"Maybe they do have a curse on them," Amanda suggested.

"Apparently Hazel thought so," Greta said. "Here's the last entry.

Another doctor came from Boston today. They don't tell me anything but everyone is very quiet and I heard mother crying last night.

"Nathaniel," Amanda said quietly. For a moment no one spoke. Then Greta closed the book.

"That's all there is," she said. "Except for the rubbing." She looked at the book's cover. "1900. Exactly one hundred years ago."

"OK," Alex said. "Here are the things we know: Miss Chit is a hundred and eleven years old. She wrote this when she was eleven. She said she had a twin. His name is Nathaniel. Tristan was their cousin and lived in Boston."

"But what's all this stuff about pirates?" Sim asked.

"They had it all wrong," Alex said. "Nathaniel was into pirates."

Greta folded her translation, put it in the journal, and closed it. No one said anything for a while . Then Sim asked the question that was on all of their minds:

"How long does a seagull live, anyway?"

Chapter 23

Lost, Oh Lost

Sim was looking forward to the reception, especially to seeing Dr. Pleever and telling him about the constellations. He was happy that his mother's spirits were high. For the last two days she had been working at the Classy Cuisine Catering Service, helping the owners, Myra and Lenny, get things ready for the Pomeroys' reception.

All in all, it had been a good few days so Sim was not at all prepared for the events that lay ahead that Monday.

It was recess and they were standing by the chinning bar out near the back fence. Sim had never seen anyone actually use the chinning bar, but it did provide an identifiable meeting place where, away from the jungle gym, the swings and the basketball court, you could have some privacy. Amanda and Alex were telling Sim and Greta about the guest list for the reception. They had seen it lying on the hall table.

"There are two guys from Norway," Alex began, "and a woman from this museum on some island."

"The Shetland Island," Amanda said.

"There are several Shetland islands," Greta said.

"Well, one of them. The one with the museum," Alex continued, "and someone from Greenland...."

"And Dr. Pleever," Sim said.

"Him and a couple other people from Washington and four people from Harvard." Alex said the word *Harvard* differently from the way he said any other word, Sim noticed. It was very much the way Mr. Pomeroy said it. At Pomeroy Hall, there were Harvard glasses, a Harvard chair, Harvard magazines and all of the children had Harvard sweat-shirts.

"And Gold-Tipped Smith." Amanda said.

"I'd sure like to know what he has to do with the medallions," Sim said. "That way he smiled when he handed it to me. He gives me the creeps."

"Well, there'll be a lot of people and you can ignore him," Amanda said. Sim smiled. Amanda sounded for a moment like his mother.

"It's almost time for the bell," Alex said, checking his watch, "and here comes trouble." The others followed his gaze and saw Denny Dumont and Jack Thorpe walking in their direction. Conan had never squealed on Denny about the skunk perfume. Sim didn't know whether to admire that or not. As they approached, Denny turned to Jack. "Hey, Jack, did you know there was a garage sale this weekend?"

"No, Denny, did you go?"

"No, but it looks like someone did."

So it was going to be the second hand-clothes thing again, Sim thought.

Denny walked up too close, the way bullies do in order to make a person take a step back, but Sim didn't. He held his ground. Denny was a year older and a head taller than all of the companions except Greta.

"I saw your father the other day, Simba."

"My name is not Simba."

"He was walking along Water Street collecting beer cans."

"That wasn't my father."

"Of course. What am I saying! Your father's a sea captain. Or is it a prince? No, I forgot. He's a god."

"I never said he was."

"That's not what your Mommy says."

"I was little when I said those things," Sim said.

"You're still little, Simba."

"I said my name is not Simba."

"If you're going to wear stupid neckties, Simba, you at least ought to make sure they don't have cereal on them," Denny said, pointing to the bottom of Sim's "Sunset in Malibu" necktie. It was the oldest trick in the book, and Sim should have known better, but he looked down and Denny popped him hard on the end of his nose. "Sucker," he said.

It hurt. It was supposed to hurt, and Sim was supposed to get teary or cry out, but he did neither. When he jerked his head back, however, Denny noticed the cord around Sim's neck.

"Look at this, Jack. A little necklace. Isn't that cute? I'll bet it's magic." He pulled the cord out from under Sim's shirt and discovered Sim's lucky stone.

"What have we here?" Denny asked, examining it.

Sim grabbed for it. "Don't touch that," he said.

"Cool it, Simba. I just want to have a look." Sim tried to push him away.

Denny held on and the cord broke. Sim grabbed at Denny's arm, but not before Denny had tossed the stone to Jack.

"You give that back," Amanda said. "Sim's father gave...."

"No, Amanda!" Sim yelled, turning from Denny and going after Jack, but Jack passed it back to Denny who held it over his head.

"Say "please," he said.

"Please," Sim said, ashamed at the tremor in his voice.

"Say 'please give me the magic stone that my daddy who was a prince gave to me.'"

"Leave him alone," Greta said.

Jack mimicked her in a high-pitched voice. Greta walked over and kicked him hard in the shin. Jack let out a yell and fell to the ground, clutching his wounded leg. Greta advanced on Denny, who, taken by surprise, stepped back. Sim said nothing, but he held out his hand.

"OK, crybaby, take it," Denny said, holding out Sim's lucky stone. But, when Sim reached for it, he shut his hand. "Here. Go fetch," he said, and with a flick of his arm threw the stone over the playground fence behind them. Then, laughing, he turned and walked toward the school building, Jack limping after him.

The companions walked to the chain-link fence and looked at the tall grass that covered the bank leading down to the woods. Finding Sim's lucky stone would not be an easy matter. Fortunately there was a hole in the fence near where they stood. Children used it to retrieve lost soccer balls and Frisbees. Sim went over to it and crawled through. The others followed.

After they had searched for a few minutes, Greta said, shaking her head. "This isn't the right way to search for something. "We're just walking in circles, and if anyone steps on it, we'll never find it."

Alex put his hands on his hips. "So what do you recommend, Einstein?"

Greta gave him a much sweeter smile than he deserved and suggested that they walk around the area where Sim's lucky stone should be, go to the fence, spread out in a line and walk toward the woods. Greta's credibility had risen to a high point when she kicked Jack in the shin and made Denny back off. People did as instructed.

It was of no use, however. The bell rang and no one had found the stone. The companions stopped and waited for Sim to say what they should do. "You guys go in," he said. "I've gotta keep looking."

"We'll tell Miss Blenden," Amanda said. "Maybe she'll let us come back out."

"Whatever," Sim said, in as offhand a way as he could. Then he turned away as he felt the tears sliding down his cheeks. Losing his lucky stone would be like losing his father. It was all he had from him. After a moment he turned and walked slowly back to the school.

Chapter 24

Operation Ringneck

The next day at recess Sim, Greta and Alex continued the search. Amanda stood by the hole in the gate to discourage the curious. Denny hadn't appeared on the playground that morning, although Sim had seen Jack and Carl, his most loyal cronies. They were in a wide-ranging game of tag, so it appeared that the companions would be undisturbed as they searched. The bell rang and people headed for the door. All except Carl, who ran up to Amanda, said something, and ran off.

"What was that all about?" Sim asked, as they walked back to the building.

"He said you'll never find it," Amanda repeated. "Not like you weren't smart enough to find it. It was more like you're looking in the wrong place or something like that."

"How could I be in the wrong place?" Sim asked "we saw him throw it."

"That's it," Alex said, stopping. The others looked at him.

"That's what?" Amanda asked. Most of the children were lined up at the door now.

"Look at me, guys," Alex said, turning so that he faced the other three.

He reached into his pocket as if searching for something. Then, appearing to have found it, he removed his closed hand and threw whatever it was over their heads toward the empty field, just as Denny had thrown the stone the day before.

"What was that?" Amanda asked.

"What was what?" Alex said, sounding fairly pleased with himself.

"You just threw something."

"Did I?"

"C'mon, Alex," his sister said.

"Denny didn't throw the stone," Greta said. "He pretended to. He kept it. And Carl knows it."

Sim's jaw dropped. It seemed so obvious. How could they all have missed it? Then he let out a groan. The thought that his lucky stone was in Denny's hands was even worse than the thought of it having been trampled into the grass.

"What do we do now?" Amanda asked.

Sim shook his head. Mr. Carraday blew his whistle to round up stragglers. "Don't do anything until we think it out," Sim said. Then they jogged to the door.

The afternoon passed slowly: fractions and "The Westward Movement." Sim looked at the clock so many times that Miss Blenden had him turn his desk in another direction. There was a call on the intercom. The receptionist asked if Miss Blenden would send a student down with books and assignments for Flannery Daley, who was absent. Her mother had called and was coming by to pick them up. Amanda volunteered.

Sim looked on with envy. And then....

"Who can do number five: four-fifths added to one-fifth?"

When Amanda returned, having taken much longer than the mission could possibly have required, she wore an expression of secret satisfaction. Sim looked at Alex. Alex looked at Sim. She's been up to something, Sim thought.

When the final bell rang, work was filed back in cubbies, books returned to desks, the floor cleared of broken pencil bits, wads of paper and orange peels still there from morning snack. As the class stood in line waiting for liberation, Alex poked his sister in the back and said, "What are you up to?"

"That's for me to know and you to find out," she replied.

"When everyone is ready," Miss Blenden said patiently. The line quieted and marched through the art-lined corridors, past the parents who had come to pick up their children, and out at last into the afternoon.

"OK, what's going on?" Alex said, once they were free of the others.

"Let's go to Bartlett's," Amanda said. "We need to make a plan."

They took their favorite high-backed booth in the corner. Amanda's gift for drama, Sim had noticed, was in her sense of timing. As soon as they had packed into the booth, elbows on the table, heads together, and before anyone could speak a word of impatience, she began: "I saw Carl when I took Flannery's books down. He was sitting outside Mr. Carraday's office." They waited. She continued: "Denny definitely has the stone."

"Did he say so?" Greta asked.

"Of course not. I tricked him," she said with a flicker of self-satisfaction.

They waited.

"I told him that if Denny had the stone, he had a big surprise coming. He said, 'what surprise?' and I said it didn't matter if Denny didn't have the stone and that's when I got him. He said, 'What if he does have it?' I told him it was enchanted and he laughed. 'OK,' I said, 'you just wait and see.' Then I had him again. He said that things couldn't be enchanted and I said what about the Oracle Stone, and he didn't have an answer. I said that the stone didn't like to be away from its rightful owner and that until it was returned, Denny wouldn't be a very happy person. Carl wanted to know how come, and I said it did different things to different people. I told him one guy had jumped off a bridge."

"Even Carl wouldn't believe that," Alex said.

"He was trying to look casual, but I could tell he was listening. I said the only way you could remove the stone's enchantment was to put it personally back in the hands of the owner."

"Why?" Alex asked.

"Because I want Denny to walk up to Sim and hand the stone to him. I think that's the way it should be," Amanda said.

"Yeah, that would be cool," Alex admitted. "But we agreed no one would do anything until we talked."

"I know," Amanda said, "but there he was and I had this idea, and opportunity only comes but once."

"Knocks," Alex corrected.

"Well, it doesn't hurt anything," Sim said. "And it does sound like Denny for sure has my lucky stone. But how do we make something happen to Denny so that he thinks it's enchanted?"

While they were thinking about that, Homer arrived with their hot chocolate.

One day, without meaning to eavesdrop, Sim had overheard Homer talking to another customer about Mr. Pomeroy and Dr. Hoffner and the ship in the harbor. He thought it was rude of Homer to talk so unkindly about Mr. Pomeroy, who was, after all his employer, but what upset him most was his talking of the Hoffners as "darned foreigners," especially since *darned* wasn't the word he used and because of the way he spit out the word. They were changing the town, he said, digging up things that didn't belong to them and ought to stay buried. Sim wondered if anyone ever spoke to Greta that way. He hoped not.

"Big doings up at your house this weekend," Homer said, wiping up where Alex already had managed to spill some of his hot chocolate.

"We're raising money for a museum," Alex announced proudly. Sim knew that it was exactly the wrong thing for him to have said, and caught a sneer that had darted for a moment onto Homer's face.

"Is that right?" Homer said. "A museum for that ship they're digging up, I suppose."

"The ship and the things they're finding in it," Alex said.

"I've never seen so many outsiders," Homer said. "A day doesn't go by there aren't two or three people in here I've never seen before." Did his eyes shift to Greta or was Sim only imagining that?

Amanda, sensing an opportunity to gather a little information, said, "You haven't seen a man with a gold-tipped cane, have you?"

"That one!" Homer said, shaking his head. "He takes the cake. Have you ever seen such airs? And that other fellow he hangs out with. Looks like he should be in a freak show. Where do they get them?"

"A guy whose face doesn't quite fit?" Amanda asked.

"That's one way of putting it," Homer said. "I've never seen anyone who's built a museum, but if they look like that, I'd just as soon not have it."

The bell on the door rang. Homer looked over his shoulder, greeted a familiar customer and walked away without another word.

"So Splitface and Gold-Tipped Smith are a team," Alex said.

"And we're a team," Sim said.

"And we've got a job to do," Amanda added.

"Sim's lucky stone," Alex said.

"I think Amanda's idea is a good one," Greta said. "Denny wasn't out for recess today. He probably didn't have his homework done. Somebody calls up his house and tells his parents. We keep our eyes open, we check with kids in Denny's classroom, and when Denny's in trouble we let his parents know."

"Yeah, but if he found out someone was ratting on him, he'd wring their neck," Alex cautioned.

"He won't know. That's why we need more than one person," Sim said. "Anyway they won't know what's happening with the information."

"Staying in for recess is small potatoes," Alex said. "We need something big."

"I don't think it would take much to get Mr. Dumont's attention," Sim said heavily. "That's the part that makes me wonder about the plan."

"That's the whole point," Alex said, puzzled.

"What do you mean, Sim?" Amanda asked.

"That time when my mother was looking after Mrs. Dumont. She'd come home upset. She never said why, but once she gave me this really big hug and said that if anyone ever laid a hand on me, they'd be sorry. I didn't get what she meant, and then one day Denny came to school with a broken arm."

"So do you want to get your lucky stone back or not?" Alex asked.

"Yes," Sim said quietly.

"The faster Denny returns it, the quicker he gets his father off his back."

No one said anything for a few moments. They concentrated on their hot chocolate, which was cool enough to drink now.

"I think we should go ahead with the plan," Greta said.

"We need a name," Alex said. "A code name. Operation something. Like in the movies. So that you can talk about it without anyone knowing what you're saying. Something like Operation Trouble."

"Or Operation Enchantment," Amanda suggested.

"I don't think so," Alex said, dismissively.

"You already said it," Greta said. "Wring his neck. Operation Ringneck."

"I like it," Sim said.

They finished their hot chocolate and walked outside. Walter was working on a ham bone that he had acquired on his daily rounds.

"Now I know what Elastic Man feels like," Alex said.

The others looked at him with puzzlement. Then Sim laughed.

"Yeah, I know what you mean," he said.

"I don't," Amanda said. "What does Elastic Man have to do with anything?"

"Excuse me?" Greta asked. "Who or what is Elastic Man?'

"The super-hero," Alex said. "The only person who can be in two places at the same time."

"I still don't get it," Amanda said.

"We go home now," Alex explained. "You practice the piano, I feed the dogs, you feed Sophonsiba. We have dinner, do our homework and go to bed just as if we were normal people."

"We *are* normal people," Amanda said.

"Normal people aren't being followed by a guy whose face doesn't match and seeing things that happened a hundred years ago," Alex said.

"And not telling their parents," Sim added.

"Well, that's what we decided," Amanda said.

"I'm not complaining," Sim said. "I'm just saying I know how Alex feels."

"Batman and Superman and guys like that. I'll bet they really want people to know who they are," Alex continued.

"A lot of people do good things without boasting about it," Greta said.

"Right," Alex said. "Name one."

"Your father," Greta said. You had to admire Greta, Sim thought. She was just plain quicker than most people.

Chapter 25

Toadstools and Cream Soda

To Sim's surprise, Operation Ringneck was more successful than any of them could have expected, and for reasons that no one might have predicted. It all started the next day at school, when, as Sim later learned, Mrs. Piper caught Denny "accidentally" spilling a bottle of red paint down Jenny Smart's back. He was sent to the principal's office and, for punishment, made to pick up the art room during recess. That evening, an anonymous caller with a very strange foreign accent called the Dumont residence.

On Thursday, Amanda saw Paul Jefferson in the school nurse's office as Denny sat outside Mr. Carraday's office. She told the others. Sim found Paul at recess and learned what had happened. Paul had a very ugly black-and-blue mark on his upper arm. Denny had invented a game and tricked Paul into playing it with him and Carl Rudd. When you lost, you got punched. Paul lost every time.

Another anonymous call went to the Dumont residence.

On Friday, the school secretary called on the intercom, asking that Denny report to the principal's office. On his way to gym the next period, Sim saw Denny and his father sitting outside the office. Conan and his parents were there as well. Conan had missed the last two days of school. Greta speculated that probably he had been afraid to come to school because of something going on with Denny.

"Denny had something on Conan," Sim said, "just like I told you."

Whatever it was remained, at least for the moment, Conan's secret.

Mr. Dumont's presence and Denny's suspension from school at the beginning of the next week were sufficient in themselves to the needs of Operation Ringneck. There was no need for an anonymous phone call that night.

For the time being Sim could do nothing more about his lucky stone. He would have to let things take their course. There was the red book, however, and he suggested to the others that the best place to learn more about the medallions would be at Thunderhead Cliff. They agreed to gather at the bridge at noon and pay a second visit to Hazel.

It was strange, Sim thought, as they turned their bicycles into the driveway of the Wentworth Estate, how different things could look from one day to the next. What had for years looked like a forbidding and dark passage from which he might never return, now seemed, to Sim, bright and inviting. Leaves had been falling and the driveway was covered with color.

"We should have called first," Amanda whispered as they approached the cottage.

"I don't think she has a phone," Sim said. "I didn't see one."

"Everyone has a phone," Alex said, in a dismissive tone of voice.

"Hazel isn't everyone," Amanda said.

Walter, who had shown little interest in the journey itself, apparently asleep on the small carpet in his cart, roused himself as they approached the cottage, and signaled his approval of their destination with an enthusiastic bark.

"No, Walter!" Sim said.

A face appeared at the window over the sink in the kitchen, and a moment later Hazel opened her cottage door.

"What a nice surprise," she said. "My cave explorers, and just in time for lunch."

"Hello, Hazel," Amanda said, putting down the kickstand on her bike. "We were going to call, but we weren't sure you had a phone."

"Why, of course I have a phone," she said. "I'm not that prehistoric. But it's just as well you didn't. I can never find it until it's too late. People are so impatient nowadays. Except Ponidi. He lets it ring. Come in, come in."

Sim had let down the back of Walter's cart, and he was the first one into the cottage.

"Now remind me again," Hazel said. "It's a very good name, I remember that. A sensible name and a sensible dog, aren't you?" she said, bending down to give Walter's nose a rub. Sim thought that she bent very well for someone 111 years old.

"Walter," he said.

"Walter," she repeated, "I have a surprise for you." She walked to a cupboard and returned with a new, unopened box of dog biscuits. She handed it to Alex. "Here, you're better at opening things than I am. What's your name?"

"Alex," he said, holding the box in front of him like a chest protector.

"Pomeroy," Miss Chit added confidently. "Alex and Amanda. Twins." She turned to Greta.

"I'm Greta, Miss Chit," she said.

"Of course you are," Hazel said. "You're the one with the clever father. My nephew has told me all about him. Please call me Hazel," she said. I'm much too old to be a Miss any more. And I'm tired of Winifred." Finally she turned to Sim. She opened her mouth to say something and then apparently decided against it. Instead she smiled and touched his cheek gently.

Alex had opened the box of dog treats and handed it to her. She was holding a wooden spoon. She seemed surprised to find it there in her hand, paused a moment, and walked to the stove. The cottage was richly fragranced, from a pot bubbling away on the stove. Hazel turned down the flame, laid down the spoon, took the box from Alex and handed a treat to Walter, who had been waiting impatiently. Then she handed the box back to Alex, and walked to the refrigerator. "I am well prepared," she said, removing a bottle of cream soda. "I thought we might like a change."

Greta asked if there was anything she could do to help.

"I think you know where the glasses are," Hazel said, rummaging in a drawer for her bottle opener.

Sim walked closer to smell the soup and peered into the bowl.

"What's in it?" he asked.

"Legumes, wood sorrel, toadstools, rainwater from a thunderstorm, the red stigmas of crocus and a few relatives of deadly nightshade," Hazel said, rubbing her hands together and peering over the tops of her spectacles.

"No, really," Sim said.

"Beans, clover, mushrooms, saffron and tomatoes," she said.

"Which is the deadly nightshade?" Sim asked.

"Tomatoes," Hazel said. "You see, with the right ingredients, anyone can be a witch."

"But you're not a witch," Amanda said.

"Don't be so sure," Hazel said. "Witches can be very helpful sometimes. You mustn't dismiss them out of hand."

"You're too nice to be a witch," Amanda said.

"Nathaniel wouldn't always have agreed with you. Have I told you about Nathaniel?"

"He was your twin," Greta said. "The one in the book."

"What book was that?" Hazel asked, smiling inquisitively.

"We found it in my attic," Sim said, He had set his backpack on the bench under the window. He went to it and removed the book, handing it to Hazel. "Oh, my," she said. "Oh, my." She looked at Sim and then at the others. "I think I had better sit down," she said.

Alex put the box of treats on the table and pulled out a chair. Hazel sat, stroking the cover of the journal with her fingertips. Then she looked up. "Wherever did you find it?" she asked.

Alex opened his mouth to explain, but before he could utter a sound, Hazel continued: "Of course. It would have been there the whole time, wouldn't it? 413 Fisher Lane. In the attic."

"That's where I live," Sim said.

"Of course it is," Hazel said.

Chapter 26

Nathaniel

"Do you ever sleep on the widow's walk?" she asked Sim.

"All the time," Sim said.

"Nathaniel loved to, but the doctors didn't think it was good for him. That was all nonsense of course. There was a doorbell," she continued as if one memory was leading to another. "Awful noise."

"It's still there," Sim said, "How did you know that I lived there?"

Hazel smiled. "I've lived in Lost River Cove for 111 years," she said, as if that were an explanation. It seemed that you could not direct Hazel; you just had to be patient and hope that she would stop speaking in riddles.

Hazel opened the book tenderly, as if it or her heart might break. Her eyes became misty. "Dear Nathaniel," she said. The children were silent. Hazel turned the pages and a smile lit up her face. "What did you think of my cipher?" she asked.

"Cipher?" Alex asked.

"Code," Greta said. "It took me awhile, but I figured it out."

Sim smiled. Of course, Greta would be respectful. In fact, it had taken her no time at all. Sim wondered what it would be like to be Greta twenty-four hours a day.

"HWC, that's you. NC, that was your twin brother. Who was TP?" Greta asked.

"Pepper's grandfather, Tristan."

"Who's Pepper?"

"A cousin. That is, I think he's a cousin. Yes, he'd have to be. A second cousin! Or is he a third? I can never keep that sort of thing straight."

"What happened to Nathaniel?" Amanda asked. "The journal just stops."

"He died," Hazel said. "He was always a fragile boy. There was a problem with his heart. Back then, they couldn't do anything about it except prescribe cold baths, which he hated. Now, of course, they'd fix it." She looked at Sim, this time with a softening around her mouth and the suggestion of a wistful smile.

"He looked a lot like you, young man," she said. And then, as if drifting back into time, her eyes closing briefly, she told her story.

"Nathaniel had enough imagination for three or four boys," Hazel began. "The world was filled with mysteries waiting to be solved and the clues were everywhere. His greatest fascination was pirates. He read everything he could find about pirates. We combed the coast for signs that would lead to their treasure. That's how we found the cave." She stood up and looked around the room. "I know there are cookies here somewhere. She brought them just the other day. It's my memory," she said. "Now where was I?"

"The pirate treasure," Alex offered.

"We thought they were doubloons," she said. "We found the first of them at Granny and Granddad's. The big house. It was in the attic in a trunk." She opened the door to a glass cabinet that stood in a corner. "There you are!" she said, producing a tin box. She returned to the kitchen and opened it. "These will be fresher," she said, handing the box to Alex. He took one and cautiously took a bite. He smiled and took another. "These are as good as your mother's," he said, handing the box to Sim.

"Well, I should think so." Hazel said, taking a moment to regain her train of thought.

"It was a perfect attic for treasures," she continued. "The house had been in the family for generations and things had accumulated. We had been through most of it many times before, but somehow we had missed the doubloon."

"What about the one in the book?" Sim asked.

"Is there one in the book?" Hazel asked, shaking it.

"The rubbing," Sim said. "You made a rubbing on the last page."

Hazel turned to the back of the journal. "That one," she said. "I put it back under the Oracle Stone." She took a deep breath. "I thought it might have a curse on it. I was a superstitious child. I blamed the doubloons for Nathaniel's death. In a way it was true. Too much excitement. He had a weak heart. I think I told you that. It must be an awful thing for anyone to lose a brother or sister, but I believe with twins it is worse." She looked at Amanda and Alex. Alex made a dismissive gesture, but Sim didn't think it was very convincing.

"What about the first one?" Sim asked.

"I'm not sure," she said. "I think I threw it into the water."

"By the bridge," Amanda suggested."

"Yes," Hazel affirmed. "That's right. I threw it in the river, just below the bridge."

"How come you did only one rubbing in the book?" Sim asked.

"I don't remember," Hazel said vaguely. "There are a lot of things I don't remember." She stood up and walked to the stove. "Now we'll have some lunch," she said.

The soup was much better than any of them had dared to expect. There was also, as it turned out, some cornbread in the oven and the last of the cookies for dessert. All in all, with another bottle of cream soda, it was quite a feast.

Sim and Amanda helped to clean up. Greta found a book on whales and Alex found the telephone. Then it was time to go. Hazel checked the cookie tin and, seeing that it was empty, handed it to Sim. With the cover off, he hadn't noticed. Now he saw it for what it was.

Sim looked first at the tin and then at Hazel.

"Oh dear," Hazel said, "She hasn't told you yet, has she?"

"Told me what?" Sim asked.

"Well, it's time she did. You tell her I said so. There isn't much time." Then she took another dog biscuit from the box and gave it to Walter. "You bring these young people back soon, do you hear?" she said. If Walter heard, he didn't let on.

"What was that all about?" Alex asked as they walked their bikes back through the sun-dappled leaves.

"Those were my mother's peanut butter cookies," Sim said vaguely as he tried to unravel the past hour.

"She's friends with your mother," Greta said.

"Why wouldn't my mother have told me?" Sim asked.

"Maybe she didn't want you to know she was hanging out with a witch," Alex suggested.

"Hazel isn't a witch!" Amanda corrected.

"Yeah, but Sim didn't know that then."

"And what was it she said last time about time running out?" Amanda asked.

"You tell me," Sim said, shaking his head. "There's something my mother needs to tell me. This gets crazier and crazier."

"Maybe it has to do with the medallions," Greta said.

Sim took Orion from his pocket and held it in the palm of his hand. "You left Ursa Major at home. Right?" he asked the twins.

They nodded. "It's still not purring?" Amanda asked.

Sim shook his head.

"Maybe it's resting," Amanda said.

Sim put the medallion back in his pocket, got on his bike, and led the way down the canopied drive to Shore Road.

Chapter 27

Guna - Guna

Now it was Sunday, the day of the big reception at Pomeroy Hall. Sim, with Walter riding like a potentate behind him on his prayer rug, was pedaling up the long driveway, which was lined with cars. Monstrous SUVs apparently favored by archaeologists, sat head-to-tail along the driveway.

Sim was wearing a nearly new pair of overalls from the thrift shop, a brilliantly flowered shirt favoring blues and tangerines on a magenta background, a necktie with a speckled trout either caught or leaping for pure joy, and a pair of high-topped sneakers decorated by his own hand.

Ponidi greeted him at the door with a broad and affectionate smile. He approved of Sim's wardrobe. It reminded him, he said, of his homeland.

"Hi Ponidi," Sim said. "I'm invited to the reception."

"Yes, I know," Ponidi said. "And Miss Hoffner as well."

"What's happening?" Sim asked.

"Everyone is doing research. The house is filled with people doing research."

"Are there lots of guests?"

"Thirty-four for lunch. There were twenty-three for dinner last night. They eat and do research and then they are ready to eat again."

"And you have to do all the cooking."

"Today I am assisting the caterers. Your mother is helping them. They have gone back for more trays of food. She is very nice, your mother."

Sim felt himself blush. He was proud of his mother and glad that she was doing part of the catering. It put her in Ponidi's world - a world that he felt was both secret and safe, a world where wishes could live. His mother needed a friend like Ponidi, he thought. "This is her first time," Sim said. "The thing is that she's a practical nurse, too, so if someone chokes on a bone, she knows what to do,"

Ponidi smiled. "That is a very good thing. These scientists talk so much that they have no time to swallow properly. I would not be at all surprised to see one do as you have said."

"I hope they like her," Sim said.

"They will," Ponidi said. He often spoke with a kind of certainty that Sim didn't hear in the voices of other adults, as if he knew things that most people didn't. In Ponidi's world, as Sim had come to understand it, objects had souls, and there might, after all, be magic. It was a world more plausible to Sim, as he stood there that afternoon, than it had been two weeks earlier, a world into which he had now stepped, not once but four times. And so, on an impulse, Sim took Orion from his pocket and handed it to Ponidi.

"What do you think of this?" he asked.

After examining it closely, Ponidi held it against his forehead and closed his eyes. It was the kind of thing you might see in a movie.

Then he opened his eyes and handed the medallion back to Sim.

"Where did you get this?" Ponidi asked. His expression had changed. His smile slipped just slightly and Sim saw behind it a look of concern.

"I was looking for skipping stones in the cove and I found it," Sim said. "I think maybe it's magic." There was no other adult on earth to whom he would have said that.

"It has guna-guna," Ponidi said.

"What is that?"

"It is difficult to say in English. With it, a dukun can see things that we cannot see. He can see into the other worlds."

"What other worlds?"

"The ones that were here before and maybe, if he is a very great dukun, the ones that will be here next."

"You mean like time travel?"

"Except that the dukun does not move. The worlds are all there. He is allowed to be in more than one at the same time."

Sim felt the blood drain from his face. He stepped to the bench that sat in the entryway and sat down. Ponidi sat next to him and took Sim's face in his hands. "I have frightened you, Simeon. I am sorry," he said.

"I have been in two worlds at once, Ponidi," he whispered. "Four times. And it is because of the medallion. I saw deep water and giant trees and a cow in the library. I saw this town a long time ago." And then, remembering, "And I saw a girl about my age sitting on the Oracle Stone. It was Miss Chit, Ponidi! When she was my age. I saw her. Miss Chit! And then it all stopped."

Before Ponidi had a chance to answer, the doorbell rangThe caterers, five of them including his mother, swept before them the momentary stillness from which Ponidi had looked so deeply into his eyes. Fortunately, his mother was carrying a tray of hors d'oeuvres and could not stop to embarrass him. She smiled, told him to be a good guest, and followed the others, equally laden, into the house, Ponidi followed behind them.

Sim sat there in the dimly lighted entrance hall, thinking. He had told Ponidi. He had told an adult. He wished now that he had told Dr. Pleever earlier. He wanted to ask his friend from the Smithsonian why it had stopped - why, when so many things had been happening, there was now only stillness. No depths of water, ancient forests, or cows grazing. No more strange dreams. But how could you ask someone why a thing had stopped when you had never told him it ever started?

Chapter 28

The Reception

"How long have you been here?" Amanda asked, as she and Alex walked up to where Sim sat.

"Not long," Sim said. "I was talking with Ponidi."

Alex laughed. "Did he tell you about the spirits?"

"Don't make fun," Amanda said.

"What spirits?" Sim asked, picking up his pack. Alex started up the stairs and the other two followed.

"He thinks no one should have dug up the ship," Alex answered over his shoulder. "He says that buried things should be left alone. The town is full of ghosts."

"He didn't say ghosts," Amanda corrected. "He said old souls."

"Right," Alex said, "ghosts."

"I told him about the medallion," Sim said.

The twins stopped mid-staircase. "You did what?" they said in one voice.

"I told him. I showed it to him. He says it has guna-guna."

"Sim! We weren't going to tell any adults. That was the rule and you're the one who made it up," Amanda said.

"But Ponidi's different," Sim said. "He can be helpful. And he won't tell anyone. Anyhow he knows lots about it and what he said is exactly what happened to me."

"Really?" Amanda sat on the landing. "What did he say?"

"Dukuns use guna-guna to travel in time."

"Ponidi thinks he's a dukun," Alex said. "That's why he sees ghosts."

"It isn't like Alex makes it sound," Amanda explained. "He doesn't talk about it unless you ask him really seriously. It's not a joke. And he doesn't like it. 'It's in my life' he says, like he wishes it wasn't."

"I'll bet Dr. Pleever would know about guna-guna," Sim said.

"He's here," Amanda said. "He arrived this morning."

"Who arrived this morning?" a voice said from behind them. They turned to find Greta standing there, holding Sophonsiba, the Pomeroys' cat. Sophonsiba was not a particularly sociable animal, but for some reason she had taken to Greta from the first moment they met.

"Dr. Pleever," Amanda said.

Just then, the upstairs intercom crackled and Mrs. Pomeroy said it was time for the children to come down to the buffet. Cameron and Jerome were already in the library being given the once-over by their mother. Lily and Tad stood there too, gawking at the attendees. The four companions joined the family clutch.

People turned and smiled. Mrs. Pomeroy told Alex to tuck in his shirt, stood back satisfied and gave them their instructions: "Don't go to the buffet before the guests, unless one of them invites you to. Don't sit at the tables. There aren't enough chairs for everyone, and anyway, they will want to talk business. Sit on the veranda steps. That would be a good place. You may not take the food back to your rooms. It won't hurt you to be a little social, and don't spill on the carpets." She said this all very seriously, but Sim knew that she was proud of her children and pleased to have them on display.

After this inspection, Sim left the others, looking for Dr. Pleever. He noticed a woman wearing a khaki skirt and a many-pocketed vest looking at him. She smiled. Sim was a student of smiles. You could never take them at face value. A smile could shut you out as easily as it could invite you in. It was best to get a fix before you responded. The woman turned to her conversation partner and said something that made him turn and look as well. Sim felt the blood rush to his cheeks. They were laughing at him, at his clothes, at the fish jumping out of his necktie. He looked away, and this time saw Dr. Pleever on the other side of the room. It suddenly seemed a long way away, and it crossed his mind that Dr. Pleever, too, might think him laughable. Perhaps this was not, after all, the right occasion for a tie. Then as he turned he heard his name.

"Simeon?" It was a familiar voice. He turned back and saw that Dr. Pleever, having disengaged from his conversation, was crossing the room. And not without it being noticed, for Dr. Pleever was, among all the guests at this reception, the most eminent, as well as the most striking to observe. The smile that preceded him was not of the sort you had to figure out. It was a smile that let you think for a moment that you might be one of the most important people on the planet.

"Hi, Dr. Pleever," Sim said. He couldn't help but glance at the khaki-skirted woman and her friend. You see, he thought, not everyone thinks I'm a silly person. They weren't smiling. They looked a little puzzled. He'd settle for that.

"It's actually *Sim*, isn't it?" Dr. Pleever asked.

"I don't mind," Sim said. And then, perhaps a little too proudly, and unable to hide a smile he added, "We broke the code. The medallions are constellations."

Dr. Pleever reached out and put his hand on Sim's shoulder. "He who sees," he said. He looked at Sim as a father might, proud of his son's achievement. At least that's the way it felt to Sim at that moment. The odd thing was that his friend didn't seem surprised. It was like that first time in the library after the lecture. Maybe the medallions are looking for.... And then he had stopped. "You knew, didn't you?" Sim said.

"Not until I studied the rubbing from your medallion," Dr. Pleever said.

"Orion," Sim said

"Orion," Dr. Pleever repeated.

"I saw his belt in a pancake," Sim said.

"Remarkable," Dr. Pleever replied, as Greta and the twins joined them.

"Did Sim tell you about Orion?" Greta asked.

"Yes, he did," Dr. Pleever said, still looking at Sim for a moment before sharing his attentions with the others.

"And I figured out Ursa Major," Amanda said. "We found it under the Oracle Stone."

"At midnight," Alex said in a significant voice.

Actually, it had been well after midnight, Sim recalled. But he wasn't going to correct Alex. In fact, midnight sounded just right.

"But there are still two we haven't figured out," Greta said. "The ones that you gave Sim rubbings of."

"Well, by chance I have brought the originals with me," Dr. Pleever said. I'll just retrieve my briefcase. He walked to the window seat, where a number of guests had left packs or briefcases, found his, and rejoined the companions.

"Wait," Alex said, looking around the room. Gold-Tipped Smith was helping himself to the smoked salmon. Sim followed Alex's gaze. It seemed to him that the strange man with the gold cane had a crafty eye peeled in their direction, even as he talked to the person opposite him. "Let's go into Dad's study," Alex said. "He won't mind." And without waiting for anyone to say yea or nay, he led them across the room to a door that opened just under the staircase.

Chapter 29

Sagittarius

It was a much smaller room than the library, and quite cozy, with several shelves of books, some comfortable chairs overlooking the back lawn and a large desk upon which Dr. Pleever set his briefcase. He took out the medallions, removed them from their cases and laid them on the desk. Alex had gone at once to the bookcase and returned with the star atlas.

"How many constellations are there?" Amanda asked.

"In all, there are eighty-eight," Dr. Pleever said."

"That's a lot to look through," Amanda said.

"I suspect we can limit our research to the sky known to the medallions' makers," Dr. Pleever said. "The Northern Hemisphere."

"I'm not really sure what a constellation is," Amanda confessed. "I know it's a bunch of stars that are supposed to look like something, but...." She stopped there.

Dr. Pleever studied their attentive faces. "Where to start," he said. "How much patience do you have?"

"Some of us have more than others," Amanda said, looking at her brother.

"Let's start with the sun," Dr. Pleever said and he did. He explained that the solar system is flat like a big plate and that the sun, the moon, and all the planets move in that same flat plane, which is called the *ecliptic*. He told them about what happens as the earth moves around the sun, how the constellations play hide-and-seek, some being more prominent in one month than another, and how some emblazon the night sky and others hide in sunlight. He said a great deal more than they could absorb, but they listened patiently, asked questions when they had them and began finally to get a sense of how the heavens are set up.

Sim's mind had drifted as Dr. Pleever spoke. He and Dr. Pleever had discovered Orion at the same time. That was important. It wasn't just the medallions that made up the puzzle. Dr. Pleever was part of it as well. And Hazel. And Greywing. And what about the Viking ship? Was it, as Dr. Pleever had suggested during his lecture, how the medallions got here? And the cave with its drawings, two of which had shown up in Dr. Pleever's lecture.

Dr. Pleever was still talking about the constellations. Alex had asked a question. Sim interrupted.

"Dr. Pleever?" he said. His friend looked up from the star atlas and smiled.

"Sim?"

"There's this cave,"

"Yes?"

Sim quickly scanned the faces of his companions. They appeared to approve. "It's on Thunderhead Cliff. We swore an oath not to tell anyone else about it, but I think you need to know about it."

Alex put his finger to his lips and nodded his head toward the study door, which they had left open a crack. He covered the medallions with the star atlas and then crossed quietly and opened it, startling Gold-Tipped Smith, who appeared to have been standing there listening.

"Excuse me," he said. "I was just looking for Mr. Pomeroy. I thought he might be here. I wanted to have a word with him."

"He's not here," Alex said, rather rudely.

"He's probably in the kitchen," Amanda said. "He likes to keep an eye on things." She smiled. It was a smile with which Sim was familiar, a smile that Alex had never learned and would have little use for.

"I'll just have a look there," the man said, his eyes taking in everything that might be observed, including the star atlas around which the group was gathered. Then he walked away and Alex closed the door.

Dr. Pleever appeared not to attach much significance to Gold-Tipped Smith's appearance or, if he did, he didn't let on.

Sim was amused to hear Alex, the most cautious of the four explorers, tell the story of finding the cave. He caught Greta's eye. She smiled. Now it was Alex who had urged the others on in the face of unknown dangers, who had been clever enough to bring a flashlight.

"It was a room twice as big as this one," Alex said, taking a quick measure of the study.

"Three times," Amanda said.

Sim was watching Dr. Pleever's face as the twins argued regarding the size of the cave. It wore an expression with which Sim was now familiar. He interrupted the twins. "You've been there, haven't you?" Sim asked the scientist.

Dr. Pleever smiled, a little sheepishly. "Yes," he said. "It's on the register of ancient sites at the Smithsonian. I was there once, ten or twelve years ago." He reached into his briefcase and removed a small paperback volume. There was a picture on the cover of a large rock covered with red images, mostly of animals that looked like deer because they had antlers. There was also a picture of a man with a bow and arrow.

"Petroglyphs," Greta said, as Dr. Pleever opened the book and they gathered around.

"Yes," Dr. Pleever said. "These particular ones were carved in rocks on the north coast of Norway around 4,000 years ago."

Sim noticed the ship and pointed to it. "That's one of the ones you showed at the lecture," he said. "It's in the cave, too."

"There are actually three or four of these drawings in the cave," Dr. Pleever said.

"Are the ones in the cave that old?" Alex asked.

"That's unlikely," Dr. Pleever said. "There's no record of any civilization in this part of the world at that time. There's good reason to think that the crew of the Viking ship used the cave as a shelter, however, and they might have been familiar with these drawings."

"Do the drawings mean anything?" Greta asked.

"I'm sure they meant something to the men who made them, but it's not something we have been able to make much sense of. Perhaps they were telling the story of their voyage."

"Maybe they were magic," Amanda suggested.

"That is not at all out of the question," Dr. Pleever affirmed, before Alex had a chance to comment. "To summon friendly spirits or bar ill-intentioned ones."

Just at that moment Mr. Pomeroy opened the door and walked in.

"So here you are!" he said, without any apparent surprise at finding them in his study looking at a book about petroglyphs. "It's time for your talk," he said to Dr. Pleever. Then he winked at his eminent guest: "Fund-raising time."

"Ah, yes," Dr. Pleever said, looking at Sim significantly. "The lifeblood of archaeological research."

"And the museum," Alex added, smiling at his father.

"And the museum," Dr. Pleever said.

As they left, Greta looked up from the star atlas that she had been examining with one of the Smithsonian medallions beside it. "Sagittarius," she said.

"Hello?" Alex said.

"This medallion is Sagittarius," Greta said. The others gathered around. Sure enough. Looking carefully they could see that it matched the drawing in the book. Now they had three of them. One more to name. How many more to collect, Sim wondered. Time would tell. That's what Hazel had said. Time will tell. Like it was some kind of person.

The Smithsonian medallions were still sitting by the star atlas. Sim put them back in their cases and put the cases in Dr. Pleever's briefcase. "He may need this for his talk," he said. He carried the briefcase to where Dr. Pleever and Mr. Pomeroy were about to assemble the guests and handed it to him. Mr. Pomeroy picked up a wine glass and struck it lightly with a fork.

"Goodness," Dr. Pleever said. "I'd forget my name if I didn't get mail. Thank you, Sim." Sim turned and made his way back through the guests. The woman with the khaki skirt looked at him again. This time, he could read her smile. He smiled back.

The children stood for a moment and watched, as the guests gathered around Dr. Pleever and Mr. Pomeroy. Gold-Tipped Smith stood at the perimeter. He turned, looked at them, and smiled.

Sim wanted more than anything else to have some time with Ponidi. There were things Ponidi could tell him about guna-guna, about dukuns, and about being in two places at once. But now wasn't the time. Ponidi was busy with the reception, and, when it was over, he would be just as busy with cleaning up. Sim would have to come back on a quiet day. He kept these thoughts to himself, not wanting to engage the twins in another argument about ghosts and old souls.

They took the star atlas up to the ballroom, where first Sim and Amanda and then Alex and Greta took turns studying the many constellations, rotating the remaining Smithsonian rubbing this way and that, trying to find a match. After a while they gave up. Greta and Amanda decided that, like Hazel, a century earlier, they should make a record of everything that was happening so they found a notebook and set about making a code. Sim couldn't help thinking that with Hazel and her companions, it had all come to nothing and he wondered if taking up such a project might not seal its doom. But he kept this thought to himself. Instead, while Amanda and Greta made up the code he and Alex raced radio-controlled cars for awhile and then made a Viking ship out of *LEGO*s.

Chapter 30

Telling Secrets

When Sim returned home that afternoon, the house was empty. He was surprised - until he remembered that the reception at Pomeroy Hall could still be going on, or at least the cleaning up. He had his secrets and his mother, according to Hazel, had hers. "It's time," Hazel had said. But time for what? What was it that his mother hadn't told him?

When she returned an hour later, she was tired, but not in the way she had been for the past months. Her feet were sore but her spirits were high. She talked about the reception. She did imitations of Myra and Lenny. She liked them, and they had gotten along well. There was another event coming up in three days at the Parish Church, and they had asked her if she would be available. "I'll have to check my social calendar," she had told them. Sim laughed.

"I beg your pardon," she said. "I have a very busy social life. There's this very engaging and terribly attractive young man, and I just can't get enough time with him."

For just a moment a look of concern crossed Sim's face Then, understanding, he smiled. His mother went to the refrigerator to see what there was for dinner.

"It looks like glop," she said, filling a pot with water and putting it on to boil.

Glop was Sim's favorite meal, consisting of macaroni and whatever leftovers there were in a cheese sauce, and, if there was one in the cupboard, a can of chopped tomatoes. Sim had learned that there was much to be gained from conversation with his mother while she was cooking. First it was a kind of feel-good event, smelling the smells, watching her cook. Often, preoccupied with her preparations, she would hear only part of what he said, and her response would be amusing. She was apt to say things that, with more consideration, she might not have. Especially about people.

"Do you know Miss Chit?" Sim asked.

"I did once," she responded, pausing with the refrigerator door open and looking at him. "Why do you ask?"

"Oh, I was just wondering. We had lunch with her."

"You did what?"

"Actually, it was last week that we met her. We went exploring in the woods by Thunderhead Cliff. Walter brought her over and she invited us back to her house."

"And she didn't turn you into frogs?"

"That's all made up," Sim said. "She's just old. That doesn't make someone a witch."

"I thought children held their breath when they rode by the Wentworth Estate."

"Well, we did. But not anymore. She's very nice but...."

"But what?"

"She's a little weird. Not *bad* weird, just weird. She goes from one thing to another. I don't think she remembers things all that well."

"That's part of old age," his mother said, getting out the cheese and a leftover chunk of ham. She closed the refrigerator and took the grater down from the rack that hung over the counter. "Here, you can do this while I cut up the ham," she said.

"She's 111," Sim said, as he shredded the hard cheese onto the counter. "I've never heard of anyone being 111."

"She was ninety-eight when I met her and she still seemed pretty alert."

"You're still good friends with her, aren't you?" Sim asked.

"I check in from time to time to be sure she's looking after herself."

"And bring cookies."

His mother smiled. "That's where the cookie tin came from."

"You noticed it."

"Yes."

"Hazel said you needed to tell me something."

"Hazel?"

"Miss Chit. She said to call her Hazel."

His mother paused and looked at the pot on the stove as if there were more in it than water, and then continued. "Winifred called me in just after I completed my course in practical nursing. She wanted me to look after someone who had come to visit her. A stranger."

"What kind of stranger?"

"A sailor," she said.

"It was my father, wasn't it?" Sim asked.

"Yes."

"You never told me that's where you met him."

"I know. I thought about that. I decided it wasn't important where I met your father, and I didn't want to make things any more complicated than they already were for you. I thought it was enough to have a disappearing father without having to have a witch in the story."

"But she's not a witch."

"She was when you were five years old, when you wanted to know everything. You learned about Winifred in kindergarten. Probably from Amanda. You don't remember, do you? You had nightmares and crawled into my bed."

"I remember having nightmares."

"Well, it was Winifred."

"Hazel," Sim corrected. "She prefers to be called Hazel."

"She was still Winifred back then, but I guess if she wants to be Hazel she can be Hazel."

She turned off the burner under the water and sat down at the kitchen table.

"There are some things I haven't told you," she began.

"I know," Sim said. "Me too."

"You too?"

"You first."

"You were born in Hazel's cottage," his mother began.

"I thought I was born at Granny's. You were living there."

"I was. Until I met your father and you were about to make your appearance. Your Granny had very set ideas about the world and how people should act. One thing that young women don't do if they aren't married, is have babies. I didn't even go out with boys. Then I met your father and everything changed."

"He didn't speak English; you didn't speak whatever he spoke, and you said things like 'Drink water, take pill.' And he said, 'Pill good.' And you fell in love. That's something I've never understood."

"What have you never understood?"

"How could you could fall in love with somebody when you couldn't even talk to him."

"As you will learn all too soon, falling in love has to do with a lot more things than talking."

"But still."

"But still. When I knew I was carrying you, Winifred – Hazel – took me in. Took us in. You were born in her parlor several months later." Sim's mother looked at him with a mixture of sadness and wonder. It made him uncomfortable.

"What's wrong?" he asked.

"I was just thinking about how things have a way of their own."

"Like what?"

"Like your finding Hazel. And I was sad for all the years you hadn't known her. I should have told you."

"Why didn't you?"

"Hazel has some strange ideas. I didn't think they'd be very helpful to you."

"Ideas about what?"

"Your father."

"Like where he came from and why he went away?"

"That's part of it." She got up from the table and returned to the stove. The water was boiling now. She took the macaroni from the cupboard, measured out four cups into a small bowl, tipped the bowl into the water and stirred it with a wooden spoon. Then she turned to Sim. "You said, 'Me too.'"

Chapter 31

More Secrets

"Huh?"

"A moment ago, when I said there were some things I hadn't told you. You said, 'Me, too'"

"Right."

"And?"

"You have to promise not to laugh at me or say I'm making it up."

"Why would I do that?"

"Mom, you do it all the time. You think Amanda lives in fairyland."

"Well, really Sim. Gnomes?"

"One gnome. A very small one."

"A gnome is a gnome. You aren't going to tell me you've seen an alien, are you," she asked lightheartedly.

Sim's heart sank. An alien would be much easier to explain than his own recent adventures. "No," he said, "no aliens."

"Well then?"

"You remember that guy who came to the house that night and I fainted and Dr. Harvey said it was because I had gotten hyper-something?"

"Hypothermia. Of course I remember."

"Well, that wasn't why I fainted."

Sim told his mother about how the stranger had put his hand on his shoulder and said, 'It's you.' Then he told her about seeing the deep, dark forest.

"It was hypothermia, honey," she said. When people have a fever and pass out it's not unusual for them to see things that aren't there. It's a little bit like hallucinating."

"It wasn't that," Sim said.

"I know," his mother reassured. "It seemed very real. But that's the way with hallucination. Believe me, I once looked after a man who saw little lobsters coming out of his bedroom wall on toothpicks." She reached under the counter for her heavy pot, the one for making the cheese sauce.

I might as well be telling her about my day at school, he thought. I should have known better. Not until now did he realize how much he had wanted to tell her, to have her reassurance, her belief in his adventure. He felt his jaw tighten. He stared at the table. "He knew me," he said, dropping the words as heavily as he could.

"You probably look like someone he knew. He was quite upset when you fainted, Sim." She put the pot on the stove, measured four lines on a stick of butter, cut it, removed the paper, and added it to the pot. "He carried you into the living room. He was very concerned."

Sim felt a shiver at the thought of Splitface holding him in his arms. He put away the thought. His mother was playing the practical nurse, explaining things away as if he were a little child. Mrs. Pomeroy, who painted very large and occasionally frightening flowers, listened to Amanda's stories with interest. She asked questions. Mrs. Pomeroy wouldn't have dismissed the possibility that somehow, somewhere, two and two might equal five. "But your mother's a nurse," Amanda had explained one day when Sim was comparing their mothers. "That's what nurses do. They reassure people that everything is going to be all right. Everything in the right place. No surprises.'

For a moment, as his mother added flour to the butter and then milk to that mixture, he wished that he had both of the medallions with him now. He would put them on the counter and ask her to touch one. But he knew what would happen. She'd ask how it was done, as if they were some new kind of toy that he'd gotten from a friend. It was all beside the point.

She gathered up the cheese that he had grated, looked at him, and smiled. "Is that it?" she asked.

"You want more cheese?"

"I mean is that what you wanted to tell me? About fainting?"

"I guess so. How come you never talk about my father anymore," he asked.

She didn't respond.

"It's because you don't believe he's coming back, isn't it? You used to. You used to be so sure. But you don't think so anymore."

"Part of me does," she said softly.

"But not a very big part," Sim said. He was surprised at the tone of his voice. He could feel himself tense up. He had made fists with his hands without knowing it. He opened them and slipped them under his bottom.

"We have to get on with our lives, honey," she said. She wasn't scolding him. She should have. He shouldn't have used that tone of voice with her. His father wouldn't have let him get away with that. He didn't want to be "honey." He wanted respect.

"Well, he is coming back," Sim said with a certainty that surprised him.

"What has Winifred been telling you?" she asked patiently.

"Hazel."

"Hazel."

"What do you think?" he asked.

"Has she shown you the cave?"

"We discovered it on our own. Walter did."

"And the petroglyphs?"

"What about them?"

"She's an old lady, Sim, a very, very old lady who has lived alone for most of her life. She invents things. She lives in a world where dream and reality get all mixed up."

I live there, too, Sim thought to himself. Or I did. For a while. Suddenly he felt very sad and aware of something that he couldn't name. Maybe it was loneliness. Something had been taken from him, some promise broken. He had not put it into words, not even in his own mind, but that day, seeing the man on the bridge with the boy on his shoulders and then the gull, he had known that he would find his father. And now the magic had stopped. He no longer lived in two worlds at once, just this one with a mother who wouldn't understand.

"He just disappeared," Sim said.

"Who?" his mother asked.

"My father."

"Yes."

"And Hazel knew him."

"Yes."

"Did anyone else?"

"Her nephew. Great - nephew. He was an expert on Scandinavian languages. Winifred thought he might be able to communicate with your father. He came up from Washington to spend a weekend."

"And?"

"He couldn't understand your father any more than we could. They spent quite a lot of time together. Then he had to go back to his work. Two days later, your father left." She paused. Sim could almost see her mind working. Then a smile lifted the corners of her mouth.

"What?" Sim asked.

"I was just thinking about how frustrated Pepper was. He was sure that your father was speaking some form of Scandinavian language, but he couldn't figure out what it was. He was a real expert. He had even written books on languages of the North."

She thought for a moment, stirring the sauce. "Pepper was a very smart man. And he was very nice."

"What did he look like?"

She tested the macaroni, poured it into the colander, drained it, and added it to the cheese sauce.

"It wasn't the kind of face you'd forget!" she said. Blue eyes, like yours. Not just blue, radiant blue like they could light a room. Almost spooky. He was sort of like a ship." She laughed. "I never thought of that before. His high forehead, hair parted down the middle like a ship's wake, a nose like the bow of a ship. It seemed like he was always walking into a wind. Longest fingers I have ever seen. Not too long, just impressive."

"You sure remember him pretty well. I'll bet if my father hadn't been there, you would have fallen in love with him."

"You have a lot to learn about all that, sweetheart. And the longer it takes, the happier I'll be. I was just a small-town nurse and he was a very famous professor. I'm sure Pepper Pleever had a number of society women in his little black book."

"Pleever?" Sim repeated the name in a very small voice.

"Pepper Pleever. Of course that wasn't his real name. It's what Winifred called him."

"Hazel."

"Hazel."

"Asneath."

"Asneath? Yes, I think that's right. Asneath, that's it. Now, *how* did you know that?"

"Asneath Pleever. Dr. Pleever. The man who gave the lecture at the library. The expert on Vikings. He's my friend."

"He's here?"

"He was at the reception at the Pomeroys. He was the most important person there. How could you not have seen him?"

"I didn't see half the people there. Unlike my son, I wasn't a part of the festivities, just a scullery maid."

"But Mom."

"But Sim."

"I just can't believe it. He was there. He talked with my father!" Sim said. Memories of their first meeting swirled in Sim's head like leaves in a tiny tornado. The way Dr. Pleever had singled him out, the way he had looked at him. What was it he had said? "You remind me of someone I knew once?" And if he did think, as Alex said, that the medallions were looking for Sim, then did that have something to do with his father? He took Orion out of his pocket and laid it on the table. He touched it. Nothing. It was over.

His mother turned. "What have you got there?" she asked.

"Nothing," he said. "Just a skipping stone."

Chapter 32

A Successful Operation

On the morning of October fifteenth, a Tuesday, Sim arrived at school to discover that Denny Dumont's father had been arrested the previous evening. It wasn't until recess that Sim and Greta were able to hear the story third hand from the twins. They had gathered at the chinning bar.

"It was the library door," Alex began. "Deputy Gladstone checked it out and found that the lock hadn't been messed with...."

"So that meant the thief had to be already in the library," Amanda interrupted.

"So either someone had hidden in a work closet or a bathroom or someplace or..."

"It was Mrs. Rose or Mr. Dumont. No way could it have been Mrs. Rose," Amanda continued.

"So it had to be either a stranger or Mr. Dumont, who doesn't have a great reputation with the police department in the first place," Alex said significantly.

"How about fingerprints?" Sim asked.

"Problem," Alex said. "Mr. Dumont's fingerprints are on everything in the library except the books."

"Right," Sim said. "So?"

"That's when they called Dad," Amanda said. "Chief Turnbull wanted to know if the man from the Smithsonian was still in town."

"He's not," Greta said, "is he?"

"No, he wasn't, but he took a plane to Portland and Ponidi picked him up," Alex explained.

"What did the chief want with Dr. Pleever?" Sim asked.

"This part is so cool," Alex began.

"Dr. Pleever announced that he was donating one of the Smithsonian medallions to the library to replace the one that was stolen," Amanda said.

"Amanda!" Alex, said, hands on is hips.

"What?"

"Am I telling this story or are you?"

"I thought we both were."

"You just blurt it out. People want to know things in order."

"So he donated a medallion," Greta said. "Then what?

"He pretended to," Alex said smugly. "It was a trap. He went to the library and made sure that Mr. Dumont was around when he gave the medallion to Mrs. Rose. Then Deputy Gladstone installed a surveillance camera in the library office. And guess what was on the tape the next morning?"

"Mr. Dumont taking the medallion," Greta said.

"Give the girl a gold star," Alex said.

"So they got the first one back?" Sim asked hopefully.

"No such luck," Alex said. "He said he'd sold it to some guy. Actually the guy got him to steal it."

"Splitface," Sim said.

"Or Gold-Tipped Smith," Amanda suggested.

"Definitely Splitface," Alex insisted. From the description that Mr. Dumont gave to the chief and the chief gave to Dad."

"I just thought of something," Greta said, turning to Sim.

They waited.

"Denny," she said. "His father gets arrested. After all the other things that have been happening, he'll think it was because of your lucky stone."

"We can hope so," Sim said.

Denny Dumont returned to school two days later, at the end of his suspension. It was Thursday. The arrest had been the talk of the school for the preceding two days, but on Thursday not a word was spoken.

At recess, Sim and the companions were scattered among groups of other friends – chasing, being chased, and playing foursquare, as if they were the normal people Amanda claimed they still were. Denny stood alone by the fence. Sim walked over and stood beside him.

"I'm sorry about your father," Sim said.

Denny was taken by surprise.

"Yeah, I'll bet," he said, casting a glance back toward the building.

He wants to make sure no one sees him talking to me, Sim thought.

Then Denny reached into his pocket and produced Sim's lucky stone. "Here," he said, handing it to Sim, "you can have your devil stone back."

"Thanks," Sim said, looking at it briefly and dropping it into his pocket. That could have been it. Sim had made it possible for Denny to give it back without losing face. He thought of just walking away, but something made him stay.

"It's not really magic, is it?" Denny asked.

"The stone?" Sim said.

"What do you think I mean, your stupid necktie?"

"Yes," Sim said. "it is."

"Right," said Denny, kicking at a stick. He missed it.

Sim realized now why he had continued to stand there. There was a question he needed to ask and he was having a hard time getting around to it. "Like I said," he repeated. "I'm sorry about your father."

"He may be in jail," Denny said. "But at least I know who he is." Denny looked at Sim and then looked away, almost as if he might be sorry for what he had said.

"I know who my father is," Sim said. "He gave me this stone."

"He was stupid," Denny said. He leaned down, picked up the stick, and threw it over the fence.

"My father?" Sim asked, puzzled.

"No, pea brain. My father."

"Oh."

"It was that other guy that put him up to it. He's the one who should be in jail."

"Splitface?"

Denny looked at him with a new kind of interest. "Is that his name?"

"It's a name we gave him. His face doesn't line up."

"He paid a lot for it. More than a hundred dollars."

"He wants this one too," Sim said, taking Orion from his pocket and holding it out for Denny to see.

Denny looked at it cautiously. He showed no interest in touching it. Just as well, Sim thought.

"Same as the one my Dad swiped?" he asked.

Sim realized that Denny had probably never seen the stolen medallion. And of course he hadn't been to Dr. Pleever's lecture. "The stones are arranged differently," he said. "But yeah, they're both medallions. They probably came over on the Viking ship."

"With your daddy, right?"

"Right," Sim said. Clearly nothing had changed or was likely to change with Denny. He pocketed the medallion and turned away. As he started to walk away, Denny spoke.

"Hey, Spotswood," he said.

Sim hesitated and then turned.

Denny was about to say something. The expression on his face had changed from scorn to something entirely different. It was only for a moment, but a very important one. Then the bell rang and their classmates started toward the door. "Forget it," Denny said. He stuffed his hands in his pockets and walked away.

When Alex asked Sim about what had happened with Denny, he simply said that Denny had given him back his lucky stone. Alex made high fives and Sim matched him, but in his mind things were more complicated than they had been.

Chapter 33

Dinner At The Pomeroys

As Sim lay that night on the widow's walk, he saw in the sky a curtain of green light rising and falling at the horizon. He had read about the Northern Lights once in a story and had seen pictures of them at the library, but this was the first time they had lit his own sky. It was one of the most remarkable things he had ever seen. He stood at the railing of the widow's walk, a slight breeze stirring his hair, and watched their dance of magical lights, his heart full to bursting. Their rise and fall made him think of his lucky stone. He removed it from under his pajama top. It was awash with color, band after band sliding down its face like rain on a window. He watched the sky for a few more minutes and then snuggled into his sleeping bag, surrounded by a friendly magic whose purposes teased his imagination. "You know, you're not the center of the universe," his mother had chided him occasionally. Of course he wasn't. No one person could be. But right now, it felt that way. He put his hands behind his head and looked up at Orion. He and Dr. Pleever had both recognized it on the medallion in the same week, maybe on the same day, maybe even at the same moment. He wondered if Dr. Pleever was watching the Northern Lights.

The more Sim had thought about Dr. Pleever that week, the more confused he felt. He didn't want to think that Dr. Pleever was being dishonest with him. Not telling people things wasn't the same thing as lying, but you had to be careful. If you told people everything you thought they might not already know, you'd be talking all the time. People had to ask you a question, and then, if you didn't answer it truthfully, that was being dishonest. But what if you did answer it with part of the truth and kept the rest back? And what if you kept things back because you didn't want to hurt people's feelings? What if Dr. Pleever hadn't told him about his father because knowing about his father would make him unhappy? What if the things Denny said were true?

There was yet another possibility, and it was the one that he favored, the one at which Dr. Pleever had hinted in the library that first day: that this was Sim's adventure and that he must find his way alone. He thought of boys in the adventure stories he had read. If you asked the right questions, wise people could answer them. If you said the right words, doors would open or spirits would appear. It wasn't as if there couldn't be helpers. Like Dr. Pleever.

But now the adventure was over. Taking a rest, Amanda had said. How could an adventure take a rest, as if it were a person? Amanda always had a way of making things OK. But this wasn't – the more Sim thought about it – OK. It was mean and unfair to tease people. Whoever or whatever was behind the medallions was playing with him. Just like Denny. Just like that morning when Denny had set him up for others to laugh at, making a fool of him. Holding Sim's lucky stone beyond his reach he had pretended to throw it. "Go fetch," Denny had said. Make a fool of yourself. Go search for something that isn't there, wasn't ever there, couldn't be there. His mother was right. The world wasn't populated with gnomes; wishes were for little children. You had to be sensible to survive.

He felt incredibly sad, and then angry. How could Dr. Pleever have led him on like this with his crazy suggestion that the medallions were looking for him? Maybe he had known about Orion the whole time. Was Dr. Pleever secretly laughing at him, too?

Orion blurred. Angry tears clouded Sim's eyes. "Father," he called, soundlessly.

Toward morning, Sim had another one of his dreams. This time, he was in a cellar with stone walls. It smelled musty and a little smoky. Even though it was dark, he could see. He found his way into a tiny room with only a cot and a wooden box that served as a table. On it was a glass globe, the kind of globe he had seen in Hazel's cottage. You tilted it and got a snowstorm. Then he woke up. It was happening again! He had had another dream. He threw off the covers and ran down the stairs to his bedroom. Opening the top drawer of his dresser, he removed Orion. Closing his eyes he held it in his hand. It purred. The adventure wasn't over.

He could scarcely tie his sneakers. It was Friday. Classy Cuisine Catering Service had been asked to cater a weekend retreat in the White Mountains, and his mother was part of the crew. Sim would be staying at the Pomeroys'. Dr. Pleever would be there. And the Hoffners.

Friday at LORCES passed without event. Sim told Greta and the twins nothing about his anger and sadness of the night before. That was all behind him. The magic was back, he told them. Maybe Amanda had been right. Maybe the adventure had to pause and catch its breath.

After school, he met Walter at their usual rendezvous and explained the plans for the afternoon and evening as they walked home. It was a little too early for Walter's dinner and the Pomeroys were as generous about pets as they were about most other things. In fact, Mrs. Pomeroy had even bought a dog dish for Walter. Sim went up to his room and changed his clothes. Then he put his toothbrush, his pajamas, and clean underwear into his pack and went downstairs. He wheeled his bicycle out of the garage, attached Walter's cart, and the two of them set out for Pomeroy Hall.

He still hadn't found an opportunity to talk with Ponidi, and that was at the top of his list. He wanted to know more about guna-guna. Was Ponidi a dukun? Had he too traveled in time? He went to the kitchen instead of the front door and was lucky. Ponidi was there preparing dinner.

"Hi, Ponidi," Sim said.

"Ah, Simeon, I am so glad to see you," he said, putting down his potato peeler and wiping his hands. "I am afraid I frightened you the other day at the reception."

"No, you didn't frighten me," Sim said. "It was just that you knew about the medallions. Things that no one else knows. You knew about being in two times at once. What is guna-guna, Ponidi?"

"It is a very hard thing to describe."

"You said that a dukun who has guna-guna can be in more than one place at a time and a great one can even see the future."

"That was a long time ago, Simeon, when people still believed in things that could not be explained. The great dukuns are in the past. Hundreds of years in the past. There are only stories."

"But you touched the medallion to your head and felt something."

"Yes, that is in my life. It is in my family. Sometimes...." Ponidi looked over Sim's shoulder and out at the back lawn. He was quiet for a moment. Then it seemed to Sim that he changed his mind, for when his gaze returned, it had lost its seriousness. "I think you are a very special boy, Simeon. Good things are going to happen to you. That is what I know. That is all that I know. There are many names for what you have, Simeon. Guna-guna is the name I know. You will maybe find another name."

"Why is it happening to me, Ponidi?"

"You have been chosen, Simeon. It is not for me to say. I will only say do not be frightened. There is no evil in what you showed me. Only good. And you will have good helpers." So saying, Ponidi returned to his potato peeler. The interview was over. Ponidi had no more to say. Sim didn't understand why, but there was no more he could do. He watched for a few more moments, then he thanked Ponidi and walked toward the living room.

At Pomeroy Hall, meals were much more formal than at Sim's home. It was the time when the family got together and talked about what had happened during the day. Not gladly, Sim noticed. Especially with Cameron, who had to be coaxed to talk about things, and, when he did, never said much that you could get a handle on. Tad and Lily talked a blue streak about whatever came into their minds, which was pretty foolish most of the time. Jerome talked about his collection of small animal skeletons.

Sim liked having so many people at the table. He particularly liked Mr. and Mrs. Pomeroy. Mr. Pomeroy took people seriously, or at least gave the impression of doing so. Sim was careful therefore not simply to rattle on about things, but to think about what he said, not wanting to disappoint his host's expectations. And there was Mrs. Pomeroy, who somehow made it all work. Mrs. Hoffner talked with Mrs. Pomeroy. Dr. Hoffner talked with Mr. Pomeroy. Dr. Pleever talked with the children. It made Sim smile to watch the way the conversation arranged itself around Dr. Pleever, the way iron filings take a direction in the presence of a magnet. Dr. Pleever was a man of many talents who could converse equally well with each of the children. With Cameron and Jerome, it was The

Washington Redskins; with Greta, her travels and the archaeological sites she had visited; and with Amanda and Alex, the recovery of the stolen medallion. The youngest two had little to say, but they had taken seats to each side of Dr. Pleever, who attended to their plates as if it were the most natural thing in the world for him to cut the steak into bite-size pieces and top up their tumblers of milk from a pitcher in the shape of a cow.

Sim said little but couldn't keep his eyes off Dr. Pleever. He had made a decision but wasn't quite sure how to act upon it. He wanted to talk alone with the man who had known his father. He wanted some answers.

When dessert was finished and people began to go their own ways, Sim screwed up his courage.

"Dr. Pleever?" he asked.

"Yes, Sim."

"You said once that you'd help me with my report on the Vikings and I wondered if now would be a good time."

"I would be very happy to, Sim," Dr. Pleever replied. "As a matter of fact, I brought a couple of things with me that might be of use to your research."

"You've spawned another archaeologist, Asneath!" Mr. Pomeroy said, with a mischievous grin. "Help yourselves to my study. You won't be bothered there."

"Excellent," Dr. Pleever responded. He turned back to Sim. "Well, shall we get to work then?"

Chapter 34

A Viking

"It's not really about my report," Sim said, as they settled themselves in Mr. Pomeroys' study.

"I thought it might not be," Dr. Pleever said.

"You were there," Sim said, "with my father."

"Yes."

"Why didn't you tell me?"

"I didn't want to get in your way. When you told me you had broken the code, identified Orion, I realized that you were doing very well on your own. It's one thing to be helpful when called upon. It's another to be intrusive. And in truth, there wasn't a lot I could tell you. It's only since seeing you that first day in the library, with your medallion and your father's eyes, that I have begun to piece together your father's story. I didn't know Magnus Siglandi had a son."

"Hazel hadn't ever told you?"

"Back to Hazel is she again?"

"She asked us to call her Hazel," Sim said.

"This month. Next week it will be Winifred again. No matter. No, I knew nothing until that afternoon when I went to Thunderhead Cliff. I went straight from the library, after the lecture. She explained about your mother having had a child and that Magnus was the father. I'm afraid I lost my temper, something I rarely do."

"With Hazel?" Sim asked.

"Yes."

"What did she do?"

"She made iced tea."

Sim couldn't help smiling.

"Winifred lives in a world all her own, "Dr. Pleever continued. "She doesn't think much of science and scientists.

"I like her," Sim said. "She makes you wonder about things."

"She certainly does that."

"You were angry because Hazel hadn't told you about my being born there?"

"Yes, I was. I had an interest in the matter. A pretty significant one, I should think. I had spent the better part of a week twelve years ago trying to learn your father's story." Dr. Pleever tented his hands in front of his face and thought for a moment. Then he continued: "Your father has been sitting in the back of my poor muddled brain for some time. Ever since I came upon the second medallion."

It was true, Sim thought. Dr. Pleever was confirming it. It wasn't just a wish or a feeling. "So my father and the medallions are connected."

"Most certainly," Dr. Pleever assured him. He opened the briefcase sitting next to him on the sofa. Withdrawing a piece of heavy paper, he glanced at it briefly and handed it to Sim. It was a drawing, done with a very black pencil.

Sim studied it. "It's a medallion," he said. He rotated the paper to see if he could recognize its constellation, but he could not. "Do you know which one it is?" he asked.

"No. I've studied it ever since you and I spotted Orion, but without success. Of course, it could be that your father simply intended to represent a medallion without drawing any one in particular. It could simply be a random arrangement of dots."

"My father?"

"Sorry. Got the horse before the cart, I'm afraid. Yes, your father drew that."

Sim touched the charcoal with his finger. Some of it came away. He touched it to his lips.

"We didn't share a common language," Dr. Pleever explained, "but there are other ways of communicating. Your father picked up a quarter from the table and pointed to the drawing. Not exactly the same size, but I got the idea."

"He wanted to know if you had seen one of the medallions."

"Yes, that was clear. But of course I hadn't. It wouldn't be until two years later that I came upon the first medallion, the one Greta identified as Sagittarius. And it wasn't until five years more had passed that the coin dealer down the coast called me with the second medallion."

"That's when you discovered the synchronicity effect."

"Precisely. I realized I was dealing with something for which science could offer no explanation. It was only then that I remembered your father's drawing. I took it out and examined it. Voilla!"

"Voilla?"

"It's French. Sorry. It means 'So there! Aha! That's it!"

"Voilla! Cool."

Dr. Pleever took off his glasses, examined them, and returned them to his long nose. "So there I was with these two impossible resonating objects and your father's drawing. Where had they come from? Where had he come from? They were ancient. I could see that at once, even before we did the carbon dating. If I had only known this seven years earlier when I met him."

"You said you couldn't understand one another."

"Yes. He spoke a dialect that I had never heard. It was Scandianvian. No question about that, but one that hadn't been recorded. At the time I thought he must have come from some isolated village in the far north. Unlikely. It was, after all 1988. But I had no other way of accounting for it. So, to answer your question: yes, we communicated, but mostly with hand signs, drawings and pointing to things."

"Like the quarter."

"Precisely. I had to return to Washington for a meeting. I planned to come back to the cove in two weeks, but by then your father had left. I didn't think much more about it until seven years later when I had the two medallions. I have lived with the mystery for the last four years. I scoured ancient documents for a lost language of the north. Nothing. I sent pictures of the medallions to museums. Nothing. Then, there I am at the library talking about Vikings. I take out Sagitarius...." Dr. Pleever stopped.

"And it resonates." Sim concluded his friend's sentence.

"Yes. It's a miracle I got through the lecture."

"You did good. It was a good lecture. It was my first ever."

"And not likely to be your last. I stared at you rudely, for which I apologize."

"It was OK," Sim said.

"You have your father's eyes."

"That's what Hazel said."

"And it's not just that. If it hadn't been for the medallion I might not have noticed. But it was all coming together so fast. I saw your father, standing there all those years back with his drawing."

"So you went to see Hazel."

"I did. As I think I mentioned, Hazel isn't particularly scientific in her thinking."

"That's what my mother said, too. What did she tell you about my father?"

"The kinds of things that belong in fairy tales. Impossible stuff. However...."

Sim sat forward in his chair.

"It fit like a glove. All the unanswered questions I had piled up, the riddles that had no solution. If I accepted Winifred's impossible fairy tale, they started to make sense. You were the missing piece." Now he stopped and looked at Sim. Somehow Sim knew what was coming. "That day in the library," he began, "when you asked if you could have the Smithsonian medallion and you walked to the window...."

"I told you I was day dreaming," Sim said. "I felt bad about that. It was sort of true, but not the whole truth."

Now Sim told the rest of the truth, the truth that his mother would not have believed but that Dr. Pleever would. He began with the day by the beach and the first medallion. He told of the gull and the deepening of the river. Then he described Splitface's visit, the ancient forest, and fainting." He saw Dr. Pleever flinch, as if he himself were in pain. "It was all right," Sim reassured him. "The doctor said it was because of the cold water." He then told of the cow grazing at Dr. Pleever's feet and Winifred Hazel Chit as a little girl on the Oracle Stone. He thought of mentioning his dreamwalks but decided against it. One thing at a time. When he had finished, he studied his older companion's face. Dr. Pleever removed his glasses once again, but this time it wasn't to clean the lenses. He wiped at his eyes with his handkerchief, put it away, leaned forward and put his hand on Sim's knee.

"So what does it feel like to be a Viking?" he asked.

Chapter 35

A Case of Mistaken Identity

Sim stared at the drawing. It was true. His father, the Viking ship, the medallions, the cave, Hazel and even Dr. Pleever were all parts of the same story – his story. It was almost too much to think about all at once. So many new questions filled his head. Maybe if he spoke it out, one stap at a time. "My father was a Viking," he began.

Dr. Pleever nodded.

"He came over on the ship that's in the harbor a long time ago. A thousand years. You said a thousand years. Didn't you say a thousand years?

"More or less."

"And they lived in the cave and made the pictures on the wall. Then what?"

"You are doing pretty well. What do you think?"

"Something went wrong. The Vikings were explorers. They weren't really settlers like the pilgrims. They went looking for stuff and then took it home." An hour ago Sim would have said they were pirates, plunderers, raiders; but those words didn't come as easily to his lips now. His father was a Viking. And so was he. "Maybe something happened to the ship."

"Unlikely. The ship being excavated is in perfect condition."

"Something else." Sim's thoughts chased one another around in his head. "Wait. In your lecture you said that no other Viking ship had ever come this far before."

"At least none has ever been found."

"So how did the ship get here? It had to be the medallions. Something about the medallions. Then they got lost and the ship couldn't return. But how would they have gotten lost?"

"That is one more mystery to which we have no answer. But perhaps in time we will. There is one more picture your father drew. I'm afraid it's a little disturbing," he said.

"It's OK," Sim said, "I can handle it." He held out his hand.

Dr. Pleever handed over the drawing.

It *was* disturbing, drawn with harsh and heavy lines. It was the face of a man. The eyebrows were larger than life, the eyes as well, staring from the sheet, fixing the viewer with something like contempt. The oddest thing, however, was a line drawn from the scalp to the bridge of the nose. Clearly, it was not a feature. It was something foreign and brutal.

"Your father called him Kolbrúnarskáld," Dr. Pleever said. "It's an ancient Norse name."

His father was no great artist, but the combination of the ferocious eyebrows and the heavy line drawn through the middle of the face from top to bottom left no question in Sim's mind as to whose rough portrait he held in his hands. Once again, he felt the touch of Splitface's hand upon his shoulder and heard the satisfaction in his voice. "It's you," he had said.

"It's Splitface," Sim said. "The man who came to the house." He thought for a second and it became clear. "He thought I was my father."

Dr. Pleever stood up and walked to the window. He stood there for a few moments and then turned, a smile lighting his face.

"Dr. Pleever?"

"Right there in front of my nose the whole time and I couldn't see it."

"See what?"

His friend resumed his seat and leaned close. "We've said it but didn't hear the words we were saying."

"What?"

"The medallions are looking for a boy, not a man. For you, Sim. They're looking for the person who can be their master, a young person." Dr. Pleever threw up his arms. "Of course! That's why your father didn't stay. He wasn't looking for the medallions. He needed a son who would have the same gifts as he, who the medallions would seek out when he was of the right age, the age your father had been when he, himself was their master. The age you are now. He came so that you might be born."

"But how did Splitface get here? And what does he have to do with my father?"

"My guess is that they came together. Your father was a boy, like you, master of the medallions. But why they came...? That we don't know. What we do know is that your father returned to his own time and Kolbrúnarskáld stayed. Yes, there is much we have yet to learn. But we have come so far! It is all unfolding as your father intended it should. Everything is falling into place. And there's something else. Yet another piece to our puzzle. Have you ever heard the story of how the Viking ship was discovered?"

"Mr. Pomeroy?" Sim guessed.

"No, it was a boy. A boy about your age. I did a little research after Winifred confirmed that you were indeed Magnus's son.

Sim sat forward in his chair, elbows on his knees, head in his hands.

"I went to the newspaper office," Dr. Pleever continued. "I wanted to know exactly when the Viking ship was discovered. I had a theory. What I learned was that there was a flood back in 1988. Lost River was a torrent. It washed out the bridge and eroded the bank below the McCrory building. One day, when the rains had stopped and the tide was out, a boy was fishing from the wharf. He noticed something that hadn't been there before the flood. Sticking up in the silt were the blackened tips of ancient timbers."

"The Viking ship," Sim said

"Precisely," Dr. Pleever said. "The ship emerged after nearly a thousand years beneath the silt of Lost River right around November the second, 1988.

Sim's eyes widened. "But that's the day I was born."

"Precisely."

Sim suddenly remembered something Hazel had said. "There's not much time," he said out loud.

"What your father set in motion when he visited twelve years ago is about to come to its conclusion."

"On my birthday," Sim said, his head in a daze.

"On your birthday."

"But I don't even have all the medallions. I don't even know how many there are. And I've never really time-traveled. It's always been half here and half there. And if I do go, how am I going to get back?" He stopped and did a quick calculation. "And my birthday's in two weeks!"

"Exactly two weeks," Dr. Pleever said, smiling. "So we must get to work." He reached again into his briefcase. "Your father did three drawings, Sim. Here is the third." He handed the drawing to Sim.

"There's a picture like this in the cave," Sim said.

"It appears on a number of stone tablets unearthed in various places the Vikings visited. You may recall I showed a slide of it during my lecture," daid Dr. Pleever. Next he removed a book, opened it and turned it so that Sim could see the writing.

"What's that?" Sim asked.

"An ancient form of writing," Dr. Pleever explained. "It's a Skaldic poem. This is the only carving known to have been written down in the Viking age. It dates from roughly the year 1000."

"Where is it?"

"In Sweden. A town called Öland. Look closely."

"I see it," Sim said. "It's the same guy. Who is he?"

"No one is quite sure. He does have a name, however. He's called Starspinner."

"Starspinner," Sim repeated. It sounded familiar, as if he had heard it before, but he couldn't think where.

"My own guess is that it has to do with navigation," Dr. Pleever said. "But that is only a guess. Your father wouldn't have drawn it if it weren't important. I have inquiries out. I'll let you know what I learn."

"There's something I don't get," Sim said thoughtfully.

"Only one thing?" Dr. Pleever asked, smiling broadly.

"Where did my father go?"

"I suspect he went back to wait things out," said Dr. Pleever.

"Back where?"

"Probably to the cave. The drawings suggest that the ship's crew lived there. But a thousand years ago."

"And somehow the medallions got lost."

"So it appears."

Sim looked at the picture of Starspinner for a long time. He had had the same feeling the day they had discovered the cave – a feeling of rightness, of familiaruty even. As if this had all happened before in a dream. He looked up at Dr. Pleever.

"Will you stay here?" Sim asked. He tried to speak casually but felt the appeal in his voice.

"Yes," Dr. Pleever replied, going one last time to his briefcase. "I couldn't imagine being anywhere else. As it turns out, I have quite an acceptable reason. Acceptable, that is, to my colleagues back in Washington. Mr.

Pomeroy, generous and farseeing man that he is, has agreed to put up much of the money for a museum here in Lost River Cove. But only if the Smithsonian will adopt it as a satellite project. The Viking ship has generated a good deal of interest in Washington. So, yes, Sim, I will be here for at least the next fifteen days. Not that I think any of this is an accident. I suspect your father had it all figured out some time ago. Dr. Pleever removed two small cases, one of which Sim immediately recognized.

"These belong to you," he said, opening one of the cases and looking for a moment at Sagittarius. He put the two boxes in Sim's hands and enclosed those smaller hands in his own.

"Thanks," Sim said. He looked up at his older friend and smiled. "The day I found the first medallion, there was a man walking across the bridge," he said. "He had his kid on his shoulders. I never got to do that. I felt sad and I felt angry and all sorts of other things. Then I knew it meant something. I knew I was going to see my father."

"Like the sleeper awakened, we actually see the people of whom we have dreamed with such ardent longing," Dr. Pleever recited, his hands clasped before him.

"Is that a poem?" Sim asked.

"It is a line from the longest book ever written," Dr. Pleever said, smiling. By a man named Marcel Proust. Some day you will read it."

"I like it," Sim said.

Chapter 36

A Note From Travelstar

The medallions safely tucked in the bib pocket of his overalls and the precious folder of drawings under his arm, Sim found Greta and the twins in the library. The girls were playing mancala. It was the official game of Pomeroy Hall. Even Mrs. Pomeroy played now and again. Alex was building a tower out of playing cards.

"Well?" Greta asked. "What did he tell you?"

"Lots."

"Like what?"

Sim looked around the library. Cameron was on the phone at the other end of the room. "I don't think this is a good place to talk," Sim said.

"Let's go up to my room," Amanda suggested.

When they were settled – Amanda and Greta in her beanbag chair, Alex on her lower bunk and Sim at Amanda's desk – Sim reported the main points of his conversation with Dr. Pleever. When he finished, they were silent. Then Alex spoke.

"That means you're a Viking," Alex said.

"Half Viking," Sim corrected.

"That's more than anybody else," Alex pointed out, "on the entire planet!"

"Except Splitface," Greta reminded them.

Then, remembering, Sim reached into his pocket and removed two small boxes. "And he gave me these. He said they belong to me because they were my father's. By the way, I told him about my time trips. I'm sorry we didn't talk about it first the way we agreed. It just happened."

"It's OK, "Amanda said, "we were pretty sure you would."

Sim showed them the drawings and told about the Viking ship having been discovered on the day he was born.

"Is that when it's going to happen?" Amanda asked.

"That's what Dr. Pleever thinks," Sim said.

"Excuse me?" Alex said, looking at each of them in turn. "It?"

"That's when I have to have all the medallions," Sim said.

"It?" Alex persisted.

"That's when Sim is going to see his father," Amanda said. "Haven't you been paying attention?"

"It's not for sure," Sim said, partly trying to keep the peace and partly not wanting to put his hopes out in the world where they might get dropped and broken.

"Well, if you don't see him, how are you going to give him the medallions?" Amanda asked.

Sim could tell that she was a little annoyed with him. Amanda didn't like foot-dragging when extraordinary events were just around the next corner.

"I don't know, Amanda," Sim said. "There are a lot of things I don't know."

"Well, there isn't very much time to find them out," Amanda persisted. "By the way, have you told your mother any of this yet?"

"No," Sim said. "You know what my mother's like."

"This is the most important thing that has ever happened to you, Sim," Amanda said. "You can't not tell her. She's always told you that someday your father would come back. You'll just be telling her how it's going to happen."

"It's not that simple, Amanda," Sim said. His words came out a little more sharply than he had intended. "First off, he's not coming back. I'm going to him. Second, my mom's not invited. At least I don't think she is. Third, she won't believe any of it. She'll probably put me in the hospital. Fourth...." He stopped.

"Fourth," Greta repeated.

"I can't think of it right now. But there are lots of problems here, guys. Lots of them."

"Get Hazel to tell her," Greta suggested. "Woman to woman. After all you were born there and she knew your father."

"I think Hazel tried to tell her, a long time ago. She really loves Hazel, but she doesn't pay much attention to what she says. I tried to get her to tell me about what Hazel said about my father."

"And?" Alex asked.

"She asked if Hazel had shown me the cave. The drawings, you know."

"Petroglyphs," Greta said.

"Yeah, those."

"She probably told your mother the whole story," Amanda said. "All the stuff that Dr. Pleever told you."

"But how would Hazel know any of it?" Sim asked. "She couldn't talk to my father any more than my mother or Dr. Pleever could."

"She's a witch," Alex said.

"Yeah, right," Sim said.

"OK, then how about Dr, Pleever?" Greta persisted. He's not a nut case. Your mother would listen to him."

"Not a bad idea," Alex said.

"She'll be really upset," Amanda said.

"Because I didn't tell her myself?" Sim asked.

"No," Amanda said. "Because if you disappear the way your father did she'll be afraid you'll never come back."

"She and me both," Sim said quietly.

They talked for another hour, trying to make sense of the adventure that had taken over their lives.

After awhile Alex let out a big yawn. The others realized that they were tired, too, so the boys went to Alex's room and, after brushing their teeth and changing into pajamas, climbed into bed. Alex had given Sim his own lower bunk so that Walter wouldn't feel too far away from him.

Sim's mind went round and round on the day's events. Sleepless after fifteen minutes and not having before him the night sky or the progress of the moon across the ships and seas of his own wallpaper, he remembered the book, the one that Mrs. Rose had given to him. He had been carrying it for days now, intending to read it but never having time. He turned on the light by his bedside and removed it from his pack. "*The Poetry of Henry Wadsworth Longfellow.*" He opened it to the first page and read:

I was a Viking old!
My deeds, though manifold,
No Skald in song has told,
No Saga taught thee!
Take heed, that in thy verse
Thou dost the tale rehearse,
Else dread a dead man's curse;
For this I sought thee.

"Far in the Northern Land,
By the wild Baltic's strand,
I, with my childish hand,
Tamed the gerfalcon;
And, with my skates fast-bound,
Skimmed the half-frozen Sound,
That the poor whimpering hound

Trembled to walk on.

"Oft to his frozen lair
Tracked I the grisly bear,
While from my path the hare
Fled like a shadow;
Oft through the forest dark
Followed the were-wolf's bark,
Until the soaring lark
Sang from the meadow.

Sim closed his eyes and saw again the ancient forest that he had seen on that first night, the giant chestnuts, the light and shadow of the forest floor. He started to close the book and discovered a small white card sticking out at the top. He removed it. *TRAVELSTAR FOUNDATION* it said, Adrian Smith, President. Curious, Sim thought. Gold-Tipped Smith must have stuck it in the book before he handed it to me that day at the library. Sim turned the card over. Four lines were written in a very fancy script. That would fit Mr. Smith, Sim thought. Then he read the verse:

The Starlight Medallions number nine
Some are yours and some are mine.
Eight encircle the ninth in a round
Powerless till the lykill's found.

Chapter 37

Pegasus

At breakfast the next morning, Sim's mother reminded him that he had volunteered to help out with the annual library book sale.

"You mean you volunteered me," Sim replied. He didn't say it in a complaining voice. He wasn't looking for an argument or a speech on the importance of community service. But it was true, she had. Mrs. Pomeroy had told her that the twins would be helping out. If Mrs. Pomeroy dyed her hair purple, Sim thought at the time, my mother would do the same. It was embarrassing.

But embarrassment was as far from Sim's mind this morning as was argument. In fact the book sale was perfect. Greta would be there as well. Greta never missed anything that had to do with the library or with books. She was never without her library card. She had taken it to a store and had it laminated. Once when Sim had kidded her about it, she had said that it was like having a driver's license. Greta would always surprise you with ideas like that.

They would all be there, and Sim could show them Gold-Tipped Smith's card. Dr. Pleever had been right.

Things were speeding up. Now he knew how many medallions there were. But what was "the lykill?" As he ate his Nutritious Nutcake Cereal, he counted up in his head. Mr. Smith had "some." That meant more than one. Sim had four. That was at least six. Splitface probably had the others. He would have to pay a visit to the Travelstar Foundation.

He kissed his mother goodbye, called to Walter and stepped out into a bright fall Sunday morning.

There were twenty other volunteers at the library when Sim arrived. Alex was waiting for him. The two of them had been assigned to ride in the cruiser with Chief Turnbull. Greta and Amanda were put on the sorting-and-pricing crew, headed by the Chief's wife, Virtue. "You Pick Them Out! We'll Pick Them Up," several posters around town had announced for the past week. People had called in and their names had been put on a pick up list. Sim was frustrated, not being able to show the others Gold-Tipped Smith's card, but Chief Turnbull was eager to get going. Walter, declining an invitation to ride in the police van, set off on his daily rounds.

They had driven to the north side of town, where the houses weren't quite as nice as in the town's center or along the ocean. It was a place where Sim had never ridden his bike but had a vague sense of having visited with his mother when he was much younger. As they turned one corner and started down a street, Sim knew that he had been there before, and recently. But that was impossible.

Chief Turnbull pulled to the side of the road in front of a neatly kept cottage with a glider on the porch.

"Who lives here?" Alex asked.

"Gladys Perkwell," Chief Turnbull replied, opening his door. "I'd better come with you. She's a little forgetful sometimes. She did call the library, though, and said she had a box of books."

As they started up the driveway, Sim looked around and saw, across the street, a broken bicycle lying in the grass in front of a house. He gasped. It was the house he had visited in one of his dreamwalks, the one from which angry voices had emerged, and the sound of someone crying. In the dreamwalk, it was the garage that had wanted his attention. It was closed up tight. There was no sign of life.

The next thing he knew, Alex was calling his name. "Earth to Sim Earth to Sim," he was saying. He was carrying a small box of books. The chief was smiling.

"Maybe Denny would like to help us out," the chief said, following Sim's gaze. "It would be good for him."

"Denny?" Sim asked.

"That's the Dumont place," the chief said. "I thought that's why you were looking at it."

"That's where Denny lives?" Alex asked.

"Sure is," the chief said." He opened the back of the van and Alex added the small box of books. Then they all got in to continue their pick ups. Sim was lost in thought. Why would he have dreamed about being at Denny's house? Why the garage? Then it came to him. "Omigosh!" he said out loud. He saw the chief's face in the rear-view mirror.

"Forget something?" the chief asked.

"No," Sim said. "I just remembered something I have to do."

"What?" Alex asked.

"Oh, just clean my room. Before my mom gets back. It's nothing." Alex looked at him skeptically.

It was the stolen medallion, Sim realized. Denny's father had hidden it in the garage before selling it to Splitface. That's what my dreams are about, he thought. Showing me where the other medallions are. Hazel has one. And of course. My first nightwalk: the McCrory Building. Gold-Tipped Smith! How could I have missed it? Right in front of my nose. He was on overload with stuff to tell Greta and the twins.

When they returned to the library three hours later, they found Greta assigned to history books and Amanda to fantasy. Sim couldn't help smiling. Mr. Pomeroy had arranged for Bartlett's to provide sandwiches, soft drinks, and ice-cream sandwiches for the volunteers.

When lunch was over, Mrs. Rose thanked the volunteers and announced, to general applause, that they had collected and sorted almost 1,500 books.

Greta had ridden her bicycle to the library and now walked it alongside the other three as they headed down the hill. Half way across the bridge, Sim stopped. The others walked on a few paces, stopped, and turned. "There's something new," he said.

"And it's not cleaning up your room," Alex said.

"Right," Sim confirmed. He took the card from his pocket and held it up.

"Travelstar Foundation?" Alex asked. "What's that?"

"Adrian Smith," Greta said. "That's Gold-Tipped Smith. Where'd you get it?"

"That day Amanda and I went to the library, Mrs. Rose had this book she thought I'd like to read. She had put it on the counter and Gold-Tipped Smith had picked it up. He must have stuck the card into it then. He handed the card to Greta, who read out the verse:

The Starlight Medallions number nine
Some are yours and some are mine.
Eight encircle the ninth in a round
Powerless till the lykill's found.

"Starlight Medallions." Amanda repeated the phrase, slowly, with a little touch of drama. "It's so beautiful. That's what they are, Sim. Starlight Medallions."

"I know," Sim said. He knew how Amanda felt. It was the way he had felt that night lying in his bunk at the Pomeroys', reading the verse for the first time.

"What's the lykill?" Alex asked.

"No idea," Sim said.

"Gold-Tipped Smith wants to talk to you," Greta said.

"I know," Sim said, "and I want to talk with him. He knows more even than Dr. Pleever."

"So let's check out this Travelstar Foundation," Alex said, turning to walk back across the bridge.

"I'm not done yet," Sim said, making a face.

"There's more?" Alex asked.

"There's more," Sim echoed. "We saw where Denny lives," Sim told the girls. "When we were collecting books. It was like I had been there before," he said, now turning to include Alex. He hesitated, considering for a moment, and then continued. "I didn't tell you because I wasn't sure what was happening, and things were already pretty weird. You would have thought I was crazy. Crazier. But when I saw Denny's house I understood what was happening." Sim had his friends' full attention.

"I've been having these dreams. They're not really dreams. They're too boring to be dreams. Like the first one. I was standing outside the McCrory Building, on the sidewalk across the street. No one noticed me. I just stood there looking at it."

"What happened?" Alex asked.

"Nothing. That's what I'm saying. I was just there. Like watching television or something."

"What about the others?" Greta asked.

"The second time was Denny's house. Someone inside was crying. It must have been Denny. I stood there looking at the garage as if it were going to do something."

"That's all?" Amanda asked.

"That's it. But today, when we were there collecting books, I figured it out. It's the medallions. They're showing me where they are."

"The one Mr. Dumont stole," Alex interjected. "It was in his garage."

"Precisely," Sim said. Hearing Dr. Pleever's voice at the back of his head, he couldn't help but grin.

"What's funny?" Alex asked.

"Nothing."

"Cleaning your room again."

"OK. I just realized I sounded like Dr. Pleever. That's his word."

"And the third one?" Greta asked.

"I was outside Hazel's cottage."

"Of course," Amanda said. "Good old Hazel."

"Any others?" Greta asked.

"Only one. I was in a cellar. There was a cot and a small table. And stuff you find in an attic. Odds and ends. One of those snow globes."

"Where was the cellar?" Alex pressed.

Sim shook his head. "Totally unfamiliar. Except for the smell. But I guess most cellars smell that way."

"What way?" Amanda asked.

"You know: musty, damp. Just that."

"This is heavy duty stuff," Alex announced. "How could you not tell us before now?"

"I told you," Sim responded, a little irritated. "It didn't make any sense until this morning. Anyway, I've told you."

"Is there anything else you're sitting on?" Alex asked.

"Back off," Amanda said. She turned to Sim.

"Thanks for telling us, Sim. But you didn't have to worry. No one" – she looked significantly at Alex – "thinks you're crazy."

"Wait a minute," Greta said. "That's four medallions. Gold-Tipped Smith, Hazel, the stolen one, and the cellar. With your four that makes eight. Gold-Tipped Smith says, 'Some are yours and some are mine.' So he's got more than one. You think Splitface had more than one before he got the one from the library? That's too many medallions."

"Not if Splitface lives in a cellar," Alex said.

Sim nodded his head, slowly. "Good, Alex. Very good. Excellent."

"I think we should have a look at the McCrory Building," Amanda said.

They retraced their steps to Water Street and stood on the sidewalk opposite where Sim had stood in his dreamwalk just a few nights earlier. The building seemed to him less spooky now, but nonetheless empty of life. Greta noticed that there was a new sign on the glass panel in the door at the center of the building, and they crossed over to read it. *Travelstar Foundation*, it said in bright new gold letters that were out of keeping with the chipped and faded paint of the door itself. Under the name was an image of a winged horse.

"That's weird," Amanda said.

"What's weird?" Alex asked.

"Why would anybody want to open up a travel agency right across from Friendly Travel?"

They followed her gaze across the street to where Jimmy and June Bradley sat at their desks behind the plate-glass window surrounded by travel posters. "You hardly ever see anybody in there," Amanda added.

"Maybe Travelstar does time travel," Alex said.

"Pegasus!" Sim said.

"Hello?" Alex said.

"The flying horse on the window. It's called Pegasus. I don't know how I missed it. It's the constellation on the second Smithsonian medallion."

Chapter 38

Bulldozers and Cranes

It was state testing week at LORCES. The tests were spread over four days, two mornings and two afternoons.

Testing meant sitting still for a long time and concentrating. After Sim's third trip to the bathroom in the first two hours, Miss Blenden asked if he needed to see the nurse. Sim actually considered the invitation for a moment before declining - not because there was anything at all wrong with him but because it would provide a reason to move around a little.

The morning, however, had not been entirely wasted, for Sim had come to a conclusion. He was going to talk to Denny Dumont at recess. This decision was the result of a long thought-out process to which the test had not proven a great obstacle.

When the companions met at recess, Sim announced his decision. Time was running out. Fast. And Denny knew things that they needed to know.

"What makes you think Denny will talk?" Amanda asked. "Just because he gave back your lucky stone doesn't mean he's all of a sudden going to stop being a jerk."

"I don't know," Greta said. "Look over there." She indicated the fence along the south side of the playground that separated the school from the town garage. Denny was standing there alone watching a couple of workmen load a bulldozer on to a flatbed. Jack and his other cronies were playing foursquare.

They watched him for a moment without speaking. He had become an outsider. None of them could fail to see his unhappiness. Alex was the first to speak. "However bad he feels it isn't bad enough, if you ask me."

"I don't know," Sim said.

"What do you mean you don't know?" Alex said, impatiently. "You're the guy he's picked on the worst. He's crud."

"Alex!" Amanda said.

"Crud is not a swear word, Amanda, in case you didn't know."

Greta turned to Sim. "You don't have to be friends with him," she said. "He could be useful. You're right about Mr. Smith and Splitface. We really need to know more about how they're connected. What have you got to lose?"

"I'll tell you in a couple of minutes," Sim said, and walked toward the fence.

He stood beside Denny and watched as the men removed the treads that had provided a ramp for the loading of the bulldozer. They slid them underneath the truck's flatbed. Sim had been working on something to say as he walked over, but he couldn't come up with anything that didn't sound stupid, so he just watched as the men got into the cab of the truck and drove away. Denny stood there, not acknowledging Sim's presence, as if waiting for some other maintenance event to occur.

"You can make good money doing heavy equipment," Denny said at last, still not looking at Sim. "My uncle knows a guy who runs a crane. He loads stuff onto ships. He is so high up that people look like little ants walking around. He's got a big SUV and a boat. He makes good money."

Then the bell rang. Denny turned, still without looking at Sim, and walked toward the building. Well, Sim thought, at least he didn't call me pea brain or tell me to get lost. He smiled. It was a start.

On Tuesday morning, they did their regular classwork. Testing would take place in the afternoon. Miss Blenden introduced their main fall project on immigration. They would read about immigrants in the early part of the country's history, mainly those who came to San Francisco and New York City. They were also to ask at home about their own ancestry and find some object that had come down through the years that they could write about. Sim looked at Amanda and smiled.

At recess Denny was again standing at the fence, and Sim would have sworn, as he stood with his friends some distance away, that Denny had actually glanced in their direction once or twice. Taking this as encouragement, he walked over once again and stood beside the boy who had once made his life so miserable.

Nothing of interest was happening in the maintenance yard. Two of the town's dump trucks were parked by the garage, facing away from them. Each had a sign on its back: *Construction Vehicle Do Not Follow.*

"That sign is so dumb," Denny said. "So what are you supposed to do? Pull off the road? Pass them?" Sim felt called upon to comment. It was one thing not to take the initiative but another to remain dumb when he was clearly being called upon to agree with Denny's remark and perhaps even add something of his own. But all he could come up with was a simple, "Yeah!"

He felt like one of Denny's goons. Denny half looked at Sim as if noticing him for the first time. "You've got something on your stupid necktie," he said matter-of-factly.

"Right," Sim said, without checking. He wasn't going to fall for that one a second time. He was disappointed. They said no more. The bell rang and they walked back toward the building, not together. As he walked, Sim looked at his tie. It was his most conservative necktie, the kind you might wear to a funeral or a week of state-mandated testing: dark blue, undecorated except for a brown pendant of hot chocolate right at the middle.

On Wednesday there was no question about it. Denny was looking for Sim, who had purposely dawdled in the classroom before coming out. From the door of the building, he saw Denny scanning the playground, his gaze returning repeatedly to the other three companions.

Sim walked over to the fence where Denny had again taken up his position. The entertainment today was provided by one member of the road crew who was washing out the bed of his truck with a hose. It wasn't a scene that inspired Denny to an opinion. Instead he got right to the point.

"That stone," he said, as if he weren't really very interested in it.

"Yeah." Sim tried to match his indifference.

"So what does it do?"

"I don't know," Sim said.

Denny seemed to hesitate, unsure of himself. Then he spoke. "It sort of glows like it's alive or something."

"My mother says they had things like that when she was a kid," Sim said. "They were called mood rings. Body heat makes them glow."

"So what does it do?"

"I think it's supposed to protect me," Sim said on an inspiration. In fact, the thought was one he had never fully formulated.

"It did that pretty good," Denny said. "That thing my father stole from the library?"

"The medallion."

"Yeah, that. I thought that was the same thing you were wearing. I heard the guy with the face say you had one. I thought if I gave it to my father, he'd think... I dunno. Think I was cool."

"Did it work?" Sim asked.

"Are you kidding? Nothing I do is cool. He kicked my butt. It wasn't one of those things."

"Medallions."

"Yeah, one of those."

Sim wondered whether it had been the night he had dreamwalked and heard Denny crying.

"The guy he sold it to," Sim began.

"The guy with the face."

"Yeah. Did he ever talk about anyone else?"

"The face and my dad had this argument about how much the face was going to pay my dad. He said he had to talk to someone else. My dad didn't like the idea that there were other people in the deal. What's so cool about those things, anyway?"

"I think if you get all of them, then they become really valuable," Sim said. That was probably about as much truth as Denny could have handled. Telling him more would have done neither of them any good.

"You mean like getting a complete set of baseball cards?" Denny asked.

"A lot like that," Sim said. "At least I think so. That other guy – the one with the money – he's trying to collect them too."

The bell rang. They stood there for a moment longer; then Denny turned to him. "You know, Spotswood, just because we talked doesn't mean we're friends."

Sim could think of nothing to say. Denny grinned and walked toward the school building.

The four companions gathered at Bartlett's after school and Sim reported on his conversation, realizing as he did that they weren't much farther along. He said as much.

"What's the next step?" Alex asked.

It was his question to answer, Sim knew. "I think it's time to try out the medallions," he said.

"Four is twice as many as you had before," Alex said. "Something should happen."

"I had this idea," Sim went on. "Oktoberfest starts Friday afternoon. Water Street will be empty."

"So?" Alex asked.

"I think I should do it near the ship. It makes sense."

"And there's at least one medallion in the McCrory building," Greta said.

"Yeah, but we don't have it," Alex countered.

"Still, it's nearby. It could help," Sim said.

"Are you sure you're ready?" Amanda asked.

"Yes," Sim said. "I'm sure."

Chapter 39

Four Medallions and a Seagull

With the building unoccupied for the last two years, the McCrory wharf was little used except by the occasional fisherman, and tourists who wanted to get a closer look at the Viking ship. It was true that most everyone would be up on the Town Common for Oktoberfest, but there might be the odd stroller, so the companions decided that they needed a cover. Alex suggested fishing.

Sim was the first to arrive. He had brought two fishing poles because Greta didn't have one. The twins arrived next with a bag of broken clams that Alex had gotten from Homer the previous afternoon. Greta arrived last. She had never held a fishing pole so Alex gave her, to Sim's surprise, a considerate and efficient lesson. Alex wasn't always like that. Often if he knew something you didn't, he couldn't resist talking down to you. He hardly ever had an advantage over Greta. Now here he was being Mr. Nice Guy, showing her how not to put the hook in the clam's belly. And Greta was just as nice back to him, letting him show her stuff that she could easily have figured out herself. Go figure, Sim thought.

As Sim had predicted, Water Street was almost deserted. The plan was that Sim would sit on the front of the dock with the others strategically placed behind him. He walked to the edge and looked down into the clear, cold water. He could see the barnacle-encrusted rocks on the river bottom and was reminded of the day he had found the first medallion and how the bank of the river had suddenly disappeared to reveal the river's ancient and unsilted depths. He took a step back. "I just thought of something," he said. "This may not be a great plan."

"What's the problem?" Amanda asked.

"I was just thinking that with four medallions, things might be a little bit different. I mean if it works at all."

"Different how?" Alex asked.

"Before, I was always here. I'd see someplace else and some other time, but I wasn't in it. It was like watching a movie or something. But what if it gets more real with more medallions and I'm actually in this other place?"

"You're afraid of not being able to get back, aren't you?" Greta suggested.

"I hadn't thought of that," Sim said. "Thanks a lot, Greta."

"Sorry."

"It's OK. I'm not really worried."

"Remember what Dr. Pleever said about your birthday, Amanda reminded him. "It's still over a week away. The medallions need you here."

"Right," Sim said. It was true. He wasn't really worried. He felt much more excited than frightened. It was like the day they had discovered the cave. He had known then that nothing bad was going to happen. He felt that way now. His concern was more down to earth. "It's the pier," he said.

"What about it?" Alex asked.

"I was just thinking that if I go back like I have been, there might not be any pier here. I might get a little wet." The companions laughed, as he hoped they would.

"Amanda, take Walter's collar," he said. "I don't want to freak him out." Then, leaving his friends on the pier, he walked to the blacktop that extended out from the McCrory Building.

On his first four time trips, the medallions had decided when and where he would go, and Sim had never really left the present. He had only glimpsed the past. Briefly. That was with two medallions. Now he had four. He arranged Sagittarius, Orion, Pegasus, and Ursa Major in front of him and sat cross-legged, the way he remembered Aladdin sitting on his flying carpet. He took a deep breath and waited for something to happen. Nothing. Then he had a thought. Maybe when you had more of them, the medallions had to be arranged in a special way. He stacked them one on top of the other. Nothing. Then he changed their order. After eight or nine attempts, he realized how little he knew about any of this. Maybe you couldn't control the medallions after all. Maybe they really *did* have minds of their own.

Then he remembered the picture his father had drawn of Starspinner, with his arms crossed. "They are definitely connected," Dr. Pleever had said. "the medallions and Starspinner... and your father." Sim had an inspiration. He stood with his feet apart, put two of the medallions in the side-by-side pockets on the bib of his overalls, held the other two in his hands, and crossed his arms over his chest.

A gull lasnded a few feet away and looked at him. It cocked its head to one side. "Hello, Greywing," Sim whispered. The gull took off and flew out across the harbor. He followed it with his eyes. Then came that tickling sensation once again, like an ant crawling up his chest. He was vaguely aware of the sound of Greta's voice without actually hearing her words. Apparently she had caught a fish. He heard Walter bark.

He was no longer sitting on the hard blacktop of the parking lot, but rather in a field of wildflowers above the river. There were no buildings and no sign of life – that is, of human life. Several white-tailed deer were grazing just outside the woods that began about fifty feet behind where he stood. He looked toward where the library had been only moments earlier. Sure enough, now dwarfed by the giant trees that stood surrounding it, there was the Oracle Stone. The river was the same, but now he could see it wind out from the forest, uninterrupted by the Shore Road bridge.

This was a very different time skip from the others, and his legs felt a little wobbly. Always before, he had remained safely in his own time, visible to anyone who might have cared to glance at him. Alex had called it double-timing, being both places at once. This time he had left his own world behind.

There was a chill in the air and a mist rolling in from the sea. He watched as the gull disappeared in its whiteness. I'll have to begin bringing a backpack with a warm jacket if I'm to go on these adventures, Sim said to himself, with a fragile lightheartedness.

Then the fog bank seemed to take on a shape and substance. He would have sworn it was the head of a dragon, but it vanished as quickly as it had appeared, like someone peeking momentarily from between the curtains at a window. He stared as the fog coiled and rolled onto the shore. It had cleared for a moment; surely it would again. He heard a rush of wings behind him and turned. The gull had alighted once again, its attention now directed, as was his own, at the coiling and uncoiling of the sea mists. As they watched, the dragon emerged once more. Only there were two dragons: one on the bowsprit and one emblazoned upon the sail of the Viking ship that moved soundlessly into the harbor.

Sim's first impulse was to point it out to his companions, so, he turned, forgetting for a moment that they were fishing from the McCrory wharf a thousand years in the future. When he looked back, the sail was being taken down and he could hear the commotion of oars being fitted into their locks. Then there was the sound of something being struck, perhaps a drum or a hollow log. He watched, amazed at the elegant movement of the oars as if one man rather than many were working them, so perfectly did they crawl upon the water. It was to the rhythm of the beat, he realized. His father was on that ship, and that thought, for a moment, drove out all others.

The ship was now approaching the bank of the river, and portside oars were pulled in. Two men were in the water. They held long sticks with sharp iron tips, which they drove at an angle into the riverbank. Then two other men threw ropes to them so they could moor the ship. Next, someone put a gangplank over the side and the sailors began to disembark.

Some of the men were dressed colorfully in long coats that came down to their knees and seemed to button down the front. Their shoes didn't look so different from his own, though he was too far away to see very much. They wore broad belts, some with swords hanging from them. Almost all of them had hats that fitted tightly over the tops of their heads. Two or three wore helmets. One man wore a cloak decorated along the edges with red and yellow animals, and a red skullcap. He had an ornament of some kind hanging around his neck and he carried a leather pack. He barked orders in a strange tongue and the men responded, some mumbling under their breath.

Sim had read that holding out your hands, palms up, was considered a peaceful gesture of welcome in most parts of the world. He did that now, approaching the ship. No one seemed to notice him. "Welcome to the new world!" he said, in the deepest voice he could summon. "I am Simeon, master of the Starlight Medallions, son of Magnus Siglandi." He might as well have been talking to the trees. No one paid the slightest attention. Each man went about his business as if Sim didn't exist.

But he did exist, and he was here in this time and the sea mist brushed his face. It wasn't fair. It was a trick. The medallions were playing with him. No, it was his problem. He wasn't doing something right. He spread his legs apart and folded his arms, repeating his speech. Nothing. Several of the men were laughing. At him? That would be too much. No, it was at something one of them had said. He kicked a stone, in frustration. His foot went right through it. He bent to pick it up. He couldn't. His hand felt nothing. He was here and he wasn't here.

Two men wrestled a large trunk onto the ship's gunwales and two other men carried it to the shore. Another man emerged carrying two cloth sacks, and then one with a string of fish. Dinnertime, Sim thought.

Now the man with the skullcap looked around him. It was a look of satisfaction, but at the corners of his mouth was something like a sneer. As if he had bettered somebody.

The man snapped out an order. He kicked one of the men with the toe of his boot. He was the captain. Or the chief. Or whatever they would have had. Sim reconsidered his situation. Maybe it was just as well that they couldn't see him. The man called loudly for someone or something. The word meant nothing to Sim. He called again, summoning with his arm. Sim followed the man's gaze. There was a boy. Focused, as he had been, on the man with the red skullcap, Sim hadn't noticed him before. He stood behind the ship, skipping stones over the calm water. Suddenly Sim's heart pounded in his chest The man called again, now angrily. The boy turned.

The boy was no older than he. The man with the skullcap called yet again. The boy approached. His hair, though long, was as fair as Sim's own, and he appeared to be about the same height and weight. He wore tan cloth leggings fitted into his boots, which looked soft and comfortable, tied around the top with a cord or perhaps a piece of rawhide. The most striking thing was his coat.

It was the most beautiful coat Sim had ever seen, lighter than the tan of his leggings and embroidered at every edge with decorations and patterns in bright reds and blues. There was a kind of belt, low on the boy's hips, which emerged from the sides of the coat and cinched at the front. Then Sim caught his breath. Just above the belt a figure of a man was embroidered in black, his legs apart, his arms crossed over his chest. It was Starspinner!

The man held out his hand and the boy removed the coat, handing it to him. The man stuffed it into his pack, examining it first as if to be sure something wasn't missing. The boy stepped back, looking at the ground. He was fully dressed, but, it seemed to Sim, incomplete without the coat. Sim felt a chill. The boy hugged himself against the cold.

Then the boy looked and their eyes met. Or so it seemed, for neither looked away. "I am going to be your son someday," Sim said. There was no indication that his father had heard him, but still their eyes locked.

The man with the skullcap called again. The boy didn't move. The man strode up behind him, struck him across the face with his hand, and pushed him in the direction of the ship. Sim let out a yell of pain. The boy made not a sound. Sim put his hand to his face. It burned like fire. He looked at his hand. There was blood on it. Sim ran to where the ship was moored. The stake had a sharp iron point. He tried to grasp it, but his hand made no contact with the surface. He felt tears of pain and frustration on his cheeks. He wiped at them with his hand. He looked at the man, standing there so sure of himself, so scornful of those around him. Then he saw it. The man wore a ring with a large red stone. Sim looked at his hand. Blood. "Someday," Sim said.

There was a rustle of wings behind him. It was the gull, ascending once again toward the mists that swirled in the harbor. One of the men pointed at it and made a sign. Sim watched it as it disappeared high above the ship. When he lowered his eyes, it was to a familiar landscape and when he raised them, it was to a clearer October sky. Something drew his attention to the building behind him and he turned. Not everyone was celebrating Oktoberfest in the park. Gold-Tipped Smith was standing in an open window on the third floor of the McCrory Building, watching.

"There he is," Alex yelled and waved. Sim took a second to collect himself. He reached down and touched the blacktop of the driveway and then walked to where his friends stood.

Chapter 40

The Graveyard

"You disappeared!" Alex said, hardly able to contain himself. He touched Sim on the arm, cautiously, and then noticed his cheek. "What happened?" he asked, stepping back. Sim realized that he had never before seen a frightened Alex. It was more than a little upsetting to see the look on his friend's face - a mixture of surprise, confusion and suspicion. He looked at the girls. Amanda and Greta were staring at his face, their brows furrowed. Gteta took out her hankie and handed it to him.

"That's a deep cut, Sim," she said. "What happened?"

Sim wasn't sure where to start. "My father was a kid," Sim explained, dabbing at his cheek with the hankie. "And he had this coat. You wouldn't believe the coat. With Starspinner on the front. And this guy hit him. Really hard."

"You're going to need stitches," Amanda said, looking at Sim's cheek.

"What's crazy is that I wasn't really there. I mean my feet didn't even bend the grass. But I got this," he said, dabbing again with the hankie.

"You're sure to have a scar," Alex said. It will be cool."

"Right," Sim said. Alex had regained his composure. That was reassuring. All of a sudden he was feeling a little weak in the knees. There was quite a lot of blood on the hankie. A slapping noise came from the pier and Sim turned. The flounder that Greta had caught continued to flick its tail fin as it expired on the end of her line. Sim furrowed his brow and looked back at his friends. "I wanted to kill that guy," he said. "I've never had a feeling like that before. I tried to grab one of those poles with a pointed end. Stupid. My hand went right through it."

"Because of your cut," Amanda said, "that's not strange. Nobody's ever hit you before. No adult."

"It wasn't that," Sim said.

"It was because he hit your father," Greta said.

Sim nodded. He couldn't have spoken right then. His friends gave him a moment and he was grateful. He was also glad when Alex put the conversation back on a normal track.

"OK, guys, we know some new stuff. Four medallions can take you all the way back but you're not there. Except for that cut on your cheek. So to really be there, you have to have more. Another thing: the medallions are deciding where you go and what you see. Just like with Hazel on the Oracle Stone. They wanted you to see your father when he was your age. And maybe they wanted you to see that other guy, too. They probably didn't plan on the cheek part."

"Maybe they did," Greta suggested thoughtfully, still appearing to work out her thought. It proves you have a deep connection with your father. You said that you looked at one another. Maybe he saw you. Maybe seeing you planted an idea in his head. Something that would stay with him until he was older."

"And the coat," Amanda said. "You were supposed to see the coat with Starspinner on the front. The guy took it away from your father. Why did he do that? Maybe the coat is connected to the medallions. Maybe you have to wear the coat to make the medallions work."

"But Sim doesn't have a coat like that, and they work for him," Alex observed.

"I'll bet they do more stuff than we know about yet," Amanda continued. "Every time Sim adds another medallion things get more complicated. Like standing the way you did this time. Remember what you said when you had Dr. Pleever's medallion in the library?"

Sim shook his head.

"You said you could almost smell the flowers, that it was almost like being there."

"Oh, right," Sim affirmed.

"Well, maybe with the coat, something really big happens."

"But the coat is back there a thousand years," Sim said.

"Maybe not," Greta said. She had been silent for awhile, Sim noticed. Sort of zoned out the way she was when she was working something through. He looked at her hopefully.

"I agree with Amanda," she began. "The coat is important, mainly because of Starspinner on the front but also because that guy took it away from your father. He can take it away but he can't wear it. Only a small person can wear it. Like you. Remember that Dr. Pleever said your father didn't come to the future to collect the medallions; he came to make you. Only you can wear the coat."

It was no surprise to Sim that Greta should be the one to offer the most important idea yet. After all, she was Greta. "Greta, you are amazing," he said.

Just then, Sim heard a window close above them. A few particles of dust descended. There was no sign of Gold-Tipped Smith.

"What?" Alex asked.

"Gold-Tipped Smith," Sim said. "He was watching."

They all looked at the window. Finally Amanda spoke. "What are you going to tell your mother about the cut on your cheek?" she asked.

"I have no idea," Sim said. He removed the hankie. It was wet with blood.

"Keep it," Greta said.

They packed up the fishing equipment and prepared to go their own ways home.

Sim's mother would be home around seven. It was already five and Walter was ready for his dinner.

Sim was glad for Walter's company as he walked home, for the days were getting shorter already, and the shadows were lengthening along Threadneedle Street. Halloween was everywhere you turned. Ghosts made of sheets and balloons hung from branches, skeletons leaned against trees, and pumpkins flickered their gap-toothed smiles from porches.

"I don't even have a Halloween costume yet, Walter," Sim said. He and Alex had talked about being surfers because Alex had two wetsuits and two boogie boards, but Amanda had said wet suits weren't really Halloween costumes. Then Sim had found the first medallion and Halloween had lost its magic.

Sim was surprised at how dark it had gotten, until he realized that another of the famous Lost River Cove fogs was rolling in, hiding the last rays of the sun. As he approached the Parish Church cemetery, he hesitated. Perhaps tonight it would be better to take a more lighted path. But Walter was already out of sight among the gravestones, so Sim followed. Walter's pace always quickened on this part of the homeward journey - not from superstition, but because dinner was now only two blocks and one cemetery away.

It was a good thing there was a path, Sim thought, for this fog was unusually dense. More and more he relied upon the feel of gravel beneath his feet to guide him.

Then he heard Walter's growl. Only once had he made the sound that now came to Sim's ears, and Sim suddenly felt as if some small furry creature were making a nest for itself in the bottom of his stomach. He heard a small whimper and realized it was his own voice. He wanted to call Walter back to him, but he was afraid to make a sound.

If it was Splitface, and if Alex's reasoning was correct about his finding Sim that first time because of the medallion, there was no point in pretending that with four of them he could hide, even in this dense fog. That thought was confirmed when suddenly he felt a presence. His fog-shrouded visitor was ahead, slightly off to the right and drawing closer. For a moment, Sim thought he might take the medallions from his overalls and hide them. Then Splitface – if it was Splitface, and he had little doubt of that – would not be able to find him. But that would be cowardly and stupid. He might as well just hand them to him.

"What do you want?" he said in a voice that was a little shakier than he had planned it.

"The lykill," came the reply, "and of course the medallions."

"I don't have a lykill," Sim said. "I don't even know what it is."

"We won't play that game anymore. You were so very clever, weren't you. Just a few skipping stones in your pouch. Well, that won't work anymore. Give it to me. Now."

Sim was baffled. Yes, he did have a few good skippers in his pants pocket. How did Splitface know that? Just stones from the beach. He needed time to think. "Here," he said, "you can have them." He reached into his pocket and threw the stones on the ground in front of him, stepping back. Now he could see the vague outline of a human shape in the grey mists, a red skullcap the only hint of color. It knelt, searched the ground like an animal fended off with bits of meat, scratching among the leaves, mumbling to himself. Then it stood, holding the stones.

"Which one is it?" he asked. "We are done with hide-and-seek."

"I don't know what you want," Sim repeated. "I'm not who you think I am." Or was he? He touched his cheek. There was blood again. He took a step back and felt a gravestone behind him. He flinched and stepped to the side. Splitface reached. His hand closed about Sim's wrist; on his middle finger was a ring with a sharp red stone.

"Let me go," Sim yelled, trying to free his arm. Splitface drew his other hand back, preparing to strike Sim as he had earlier struck Sim's father but just at the moment Walter grabbed the man's ankle and pulled. Splitface lost his balance and would have pulled Sim down with him if, in trying to regain it, he had not loosened his grip on Sim's arm. Sim wrenched his wrist free, took a step back, spread his feet, and crossed his arms, in the Starspinner position.

He heard Splitface's curses become fainter as the mists of time enfolded him.

Sim reached down and picked up a handful of twigs and leaves, the kind of ground cover upon which he and the twins had walked the day they discovered the cave. Then the fog began to thin and the great chestnut trees seemed to step out, as upon a stage, from behind that diaphanous curtain. A curious thought occurred to him, and he smiled. It isn't, he thought, a question of *where* I am, but *when* I am. He had done enough time-traveling by now to be pretty sure he was standing a hundred feet or so into the Parish Church cemetery, but long before the people who lay buried there were even born.

Now he tried to piece together what had just happened. He had crossed his arms over the medallions, just as he had an hour earlier, and stepped into a parallel time. Splitface had not followed him. Splitface had been unable to follow him. That explained his curses. Poor Walter. This was the second time in less than an hour that his master had left him behind. Or was it ahead? What must poor Walter he think? Sim smiled again, his confidence renewed.

So what did it mean, he wondered. Was it because he had more medallions than Splitface or because there was something like loyalty involved? The medallions had protected him from Splitface. Sim felt that he was beginning to find his way in this adventure, that he and the medallions had one another's best interests at heart. Together they had outsmarted Splitface. But what was the lykill? Gold-Tipped Smith knew about the lykill. He had the answers Sim needed, But what now? Perhaps just wait until Splitface would have given up, and then go back? He sat at the foot of one of the giant chestnuts, pulled up his legs, cradled his head in his arms, and, thinking again about his father, the coat, and the seagull, slept.

Sim dreamed that he was a small child again. He had just finished a bowl of coffee ice cream – his favorite flavor – and his mother was wiping his face with a wet cloth. He tried to push her hand aside and encountered instead the cold nose of a basset hound. Walter, his front feet on Sim's chest, his tail wagging a semaphore of happy discovery, was licking his face. It was night, but the fog that had shrouded the graveyard had dissipated and the sky was brightened by a quarter moon. He felt a little stiff and realized he was leaning against a gravestone. This was not a happy discovery, and he stood up quickly, stepping back, remembering that only minutes or perhaps hours earlier, it had been the trunk of a giant chestnut.

Less superstitious than curious, he looked more closely at the stone. The inscription was simple. "Nathaniel Chit" it said, "beloved son of Arthur and Mabel, twin of Hazel Winifred. 1889-1900." He paused, overcome for a moment by the coincidence. He knelt before the granite slab, Walter next to him. On an impulse he took the medallions from his pocket and laid them across the top of the stone. "They're medallions," he said aloud. "I wish they could have helped you get better. They're going to help me find my father." Then he put them back in his pockets and stood up. His watch said 6:30. He had slept for more than an hour. There was no sign of Splitface.

His mother was on the phone talking to Lenny when Sim entered the kitchen. "Luckily the Toyota has fog lights," she was saying, the phone in one hand and her coffee in the other. She turned. Her smile disappeared. Sim touched the wound on his cheek.

"I'll call you back, Lenny. Something's just come up," she said, reaching behind her to put the phone back in its cradle. She set her coffee cup on the edge of the sink so that it crashed into the basin and ran to Sim. "Sim, what happened to you?!" she asked, touching his wound.

"The fog," Sim said suddenly inspired. "I was coming home. I was late, so I started running. Right into a tree. It must have been a broken branch. I guess it was sharp."

"You guess!" She examined his cheek more closely and went to the phone.

"Mom, It's just a scratch," Sim pleaded.

When they returned from the emergency room he had a real dish of coffee ice cream and his mother made a toasted cheese sandwich. Sim didn't feel up to a night on the widow's walk. He wanted familiar walls around him. Walter followed him up the stairs.

Chapter 41

Gold-Tipped Smith

"Three stitches," Amanda confirmed, examining Sim's cheek. He probably could have done it with two, but this way there won't be a scar. Did it hurt?"

"Only the Novocain. A little. It was nothing."

"Pretty good about the tree branch," Alex said.

The companions had met at Bartlett's to plan the next step – Gold-Tipped Smith. Walter was off on his daily rounds.

Sim told them about his encounter with Splitface in the graveyard, the strange episode of the skipping stones, about seeing the ring on Splitface's finger and, later, Nathaniel's gravestone.

"So about Splitface," Alex began.

Sim and the girls looked at him, wiping up with his paper napkin where he had slopped his hot chocolate.

"When you saw him that day the ship landed, his face was normal, right?"

"What do you mean by *normal*?"

"You know. He wasn't Splitface. But he had the ring."

"Right."

"So something major happened to him either before he left the past or after he got to the future."

Sim's mind flashed back to that moment when he had reached for the pike that moored the Viking ship, blood running down his cheek. He had wanted to hit back but he couldn't grasp the pike. Maybe his father had done something like that. Maybe the next time Splitface struck him he had struck back. His hand would have been able to grasp the pike. "It had to be before," Sim said.

"Sim's right," Greta said. "Sim's father had seen him like that. He drew the picture. It had to be when they were together."

"Maybe they came to the future together," Alex said.

"There's a lot we don't know about Splitface," Sim said. "And time is running out."

"So," said Alex, "Gold-Tipped Smith."

"Right," Sim confirmed. "I need to go alone."

"I don't think so," Amanda responded. "I trust him about as much as I trust Splitface."

"I think I have to," Sim said. "For one thing, Mr. Smith knows your father and I don't think he would talk the same way if you were there. And he knows some stuff about me that nobody else knows."

"Like what?" Alex asked.

"Like disappearing." Sim said.

"I think Sim's right," Alex said. "Here's my plan. We all go to the McCrory building. There are only two doors: the one that goes out to the parking lot and the one at the front. We stay outside the doors so that Mr. Smith doesn't try to kidnap Sim."

Sim had a sense that Gold-Tipped Smith was very different from Splitface, and he wasn't particularly frightened about seeing him, but he was grateful to have the others there. They walked down the library lawn past the Oracle Stone to Water Street and stood opposite the McCrory building. Sim noticed that two pedestrians on the sidewalk opposite, observing the children's focused attention, had also stopped to look at the building.

"Hey, guys," he said. "I don't think we're doing a very good job of being invisible."

'Huh?" Alex said. Sim nodded his head in the direction of the pedestrians. Now there were four of them. "Right. Time to disappear. Good luck, Sim."

Alex and Amanda walked in the direction of *Bob's Sweet Shop,* which they had chosen as their observation post. You could sit at one of the tables by the front window and see the McCrory building perfectly without anyone suspecting that you were doing surveillance. Greta and Sim crossed the street, she to guard the back door.

There was a bone-colored button beside the door, and Sim pressed it, listening for a sound within. He heard nothing. It probably doesn't work, he thought. Or if it does, he doesn't hear it. Or he isn't there. He found the thought reassuring but then screwed up his courage and knocked. Finally he tried the handle. It turned easily. He pushed the door open. Inside was a short entrance hall, narrow and undecorated. The walls were yellow, flaking here and there to reveal a white undercoating. The stairs will creak, he thought, so he stepped on the first of them gingerly, but it was silent.

So were the others. He ascended.

As he opened the door on the second-floor landing, a smell of dampness gave way to a more pungent aroma. There was a flapping of wings as several pigeons, not used to visitors, left their perches, circled briefly, and once again alighted. A window on harbor side was broken, had been for some time, it appeared, from the whitewash of bird droppings on the floor. Ghosts of fog drifted into the room, seemed for a moment to take shape and dissolve.

He climbed a second staircase and found himself in a large attic, bare of any improvement, its rafters covered with cobwebs. At the far end of the room was a circle of light. A cord hung from one of the beams, and at its end was a green metal lampshade. It looked to Sim like an island, upon whose shore had been piled the salvage of a shipwreck: boxes, some filing cabinets, a desk, a few chairs, a table, stacks of books, and, at the exact center, an umbrella stand from which the unmistakable gold tip of a cane protruded.

Gold-Tipped Smith sat hunched over a table on the far side of the island, just feet back from the sea of darkness beyond, his back to Sim.

Sim crossed the room quietly and stood in front of a desk at the edge of the light. It was rude, but nonetheless interesting, to observe someone who was unaware of your presence.

Smith was examining a document with a large round magnifying glass. He snorted, a sound that could equally signify satisfaction or annoyance. He scratched the back of his head, stood, and turned, seeing Sim for the first time.

"I rang the bell," Sim said. It couldn't hurt to be polite, he thought.

"Doesn't work," Mr. Smith responded. He studied Sim for a moment and smiled. "I should have it fixed."

Gold-Tipped Smith was as formally dressed as he had been that first they had met at the library, except now there was no flower in his buttonhole.

"What's the Travelstar Foundation?" Sim asked.

"I'm afraid it's not much, yet. As you can see." Mr. Smith indicated the meagerness of the room's furnishings with a dismissive gesture. "We are still at the research and development stage."

"What kind of research?" Sim persisted.

"Not unlike your own," Mr. Smith said, approaching and placing his hands on the back of the wooden desk chair. "We've been at it longer, of course, as has your friend Dr. Pleever. Not, I might add, without some success. But you know how these things go. Theories that look good one day and fall flat the next. Leads that run you in circles or down blind alleys. It's painstaking work, I'll tell you."

"Am I a part of your research?" Sim asked.

"You are a very direct young man."

"I found your card in my library book," Sim said, producing it from his pocket and laying it on the desk.

"I'm not sure it strikes just the right tone," Mr. Smith said, glancing at the verse. "Fairy tales, adventures, riddles. Things for children."

"So am I?"

"A child?" Mr. Smith said.

"A part of your research."

"It seems that you are," Mr. Smith said, the way one might report the likelihood of bad weather. "The simple facts are that neither of us can achieve his goal without the other." He studied Sim, as if trying to decide how to proceed. Sim waited, curious. He had expected to be a little frightened, but Mr. Smith was more puzzling and amusing than frightening.

"By the way, what have you done to your cheek?"

Sim touched the three threads. "A tree branch," he said.

"Good thing it missed your eye."

"Yes," Sim said, wanting to get on with the conversation.

Smith looked at him with a sympathetic smile. Sim didn't trust it. "Do you remember the stories your mother and father read to you when you were little?" Mr. Smith asked.

"My mother did, sometimes," Sim said.

"Surely she must have read you stories about children who get three wishes and very often make the wrong choices. I've never understood writers persist from one generation to another in making that mistake."

"Why is it a mistake?" Sim asked.

"Well for one thing, it reveals a prejudice that one rarely encounters in real life. How many children do you know who get to decide how things are going to be? The important decisions are left to adults, as they should be. Think about it. Do you want your mother turning to you every time there's something to be decided? Wouldn't that leave you a little anxious, given your limited experience of the world?"

"I guess so," Sim said, a reluctant accomplice in this line of reasoning.

"Oh, I'm quite certain of it. No. Important decisions should definitely be left to adults."

"About things like the medallions?" Sim asked.

"They contain great power, my boy. In the right hands, they could change the world."

And in the wrong hands? Sim wondered. What would they do in Splitface's hands? "You and Splitface are partners, right?" Sim asked.

Smith looked confused for a moment and then laughed, actually threw his head back and laughed. It was a big laugh for a small man. "Oh, my," he said after a moment, "you mustn't call him that to his face. He's very sensitive about his appearance. Splitface! The poetry of children. Wonderful." Then, recovering his composure, he continued in a businesslike way, "But to answer your question. Yes, in a manner of speaking. As much as one can with a barbarian. He came looking for me a little over a year ago. He had read my book on lost legends. Not a great many people have," Mr. Smith said sadly. "I must remember to give you a copy before you leave. I'll inscribe it for you."

"Thanks," Sim said. The conversation wasn't going at all the way he had anticipated.

"One man's legend is another's personal history," Mr. Smith continued. "Kolbrúnarskáld has spent over twenty years looking for the medallions, which you have recently begun to collect with uncanny success."

"That's how long he's been here?" Sim asked.

"Give or take a year or two. Kolbrúnarskáld doesn't keep track of time the way most people do." Mr. Smith paused, considered for a second, and smiled. "That's rather good, if I do say so myself. 'Keeping track of time.' Time-traveling." He looked at Sim. "Yes, well. Where were we?"

"The medallions," Sim said.

"Ah, yes. So what is your secret? X-ray vision or something like that? You must have four or five by this time. I should think it must take at least that many for that disappearing trick you did the other day. "

Sim recalled the face at the window. He wondered what other things Mr. Smith had seen over the past weeks.

Chapter 42

Kolbrúnarskáld

"What was the legend that you wrote about?" Sim asked Gold-Tipped Smith.

"One of them was about the god Starspinner," Mr. Smith said. He looked at Sim and smiled. "You will never be any good at cards if you can't keep a straight face," he said.

"Cards?" Sim asked.

"Your eyes got somewhat larger when I said *Starspinner*. I gather you have heard the name before."

"Dr. Pleever said something about him." Sim said.

"Perhaps he's read my book," Mr. Smith said. Then he considered for a moment. "No, I don't think so. My book was not highly regarded by the scholarly community. In fact, you might as well know that I'm considered something of a quack. But Mr. K. didn't think so."

Gold-Tipped Smith knew about Starspinner, and it was information that Sim needed. On the other hand, there were things that *he* knew and that Mr. Smith probably didn't. Was this what their meeting was all about? A matter of trading information?

"Who is Starspinner?"

"All in good time," Mr. Smith said. He stood up and walked to the other side of his island. "I don't suppose you drink coffee at your age." He poured himself a cup, as if to give Sim time for thought. "I'm sorry I don't have any other beverages."

"It's fine. I'm not thirsty." Mr. Smith was as strange a man as Sim had ever met, but certainly not frightening.

Mr. Smith returned to his seat and leaned back. "As I was saying, Mr. K. had read my book. There's a bit about the Starlight Medallions. Mr. K. had two of them with him. I was, to say the least, interested. Finding evidence for the truth of legends has been my life's work."

Sim had to set his jaw to keep from smiling. The expression "life's work" hardly seemed appropriate to someone not many years older than he.

Smith continued: "He showed me that little trick that the medallions do when more than one of them is present."

"It's called synchronicity," Sim said, instructively.

"Is that right? Synchronicity. I'll have to make a note of that."

Smith seemed amused.

Mr. Smith was making fun of him. Sim had tried to show off and botched it. It was to recover his pride that he continued, sorry even as he heard the words leave his lips: "For most people, it takes two," Sim began. "I can do it with one. It's because the medallions are looking for me."

"Are they now?" Mr. Smith said.

Sim felt the blood rise in his cheeks. He was not as clever at this game as he had thought. He needed to get the conversation back to Splitface. "You were telling about how Splitface came to visit you."

"Right." Sim could almost hear the wheels spinning in Mr. Smith's head. He looked at Sim but his gaze was inward, his eyes unfocused. Then he blinked and continued. "Yes, well, I listened to his story." Mr. Smith leaned back in his chair. "Mr. K. was a shaman," he began. "You're sure you don't want to sit down?"

"I'm fine," Sim said.

"Very well. Do you know what a shaman is?"

Sim had thought of asking Dr. Pleever that question after the lecture but he had forgotten to. He shook his head

"A magician, medicine man, fortune-teller. Every society has them," Mr. Smith instructed.

"Like a *dukun*," Sim said.

"Not a term I've heard," Smith admitted.

"Indonesia," Sim said.

"I must look into that," Mr. Smith said, as if he meant it. Then he continued with his story. "Mr. K. was in what we would now call Norway. Near the Arctic Circle. Every village had a shaman back then, doing the same tricks that had come down for generations: predicting an eclipse, taking credit for an April shower or a good catch. One day, a boy showed up in the village. He was about your age I gather. It seems there had been a meteor shower the night before, so his appearance was taken as a good sign. The boy could say nothing about where he had come from, who his parents were, or anything else that might have identified him. Today we would probably ascribe this to some kind of post-traumatic stress syndrome."

Smith finished his coffee and continued. "The villagers, with little encouragement from Mr. K., applied a more poetic interpretation. The boy's voyage to the village had been celestial, they concluded. He was a child of the gods, or perhaps an incarnation of one of them. Partly it was his coat. Not unlike coats of the times, I gather. Or, for that matter, of our own times among the Sámi." Mr. Smith had been arranging the several objects on his desk in a pattern as he spoke. "The Lap. You have heard of Lapland."

"Yes. They herd reindeer."

"They are actually called the Sámi."

"Oh."

"The difference in the boy's coat was its embroidery. Very fine. Lots of decorations. It alone would have made him stand out."

"I've seen it," Sim said.

"I beg your pardon?"

"The coat. I've seen the coat."

Smith's jaw dropped. "You've seen the coat?" He said it as if he were speaking each word for the first time. "Where?"

"All in good time," Sim said. He felt pleased with himself. He was beginning to get the hang of it.

"Yes, well. Seen the coat." Mr. Smith mumbled to himself as he walked once again to the coffeepot. When he returned, he appeared to have regained his composure. "Well, well, well," he said.

"What about the boy?" Sim asked.

"Ah, yes, the boy, Mr. Smith continued. "Well, Mr. K. realized that the boy was pure gold. You have to understand that Mr. K. was a bit of a hustler. He could have sold an elephant to a fisherman if there had been any elephants around to sell. The villagers had decided the boy was magic; it only remained for Mr. K. to put that magic to work, and the money or whatever they used for barter would start rolling in. Mr. K.'s intention was to make the boy a kind of child oracle. It was all hocus-pocus of course." Mr. Smith chuckled to himself. Sim noticed Gold-Tipped Smith had a way of being his own audience. He could imagine his host in the room all alone carrying on the same conversation.

"Imagine Mr K.'s surprise the first time the boy did his disappearing act."

Sim looked puzzled. "Did my fa.... I mean did the boy have the medallions?"

"Oh, yes. But neither he nor Mr. K. knew it at the time. I'll come back to that." Mr. Smith gathered his thoughts for a second and continued. "So the boy does his disappearing act. You have to understand that no one is more skeptical of magic than a magician. He knows it's all sleight of hand, so imagine his surprise. One night, he wakes up and sees the boy standing in the middle of the hut, his arms crossed upon his chest and his eyes closed as if he were communing with spirits. What's all this about? Mr. K. says to himself. He doesn't disturb the boy. And then the boy disappears. Just vanishes right before Mr. K.'s eyes. Well, we know all about disappearing, don't we?" Mr. Smith said with a wink. "Of course. Mr. K. has no idea what is happening. He walks over to where the boy was standing and explores with his hands. Carefully. Nothing. Where has the boy gone?"

Gold-Tipped Smith, who had talked a blue streak for the last five minutes, became silent. The question hung in the air. Smith looked at his folded hands and then raised his eyes to meet Sim's. Sim smiled. Yes, he was beginning to understand how this game was played. Then Mr. Smith spoke again.

"This story is getting very long, isn't it?"

"That's all right," Sim said. "What happened next?"

"Well, needless to say, the boy came back. He walked through the door of the hut. He could not say where he had been. He had opened his eyes on the same landscape in which he had closed them, but there was no hut, no shaman, and no village. There was only the night sky. The boy had stared at it and it seemed to him that he had seen the stars move.

"So what about the medallions? Sim asked. "You said he didn't know he had them."

"They were in the coat. Sewn in the lining. But if I may proceed with my story."

So Greta was right, Sim thought. Of course they would have been in the coat. He nodded.

"Under Mr. K.'s guidance, the boy learned to navigate – not the best word, but it will do – these time journeys as he called them. By the way, what do you call them?"

Sim thought for a moment. What did he call them? Time-shifting? Time-traveling? Alex had called it double-timing. He realized he hadn't actually settled on an expression. "Time-skipping," he said, so as not to appear wishy-washy.

"Time-skipping," Gold-Tipped Smith repeated. "How apt. Who would have thought. My goodness. It's all quite remarkable. Skipping!"

"What is?" Sim asked.

"Later, later," Mr. Smith said. "Well, the boy got the medallions somewhat under control. He reported to Mr. K. things that he had observed happening weeks, months or years earlier in the village. Things lost were suddenly found. Petty crimes were revealed. Perhaps you've heard of the word *blackmail*."

Sim nodded. He thought of Denny Dumont. "You learn things about people and then make them give you money to keep quiet," he said.

"What a clever boy you are," Mr. Smith said.

"Why did the boy let himself be used like that?" Sim asked, ignoring Mr. Smith's sarcasm.

"Probably he was frightened. Mr. K. had appointed himself the boy's guardian. If we are to believe K., the boy had no past that he could recall. He had no place to go, no one else to turn to. He became Mr. K.'s property. And the medallions as well. Mr. K wanted to be sure that his precious boy didn't wander off into a more friendly time. He re-did the lining of the coat so that the medallions could be removed, returning them to the coat when he wanted the boy to do his time trick."

Sim recalled the scene on the beach, his father taking off the coat and handing it to Splitface. How he himself had felt a chill, how his father had hugged himself, how their eyes had locked.

"It was a small village," Mr. Smith continued. "Mr. K. was ambitious. He decided to buy a ship, hire a crew, and go in search of treasure. If the treasure were buried in a city overtaken by vegetation, the boy would be able to find it by traveling to the past. There were stories drifting back of a new world across the ocean and of cities of gold. He bought The Midnight Sun."

"What is that?"

"The name of the ship sitting out there in the harbor."

"The Midnight Sun," Sim repeated. Of course, the ship would have a magical name.

"There was never a shortage of willing seamen," Gold-Tipped Smith continued, "as long as there was a promise of treasure. And there was such a promise."

So Nathaniel was right, Sim thought. It was a treasure hunt after all. It's he who should be here, and not me. In a way he is, I suppose. He smiled at the thought.

"What are you smiling at?" Mr. Smith asked.

"Oh, just the idea of buried treasure," Sim said.

"And pirates, and Peter Pan," Mr. Smith said dismissively.

Sim looked at him soberly. "And boys who die of broken hearts," he said.

Chapter 43

A Tomahawk

Mr. Gold-Tipped Smith looked puzzled and somewhat taken aback by the sudden change of tone. Sim had surprised himself as well with his last remark. Nathaniel Chit had been on his mind since the evening before, when he had discovered his gravestone in the Parish Church cemetery. It made him sad to think of the boy and of Hazel's loneliness those many years ago. And there was more. It wasn't only of Nathaniel that he had just spoken, he realized. It was of himself as well. For surely, if all that must happen in the next few days did not, then he would fail in the task his father had set for him. He would never see his father. That would break his heart. He shook these thoughts aside and looked at Gold-Tipped Smith. "They came to Lost River Cove," Sim said.

Apparently glad to have the conversation back on a more matter-of-fact footing, Mr. Smith continued. "Yes," he said. "The ship arrived in Lost River Cove about a thousand years ago, give or take. As Mr. K. tells the story, they set up camp in a cave and then he, the boy, and several members of the crew set off on a reconnaissance expedition. There were several in the months following, without much result, and then one day they traveled farther afield and came upon a village of natives. Probably Moratiggon. It's thought they had an encampment in this area."

"Communication, as you can imagine, was something of a problem," Mr. Smith continued. "Relations became strained, one assumes. Mr. K. tells it from his point of view, of course. He apparently made some enemies, or at least one. A rival shaman. They called them medicine men. Got a tomahawk in the head."

Smith punched out the last phrase and looked at Sim. "Right between the eyes, so to speak. Next thing Mr. K. knows he's in a hospital bed in what is now Newburyport, Massachusetts, and it's 1978 or thereabouts."

"The boy took him there," Sim concluded. "Into the future."

"Right on the money," Mr. Smith said.

"But why...," Sim began.

"Not why. How!" Mr. Smith corrected, in an entirely new voice. His eyes blazed. Sim almost took a step back. "The future, boy! The future. He had never traveled to the future before. Don't you see?"

Sim was confused. It was the *why* that puzzled him, not the *how*. Why would his father have wanted to save the man who had enslaved and abused him? He touched his cheek and thought once again of the pike with the steel tip. There was something he didn't know. Something he didn't understand. It wasn't something that Gold-Tipped Smith was going to be able to help him with. As to his father traveling into the future, what was the marvel in that? No, much more important than the direction of travel was that you could take someone with you. Could he bring his father back with him? Would he want to come?

He hadn't heard a thing Gold-Tipped Smith had said for the last minute, stunned as he was with these new revelations. Now he looked at Mr. Smith, who was waving his arms and repeating, "the future! Think of it, boy! The possibilities. The fortunes to be made!"

"That's what you want, isn't it?" Sim asked, with a studied calmness. "That's the Travelstar Foundation."

Smith regained his composure as quickly as he had lost it, with a long clearing of his throat and after pouring yet another cup of coffee, he continued with his story.

"They fixed him up," he began. "Not the best example of plastic surgery that I've ever seen, and I don't think the experience did much for Mr. K.'s disposition. It took awhile as you can imagine. About a year, I gather. Time enough for our Viking shaman to begin learning the language of the land he had set out to plunder."

"And?"

"They put him in a psychiatric hospital."

"What happened to the medallions?"

"Ah, yes. The medallions. Well, there are several possibilities. It's unlikely the boy stayed around after delivering our friend to the hospital. But who knows? He might have found the twentieth century somewhat more interesting than his own. That was Mr. K.'s guess. He spent a year looking for him. Inquiring of anybody in the vicinity of the hospital who might have seen him. No luck."

"So the boy went back to the ship."

"That would be my guess. Back to his own people."

"But the medallions got lost. How would he have let them get lost?"

"I've no idea. If I had to guess, it would be that the natives whom Mr.K. had offended in his search for the buried city of gold came after them. He had done some tricks for them, some of his shaman carnival acts and shown off the medallions. Risky and stupid, of course, but Mr. K. is above all things a showman."

"So you think they took them from the boy."

"That would be my guess. They couldn't make them do any magic, of course. I suspect they got passed around for a few generaltions and gradually lost."

"How many medallions does Splitface have?" Sim asked.

"You are a very direct...."

"...young man. Yes, you said that before," Sim retorted.

"Two. Now."

"Including the one Mr. Dumont stole from the library?"

"A very stupid thing to do, by the way. But yes, including that one." said Smith.

"And you?" Sim asked.

"Quid pro quo."

"What does that mean?"

"You tell me, I'll tell you."

"Four."

"Four?"

"Four."

"You did that disappearing trick with only four?"

"How many do you have?" asked Sim.

"One. Mr. K. and I made a trade. My knowledge for one of his medallions."

Mr. Smith paused and looked at Sim, a twinkle in his eyes. "Who knows, if all the medallions were together again, what surprises there might be. If we could just find a way of sharing our...." He paused, as if searching for the right word. "Experiences."

Sim picked up Mr. Smith's card from the desk and read the verse aloud:

The Starlight Medallions number nine
Some are yours and some are mine.
Eight encircle the ninth in a round
Powerless till the lykill's found.

"What is the lykill?" Sim asked. Mr. Smith was leaning back in his chair, his hands folded neatly in his lap, smiling. "Sure you don't want to sit down?" he asked again.

"I'm fine," Sim said.

"Very well. You recall my telling you that Mr. K. had sought me out because of a little book I had written."

Sim nodded. Mr. Smith got up and walked back to the desk at which he had stood when Sim first entered the room. He rummaged among a pile of books, chose one and returned, holding it up. "This book. He held it up so that Sim could read the title: *Forgotten Legends, Unforgettable Gods: Stories from Behind the Northern Lights*. Mr. Smith leafed through the book, humming to himself. "Mmmm. *... asked the greatest of the dwarf artisans, Brokk, son of Ivaldi, a superb smith and jeweler, to fashion nine medallions from the ores and jewels of Asgard to represent the procession of the stars and as a gateway into time past.* Ah, here it is: *He himself fashioned a stone from the Northern Lights as a gateway to the future. To it the others would respond, for it was indeed the lykill,* "The word is from ancient Norse. It means *keystone*," Mr. Smith explained.

"Did the boy have that as well?" Sim asked.

"Until I read him that passage, Mr. K. had never heard of a lykill. It was the boy's secret. Without it the medallions would have been useless."

"But how could he have it without Splitface knowing?" Sim asked.

"Good question. Very good question. I asked Mr. K. to tell me more about the lad, looking for a clue. There was one. A rather promising one, though my theory is only conjecture. I suspect the boy was no dunce. In fact, the lad was quite shrewd as well as extraordinary. But at heart he was just a boy and he loved the things that boys love."

"Like what?"

"Like skipping stones," his host said.

Sim felt his legs go rubbery and the color drain from his face.

"Is something wrong?" Gold-Tipped Smith asked.

"Maybe that chair," Sim said.

Mr. Smith hurried around his desk carrying a folding chair. He opened it. "Feeling a little faint?"

"It's just that I've been standing for a while," Sim said.

Smith seemed sincerely concerned. He walked back to the coffeepot. There was a water cooler beside it. He poured a cup of water into a paper cup and handed it to Sim.

"Thanks," Sim said, taking a sip. It was cold. A picture had appeared in his mind – of Splitface on the grounf in the graveyard poking among the leaves for the handful of skipping stones Sim had tossed on the ground.

"Shall I continue?"

"Please," Sim said. It was all becoming very polite, Sim thought.

"According to Mr. K., the boy never missed a chance to pick up a flat stone. He had an eye for them. He had a small leather pouch. Had it when he showed up at the village. He'd compete with the village boys. No one could beat him."

"What does that have to do with the lykill?" Sim asked.

"My guess is that it looked very much like a skipping stone. It certainly would have had other properties, but not to the eye of the common observer. I suspect the boy kept it among his skipping stones. They provided camouflage, as it were. It was one stone among several. Mr. K. would have attached no significance to the boy's fascination with flat stones. As we know, he thought the medallions were sufficient for the boy's magic. He wasn't looking for the lykill. And it makes sense. We have to imagine that Mr. K. had tried to use the medallions himself. They didn't work for him. He thought it was the coat, but of course it didn't fit him. When I read him the legend, he was quite excited.

It wasn't the coat. It was the lykill. If only he could get the lykill, he could be master of the Starlight Medallions."

Gold-Tipped Smith continued talking, but Sim heard nothing of what he said. It was as if someone had opened a dusty window in a closed and quiet room. Sudden brightness, a rush of wind and the sea pounding on rocks. Or was it the pounding of his own heart? He put his hand behind the bib of his overalls and felt his lucky stone, the lykill stone. Why had it taken him so long? It was so obvious. The ant crawling on his chest. The only thing he had of his father's. The most important thing. Everything suddenly made sense. The adventure had stopped when Denny had the stone. Of course. The stone. His lucky stone. That was what his mother had heard his father say. Lucky. But his father spoke no English. Lykill, he had said. Lucky she had heard.

"Are you all right, young man?" Mr. Smith was saying.

Sim looked at him. "Yes," he said, "I'm fine."

"You look a little peaked."

"No, really."

"Well," Mr. Smith said, opening the book. "This may be useful to you. Perhaps after you have read it, we might talk again." He withdrew a fountain pen from the inner pocket of his jacket and wrote a few words inside the cover. He handed the book to Sim. "I think you will find Chapter 45 of particular interest."

Sim examined the table of contents. Starspinner?" he asked.

"Yes. And read it sooner rather than later. Our ancient Viking friend is impatient. He seems to be aging. His squash seems to be buckling." Mr. Smith chuckled to himself. "Not bad. Not bad."

"I don't get it," Sim said.

"Squashbuckling. Pirates."

"I thought you said Splitface was a shaman."

"Shaman, magician, vaudevillian, pirate. Humor requires a certain latitude of attitude, boy."

Sim shook his head, opened the book, and read the inscription. *To Simen. Safe travels. Best wishes, Adrian A. Smith.* "It's Simeon," he corrected. "but thank you. "

Smith smiled. "Names change over time," he said. Then he folded his hands and looked up in a way that reminded Sim of Walter. The expression that said, "how about a little gravy on the kibbles." His eyes softened into an almost winning smile. "I have emptied my treasure," he continued, opening his hands before him. "Have you nothing to offer in return for all you have learned this afternoon?"

Sim thought for a moment and then smiled. He reached into the pocket of his overalls, removed four nearly perfect, grey skipping stones, and tipped them onto Mr. Smith's desk. Mr. Smith stared at them without speaking. Then he looked up. He smiled. "Of course," he said.

Chapter 44

Behind The Northern Lights

Forty minutes from the time he had entered the McCrory Building, Sim emerged, closed the door behind him and looked once again at the newly installed sign. Did Gold-Tipped Smith really expect to offer travel vacations to the future? It didn't make sense, but then not much had for the last few weeks.

If Dr. Pleever's theory was correct, if his father had come to the future twelve years ago so that Sim might be born to retrieve the medallions, why? Not simply so that Sim could travel to wherever his father was. If it was just their being together, he could simply have stayed around for the past 11 years the way fathers are supposed to do. No, there was more to it. His father needed both him and the medallions for some purpose. There was something else, something his peculiar host had held back. "I have emptied my treasure," Mr. Smith had said. Not quite, Sim thought, nor would he have expected him to.

The twins emerged from the sweet shop seconds after Sim closed the door of the Travelstar Foundation. They crossed to where Sim stood.

"Well?" Alex inquired.

"You were right," Sim said.

Alex looked puzzled.

"When you wondered if he was opening up a time travel agency."

"You're not serious," Alex said.

"I don't know," Sim said. "He's a really strange man. I mean *really* strange." They walked around the side of the building to where Greta stood patiently leaning against the railing, her fishing pole crooked under her arm, watching the clam that dangled from the end of her hook three feet under the water.

"I hope you guys had more luck than I did," she said, as they approached. "I didn't see a single fish." She cranked in her line, removed the clam, and seated the hook in the cork handle. "Well?" she asked.

"Let's go up to the Oracle Stone," Sim said. "I think we need a place where nobody's going to be around. He glanced up at the window at which Gold-Tipped Smith had stood watching him the previous day. Perhaps he was standing out of sight watching them. Sim hoped so. He was glad to be with his friends. They looked out for one another. He wondered whether anyone looked out for Mr. Smith.

"What's the book?" Alex asked.

"Gold-Tipped Smith gave it to me," Sim said. "He wrote it." He handed the book to Alex.

"*Forgotten Legends, Unforgettable Gods: Stories from Behind the Northern Lights*," Alex read. "It might be pretty good. How come he gave it to you?"

"There's a story in here about Starspinner," Sim said.

"He knows about Starspinner?" Amanda asked.

"I think he knows a lot about Starspinner," Sim said.

They went to the Oracle Stone as Sim had suggested. It wasn't a bad place to be if you wanted to catch the afternoon sun. It was October and the days were getting shorter. When they were seated, he took the lykill out from beneath his shirt and the two skipping stones that remained in his pants pocket, and laid them on the Oracle Stone. Apart from the fact that it had been pierced so that he could wear it around his neck, the lykill looked very much like the skipping stones next to it.

"So?" Alex asked.

Sim told them the story Gold-Tipped Smith had told him about his father being a stone skipper and hiding the lykill in his pouch of stones. He wanted to add that his father had been the best stone-skipper in the village but decided it would sound like building himself up.

"Powerless till the lykill's found," Greta recited. "So you've had it all along. That explains why you could feel the resonance when you had only one medallion."

"It explains lots of things," Sim said, "like why it was the one thing my father left for me."

"And why Splitface went crawling around on the ground looking at the stones you tossed out," Amanda added.

"And when Denny had it, everything stopped happening," Alex said.

"I just can't believe I didn't figure it out before this," Sim said.

"Well, none of us did," Greta said. "Mr. Smith's verse didn't say lykill stone. It said lykill. It could have been anything."

"So why does Smith want the medallions?" Alex asked. "Is that what Travelstar is all about?"

"He never really said," Sim responded. "He talked about their having great power and how adults ought to make decisions. He says we need one another."

"Right," Alex said, "like a hole in the head."

"Did he say why Splitface wants them?" Amanda asked.

Sim shook his head.

"Maybe he wants to settle up with those guys who put the tomahawk in his head," Alex suggested. "You couldn't blame him for that."

"Maybe," Amanda said, "but I'll bet he just wants to go back to his own time."

"He'd really be crazy if he wanted to do that," Alex said. "No cars, no TV. They didn't even have toilets back then."

"I don't think Hazel would mind going back a hundred years," Greta said. "She's not all that impressed with modern things."

Sim put the lykill stone back around his neck. "Gold-Tipped Smith says he and Splitface have a partnership." He thought for a moment and corrected himself. "No, he said that Splitface thought they did. Almost like he was putting one over on him."

"What I don't get," Alex said, "Is why your father brought Splitface into the future if he was such a jerk."

"Maybe because he didn't have anybody else," Amanda suggested. "Or maybe he was just a very unusual person." Sim knew she was looking at him as she spoke, but he didn't look up.

"We've got to get going," Alex said, jumping down from the Oracle Stone. "If we don't feed the animals on time today we get grounded."

"Me too," Sim said. "Walter is getting pretty confused by all of this too."

"I think this is the first time ever that I'm the one who didn't have to go home first," Greta said. "So what's the plan for tomorrow?"

Sim thumbed through the book quickly. "I'll know after I've read this," Sim said, holding it up.

They climbed down from the stone and, without any further conversation, went their separate ways.

Walter was waiting for Sim on the porch and greeted him with more affection than Sim felt he deserved, having been of late a little neglectful. But Walter was a forgiving creature. Sim found a little bit of left over ground beef and added it to Walter's dish.

There was a note on the table from his mother reminding him that she had a catering event, and would not be home until after ten. His dinner was on a plate in the refrigerator. He should microwave it for exactly four minutes, the note instructed. There were peanut butter cookies in the cookie jar.

He had left his homework, as usual, till the end of the weekend. It took him about an hour. When he had finished, he realized what an eventful day it had been and welcomed the idea of going to bed a little early. There wouldn't be many more nights when he could sleep up on the widow's walk, and he wanted to make the most of them. He hauled his bedroll up the stairs and then, remembering Gold-Tipped Smith's book, retrieved it, along with his flashlight. Snuggling into his sleeping bag, and using Walter as a pillow, he turned on his flashlight and opened the book. There were about fifty legends in the table of contents. He opened the book to *Chapter 45: Starspinner*.

Chapter 45

Starspinner

Once long ago in the northern lands there was a boy named Simen. He lived with his father and mother in a small fishing village. His mother sewed their clothes and his father fished from his small boat. They had a vegetable garden that Simen tended. Simen's eyes were blue like his mother's and his hair the same flaxen gold. But he looked nothing like his father, who had come from the South and who was dark. It was said by some that the man with the fishing boat was not Simen's father at all, but no one said that to the man's face, for he was powerful and his temper was easily stirred.

Simen loved the stars, and when the moon was dark and the stars were brightest, he would lie wrapped in his bedding by the forest's edge, animating the heavens with stories he made up. It was a good and simple life and on his eleventh birthday Simen had much to be thankful for. But it is the lot of mankind that for each measure of happiness apportioned by the gods, there is an equal measure of sorrow that – like water hidden in the crevices of rock – one day freezes and shatters what seemed unbreakable and timeless.

So it was that one moonless night, raiders from the South landed their ships, and with torches shattering the soft starlight, set ablaze the homes of the villagers. They took such livestock as would fit in their boats and killed the rest. Some villagers were fortunate enough to escape into the forest, as had their ancestors on occasions in the past, emerging days later to bury the dead and rebuild their homes. Others, including Simen's parents, were not so fortunate. They either died in the fires or were taken as slaves by the raiders.

Simen watched helplessly, wrapped in his blanket, tears running down his cheeks as his own home burned.

There now came from out of the night behind him a great wolf whose eyes glowed like stars. The wolf stood beside him, and, when one of the raiders approached with his torch, bared his teeth and growled so deeply that the earth seemed to shake beneath them. The man took a step toward them holding out his torch to frighten the wolf, but the wolf howled and the torch went out. The wolf howled again and other torches were extinguished. He howled a third time and every flame expired. Now the men were very frightened, for they knew they were in the presence of a god, perhaps even Fenir himself.

They went quickly to their ships and put out to sea. The wolf approached Simen and nuzzled his hand, then turned again and walked away. Simen understood that he was to follow and he did. He grasped the fur at the back of the wolf's neck and walked close beside him. They walked northward for many hours, and when Simen was too tired to walk any farther, he rode upon the wolf's back. The wolf carried him to the back of the north wind, behind the curtain that is called the Northern Lights and in whose folds all times are as one, to a land called Hyperborean.

They came to a field of soft and fragrant grasses by a crystalline lake. Simen walked among the grasses and along the shore of the lake, wiping the tears from his face, wondering at the strangeness of it all. He picked up a stone and skipped it across the water where the night sky was reflected. Then he lay on the grass and looked at the stars, in hope that they might comfort him. He had never seen so many nor felt that they were so close. A curtain of colored light danced around him, and he fell asleep.

Some say that the gods made the stars. One legend has it that Odin once threw the eyes of the giant and shape-shifter, Thjatsi, into the sky after he kidnapped Idunn. Some say the stars belonged to the Danish king, who fashioned them from gold in a great mill. Still others say that it was Rida Stjarna who speckled the night with light, each star a stone skipped across the celestial sea. It was he, some say, who created the constellations to amuse men and tease their imaginations. This great work he signed with his own image.

Rida Stjarna was also called Starspinner. He stayed aloof from the struggles at Odin's palace, which was called Valhalla. He lived behind the north wind and fashioned for himself a curtain of light called the Northern Lights. There he was content to contemplate and continue his work, for the heavens are forever being made anew. Some say that he was the oldest of all the gods and also the youngest. Now and then he would be visited by a child, for only children can travel behind the Northern Lights to the land of Hyperborean. When the child grew older, he would not remember that visit, for he or she would have achieved what adults call common sense, and common sense knows that no such place as Hyperborean could exist and that Starspinner himself was but a legend.

Rida Stjarna was the keeper not only of the stars but of time itself. He asked the greatest of the dwarf artisans, Brokk, son of Ivaldi, a superb smith and jeweler, to fashion nine medallions from the ores and jewels of Asgard to represent the procession of the stars and as a gateway into time past. He himself fashioned a stone from the

Northern Lights as a gateway to the future. Because it controlled the others, he called it the lykill.

When the giants who had built Odin's palace demanded payment, Odin sent his messengers out among the gods to gather together all the treasure that could be found. Knowing that these collectors would come for the medallions, which already had become legendary, Starspinner devised a strategy for their protection. He wove a coat of the kind worn by the mortals of the north, a colorful coat of which its owner would take great care. He made it to fit a child, and in its lining he sewed the nine medallions.

As everyone knows, the gods often visited the underlands, taking the form of a mortal and, through some act, redirecting the affairs of men when they went awry. Often they slept with a mortal woman who would later conceive a child. The child, being half god and half mortal, could do the god a service that an ordinary mortal could not. Starspinner, being master of the stars and therefore of time itself, knew always what was past, passing, and to come; and it was with this foresight that he had fathered the boy, Simen, who now slept in the fragrant grasses behind the Northern Lights.

Anyone who has ever seen a gull perfectly still in the air while the clouds rolled above and the sea crashed below, as if free from the currents of time, will understand why Starspinner had chosen the gull as his form in the world of mortals. And so, when the boy awoke, it was not the boy-god Starspinner, in his radiance he beheld, but instead a lowly gull, its head cocked slightly to one side. In the grass lay a coat. Simen looked at it with wonder and then searched the vast plain for its owner. Who could he offend by trying it on, he asked himself; and, being able to imagine no answer, he picked it up. As he did, a perfect skipping stone fell to the ground. He retrieved it, holding it in is hand. Waves of light washed down its surface. Slipping it into his pocket, he put on the coat and as he did, a wonderful feeling swept through him, of being embraced and protected as if the coat were a living thing. A shiver of joy ran down his spine, and he hugged himself for pure gladness. As he did, the gull rose in the air. He watched it as it circled higher and higher and disappeared into the sun. Then he heard the sea crashing upon the shore and realized he was once again at the forest edge by his village, where people went about their daily tasks.

The village was as it had been the day before. Had it all been a dream? Simen walked to his home, but even as he approached, he heard his own voice and the voice of his mother. He entered and saw them having their morning meal, his father already out in his fishing boat casting his nets. He spoke, but his voice made no sound. He walked to the table and stood at his mother's side. He put his hand upon hers, and, for a moment she paused in what she was saying, but then, shaking her head, continued.

It was very strange, because it was of such recent memory that he knew each word that would be spoken. Simen did not understand why this was happening to him, but he was glad to see his mother again and to be able to put this picture of her in his mind.

Knowing what it would mean to him to see his mother again, Starspinner had given him this gift.

Simen realized that he could not stay, for staying would mean watching helplessly as the day unfolded and disaster drew near. He stepped outside. A gull sat on a rock opposite. He looked at it and spoke. "Take me away," he said.

Sim put the book aside and lay there staring at the stars. If Sim's father was a Viking who had lived a thousand years ago, at least he was a man of flesh and blood. And if Splitface had been transported to Sim's own time with a hatchet in his head, at least it was a real hatchet and, however disagreeable, a real head. But here was a story of gods who took on the shapes of wolves and gulls, who had lived for perhaps thousands of years, who inhabited places behind the north wind and the Northern Lights. Still, for all of its strangeness, there was something in the story that felt very real to Sim. It was the cottage: the boy and his mother at the table. It was almost as if he had been there before. It was the same feeling he had had that first time in the cave.

Sim picked up the book again and looked at the inscription. "To Simen. Safe travels. Best wishes, Adrian A. Smith." Sim had corrected him. "Names change over time," Gold-Tipped Smith had said.

Sim looked at the sky. Orion, his sword drawn, stood above the horizon to the east. He closed his eyes.

Chapter 46

The Runaway

Sunday and Monday were without incident except that Twist and Shout, the Pomeroys' pet anacondas, were on the loose again, and the lady who did the Pomeroys' laundry refused to enter the house until they were found.

The big news came on Tuesday. Fred Dumont was out of jail. Mr. Pomeroy had announced it at breakfast and the twins dutifully reported to Sim and Greta at recess. Sim looked around the playground trying to spot Denny, but he could not. He kept his worried thoughts to himself.

Amanda asked Sim about the book that Mr. Smith had given him, and Sim summarized the story. Amanda was enchanted, Alex rolled his eyes, and Greta seemed thoughtful.

Sim met Walter at the regular place after school and they walked home together. It was then that things took an unexpected turn. As soon as Sim closed the gate to 413 Fisher Lane, Walter made a beeline for the small stable behind the house that served now as a garage and toolshed, and started barking. It was a bark more of curiosity than of disapproval, certainly not his Splitface growl.

Sim opened the door cautiously, ready to beat a quick retreat if necessary. Walter trotted up to what had once been a horse's stall and Sim followed. In the corner sitting on a bale of straw, which Sim's mother had bought to keep slugs from eating the strawberries, was a boy, his legs drawn up to his chin, his arms wrapped around them as if they might suddenly, with a mind of their own, take flight.

"Denny?" Sim asked.

"Hi," came the uncharacteristically meek reply.

It was a very different Denny Dumont from the one he had last seen. There was a cut on his right cheek and the area around that eye held promise of an ugly bruise. More startling to Sim than either of these, however, were the tear tracks on his cheeks.

"What happened?" Sim asked.

"I'm running away," Denny said.

It was clear enough from what Sim had already guessed just what Denny was running away from.

"I'm sorry," Sim said.

"Don't be," Denny replied. "I'll make out OK. "

"I mean about the stone," Sim said. "Isn't that why your father beat you up?"

"No. It was because I talked back. Me and my mom had been getting on good with him away. He came back and was just like he had been before. I don't even know what I said. Anyway …."

"Where will you go?" Sim asked

"I don't know yet."

Sim didn't know what to say. In his moment of need, Denny Dumont, the terror of LORCES, had come here. Maybe Denny hoped that Sim really did have magical powers and could make everything OK. Well, he could try. But it wasn't magic that was needed. It was a first-aid kit.

"The first thing we need to do is clean you up," Sim said. "My mom won't be home till after dinner. She's working. C'mon."

Denny followed him out the door and into the house, Walter trailing behind. Sim had never fixed up anyone before, but from time to time he had been the fixee, so it was just a matter of switching roles with Denny in a kitchen chair, the first-aid kit on the table, a washcloth, some swabs, disinfectant, and a Band-aid. Denny wore a lot of faces, most of them designed to frighten or charm. Tear tracks did not figure in any of them. As Sim wiped them away so that he could clean the cut, he felt something to which he could not have given a name.

Denny winced. He was going to have a major black eye. Not much was said. It was just too weird, Sim thought to himself. Here he was time-skipping all over the place, trying to find his father, and Denny was running away from his. Go figure. He thought of suggesting that Denny go to Chief Turnbull and turn his father in. There had to be a law against beating up on children.

"What's that?" Denny asked.

Sim realized that he had absent mindedly reached up to touch his own cheek. Denny had followed his movement. "Ran into a tree branch," he said. No, he thought. I got smacked across the face by a bully, just like you did.

"Stitches?" Denny asked.

"Three," Sim said.

"I need a place to hide out for a few days," Denny said.

It couldn't be here, Sim decided. One more secret from his mother was more than he could have handled. Then he thought of Hazel. Hiding a runaway wouldn't bother her. She'd like the mischief of it. But he felt some responsibility for Hazel and wouldn't have wanted to get her in trouble. Then he thought of the cave. The twins would have a conniption fit. Denny, of all people! Sim breaking the rules of secrecy. But he could think of no alternative, and the idea of hiding out in the cave appealed to his imagination.

"There's this cave," he said.

Halloween was only one day away, and, it provided a good strategy for getting out of town. Children had been out trick-or-treating already now for two nights. There was a Dracula costume that would fit Denny more or less, since it was mostly a cape and a mask with teeth that dripped blood. There was also a skeleton mask from two years back. He'd wear that himself, and then he had an idea. "I'll be right back," he said and went up to his room. When he returned, he looked like a fat ghost. Two shopping bags would look like trick or treat bags. They filled them with provisions for Denny's retreat: peanut butter sandwiches, a box of cereal, several Cokes, a canteen of water, a flashlight, a couple of bananas and some tangerines.

"Do your parents know you weren't at school today?" Sim asked.

"With this?" he pointed to his black eye and the cut on his cheek.

"Right," Sim said, "I was just wondering what they're doing right now."

"Fighting," Denny said, bitterly.

"Oh," Sim said. "What do you think they'll do when they figure out you're not coming back?"

"My dad will come looking for me."

"You don't think he'll tell Chief Turnbull?"

"What do you think?"

"No,"

"No is right."

When they reached Shore Road, they removed their masks and took a rest. It was a lot longer trip without a bicycle. Sim thought it would have been nice to have Walter go along with them so he would not have to walk back alone, but that hadn't been a good idea. What would the point have been in wearing a disguise with Walter walking behind him?

Denny was impressed with the cave. Sim was going to tell him about the secret society and the pledge but thought better of it. Denny didn't realize, until Sim took off his costume, the reason behind it: sheet, blanket, pillow. "We can make you a bed out of leaves," Sim said. Denny stood for a moment looking at the pile of bedding, then together they gathered the leaves. Denny decided he'd sleep just inside the entrance, protected if it should rain, at least until he had a better chance to explore the cave. He assumed that children had done the drawings on the cave wall, as Sim and the companions originally had thought, and Sim didn't contradict him.

Sim had kept an eye peeled for Greywing but saw no sign of him. He was sorry. He would have liked someone to be there to protect Denny. He stayed around for awhile and Denny talked boldly about the adventures he would probably have once he hit the road. Sim wondered, but not very long, why Denny didn't hit the road tonight. Why hang out in a cave? But then he realized the answer. Denny still held on to the hope that things would get better.

I could tell you some stories about traveling, Sim thought but didn't say.

Finally it was getting toward dusk and since they had not thought to bring a second flashlight, Sim thought he should start back. He held out his hand. Denny shook it. "Good luck," Sim said.

"Thanks," Denny replied, and then, indicating the provisions, "Thanks for the stuff."

Sim started away and then turned. Denny was watching him. He looked smaller than he had a few days earlier.

"I'll check up on you," Sim said.

"I'll probably hit the road in a couple of days," Denny said, in a voice he might have been practicing for his new gypsy life. An easy-come, easy-go voice. A cool voice. But he didn't have it down quite yet and that was what Sim heard.

"Well I need to come back for the stuff anyway," Sim said.

"Right,"

"Well."

"Be cool," Denny said.

Sim turned and walked into the woods.

"Hey, Spotswood!"

Sim stopped.

"Thanks."

Chapter 47

Dreamwalking

That night, Sim thought of Denny and his one thin blanket as he hauled his sleeping bag up to the widow's walk. It was definitely getting colder and the air was fragrant the way it is sometimes before a storm. There was a sliver of moon across which clouds skidded, driven by some higher secret wind.

The green lights that Sim had seen a few nights earlier at the edge of the horizon had become brighter now and more colorful. The Northern Lights. *The Lost River Cove Clarion* reported that there had not been such a display for more than eighty years. People could be seen standing outside or sitting in lawn chairs, awaiting their appearance. Children were awakened so they wouldn't miss the event. Sim wasn't the only child in Lost River Cove who was beginning to suffer a little bit from sleep deprivation. Now, as he lay there staring at Sirius, his eyes closed and he slept.

He was in a dark room with a familiar fragrance of bird droppings and the residue of machinery long gone. He knew at once that he was standing on the second floor of the McCrory Building where printing presses had once stood. There was a creak of boards from the floor above, the rolling of a desk chair, the sound of footfalls. And then voices. It had seemed in these dreamwalks that he was invisible to those whom he observed. Still, he was cautious and climbed the stairs halfway to the third level as quietly as he could. There was no need to see them. Neither did he wish to. He sat on the step and listened.

"Time is running out," Kolbrúnarskáld said.

"You don't know that," said Gold-Tipped Smith. "It's pure conjecture. Just more of your superstitious nonsense."

"You've been pretty interested in what you call my superstitious nonsense up until now. How many times have I been mistaken?"

"You really don't want me to run an inventory, surely," Mr. Smith said. "You have been bumbling around for over twenty years with very little to show for it until you sought my advice. And now you're willing to cast it aside and act rashly as you did the other night, risking everything we have worked for."

"Your method is not working," Splitface said. "You coddle and seek to charm the boy with your cleverness. We don't need him; we need the lykill."

"And five more medallions."

"You said he has four."

"And he will find the fifth, given time."

"You are so sure of yourself."

"It seems certain from what we have seen that they are seeking the boy. So, rather than frightening him, we should get out of the way until he finds it or it finds him."

"Is that why you invited him to your office with that silly verse?" Splitface asked in a dry and cynical voice.

"He is a child. I appealed to his imagination. And it worked. He is quite charming. And bright. You have convinced yourself that once you have the medallions and the lykill, you'll be able to go skipping through time the way your boy did. What if you are wrong? What if there's more to it?"

"What more can there be?"

"The coat," said Smith.

"The coat was merely a hiding place for the medallions. It is of no importance."

"And the boy?"

"What about him?"

"How do you explain his collecting in a few weeks more medallions than you have been able to turn up in twenty years?"

"What are you suggesting?"

"I should think it was obvious. You persist in confusing him with the boy who, for some reason I will never understand, saved your life, and yet you dismiss him as unimportant. We need the boy."

"Aren't you forgetting your brilliant discovery, the answer to the riddle? Kolbrúnarskáld reminded. "The lykill. I couldn't make the medallions obey because I didn't have the lykill. It wasn't the boy or the coat or anything other than the lykill. When we have that, we will be masters of the Starlight Medallions."

"The boy says he doesn't have it."

"He lies. He has traveled. You saw him. We are wasting time."

"So why are you here? I thought we had agreed that you would stay in your little cottage until the medallions had all been found."

"My little cottage."

"I think it's brilliantly appropriate."

"Speaking of my little cottage, we know very well where to find the last medallion," Kolbrúnarskáld said.

"We have been through this. That Winifred Chit is 111 years old has nothing to do with the medallions. She has a good gene pool. If the medallion is at Wentworth Hall – and I'm not suggesting that I think it is – then the boy will find it just as he has the others. If you are thinking of paying her a visit I remind you how badly you botched your last such attempt and put this whole plan at risk."

"I got the medallion, didn't I?" Splitface said.

"But the medallion was perfectly safe in the library. We could have had it any time we wanted it. All you accomplished was to focus attention on them. Are you aware that Dr. Pleever has moved into Pomeroy Hall? He would be back in Washington and we would have the boy to ourselves if you hadn't created this little drama. Winifred Chit is no fool. She is a very strong-willed old crone and you might very well come out the worse for an encounter."

"Your concern warms my heart."

"I didn't know you had one. In any case, it's not concern. It's a matter of practical strategy. I tell you the boy will find the medallion."

"I don't have time to wait. I am aging."

"Nine hundred and what is it? Forty-two years. I should think you're doing rather well."

"You misunderstand me. I have only days."

There was a different tone in Kolbrúnarskáld's voice and Smith was silent for a moment, then he spoke with something like concern: "Look, for better or worse, we are in this together. When the boy has the remaining medallion we will acquire it along with his others, if not by my method, then by yours. He is, after all, only a child."

"You talk too much, Smith," Splitface said. "If you were half so dedicated to the plan as you were to the sound of your own voice, time might still be on our side."

"The plan? When have you paid any attention to the plan? Everything you have done has been on impulse. Harassing the old lady is certainly not a part of the plan." Mr. Smith put a particular emphasis on the word *plan*.

As if it had materialized from his imagination, Sim heard a rumbling, the unmistakable sound of distant thunder. Although he could not see a window from where he sat on the stairs, he could see the room brighten with flashes of lightning.

"I think we have nothing more to say to one another," Splitface said. Sim could hear the scraping of a chair as he stood up. There was no sound to indicate that Mr. Smith had paid him the courtesy of rising as well.

"The arrangement we have is not a bad one. Our aims are compatible. And they're not entirely incompatible with those of the boy," Mr. Smith said. "Give me a week. If at the end of that time I've not brought the boy around to our way of thinking, I will leave the field to you. Is that agreeable?"

"I will give you two days with the boy. "

Then Sim realized, to his horror, that Splitface was about to leave the room and there was only one exit. He had been sitting on the fourth step down. Now he stood and pressed himself against the wall as the shaman drew nearer. Splitface descended the stairs, mumbling to himself words that Sim could not understand, perhaps in the same language Sim's father had once spoken. He seemed bent, haggard, and much older. Halfway down the staircase, he hesitated, turned, and looked back up toward the door. Then he shook his head and walked out of sight behind the stairs. Sim continued to listen as Splitface descended to the first floor and then as the door closed behind him.

So he couldn't be seen. Good. He climbed the last five steps to the third floor. It was as he had remembered it – the circle of light within the shadows and cobwebs of the attic like room. Mr. Smith had his back to him, standing at his desk. He opened the top left drawer and took something out. It was a key, Sim realized, as Mr. Smith went to his filing cabinet and inserted it in a small lock at the top. He could hear it snap open. Then Mr. Smith opened the top drawer and withdrew a small purse of the sort that he had seen ladies produce in the grocery store. He removed a medallion from it and held it so that the light caught its gems. Sim wondered which constellation it might be.

Now the thunder was overtaking the flashes that filled the sky at regular intervals. Then there was a crack, as if from a large gun. Sim covered his ears. The lights went out. Then another flash. The medallion glowed in Mr. Smith's hand.

The heavens opened and the rain fell in large loud pelting drops. Sim could feel them. Had the roof blown away? He looked up and the rain pelted his face. Someone was calling to him. He sat up. His mother stood in the doorway below the widow's walk. "Sim, for goodness sake, you're drenched. Come down here," she said. It took only a moment for him to come to his senses. He crawled out of his sleeping bag, sodden already with the downpour, gathered the bag and his pillow, and ran for the staircase. His mother had not thought to bring a towel, but she took off her bathrobe, rubbed his head with it, and then wrapped him up.

"How could you have slept through that?" she asked.

"I was dreaming," he said. "The thunderstorm was in my dream. I didn't know it was real. "

"I think it may be getting a little late in the year for camping out on the widows walk," she said. He got into dry pajamas and crawled gladly into his warm bed. His mother stood there, looking at him, her eyes filled with concern. He wanted so badly to tell her.

"Is everything all right, Sim?" she asked.

He nodded.

"I love you," she said.

"I love you too," he answered.

"Shall I leave the door open?" she asked.

"Please," he said.

He lay there for a while before going back to sleep, thinking of Hazel.

Chapter 48

Protecting Hazel

By the time Sim awoke on Halloween morning, the storm had passed and the day was clear, the air freshly washed and fragrant with fall. Sim lay there, his hands behind his head, studying the ships on his wallpaper. There was now a great deal more to think about, and he tried to put his memories of the past night into some order. The main thing was Hazel. Splitface did as he pleased. That was clear from the conversation he had heard on his dreamwalk. Hazel needed to be warned. She needed to be protected.

If there had been any doubt about his dreamwalking before, there was none now. He had seen Gold-Tipped Smith's medallion.

Did Hazel know about her medallion, or, like so many other things, had she forgotten? But not the promise. She had not forgotten the promise. She had looked at him. "A promise is a promise" she had said. A promise to his father? Maybe the promise was the medallion. And when she had kept her promise, what then? Would she die? Apart from his mother, there were only two other people who had known Sim's father. For that reason alone she had taken on great importance in his world.

When the topic of the thunderstorm came up at breakfast, as it most certainly would, and his mother said that the time for sleeping out had come to an end, he would not know what to say. The stars had become everything to him. And now there were the Northern Lights as well, brighter every night.

When he arrived in the kitchen, his mother was on the telephone, talking to Myra about a catering job. Sim fed Walter and made himself a bowl of Nutritious Nutcake Cereal.

His mother put her hand over the receiver for a moment and turned to him. "Hi Sweetie," she said. "Amanda called. She wanted to know what you were wearing today."

For a moment Sim was baffled, and then he remembered that it was Halloween. Miss Blenden had encouraged the children to wear their costumes to school that day, but Sim suspected not very many would. He and his friends were getting a little old for that kind of thing. Even walking through town with Denny the day before, he had felt a little foolish.

"I'm not doing Halloween this year," he said, walking to the sink, cleaning out his cereal bowl, and putting it in the dishwasher. Fortunately, Myra was waiting on the other end of the line, so there didn't have to be a conversation about not growing up too fast. He walked over and gave his mother a hug. "I've gotta run. See you later. "

"When later?" his mother asked.

He had to think quickly. He didn't really know. "We might be going to visit Hazel," he said. His mother smiled.

"That's sweet," she said. "Tell her I'll be over later in the week."

Arriving at school, Sim was confirmed in his prediction. Only Morty, Conan, Felice and Miss Blenden wore Halloween costumes. Miss Blenden was the Wicked Witch of the West and had a green face. Morty, who took every possible opportunity to look like a policeman, was a policeman. Conan was a leprechaun. It was obviously a costume his mother had made, and a very good one, fitting him in more ways than one. Felice was a hockey goalie, but only very briefly, since the padding in her brother's outfit made it difficult to do anything except stand around looking like the Michelin Tire Man.

There was a midmorning assembly where those who had worn costumes had an opportunity to parade before the rest of the school. Prizes were given for the most original, the scariest, and the funniest costumes. Conan won for the most original, receiving a box of ice-cream sandwiches to be shared with his class.

At the end of the assembly, Alex remarked that Denny was absent again. Sim nodded and said nothing. Now he was keeping secrets from his friends as well as from his mother. It wasn't a good feeling.

After school, as they walked down Threadneedle Street for a hot chocolate at Bartlett's and Sim reported his dreamwalk, Amanda said that if they were the only ones who knew Hazel might be in danger, they had a responsibility to protect her. No one could disagree. They talked about guarding her in shifts, secretly, but realized quickly how impossible that would be. You couldn't just take a day off from school – although Alex thought they should carefully consider that possibility – and you couldn't stay all night. There had to be another way.

Amanda suggested that their parents should invite Hazel to come and stay for awhile . Or if not their parents, then Sim's mother. But the idea that Hazel, after 111 years, would suddenly go visiting people didn't hold up well.

Sim thought about Dr. Pleever. Had his Smithsonian friend been in town, he would have been the perfect person to look after Hazel, but he had returned suddenly to Washington two days ago, and Sim had heard nothing from him.

What about Ponidi?" Greta asked.

"Brilliant," Sim said. "If anybody can deal with Splitface, it's Ponidi. Wizard to Wizard." They agreed that there was no time to waste, so they said goodbye to Homer, got on their bicycles, and headed to Pomeroy Hall.

Chapter 49

Netting The Rhododendron

Not finding Ponidi in the usual places, Alex had the idea of checking out the garage. Ponidi's little Volkswagen was gone. Mrs. Pomeroy was in the garden superintending the netting of the rhododendrons to protect them from foraging deer. Amanda led the procession across the lawn to where her mother and Roger, their gardener, were unrolling the black netting. Alex asked about Ponidi.

"Ponidi is away for the day visiting a friend," his mother answered.

"What friend?" Alex asked impatiently.

"Ponidi *does* have a life of his own, you know," Mrs. Pomeroy replied. "I have no idea what friend and it really isn't any of my business." Mrs. Pomeroy was a very proper woman and very polite, even with her children. She didn't say it was none of their business but that, it seemed to Sim, was what she meant.

They made their way back to the house just as another car was coming up the driveway. Sim didn't have to see the license plate in order to know that it said Washington, D.C. By now he knew the silver Volvo as well as he knew his mother's Toyota – not because he had seen it as frequently but because the driver had become so important to him. Seeing the children, Dr. Pleever stopped and put down the passenger side window. They gathered around, and Sim smiled as he looked at the car's disarray. It was as cluttered as Dr. Hoffner's basement was orderly. And so, for that matter, was Dr. Pleever. Not exactly cluttered, but looking like someone who had returned from a brisk walk on a windy night. His hair wasn't combed, his eyes, which sparkled no less, were now shadowed; and he had not shaved, probably for several days. He leaned across the seat.

"I've been doing some research," he said. Then he looked at Sim. "What happened to you, my boy?" he asked.

"Splitface," Sim said.

"I misjudged him," Dr. Pleever said. "I have been irresponsible. My dear boy, I am so sorry."

"It's more complicated than that," Sim said. "A lot has happened since you went back to Washington. We need to catch you up."

"Climb in," Dr. Pleever said, reaching to open the back door. Sim looked at the pile of boxes and clothing and closed the door. "We'll meet you at the porch," he said.

Sim looked back over his shoulder at Mrs. Pomeroy and Roger as they flew yet another net into the air over a rhododendron. It was the kind of disconnect that he had been experiencing more and more over the past weeks. There was the world of ordinary time and seasonal ceremonies, and then there was the world in which time knew no rules or seasons.

Dr. Pleever awaited them at the door, an over stuffed briefcase under his arm. They followed him up the stairs to the veranda, where he settled himself in one of the rattan chairs, his briefcase in his lap. The companions sat on the grass carpet at his feet.

"I saw *The Midnight Sun* land in Lost River Cove a thousand years ago," Sim began.

"*The Midnight Sun*?" Dr. Pleever repeated.

"That's the name of the Viking ship," Sim explained. "Gold-Tipped Smith told me."

"Gold-Tipped Smith?" Dr. Pleever repeated.

"Oh boy," Sim said, "there really is a lot to tell. I don't know where to start."

"Take your time, my boy," Dr. Pleever said, his face full of care and affection. He reached out and put his hand on Sim's shoulder. It was like a light switch. Sim started to laugh. He couldn't help himself. Everything was upside down, inside out. Take your time? Could you take time or did time take you wherever it wanted whenever it wanted? "Time will tell all," Hazel had said. But what would it finally tell? Then he wasn't laughing at all. He was crying, and he felt Dr. Pleever's hand on his head. He felt Amanda's arm around him. He was surprised not to be embarrassed. He had never cried in front of his friends, only his mother. His mother. She knew none of this. She wouldn't have believed any of it. He realized how alone he had felt.

Then it was over as quickly as it had come on him. Greta had her hankie at the ready. "Thanks," he said.

"You needed that," Alex said.

Only Alex could have said it. It was just the right thing.

"Sorry," Sim said, "it was just when you said 'Take your time.'"

"I can well understand," Dr. Pleever said. "You are a very brave boy, Sim. We are all very proud of you."

Sim took a moment to collect and arrange his thoughts, took a deep breath and began. He related the events of the past two days: his time-skip and seeing the ship land with Splitface and his father. He told about the coat, the wound on his cheek and his second encounter with the shaman in the graveyard. Gradually Greta and the twins joined the narration, adding things that Sim had forgotten or straightening out the sequence of events. Dr. Pleever shook his head in wonder as the story unfolded. Finally,

Sim went to his pack and took out Gold-Tipped Smith's book on legends. Dr. Pleever took the book, opened it to the title page, and smiled. "He spelled your name wrong," he said.

"I know," Sim said. He thought of repeating what Mr. Smith had said about names changing over time but remembered that he hadn't mentioned that part to the twins and Greta. Anyway it wasn't important.

"Your turn," Greta said.

"Well," said Dr. Pleever, "*my* little discoveries are not in the same league with your own, but they might answer a few of the questions we have been asking ourselves. Let's start with your friend Starspinner." He looked at them each in turn. "Do you know what a celestial event is?" he asked.

"Like an eclipse?" Alex suggested.

"Precisely," Dr. Pleever said. "An eclipse, the arrival of a comet, a meteor shower, the close approach of another planet to earth. Some events occur every year. Some are easier to predict than others. The equinoxes, the phases of the moon. Some occur every hundred years or even at greater intervals. Comets, for example. Halley's comet appears only every seventy-six years." He paused and lowered his voice. "Imagine such an event occurring every five hundred or a thousand years. Think how many generations of people would have come and gone. How many societies, for that matter. The very idea of predicting such an event is beyond conception." Dr. Pleever paused.

"But," Alex said, after a moment's silence.

"But," Dr. Pleever repeated, "indeed. Beyond our conception, but not beyond possibility."

"You mean it has happened?" Alex asked.

"Indeed I do," Dr. Pleever said, rubbing his hands together.

"On Sim's birthday," Amanda said.

Chapter 50

A Wormhole

"In so many words, yes," Dr. Pleever said. "Or so it begins to appear. It's quite complicated."

"We can handle it," Alex assured him.

"Well, here it is. Recently a Viking stone tablet was discovered in Iceland. It was about a thousand years old. Usually such tablets have on them a kind of writing."

"Runes," Sim interjected, remembering their earlier conversation.

"Precisely," Dr. Pleever affirmed. "This tablet, however, is different. Intermixed with the runes are markings that resemble your medallions. That is to say, they depict a number of the constellations and open star clusters that would have been familiar to navigators of the Northern Hemisphere."

"Like Vikings," Greta suggested.

"In fact, Vikings," Dr. Pleever responded. "They were marvelous navigators, and we have searched for years for some indication of the methods they used. So finding this tablet was of major importance. The team that studied the designs was able to identify all of the clusters and constellations except one. Needless to say, they published their findings."

"My father does that," Greta said.

"And very important findings they have been," Dr. Pleever assured her. Then he continued. "What happens when such articles appear in journals is that other scientists say, 'My goodness, that's like the thing I saw or the theory that I've been working on.' Well, that happened in this case. Three times. First a man at the British Museum in London matched the unknown open star cluster with a previously unexplained design in an Egyptian burial chamber. Then an archaeologist who works with Sumerian artifacts recognized it, and now it seems that an archaeologist in China has also matched it." Dr. Pleever withdrew a copy *of The Journal of Ancient Scripts* from his briefcase and opened it to reveal two side-by-side photographs. "The one on the left is of the tablet discovered in Iceland," he said. "The one on the right is Egyptian."

Sim studied the drawings carefully. They were even more filled with dots than the medallions and he could find no pattern. He shook his head and looked at Greta. She seemed baffled as well.

"I don't get it," Alex said.

"This might help," Dr. Pleever said, removing a photocopy from his briefcase. It was the drawing that Sim's father had made of Starspinner. They looked at the drawing and then again at the photographs.

"Omigosh!" Sim said. "Look! Here and here and here." He pointed to the largest of the dots in the photographs, which corresponded very closely with the dots his father had made on his drawing.

"Starspinner is a constellation?" Alex asked.

"No," Dr. Pleever said. "It is an open star cluster."

"What's the difference between that and a constellation?" Alex asked.

"The main difference is that all the stars in a cluster are more or less the same age. Like the four of you. Constellations, on the other hand, can be made up of stars of quite different ages. The other thing is that a constellation is always there in the sky because its stars are unvarying. Constant. The interesting thing about an open cluster is that its stars may be variable. By that I mean that they may be visible at one time and not another.

"Celestial event." Alex announced with a flourish.

"Right you are," Dr. Pleever said. "And a very rare one. Unheard of, in fact, that a cluster of this size should be periodic. But science is full of surprises."

"So what are the dates for Starspinner?" Greta asked.

"The newly discovered Icelandic tablet is roughly a thousand years old. The Sumerian about 5,000 years old."

"What about the ones in China and Egypt?" Amanda asked.

"The Chinese discovery was during the Western Han dynasty 2,000 years ago. The Egyptian is about 3,000 years old," Dr. Pleever said.

"So Starspinner shows up every thousand years," Greta ventured. She thought for a moment and then looked quizzically at Dr. Pleever. "It should be there now," she said.

"Yes," Dr. Pleever affirmed. "It should be there right between Ursa Major and Perseus, but it's not."

"Excuse me, Dr. Pleever, but how does anyone know where it should be if no one, I mean no one for a thousand years, has ever seen it," Amanda asked.

"The Icelandic tablet," Greta said. "There were other constellations on it. They were in order. Starspinner was next to Perseus."

"Give the girl ten points," Dr. Pleever said.

Greta looked quickly at Alex. It was almost a look of apology. There was something going on. Ever since that day they discovered the cave. Alex, he knew, would have denied it furiously, but there was no question. He had a thing for Greta and she for him. Sim looked at Amanda. She was his best friend, but that was all. With Alex and Greta, there was more.

"So what happened to it?" Alex asked.

"It's because Starspinner doesn't have the medallions," Amanda announced, as if reporting the time of day.

Alex made his space ship sound and rolled his eyes. "Starspinner is a bunch of stars, Amanda. What did you call it, Dr. Pleever? A cluster. A star cluster. Big rocks."

Sim didn't dismiss Amanda's explanation out of hand, though he was reluctant to support it in front of Dr. Pleever. Instead, he suggested another idea. "What if it's there but we can't see it?" he ventured.

"Excuse me," Alex said, "but how can something be there and not be there?"

Sim put his mind to the riddle. It was a good one. How could something be and not be at the same time? Maybe you had to think of it in a different way. Something could be there but not seen. Like the stars. There they were above you in the sky all day long, but you couldn't see them until it got dark. Or a house. If, on a dark night, there were no lights on, you might not know it was there. But it still would be. "It's there but its lights are out," he said.

"Hello?" Alex said.

Sim explained his idea.

"That may be as close as we will get to an answer right now," Dr. Pleever said, as Alex was about to continue his protest. "Let's speculate that in some sense it is there and see where our reasoning might take us." He settled back in his chair and made a tent with his fingers. "Celestial events have consequence," he began. "When they occur, things change. Just as the moon affects the tides, the movement of one celestial body affects another. Indeed, to go back to Sim's suggestion, scientists often detect an object that they can't actually see, through the behavior of other celestial bodies in the same vicinity."

Sim was lost. So, from the expressions on their faces, he decided, were the twins. Greta, predictably, nodded her head. Dr. Pleever seemed to realize he was losing most of his audience. "Yes, well, that's a lesson for another day," he said briskly. "To the point! We're only beginning to discover the magnitude and variety of the effects that celestial events have on space and time."

"Time. " Sim said.

"Time," Dr. Pleever repeated.

No one spoke for several seconds.

"Sim's time trips," Amanda finally suggested.

"Very possibly," Dr. Pleever replied. "No, I'll go farther than that. Very probably."

"That's what Starspinner does," Greta said slowly, as if unraveling the thought even as she spoke it. "It's a worm hole?"

"A worm hole?" Sim asked.

"It's like a shortcut in time. A sort of time tunnel. Isn't that right, Dr. Pleever?"

"So it seems," Dr. Pleever said. "At least I can find no better explanation."

"How long does Starspinner stay around?" Greta asked.

"Only the Egyptian and Chinese reports record a time span, each different from the other. The Chinese record speaks of twenty-two years, the Egyptian of eighteen. Very little to go on, really, but if I had to make a choice, it would be for the Chinese."

"You said that whatever was going to happen would happen on my birthday," Sim reminded the scientist.

"Actually, I suspect the eve of your birthday, but yes." He reached once more into his briefcase.

"There is something else I have dug up over the past few days that might be of interest." He removed a photocopy of a newspaper, and handed it to Greta. The newspaper was dated October 5, 1978. The clipping was headed "Reincarnation or just Bad Surgery?"

She started reading it aloud: *A man, discovered by a resident on his back lawn and brought by ambulance to Newburyport Hospital was in critical condition from a severe skull wound, apparently from a sharp instrument. Police are investigating what appears to have been an attempted murder and are questioning local residents. Dressed in a primitive costume, the victim was apparently in the area as part of an ethnic or tribal gathering. His identity remains unknown.*" She stopped reading and looked up.

"Splitface," Sim said.

"It fits with the story that Adrian Smith told you," Dr. Pleever said, looking at Sim.

"Twenty-two years," Greta said, having quickly done the math. "The thing they found in China. Twenty-two years. Right?"

"Precisely, my dear," Dr. Pleever affirmed.

"That's when Starspinner was supposed to appear," Sim said, picking up the thread of Greta's reasoning. And he – I mean it – didn't appear because that was exactly the time that the medallions got separated from one another." Careful to avoid Alex's eyes, he continued: "Starspinner needs the medallions so that his constellation – I mean his star cluster – can appear."

"Yes, Alex, you are quite right to roll your eyes," Dr. Pleever said, "but something is at work. All through history, people have attributed to various gods those things in nature that they could not understand. Then science has come along and replaced the god with a scientific explanation. That's a little bit like where we are now. Some day science will make sense of all this, but for the time being, what's the harm in giving credit to Starspinner?"

"You really have to read that legend," Sim said, pointing to the book that now sat on the table by Dr. Pleever's chair.

"I intend to, as soon as we are done here," Dr. Pleever said, putting his hand on the book.

"So Starspinner's medallions got lost and he needs to get them back," Sim continued, now feeling free to speak his imagination as well as his mind. "My father tried to get them but he couldn't and even if he could – this is what it says in Mr. Smith's book – he wouldn't be able to take them back to Starspinner because only kids can go behind the Northern Lights." Amanda was beaming. Alex was writhing in agony, Greta appeared to be keeping an open mind. Sim continued. "So Starspinner waited until my father was old enough to make babies and sent him back to make me."

Alex couldn't stand it any longer. "Without the medallions? They were lost, remember?"

"Starspinner can do anything he wants to," Sim continued. "Anyway, there's still stuff we don't know about the medallions and the lykill. Maybe if you have the lykill, you don't need the medallions. I don't know the answer, Alex. Just hear me out."

Alex nodded.

"OK, other stuff. Splitface. He's suddenly growing old. Time's running out, he says. When the twenty-two years are up and Starspinner closes the time tunnel, Splitface goes up in a puff of smoke."

"What about Gold-Tipped Smith?" Alex asked. "You said he didn't seem very worried. What about his Travelstar Foundation?"

"He doesn't know what we know. He doesn't know about the twenty-two years or the time tunnel." Sim stopped, out of both breath and ideas.

"When does a child stop being a child?" Greta asked. "What if Sim were going to turn thirteen or fourteen, or even ten on November the second? Is it his age or the end of the twenty-two years that make whatever is going to happen, happen?"

"A very interesting question, Greta," Dr. Pleever said. "One that I have been thinking about these past few days myself. My best guess is that this entire series of events, dating back to the discovery of the ship on the day of Sim's birth, is all elegantly timed. Consider: a thousand years ago when the Vikings roamed the seas, people lived shorter lives. There were exceptions, but as a general rule a man of fifty or even forty would have been considered quite old. A man named Geoffrey Chaucer, who wrote a long poem over three hundred years after *The Midnight Sun* landed in Lost River Cove describes a knight... you all know what a knight is, right?"

"King Arthur and the Knights of the Roundtable," Alex said.

"Precisely. Well, Mr. Chaucer tells us that his knight was twelve years old."

"You could be a knight at twelve?" Alex asked in disbelief.

"You had to get an early start on life," Dr. Pleever said. "Carpe diem!"

"Carpe diem?" the four companions repeated in almost perfect unison.

"Latin. It means Seize the day."

"Cool," Sim said, holding up his fist. "Carpe diem!"

"So it wouldn't be happening if Sim was turning thirteen or fourteen?" Greta said.

"I don't think so," Dr. Pleever confirmed.

"And that's why it is happening on the eve of Sim's birthday," Greta continued. "It has to happen while he's still eleven."

"Precisely."

Chapter 51

The Eighth Medallion

"Remarkable," Dr. Pleever said a little later, as he finished the chapter on Starspinner and handed the book back to Sim. "Simply remarkable. And you saw a boy we assume was your father wearing the coat."

"I'm sure it was him," Sim said. "I think he saw me. I looked right into his eyes and he seemed to look into mine. It was like looking into a mirror. except our clothes were different. I wonder what Simen looked like," Sim said thoughtfully.

"Very much like you, I suspect," Dr. Pleever said. "And your father, and that fellow who lives behind the Northern Lights," he added, winking at Alex.

Sim smiled. He wondered whether Dr. Pleever when he was a child had seen a gnome. He wasn't like the other adults Sim knew. Except Ponidi. They gave things a chance, left the door open a crack. His mother had too, once, years ago.

Dr. Pleever had opened the book once again to the chapter on Starspinner. "Lykill." he said. "In ancient Norse, that means keystone." He ran his finger down the page. "*He himself fashioned a stone from the Northern*

Lights as a gateway to the future. Because it controlled the others he called it the lykill."

Sim realized that he had never shown Dr, Pleever Gold-Tipped Smith's verse. Nor had any of them, in the rush to relate the events of the past two days, mentioned Sim's discovery. He took the lykill from around his neck and held it in the palm of his hand.

At first the scientist looked a little confused. Then his eyes widened and he reached to touch it. "Of course," he said.

"His mother thought his father said *lucky*," Alex interjected.

"I've always had it," Sim said. "My father left it on the table in the room where he stayed at Hazel's house." Then, with helpful comments and reminders from his friends, he told Dr. Pleever about how it was the lykill that had made a medallion resonate when there was only one, how a boy at school had stolen and then returned it and how his father had kept it hidden from Splitface among his skipping stones.

"When did your mother give you the lykill? Dr. Pleever asked.

"When I was six," Sim answered.

"So you have worn it for over 5 years without any time-traveling."

Sim nodded.

"Not until you found the first medallion."

"That day when the water got deep."

"This might help explain how your father used the time portal without the medallions. The medallions may be powerless without the lykill but that doesn't mean the lykill is powerless without all of the medallions."

Dr. Pleever looked once again at the legend. Then he read aloud. *"He picked up a stone and skipped it across the water where the night sky was reflected*. And you, Sim," he said, closing the book.

"Yes, me too," Sim said.

"So, Simeon Stone-skipper, what do you recommend we do now?" Dr. Pleever asked.

"Make sure Hazel's safe," Sim answered.

"And get Gold-Tipped Smith's medallion," Alex suggested. "If what you said about Splitface going up in a puff of smoke is true, he's not going to mess around. He'll go after that one as well as Hazel's."

"We can split up," Greta suggested. "Sim, you and Dr. Pleever go see Mr. Smith and the three of us will go up to the cliff to keep an eye out for Splitface."

They looked to Dr. Pleever for approval of the plan. He thought for a moment. "I'm sure Winifred will be glad for your company."

They parted at the foot of the driveway, Sim and Dr. Pleever in the Volvo and the other companions on their bicycles.

"It seems that we are not Mr. Smith's first visitors," Dr. Pleever said when he and Sim stepped onto the third floor landing of the McCrory building. What had previously been a more or less orderly arrangement of boxes, filing cabinets and the odd piece of furniture was now in utter disarray. Every drawer had been pulled out and up-ended, every box emptied, and even the umbrella stand lay on its side. The drawers of most filing cabinets had been pulled out, and emptied. Most, but not all. The one containing the medallion, presumably the only one that had been locked, remained intact.

"Splitface!" Sim said. "What do you suppose he did with Gold-Tipped Smith?"

"I suspect that Adrian Smith wasn't present when all this happened, which is probably a very good thing," Dr. Pleever said, picking up a chair and placing it back on its legs.

"Because Splitface would have forced him to give up the medallion?"

"Precisely."

While Dr. Pleever speculated, Sim had walked behind the desk and searched the floor for the contents of the upended drawers. As he knelt there, now out of sight, he heard a sound on the stairs. He started to stand up and Dr. Pleever waved him down. He listened and what he heard was the approach of a three-legged man, or, more likely, a man with a gold-tipped cane. Mr. Smith stopped, apparently surveying the damage. Sim would like to have seen the look on his face as he discovered Dr. Pleever and then the damage.

"You didn't ...." Gold-Tipped Smith began. He paused. Sim could imagine him assessing gentle Dr. Pleever. "No, of course not. It was that barbarian. This is what comes of trafficking with Vikings." He said it with a laugh. Still the remark didn't go down well with Sim.

"He's convinced that time is running out. He never had much patience," Mr. Smith continued. "And now...." He paused. "As you can see."

"It is," Dr. Pleever said. There was another pause. Sim tried to imagine what was unspoken: Gold-Tipped Smith looking at Dr. Pleever with a puzzled expression. Apparently he understood.

"Coming to an end?" Mr. Smith asked.

"Yes. "

"I see. There's more and more in this that I don't understand," he said. "Is the boy safe?"

I should stand up, Sim thought to himself. This could be embarrassing. It's one thing to be invisible and another to be hiding behind a desk. Sim picked up a handful of the objects on the floor and dropped them noisily into one of the desk drawers. Then he stood up with the drawer and put it on the desk.

"He's dumped everything out, Mr. Smith," Sim explained.

"Speaking of the boy," Mr. Smith said.

Sim had an inspiration. There was no opportunity to check it out with Dr. Pleever, but he thought his friend would approve. "You said we should work together and I've been thinking about that," he began. Dr. Pleever registered no surprise. Sim thought he saw a glimmer of a smile. "Dr. Pleever says that time is running out. Something is supposed to happen on my birthday. We don't know what it is, and we don't know what can happen after that." Now he was in a little over his head and had to invent quickly. "If that thing doesn't happen when it's supposed to then the medallions may lose their power, and all the good things you were telling me could happen would never have a chance to."

"So you came here to ask for my medallion. " Mr. Smith said, simply.

"Partly," Sim said. "I read the story. "

"Ah, Starspinner," Mr. Smith said. "What did you think of it?"

For an answer Sim took the lykill from around his neck. As if on cue, the grey, flat stone came to life, waves of color rolling across its surface. Gold-Tipped Smith took a step back, his eyes wide. "Your legend was right, Mr. Smith," Sim said.

"*He himself fashioned a stone from the Northern Lights as a gateway to the future.*" Mr. Smith recited. *"Because it controlled the others he called it the lykill.* " Mr. Smith reaching to touch the lykill. "May I?" But as he did the stone grew red. Mr. Smith withdrew his hand and the lykill resumed its soft flow of color. "Ah, yes," he said "*none but a child.*" Then he reached into his pocket and walked to the filing cabinet, inserting his key in the lock. He opened the drawer and removed the medallion, looking at it wistfully, and then handed it to Sim.

"Does this give me a one-ninth interest in the corporation?" he asked.

"The Travelstar Foundation?" Sim asked.

"I must say, it's all a little embarrassing," Mr. Smith said.

"I don't know what's going to happen," Sim said. "but sure. We're partners now." He held out his small hand and Mr. Smith took it.

"You are a remarkable young man," Gold-Tipped Smith said. "Remarkable."

Chapter 52

Sailing On Starlight

Whatever dreams Adrian Smith might have had about acquiring the medallions and traveling through time, he kept to himself. At least for the present. If he was a bad man, it wasn't obvious to Sim. Certainly he was a strange one. But without Gold-Tipped Smith, Sim would never have read the legend of Starspinner. Were the medallions responsible for that, too? It all depended on how you looked at things, and, right now, Sim was inclined to feel generous toward the man with the gold-tipped cane.

So he and Dr. Pleever helped Mr. Smith put his little circle of light back in order. The papers were hopeless. Reorganizing them was something Mr. Smith would have to do by himself, so they set to collecting them into straight piles and replacing them in boxes and file drawers.

Having made a gesture of cooperation, Mr. Smith apparently felt entitled to know a little more about the past weeks than he had been able to learn by himself. Dr. Pleever left the telling to Sim, who was informative to a point. There were several things he didn't mention, including his dreamwalking.

Remarkably, the coffee machine had not been tipped over, so Mr. Smith made a pot of coffee. Dr. Pleever accepted a cup. Sim declined. Then they sat down as they might have in someone's kitchen, having just returned from a Little League game or a movie, and chatted. Sim asked what it was that Splitface wanted to do with the medallions.

"He wants to go back," Mr. Smith said. "He doesn't like our world very much. Like those religionists. He doesn't like modern things. He wants the old ways." Mr. Smith laughed. "He has collected a treasure that he intends to take back with him."

"What kind of treasure? Sim asked.

"Nothing that we would consider of much value. Trinkets. One day he came in with a crystal ball, the kind of thing you and I had when we were children," he said to Dr. Pleever. "A winter scene. You tip it upside down and get a snowstorm. I hadn't seen one for years. I'm sure it would amaze an audience of Vikings."

"Once a shaman always a shaman," Mr. Smith continued. "His view of the world is very different from ours. His experience of time is something we really can't even imagine." Mr. Smith paused to reflect for a moment. "Most of us can't." He looked at Sim who was still lost in his own thoughts. He smiled. "I'm somewhere in the middle, neither scientist nor magician," Mr. Smith continued. "Somebody who writes books that nobody reads about things that nobody believes. When Mr. K. knocked on my door and showed me his medallions, I felt a little like Alice must have felt seeing the White Rabbit with his watch chain."

Smith paused, reflecting for a moment, and frowned. "He's aging. Rapidly. It seems to have something to do with the medallions. He has a great sense of urgency. I doubt that he will part with his medallions as readily as I did. Unless you include him in the partnership as well."

Sim could tell that Gold-Tipped Smith wasn't serious. He touched his cheek. The idea of having anything to do with Splitface made his skin crawl.

Dr. Pleever turned to Mr. Smith. "Excellent book, incidentally, Adrian. If you've written anything else, I'd be most interested in reading it." Mr. Smith looked first surprised and then pleased. He nodded and smiled. "I appreciate the civility you have shown me, Dr. Pleever." said Mr. Smith. "In fact I am quite touched by it. There is something I haven't told either of you." He paused for effect, still the great storyteller. "It bears on the question of the medallions and, I must confess, my interest in them. They do more than our young friend here has yet experienced. *The Midnight Sun* did not sail into Lost River Cove."

"But I saw it," Sim said.

"You saw it," Mr. Smith repeated.

"That day you saw me disappear. That's where I went."

"Ah," Mr. Smith said as if confirming a weather report. "Yes, well." He cleared his throat and thought for a moment. "That's when you saw the coat," he suggested.

"Yes, my father was wearing it."

"Your father?" He looked at Dr. Pleever. "His father?" he repeated.

"Yes, I'm afraid so. Kolbrúnarskáld's boy. Sim's father."

"Kolbrúnarskáld's boy was this Sim's father? Yes, well of course. That would explain a good many things wouldn't it? Is there anything else?"

"I don't think so," Sim said, looking at Dr. Pleever.

"No, I don't think so," Dr. Pleever confirmed.

"So, where was I?" Mr. Smith said, appearing more than a little confused.

"The ship," Sim reminded him. "You said it didn't sail here and I said I saw it land."

"Yes," Mr. Smith said, sounding a little more confident. "Yes, well. You saw it, I suspect, after it had arrived. According to our friend, the shaman, it was the boy – your father, as it now appears – who brought the ship across the sea. The ship had left northern waters and sailed for two or three days down the coast of Norway. It was night. The sea was calm. The sail was down. Suddenly the sky was awash with light. They were familiar with the aurora borealis, but this event, as Kolbrúnarskáld explains it, was a different order of magnitude. The lights rolled and danced overhead. The crew, awestruck and probably frightened, were silent. Then the boy – your father – on some inspiration of his own, walked to the center of the ship, and crossed his arms, and the ship rose on starlight. That was the expression Mr. K. used. I asked him to amplify but he couldn't. The aurora apparently withdrew gradually and the sky was unusually bright with stars. The ship was motionless, the sea no longer beneath it. Time passed. The sky above them never changed. And then, once again, they felt the sea beneath them, rocking the boat, and the sun rose in the east.

"They sailed on starlight," Sim whispered. He thought for a moment and looked at Mr. Smith. "The Travelstar Foundation," he said.

Mr. Smith looked a little sheepish. "You have found me out," he said with a smile. "But it appears that I'm a pound short and a day late."

Chapter 53

The Northern Lights

"He seems pretty sorry about what he did," Sim said, when they were back in Dr. Pleever's car.

"Adrian Smith is something of an epicurean," Dr. Pleever said, turning the key and smiling.

"You have more words than anybody I've ever met," Sim said.

Dr. Pleever laughed. "I have too many words and too few adventures. You'll find, Sim, that that's often true of people. The people who have the most to say often have the least to talk about." He moved the car out of its parking place and started down Water Street.

"I like your words," Sim said. "I used some of them in my paper on the Vikings. But you need to tell me what they mean. "

"An epicurean is someone who likes the flavor of things. And not just things you eat. I think Adrian Smith enjoys tasting the flavor of repentance and feeling that he is a better man. Some people enjoy looking at themselves in the mirror wearing different clothes. Some people like to hear themselves talk. I guess I should include myself in that category."

"Mr. Smith sure likes to hear himself talk," Sim said. "He even said so. He said he loves a good story."

"And much to his credit," Dr. Pleever said.

"Is Hazel going to die, Dr. Pleever?" Sim asked.

"Rather sooner than later I should think," Dr. Pleever replied. "She is going on 112 years."

"You know what I mean."

"We can't know that, Sim."

"Splitface thinks she's old because she has one of the medallions," Sim said.

"I wouldn't be at all surprised if she did have one. If your father had a medallion, he might very well have left it with her. But as for it prolonging her life? Winifred is a very strong-willed woman. You may remember our chat in Mr. Pomeroys' study when I told you about your father perhaps counting on me to be around these past weeks. Well, I think Winifred has had her role as well, and I know no more about it than she knows about mine. I'd guess she's stayed around out of pure tenacity. She made a promise and she was determined to keep it."

"Then what?" Sim asked.

"We will have to wait and see," said Dr. Pleever.

"She said once that she wanted a new adventure," Sim said quietly.

They were silent for awhile.

"What's the hardest part of all of this for you, Sim?" Dr. Pleever asked.

"My mother," Sim said without hesitation. "I haven't told her anything about the medallions."

Dr. Pleever turned and looked at him. "Well, of course you must. You can't go crawling down a wormhole into the tenth century without her knowing. Oh, Sim, this is an important oversight. I thought you had said something about Winifred having told her."

"I think she tried. Once. My mother didn't take her seriously. I've tried to tell her myself, but she doesn't listen.

My mother was a practical nurse. She's very practical. Time-skipping isn't practical. It's make-believe."

"Time-skipping?"

"That's what I decided to call it," Sim said.

"Of course. How perfect," Dr. Pleever said as he turned onto Shore Road and they headed north toward Thunderhead Cliff.

"She used to tell me when I was little that my father would come back some day. I believed her. I used to wish it whenever there was a shooting star. Then she stopped. I didn't notice it until just recently. She never talks about him anymore. She stopped believing. I told her the other night that he was."

"And what did she say?"

"She asked if I had been talking with Hazel."

"And you have."

"It was Hazel who asked if my mother had told me yet. I guess she thinks that my mother knows all about it. Hazel told her stuff and Hazel thinks that she believed it, but she didn't. I don't know what to do. I thought maybe you would have an idea."

"Do you mean you thought I might be the one to tell her?" he said with a smile.

"Well, you *are* a famous scientist. She'd have to take you seriously."

"Perhaps together we could tell her."

Sim hadn't been so happy for days. "Thanks," he said with a big smile. "You're one of the best friends I've ever had."

"That's the nicest thing anyone has said to me in a long time," Dr. Pleever said. He thought for a moment and continued. "Your mother will be very frightened, Sim. She has already lost one time-skipper."

"She doesn't know that about him. She says that one day he disappeared, but what she means is that he left. Something he had to do for the next eleven years." Sim could hear the anger escape in his voice. He hadn't meant to. If Dr. Pleever caught it, he didn't let on.

"I will be able to come back, won't I?" he asked.

"You always have," Dr. Pleever replied.

It wasn't the answer Sim wanted but he knew it was all Dr. Pleever could offer. How could anyone know what lay ahead? All he had to go on was a feeling, the same feeling that he had had throughout the past weeks, that he was following a path laid down by his father and that it was a safe one.

Sim took out the lykill. He still thought of it as his lucky stone. Now once again, waves of light rolled down its surface as they had for the past few days. "Have you been watching the Northern Lights?" he asked his friend.

"They have caused quite a stir in the news," Dr. Pleever said. "I believe it's a record."

"What makes them?" Sim asked.

"Electromagnetic forces," Dr. Pleever replied. Dr. Pleever slowed as they came to the top of the hill that bordered Thunderhead Cliff. He waited as a car passed going in the other direction, then turned into Hazel's vine covered driveway.

Or Starspinner, Sim thought. Nine medallions from the stars and one from the Northern Lights. "Have you ever seen a seagull fly at night, Dr. Pleever?" he asked.

"I don't believe they're nocturnal birds," his friend replied. "Why do you ask?"

"I was just wondering," Sim said.

Chapter 54

Trapped In Time

When Sim and Dr. Pleever joined the others at Hazel's cottage, they found not only the twins and Greta but Ponidi as well. Sim wondered what Hazel made of all this attention and whether anyone had told her that she might be in danger. There was no indication of tension, certainly. Everyone was in a festive mood and Hazel, though aging almost before his eyes, seemed nonetheless alert and in charge. She had made lemonade and there were cookies. Hazel was talking about the old days and how much the village had changed since she was a child.

Ponidi looked at his watch and announced that he needed to get back to Pomeroy Hall and get dinner underway. The twins and Greta said goodbye and piled into the Volkswagen. Then it was just Dr. Pleever, Sim and Hazel. While the two adults talked, Sim wandered into the parlor. There was a shelf of books that he hadn't noticed before. Surprisingly, they weren't all old. Most things in Hazel's cottage were, as if she hadn't set foot in the outside world for ages and ages. Perhaps Ponidi had bought the newer books for her, Sim thought. Or Dr. Pleever. One whole shelf was dedicated to nature. There were books on trees, wildflowers, animals, mushrooms, birds and something called perennials. He opened that one and recognized some of the flowers in Hazel's garden. Replacing it, he noticed on the shelf below, lying on its, a book on Vikings. It was the same as one of the books he had found at the library, filled with pictures of the kind Dr. Pleever had shown during his lecture. A thought crossed Sm's mind. What if this book had been here when his father visited? Might he have seen it, recognized the ship on the cover? Wouldn't he have used it as a way of explaining where he had come from, who he was?

Sim started to replace the Viking book when he noticed the book it had covered, a small paper-bound book that he knew at once. Unlike his own, this copy *of Forgotten Legends, Unforgettable Gods: Stories from Behind The Northern Lights* was not inscribed. He was about to take the book into the kitchen and ask how Hazel had come by it when he glimpsed, still sitting on the sofa where he had placed it on his first visit to Thunderhead Cliff, the small glass globe that contained a snowstorm. He tilted it and watched the snowfall. Then it hit him. He felt dizzy. How could he have missed it? "One day he came in with a crystal ball," Gold-Tipped Smith had said, speaking of Splitface's trinkets. A child's toy. Just like this. Just like the one in his dreamwalk. The musty cellar, the cot, the wooden crate on which the globe sat. It wasn't a cellar at all. Mr. Smith had teased Splitface about his little cottage. And that had reminded them of Hazel. So appropriate, he had said. Of course it was appropriate. Where else would Splitface have gone? Where else would he have kept his medallions?

Denny! Oh, what had he done!

"I've got to do something," Sim said, walking to the door. "Something I forgot." He turned the handle on the door and hesitated. "In the cave," he added. He wanted Dr. Pleever to know where to look if he didn't come back.

Denny's bedroll was not in view. A bad sign. Sim called. There was no answer. He entered the cave and shined the light on the wall of drawings. They had by now become old friends and he knew them intimately, but still he did not know their story – at least not all of it.

Again he scanned the walls of the cave. There was no sign of the bedroll or even that Denny had stayed here. No empty Coke cans, no remains of the food Sim had supplied. Not even of the shopping bags. Suddenly, there was another light behind him. He turned.

"We have been waiting for you," Splitface said. He held a kerosene lantern in one hand that threw menacing shadows on the wall behind where he stood. His other hand held a short length of rope. At its other end was Denny, hands tied behind him, a cloth stuck in his mouth. The rope was around Denny's neck. Splitface jerked down on the rope and Denny fell to his knees. The shaman had indeed aged, and he looked even more frightening – his face hollowed out, his eyes sunk so deeply into his skull as to be almost invisible. He was stooped over, hardly the giant of Sim's nightmares, hardly worthy of the shadow he cast on the cave wall. Denny was beyond being frightened. He looked at Sim with desperation.

"So here we are again, " Splitface said.

"I'm not the person you think I am," Sim said.

Splitface laughed quietly. "Always the trickster," he said.

"I am Simeon Spotswood and I live at 413 Fisher Lane. You have been to my house. You have met my mother."

"And your father," Splitface said, laughing his quiet laugh. "Just give it to me."

"I don't know what you want," Sim pleaded.

Splitface pulled on the rope around Denny's neck. Sim now saw that it was a slipknot. Denny gasped for breath.

"Don't do that," Sim said.

"It gives me pleasure," the shaman said. "He's a fool like his father. He had the lykill and didn't even know it." He pulled the rope tighter. Denny's mouth fell open and his eyes started bulging from their sockets. "Your friend's life for the lykill."

"He's not my...." Sim stopped. "I have the lykill. Let him breathe."

Splitface released the tension on the rope. Denny gasped for air, choked and gasped again.

Sim's mind raced. Maybe if he played along. He took a deep breath and tried to speak firmly. "You wouldn't be alive if we hadn't brought you here," he said.

"Maybe I would rather be dead," Splitface replied, but there was no conviction in his voice. He pulled again on the rope.

How to use that? Sim's mind raced. Where to go from here? "You can't go back without me, he said in the biggest voice he could find. The medallions have chosen me. I am their master."

"Foolish boy with your little pouch of skipping stones. Give me the lykill."

Sim removed it from beneath his shirt. It glowed. It was as if they had stepped outside in the aurora borealis itself. Sim could feel a tingle, as if the air were charged.

"The curtain falls," Splitface said with a bitter sneer. "Give it to me. Give me the stone and I will let your friend go."

Sim took the cord from around his neck and carefully laid it on the ground at Splitface's feet. Splitface released Denny who ran from the cave, his hands still tied behind him.

Splitface picked up the pendant by its cord, looked at the lykill for a moment, and laid the stone in his hand. "At last," he said. Then, with a cry of pain he dropped it and backed away.

They stood there in silence for a moment. Splitface knelt and stared at the lykill. He reached for it again, and as he did its light faded. All light faded. Darkness descended and within it another greater darkness. All was silent. Then Sim heard a sound that of all human utterances he might have imagined, was the most unlikely. Softly, almost imperceptibly, but unmistakably, Splitface was weeping. He was an old man, an evil man who would have taken, along with the lykill, Sim's one chance of being with his father; who would, without a second thought, have taken Denny's life. But he was dying. In that second, the "why" that had been hidden from Sim's understanding became clear. Why had his father brought the dying shaman into the future 22 years ago? Because he could. Because the power of the medallions was the power to create, not to destroy. to restore, not to abandon.

Then he stood before the huddled figure and held out his hand. Kolbrúnarskáld reached a skeletal hand into his coat pocket, retrieved his medallions and held them out.

Sim put them safely into his bib pocket, hung the lykill on its thin cord around his neck, and helped the shaman to stand. Then, his feet apart, he put his arms around the shaman, crossing them as he had learned. For a moment he had a sensation that he would never forget. He was standing in an ancient forest, a dying man in his arms, the man's blood on his chest.

The curtain of light descended and enfolded them. There was a smell of wood smoke. Sim opened his eyes. He took Splitface by the hand and led him out of the cave. Outside men stood and sat around a fire, talking and laughing, finishing their dinner.

Splitface approached the fire as if to warm himself, but his feet made no impression on the grass and no head turned. Sim felt pity for the old shaman. He will feel little warmth from that fire, he thought. Splitface looked back at Sim. A smile, more accepting than bitter, knitted the ravaged features of his face. He understood. This was the last trick that time, which was finally his master, would play. Would he have preferred death? Sim wondered. A gull alighted. Splitface removed his cap, which had for so many years hidden the grotesquerie of his skull, and nodded his head. Then the gull rose, and, as he did, the lights from the north climbed in the night sky to enfold him.

Chapter 55

The Coat

Sim looked for some sign of Denny. He called, but there was no answer. Poor Denny, he thought. What must he have thought? Surely not that Sim had known, had planned it all. That wasn't possible. Denny had witnessed Sim's confrontation with the shaman, seen him give up the lykill. But what Sim had seen in Denny's eyes wasn't thought; it was pure terror. Sim felt responsible. It was crazy, he told himself, but there it was. And it all had to do with Denny's father. How much fright and pain could a boy endure?

It was all about fathers. Denny's, his own, Simen's. And his father's father. Who would that have been? What had happened before his father had shown up in that village a thousand years ago, alone?

Sim called again. No, Denny was long gone. But where would he go? To Sim's house again? He should go and check. But first he had to return to Hazel's cottage. The thought of it suddenly felt like a great weight. What should he say? Should he tell them? No, not yet. Not until he had put it behind him and found the words to put in its place. But the blood. He had felt the old man's blood, the blood from his wound. He looked at his clothes, his hands, wiped at his face. Nothing. It had all been in his mind. But it had seemed so real. For just that moment.

Conversation ceased as Sim entered the cottage. Hazel held out her hand and smiled. He crossed to where she sat on the sofa and took it. Sim wondered what they had been saying, but could read nothing other than affection in their eyes. That was enough. Then he saw the coat. It had been hung on the back of a kitchen chair. It was the most beautiful coat he had ever seen but once, on a boy standing by a Viking ship, watching a seagull. He walked over and touched it.

"I have had it all these years," Hazel said. "It's beautiful, isn't it? Go on, try it on."

"Sim picked up the coat as if it might disintegrate in his hands, as if it were as fragile as his dreams. But it was real, as bright as he remembered it. He put it on. It fit him perfectly. He looked into the mirror and froze. He saw the boy. The other boy. The boy by the boat. The boy Kolbrúnarskáld believed him to be. The boy was Sim, and the boy was his father and, it seemed for a moment there was a third boy, standing behind him. But when he turned, there was no one except Hazel and Dr. Pleever.

He could see now, more clearly than when his father had stood by *The Midnight Sun*, the image of Starspinner embroidered at the center of the coat above the belt. He touched it. He felt something there. Then he felt more carefully. It was solid and round. His heart leapt. He removed the coat and looked inside at its lining. There was a small pocket behind Starspinner, and in it was the ninth medallion.

If Hazel had known it was there, she gave no sign. She looked weary and satisfied, as if a burden had been removed from her shoulders. "It might have been made for you," she said.

"Perhaps it was," Dr. Pleever said.

"That's all of them," Sim said. "I'm ready."

Close examination of the coat revealed eight other pockets, each decorated with a medallion's constellation. So this was how it would work. There were still millions of things to talk about – things about magic and the gods of the North and time travel and whether, at the appointed time, Sim would indeed meet his father.

As Dr. Pleever drove him home a few minutes later, Sim told him about his encounter with Splitface only an hour earlier. "At first I told him he had me mixed up with someone else and he said this really spooky thing. He said 'you're all the same.' Not the way people usually say it, not like 'Oh you kids, you're all the same. *Not* like that. Like we really were. And that's not the weirdest thing. When I put my arms around him, and we went back. Just for a second, I knew that I had done this before. I felt blood on my face."

"But you didn't."

"Have blood on my face? No. Not this time. Not my blood. It think it was his. Crazy, huh?"

"I wonder what Adrian Smith would say," Dr. Pleever mused.

"Names change over time," Sim repeated. The memory of that comment came into his mind from nowhere. He was as surprised as Dr. Pleever appeared to be. His older friend wrinkled his brow.

"Say again?"

"When he gave me the book. He had written 'To Simen'... and then some other stuff about traveling safely. I told him that my name was Simeon and then he said about names changing."

"What do you think he meant?"

"It's too weird."

"Given all that has happened, and hopefully all that lies ahead, it's hard to think of anything that could be too weird." Dr. Pleever smiled.

"OK, but don't laugh."

"I promise."

"I think he meant we are all the same person. At different times. Sort of like ancestors, but not exactly. Like when Splitface said 'It's you' when he thought I was my father. And there in the cave when I felt the blood that my father must have felt when he brought Splitface to the future. And the cut on my cheek when I was standing watching the ship land and Splitface hit my father."

"It's beyond my understanding, Sim. And I'm not sure that *understanding* as we usually think of it, really matters. What you feel is the important thing. Your heart has opened this adventure, your wish to see your father. It is your remarkable imagination that has brought the pieces together. More pieces than either of us could ever have imagined. The discovery of the ship on the day you were born, your father's return so that you might come into the world, the boy, Simen, in the legend, and Starspinner himself. It is all of a piece. You are all of a piece. You are all the same story told again and again." Dr. Pleever drove into the driveway at 413 Fisher Lane.

Sim's mother had not come home yet. Walter, who seemed more than a little annoyed at having been left out of recent events, was lying in Sim's small vegetable garden. There were other more comfortable places for him to have chosen, but Sim knew Walter well enough to know that his choice was no accident. Left alone for a day, Walter was as likely as not to make his bed in the middle of the freshly folded laundry. He looked at Sim as if challenging him to a scolding, but Sim went over and gave him a hug, and the three of them went up the front steps.

He was still wearing the coat and he decided to leave it on. That's where the conversation with his mother would begin. "This was my father's coat," he would say. "He left it for me."

As Sim approached the door, he realized that the house would be a mess. His mother had been busy lately with both her new catering job and Hazel. What would she think, returning to find Dr. Pleever in the kitchen with unwashed dishes, magazines scattered here and there, floors that needed sweeping? He closed his eyes, crossed his fingers, and opened the front door.

Things were not perfect, but they were all right. At least there were no dirty dishes. Dr. Pleever reminded him that the house had once been in his own family and Sim remembered that Hazel had spent part of her childhood here. It was here that Nathaniel would have lived his too few years, and it was in this attic that Hazel had left the book when they moved away. Dr. Pleever had never been in the house, however, and so Sim gave him a tour, ending on the widow's walk. It was only 5:30 so there were no stars, but Dr. Pleever pointed to the place in the sky where astronomers had expected to find Starspinner.

Sim excused himself and checked the tool shed. Denny wasn't there. When his mother returned, she found Sim on the floor, his head on Walter's back and Dr. Pleever sitting at the kitchen table with a cup of peppermint tea and a peanut butter cookie. If she was remarkably surprised, she did not show it. "Pepper!" she said. "What a wonderful surprise. After all these years."

Then she saw the coat and Sim hastily explained that Hazel had given it to him. "It's an early birthday present," he said. Then he felt his face redden. He didn't want to look at Dr. Pleever. He had chickened out. He had worked it out in his mind and then couldn't do it. He was ashamed. He bit his lip. "Actually," he began, "it's very old."

"It's probably been in Hazel's family for years," his mother said, touching the fabric. "It's a very special present, Sim. I hope you thanked Hazel."

Sim darted a look at Dr. Pleever. He raised his eyebrows in encouragement. "Actually, it's even older than that," Sim began. But his mother had turned her attention to their surprise guest. Clearly she was very pleased to see Dr. Pleever again. Sim hadn't seen his mother smile quite so warmly in a long time. The next thing Sim knew, his mother had invited Dr. Pleever to stay for dinner, he had accepted, and they were catching one another up on the last eleven years.

Dinner seemed both interminable and altogether too short. Sim had no appetite. His stomach was doing push-ups. Once or twice, he almost took the plunge but didn't. He was waiting for just the right place in the conversation. It occurred to him that he might just go to bed and leave them here together, leave it to Dr. Pleever to tell her. There was a man here now – not his father but a friend of his father's, a helper. He could do what a father would do. Explain to his mother what it was to be a boy, how hard some things were. He looked at Dr. Pleever who was laughing at something Sim's mother had said. Sim looked away. He didn't want to meet Dr. Pleever's eyes right now. He was ashamed of his weakness. He knew what had to be done and who must do it.

"Mom?" he said. She turned and looked at him. She was enjoying having Dr. Pleever here as much as he was. She looked happy.

"Yes, Sweetie?" she said.

"The coat."

"It's very beautiful. What a lovely gift."

"It isn't really from Hazel," he said.

"Oh?"

"It's from my father."

"Your father."

"He left it with her when he came here, when you took care of him and Dr. Pleever got to know him. Before he went back."

"Oh, Sweetie, you've been talking to Hazel again." She looked at Dr. Pleever with that expression adults use, the one that says, "here we go again" or "what's to be done?"

"I was afraid she'd do that and upset you." Her eyes were full of concern. "And she has, hasn't she?" She reached across the table and took Sim's hand. "Your father was not a Viking or a Norse god, Sim. He was just a man, a sailor. A wonderful man whom I have always hoped you would get to know, but just a man." She looked at Dr. Pleever. "Your aunt is a wonderful woman, Pepper, but these last years, unkind as it is to say it, she has earned her unfortunate reputation. She lives in a fairy tale."

"Perhaps we should go into the living room, Linda," Dr. Pleever said, standing up. "My stopping by isn't entirely coincidental. Sim asked me if I would help him tell you a story, an unlikely and quite remarkable story, and I think he's ready to do that now."

Had Sim any inclination to sleep, he would have exchanged Walter for his pillow, but sleep was the last thing on his mind. His mother had cried, and that had been hard to watch, hard to be responsible for. Dr. Pleever had been right about that. Sim thought that the hardest part for her would be the story itself – its strangeness, its impossibility. Yes, it was a fairy tale. Hazel's fairy tale. That might have been the case if Dr. Pleever hadn't been there, but he used big words – words even bigger than *celestial event* and *synchronicity effect* – which made it all somehow sound reasonable. It wasn't that she didn't believe the story; it was that, when they had both finished, she did. And then she knew that he, like his father, would disappear. Not disappear out the front door in the middle of the night, but, as his father had, in an instant from the place where she had just seen him.

"I couldn't stand it," she said. "Not again. Not my Sim." He had gone to her and she had held him a long time, he reassuring her that he had always come back, that it was just to complete the task his father had set, to return the medallions. The only place he wanted to be was here with her, he said. But he couldn't let his father down. In fact, it was at that moment he realized that what he said was true. He had held in his mind until now the possibility that he might stay. Two weeks there and two weeks here, like children with divorced parents. But that was crazy. No, he wanted to see his father, to have his father know that he had succeeded, but he didn't want to stay. His life was here. With his mother and his friends. And Dr. Pleever.

Finally he carried his sleeping bag and pillow up to the widow's walk. Dr. Pleever stayed. He was glad of that. He didn't want his mother to be alone. What would it be like, traveling through a worm hole? He liked the term, *time tunnel*, better. What would happen when he met his father? Would his task be, like his father's when he was a boy and wore the coat, to make the ship travel by starlight back to Norway? And what of the medallions and the lykill? How would they get to Starspinner? Would he, like Simen, travel behind the Northern Lights? And when it was all over, what then? How would he return?

It wasn't until some time later that the curtain of the Northern Lights began to rise in the north, now even brighter than it had been for the last several nights. Again he had the sensation he had experienced in the cave, not unlike the gentle hum of the medallions but suffusing his whole body. He lay atop his sleeping bag and a slight breeze caressed him. He took the stone from beneath his pajama top. It was like a mirror reflecting the spectacle of the heavens in miniature.

Time had not run out after all. Everything was as it should have been. With Kolbrúnarskáld back in the time for which his life was intended and no longer a threat to the medallions, and with the medallions gathered together once more, Sim and his friends had only to assemble tomorrow night beneath the stars. There was no more he could do.

A meteorite shot across the sky. Well, there was one more thing he could do, one more time. He made his wish.

Chapter 56

Six Hours Till Twelve

Sim got the news from the twins first thing the next morning. Deputy Gladstone had found Denny Dumont curled up among the wild raspberries in the vacant lot across from his house. He had a Class A shiner as well as the cut on his cheek and red marks on his neck. When the deputy had asked if his father had done this to him, Denny apparently had nodded. Sim guessed that in Denny's imagination his father and Splitface had morphed into one demon. The twins also reported that Mr. Dumont was back behind bars. It's funny, Sim thought, how bad things can produce good results. Denny would have a safe home now – at least for awhile –and Splitface had played a part in making that happen.

Now it was the eve of Sim's birthday, and they were all gathered at Hazel's cottage: Greta, the twins, Sim and his mother, Dr. Pleever, and Ponidi. Hazel had made lemonade but no one was very thirsty. By comparison to the others, Walter was a bundle of energy, managing to wheedle four dog biscuits from Hazel's stash. Hazel was quite energetic as well. She had waited longer than any of them for this moment, for it was to her that by some strategy Sim's father had communicated his message. It was with her that he had left the coat.

Sim's mother had spent the morning with Hazel, and it seemed to Sim that she was calmer than she had been earlier, when he had noticed tears quietly dripping into her bowl of Nutritious Nutcake Cereal. He had reassured her that he certainly would come back as soon as he had completed his mission. He reminded her that they had talked for his whole life about his someday seeing his father. "Yes," she had said. "I know, and I am glad, but it is all so strange and new." Then he had gone over and given her a big hug and she had smiled.

Then she had gone to talk with Hazel.

Dr. Pleever said that the forecast was for clear skies and a moonless night – perfect for seeing the stars.

"And the Northern Lights," Alex added.

"Yes," Dr. Pleever said. Then it was quiet again.

Ponidi got the companions to help him gather rocks for an outdoor cooking fire. Then he showed them how to cut sticks for holding hot dogs. Sim's mother had brought a salad and cookies. Alex had pinched a bag of marshmallows from the pantry at Pomeroy Hall, but he and Hazel were the only ones who had an appetite for them.

The twins took Ponidi off to show him the cave, Greta and Hazel cleaned up the meal, and Sim, his mother and Dr. Pleever walked off to be by themselves. Dr. Pleever was older and wiser, but Sim knew his friend didn't have answers to the questions that filled his mind and, despite the warm night, gave him the shivers. Dr. Pleever had taught him, *Fa*, the Norse word for father.

"What will it be like?" Sim asked.

"There will be no path to Wentworth Hall, no Wentworth Hall, no road, nothing but the cave and the trees and the stars."

"And the Northern Lights," Sim added.

"And the Northern Lights," Dr. Pleever said, as the sun's last rays flickered in the treetops.

"What if he isn't here?"

"He will be," his mother said, pulling Sim close to her.

"It's remarkable to me that we have actually come this far," Dr. Pleever said. "It would be even more remarkable to think that the most important part might not occur. Your mother is right, Sim."

"What has your fondest wish been for these last eleven years?" his mother asked.

"To see him."

"Without that wish," Dr. Pleever said, "maybe even the lykill would have been powerless."

"Look at the stars!" his mother said, craning her neck.

"And the aurora is rising again," Dr. Pleever said, pointing to the horizon from which green lights were beginning to climb into the sky. "I guess we expected that, didn't we?"

Sim nodded. Dr. Pleever put his hand on Sim's shoulder. "I believe you will travel and return safely." He looked at Sim's mother and smiled. "There are a number of people here who are quite fond of you. I think their own wishes may have something to do with all of this."

"Thank you," Sim said.

There wasn't much more to say, so it was just as well that the twins and Greta came running up just at that moment. "We've been looking everywhere for you," Alex said. "Hazel says it's almost time."

"We lost track," Dr. Pleever said. "Imagine, here we are about to launch Sim into another time altogether, and we can't even keep track of our own."

They returned to find Hazel in the entryway of the cottage, examining her hats. Finally she selected the one she had worn on that first day, the one with the silk flowers and the precariously perched cardinal. She took the long pins from its side, put them between her teeth, placed the hat on her head, pinned it and looked in the mirror. "I think that will do quite well," she said, turning back to them.

"What do you think, Greta?"

"I think it's perfect," Greta said.

"Good," Hazel said. "Let's get this show on the road. I have been waiting a very long time for this occasion. I promised I would stay around, and I'm glad I have, but 111 is at least ten years too many."

They walked to the cave with Sim and Walter leading, then Hazel and Sim's mother. Next came the two girls, Ponidi, and Alex with Dr. Pleever bringing up the rear.

Chapter 57

The Starlight Medallions

Sim helped Hazel over the log, just as he had when they first met. "Have we met?" she had asked then. "No," he had said. But they had, of course. Exactly twelve years earlier. She seemed to Sim even more insubstantial than on that first occasion – as if, but for her great flowered hat, she might have floated away. They stepped into the clearing and waited for the others. The tide was full and roared into the grotto beneath Thunderhead Cliff. Sim stood at the center with the others around him. He looked at his mother and then up at the night sky. The Northern Lights were now a tapestry of color that filled the sky. Sim was about to cross his arms when he remembered something. He turned and looked back toward the cave. A seagull perched on a rock by its entrance, its head cocked to one side. Sim smiled.

Then he raised his head, spread his feet apart and crossed his arms over his chest, reciting as he had so many nights, the verse his mother had taught him.

"Star light, star bright, First star I've seen tonight. I wish I may, I wish I might get the wish I wish tonight."

Was it possible that at last it might come true?

His mother told him later that it was as if the aurora itself had embraced him. Suddenly he was covered with light and the next moment he was gone.

The night was quiet. The sea, which but moments ago had roared in the confines of the grotto, was now soundless. Above him was a forest of giants – not the chestnuts that he had earlier seen farther inland but great pines whose trunks it would have taken three or four boys to circle with their arms. He half expected to see a pterodactyl sweep down from their branches or hear the earth-shaking tread of *Tyrannosaurus Rex*.

Mainly he felt small. Even the cave seemed somehow larger, though he knew it could not have been. Things often were, as Dr. Pleever said, as much the way you felt about them as the way they really were, whatever "really" meant.

He turned toward the sea. A man was standing there looking at him. The Northern Lights still danced in the sky. The man had long blond hair that appeared to blend with the fawn color of the vest he wore. It was, Sim guessed, a deerskin. It had been embroidered simply, but in the same fashion as the coat he now wore that had once been his father's.

"Fa?" Sim said. His father smiled. His face was not the cartoon face, carved from rock, as certain as sunrise and as constant as the tides, that Sim had conjured, but his smile was the one Sim had hoped for. And the voice. "Simen," the voice said.

Sim took two steps, slowly, but when Magnus Siglandi opened his arms, he ran. Sim felt himself lifted as if he were no more than an infant, held against the Viking's chest. He buried his head in the vastness of his father's beard. It smelled of things he had never smelled before, not all of them pleasant, but none of which he would ever forget. Then his father put him down and they studied one another. There was a scar on his father's left cheek where the beard didn't grow. His father touched Sim's cheek, then his own. Then he touched the coat. "Winifred Chit," he said.

Sim nodded. His father examined Sim's Winnie The Pooh necktie and laughed. Sim had not meant to have it showing. He felt himself blush. "Good," his father said. On an impulse Sim loosened the knot, removed the tie, and handed it to his father who put it around his own neck over his deerskin coat. His father smiled. Sim laughed.

They stayed there for some time without any words. There is so much that can be said through the eyes with never a chance of deceit or of holding back. All of Sim's loneliness spoke, all of his anger at having been abandoned by the person who should have walked him into manhood, all the worship and fantasy and all the love. Then his father took Sim's head in his great and gentle hands, looked him in the eyes, and said 'good.' Sim saw a tear, nestled in the scar on his father's cheek.

At last his father pointed toward Lost River Cove. Sim nodded. His father made a dumb show of picking him up and carrying him on his shoulders, but Sim shook his head and took his father's hand. It was a hard thing to do. He would have liked to see the world from up there, have at last the ride of which time had robbed him. But he wanted his father to know that he wasn't a child any more.

His father nodded, and they proceeded down a well-worn path toward what would someday be the village of Lost River Cove.

Nothing except the Oracle Stone offered a familiar landmark, and not until he could see it in the distance did Sim know where the cove lay. Then, a moment later it emerged and he saw the ship. It was smaller than he had remembered. Once it had been painted bright colors, but now they had faded. A primitive dwelling had been made on the shore, much resembling one he had seen in a book.

As they neared the shore his father called out and men emerged from the dwelling. They were dressed, like his father, in animal skins, mostly deer, but here and there he saw signs of black bear and smaller animals, not all of which he recognized. A fox's tail adorned one man's leather skullcap, the tail of a raccoon another's. The men were very animated, though whether at the sight of him or the familiar coat he could not tell. The necktie received a great deal of attention, as did Sim's high-topped sneakers. "Bam" one of the men said, pointing to Magnus's tie.

"Bam?" Sim asked.

The man got down on all fours then reared up and waved his arms.

"Bear!" Sim said. "Pooh," he said, pointing to the tie. The men looked at one another, mumbling, then laughed.

Now Sim noticed that women were emerging from the long house, and with them, children, none older than he. They were moving to the ship, carrying small packages of their belongings. His father spoke to the men, who nodded and also made their way to the ship, each of them touching Sim on the head as if for good luck.

Then his father pointed to the sky. It was the same sky, awash with color, that Sim had looked at just an hour earlier when he made his wish. That wish had come true. Now it was time once again for the small ship to rise on starlight, as it had a thousand years ago.

He followed his father to the boat. It was not as crowded as Sim had expected, with wives and children now included, but then he guessed that many of the crew had gone off to make their way in this new world without a thought of returning to Norway.

A place was left in the middle of the ship, and his father led him there. His father spoke to the crew and their families in a kindly and reassuring way. He even joked, which surprised Sim. He hoped someday he might be like his father. As he stood there listening, he caught the gaze of a small boy about seven or eight. The boy smiled at him and then at his father. Sim looked from one of them to the other. "Omigosh!" he said. The boy looked at him and laughed.

"Anne sonne," their father said. "*Broder.*" Sim nodded. His father took Sim's head in his hands and looked long and lovingly into his eyes. Then he looked up at the sky and Sim followed his gaze. The aurora parted as if it were the curtain of a vast celestial stage. His father stood facing him, his brother behind. Sim crossed his arms. "Star light. star bright." he said, in a full and confident voice, feeling the strong hand of his father on his shoulder. "I wish we may. I wish we might, have the wish we wish tonight."

It was as if the stars dropped threads of light upon the ship's deck like a million fireflies in the night. Sim felt a wind on his face, a kiss on the top of his head, and all was still. The ship rose on starlight, high above the coast and the sea, and floated upon the Northern Lights. No one spoke. Then he felt it descend, he smelled again the salt air, and the ship settled gently upon the sea. He guessed that they must be where the voyage had begun when his father was the same age as he and wore the coat he now wore.

Chapter 58

A Skipper of Stars

They disembarked and stood on the shore. Now the Northern Lights seemed almost close enough to touch, no longer an aurora, more like a curtain, as substantial as the forest behind him. It moved. It danced with light as his lykill had danced atop the widow's walk. He looked at his father. What would happen now? He needed somehow to communicate with his father, to let him know that there were people who needed him in another time. And whom he needed as well. He started to take off the coat, thinking that doing so might signal that he had finished with his task, but his father stayed his hand, all the time staring into the curtain of light. Then he called out, using words that meant nothing to Sim. The same words three times. Then Sim saw it and stepped back behind his father, holding onto him like a child. Never had he seen so frightening a creature. His father spoke again. This time Sim recognized two of the words: Rida Stjarna, Starspinner.

Sim's voyage was not over. He knew what must happen now, and he stepped out again beside his father. The wolf approached; its coat glowed as if it were made not of anything substantial but of light itself. Its red eyes burned like the last coals of a fire. It showed no emotion, revealed no intention of its own. It seemed indifferent to everything around it. It approached. In terror, Sim held out his hand. The wolf's muzzle was moist, soft, gentle. Sim thought of a basset hound one thousand years in the future.

Before he was aware of it happening, his father had lifted him onto the wolf's back. Then he kissed him again on his forehead. The wolf turned and walked toward the curtain of light. It was what Sim had to do, but it was much harder than he had ever dreamed. His heart was breaking. He turned. His father waved. "I love you," Sim called. His father bent down, picked up a stone and skipped it onto the calm waters of the inlet. Then the curtain of light parted, the great wolf, Fenir, stepped into Hyperborean, and the world of men past present and future, disappeared from view.

The next thing Sim knew, they were in a field fragrant with wildflowers beside a still and crystalline lake. The Northern Lights were no longer above his head but formed a great wall behind him – a wall of ever-shifting images, as if all the stories ever told were captured there in eternal repetition. He looked up at the sky and gasped. It was as if he could touch the stars. Even more remarkable was the way the constellations stood out from the millions of stars surrounding them, as if in a children's book. Now the wolf stood beside another boy who could have been himself.

The boy smiled at him and held out his hand. Sim understood, or thought he did, but when he began to take off the coat, the boy stopped him. The boy looked up at the constellations arrayed above them. Then Sim understood. He removed Orion and handed it to Starspinner who smiled, drew back his arm and threw it among the stars. Sim could see it skip as if upon a lake. It came to rest between Ursa Major and Perseus. Then he removed the others one at a time and Rida Stjarna skipped each of them to its proper place in his own constellation. No, Sim thought to himself. Not constellation. Star cluster. Now there was only one medallion left. Sim held it out to Starspinner, but the boy-god who was both the oldest and the youngest of all the gods, who was master of the stars and therefore of time itself, who knew always what was past, passing, and to come, held up his hand and pointed to the cluster that now, but for one last star, had taken its rightful place in the heavens.

"Me?" Sim asked.

Starspinner smiled and stepped back. Sim crooked the medallion in his forefinger, felt its weight, looked up into the heavens, and skipped it a thousand thousand leagues above him, into the night sky. He looked. The star cluster, Starspinner stood bright and clear between Ursa Major and Perseus. Sim looked at Rida Stjarna and smiled. Remembering the lykill, he reached to remove it from beneath his shirt, but again Starspinner stayed his hand. Then he took Sim's hand in his own and placed in it something that Sim could not identify, for its brightness was greater than its form. Starspinner closed Sim's hand, smiled, and removed his own. As he did, Sim was again enveloped by light and again he felt the wind in his hair.

Someone had gotten Hazel a blanket. She was asleep, leaning against a log, snoring delicately. Greta sat beside her. The twins were sitting by Sim's mother, one on each side under an arm, sound asleep. Dr. Pleever was standing exactly where Rida Stjarna had stood one moment before. At his side – patient, expectant and vigilant, sat Walter.

Sim opened his hand and a feather fell to the ground. He bent and picked it up. He could hear the waves crashing in Thunderhead Cove, and in the sky, from which the aurora had withdrawn, he could see the immense secrecy of the stars. He looked at his mother, then at Dr. Pleever, and smiled.

Sim looked up into the night sky, clear and bright with stars. The aurora had disappeared as mysteriously as it had arisen. He searched for a moment and then saw it. He pointed just between Perseus and Ursa Major. "Starspinner," he said.

Epilogue

There was a great stir in Lost River Cove on the morning of November second. First, there had been the light show, a display of the Aurora Borealis witnessed from southern Maine all the way to Newfoundland, already distinguished by the mullahs of meteorology as the most dramatic display on record. As people see shapes in clouds and figures among the stars, that evening several residents of Lost River Cove claimed to have seen the head of a dragon among the lights and others the sail of a ship. Homer Dunn saw a giant bird the size of a football field hovering within the lights.

Ordinarily shy and private people came forward in the mild hysteria of the occasion to speak of things that they remembered seeing in weeks past: bright lights in the sky, strange humming noises and misbehaving pets. Myron Purdy swore that two whales had spouted just outside the cove. Newspapers had sent reporters and there were television cameras everywhere.

"It ain't the only strange thing that's been going on in this town since all them scientists arrived," Homer Dunn was heard to say in an interview on a Portland midday news program. "I've got nothing against scientists, or foreigners for that matter, but sometimes it's best just to leave things alone, if you know what I mean."

Virtue Turnbull, the police chief's wife, who had no imagination at all, was one of several people who claimed to have seen the ship, and she would not be shaken in her conviction that Dr. Hoffner and his associates had disturbed spirits from the past.

The discovery and excavation of the Viking ship would be known far and wide in the months to follow, and the Lost River Cove Chamber of Commerce would take full advantage of the publicity.

Also in the months to follow, new scientists and parapsychologists would turn up in this small coastal village. Some of them would have made Gold-Tipped Smith look downright legitimate.

Had people known what actually happened, they would have found it no easier to believe than the rumors that abounded. It was just as well that they didn't, for the sailing of The Midnight Sun on a sea of starlight would have meant nothing to them, anymore than the boy who stood at mid-decks, his arms crossed, wearing a magical coat, or the gull, its head cocked to one side, perched at the top of the ship's mast.

More interesting to Dr. Pleever and the companions, however, was a newspaper story that had no apparent connection to the events in Lost River Cove. It announced a new star cluster in the night sky. The event had been predicted for some time, based upon certain archaeological research. According to that same research, it should have been visible for a number of years. And yet it appeared for only one night, the second of November, and disappeared as suddenly as it had arrived.

At 3 p.m. on the second day of November, Simeon Spotswood turned twelve. That afternoon, Hazel arranged a small birthday party at Thunderhead Cliff. Hazel reminded Sim of those mists that now and then cloak and fragrance the coast of Maine, so frail had she become. Her spirits had never been higher, however, and somewhat relieved the sadness that Sim felt. It seemed to Sim that he was losing more people than he was getting. But in the same way that he understood his father's need to complete the journey he had begun a thousand years ago, he understood Hazel's desire to complete hers.

"I still don't get it," Alex said, when they had all assembled in Hazel's garden. They had brought out chairs and the bench from the kitchen. Sim's mother had set up a card table for the cake and beverages.

"What don't you get, Alex?" Dr. Pleever asked, pouring himself lemonade and offering a glass to Hazel.

"How the ship could go away and still be here. I sort of understand just a little bit about how there can be more than one time at a time. But how can things from one time get mixed up with things in another time? I mean the boat was here and it sank and it got buried and dug up and it's still sitting there in the harbor."

"I wish I knew," Dr. Pleever said. "I don't. That's the fact of the thing. I don't have anything close to a theory that could explain any of this. We understand very little about time. It's not just clocks and calendars, as Dr. Einstein showed us almost a hundred years ago. It's all tangled up with space, and space is filled with things that play tricks on time and with time."

"I don't think it's science at all," Amanda said.

"What *do* you think, Amanda?" Sim's mother asked.

"I think we are all a story that someone is telling and she doesn't always tell it perfectly and things get confused. You couldn't figure the story out unless you could figure her out and nobody can ever figure anyone else out."

It was a refreshing suggestion, and they all laughed. All except Alex, who made his spaceship hovering sound. Walter, sensing a change in the mood of the crowd that might possibly result in a sudden kindness to animals, barked. His guess was right. Hazel produced one of her new dog biscuits.

"Presents," Alex said. "It's time for presents." He got up and started toward the house, turning to see if anyone was following. No one was. Sim wasn't, because it was his birthday. Amanda wasn't, because it had been her brother's idea. The adults weren't, because it seemed that Alex was doing very well by himself. "Well?" he said.

"You get mine, please, Alex," Hazel said. "They are in a box in the parlor."

Alex went indoors, reappearing in a moment with Hazel's box to which he had added several other presents.

He handed Sim his own present first standing by while Sim carefully removed the ribbon.

"It's something that you really need," Alex said. "I was going to get one for myself as well, but then I decided we can share yours. My dad helped out. It's from him, too."

Sim removed the paper to reveal a box containing a small instrument.

"It's a GPS," Alex said, "a global positioning system. It tells you where you are anywhere on the whole planet. They use them on ships and planes and cars. Dad has one in the Land Rover. This one isn't as fancy, but it still works."

"It's great, Alex. Thanks," Sim said.

"It only works in the present," Alex said.

"That's OK," Sim said. "I'm not going any place else for a long time."

Amanda gave him hers next, a piece of paper rolled up. It was a picture she had drawn of his father. Of course, she had never seen Magnus Siglandi, and she wasn't very good at art, but it meant a great deal to Sim because she had drawn him as Sim had described him: blond hair, wearinga deerskin jacket and standing with his legs apart and his arms crossed. Sim didn't say anything for a moment, and then he said a very quiet "Thank you," which was all any giver could have asked for.

Greta's present was a small journal bound in red leather which she handed to him unwrapped. He opened it and read the first line,"Once upon a time in a small village on the coast of Maine lived a boy named Simeon Stoneskipper." It was done in beautiful script. Sim couldn't think what to say. He hugged it to his chest.

The present from his mother was a beautifully framed print of *Starry Night*, by a man named Van Gogh, for his bedroom.

Dr. Pleever cleared his throat and everyone settled in for a speech, but none was forthcoming. He spoke simply: "My present to you, Sim, is a trip to Washington with your mother, to visit with me for a week this summer. I'd like you to get to know my museum, and, quite selfishly, I'd like to get to know you and your mother a little better. You are quite a remarkable young man. It would be hard just to walk away now that the medallions are back in their own time and this adventure is over."

Sim looked at his mother. She smiled. He had told Dr. Pleever that he had a brother. It was better, he thought, not to tell his mother. Dr. Pleever had agreed. "That would be very nice," Sim said. "really nice." He walked over and gave Dr. Pleever a hug. It may have been the first such hug Dr. Pleever had had in some time. He was a little awkward and did a kind of "tut tut hmmmm. Yes, well." The others couldn't help smiling.

"Bring me the box, would you, Alex?" Hazel said.

He did, and she removed four packages. They were wrapped in newspaper and tied with string. Hazel explained that she had run out of gift-wrapping paper twenty years ago.

The twins opened their boxes. There was a set of silver brushes for Amanda, a silver belt buckle for Alex, a gold-plated fountain pen for Greta, and a watch that chimed on the hour for Sim.

"It's so that you can keep track of time," Hazel said, "and so that time can keep track of you." She turned to the other three children. "I've given you all presents for a selfish reason. I want to know that you will think of me now and then," she said, not sadly, but seriously. And then, more light-heartedly, "and of course they are all enchanted. I'll be keeping an eye on you."

Then she turned to Sim. "I have something else for you, Sim. I'm afraid it may prove to be more of a burden than a gift, but I have no one else to give it to."

She looked at Dr. Pleever, who handed her a very large red envelope surrounded by a rubber band. Sim walked over to where she sat. She rested the envelope on her lap and took his hands. She examined them. "These are very competent hands," she said, "and they belong to a very courageous young man who was worth waiting for. This was a beautiful place once," she said, indicating the woods that had once been a field that had once been lawn and the great estate that sat between her small cottage and the cliff edge. "Pepper thinks it could be again, in the right hands. It will take time and money, and there should be enough of both. Pepper has looked after things for me these too many years."

Sim was only beginning to understand what she was saying. She continued. "At twelve you can't be either a king or an owner of real estate," she went on. "Princes who became king when they were underage had regents."

Sim moistened his lips with his tongue.

"Your mother will be your regent. That should meet with your approval. And Pepper will be your banker. Do you understand, Sim?"

He nodded.

"You had your father briefly. Long enough to know the kind of man he was and how much he loved you. You will have Thunderhead Cliff as long as you wish. It was the place where you were created, Sim, where for a time your father lived. It is your rightful home."

"You're giving him the whole thing?!" Alex could not restrain himself.

"I am, Alex. What do you think of the idea?"

"The cave too?"

"The cave too," Hazel affirmed.

"Cool."

And with that, Hazel declared the ceremony of gift-giving over. It had been a long and busy twenty-four hours, she said, and she was ready for a nice, long nap.

Sim stood there during all of this, still not knowing what to say. Having had his most important wish granted, he could still not grasp the fact that his other wish, for a home of their own, could have been granted as well.

And not only a home, but a home right next to where his father lived, only a wish and a thousand years away.

Chat with the author. Learn more about Vikings and the night sky.

www.starlightmedallions.com

CPSIA information can be obtained
at www.ICGtesting.com
Printed in the USA
FFOW05n0743241213

9 781450 200523